# The Way We Were

### SINÉAD MORIARTY

PENGUIN
IRELAND

PENGUIN IRELAND

UK | USA | Canada | Ireland | Australia
India | New Zealand | South Africa

Penguin Ireland is part of the Penguin Random House group of companies
whose addresses can be found at global.penguinrandomhouse.com.

First published 2015
001

Copyright © Sinéad Moriarty, 2015

The moral right of the author has been asserted

Set in 13.5/16 pt Garamond MT Std
Typeset by Jouve (UK), Milton Keynes
Printed in Great Britain by Clays Ltd, St Ives plc

A CIP catalogue record for this book is available from the British Library

ISBN: 978–1–844–88349–3

www.greenpenguin.co.uk

MIX
Paper from
responsible sources
FSC® C018179

Penguin Random House is committed to a
sustainable future for our business, our readers
and our planet. This book is made from Forest
Stewardship Council® certified paper.

To all aspiring writers. Believe in yourself.

*Sometimes even to live is an act of courage.*

Seneca

*London, Holland Park, November 2014*

Dan reached over and took two glasses of champagne from the waiter. Handing one to Alice, he smiled reassuringly at her, then tapped his to get everyone's attention. He cleared his throat and made a toast: 'I'm so happy that you, my closest friends, could be here tonight to meet Alice properly. You all know my story, and you also know from me that Alice has had a very difficult time. I feel very lucky to have met her. Second chances are hard to come by in life, and I'm grabbing this one with both hands. Here's to new beginnings with the most wonderful woman in the world.'

He pulled her close and kissed her as his friends clapped and cheered.

Alice glanced over at Jools and Holly, who were standing in the corner with Dan's daughter, Stella. Jools smiled crookedly at her mother, while Holly gave her a double thumbs-up. Alice smiled back and allowed herself to breathe. Everything was going to be fine. She had made the right decision.

Alice leaned into Dan and said, 'Thank you for . . . well, for everything. For saving me and for making me see that I could be happy again . . .' She stopped as her voice quivered.

Dan kissed her hand. 'You're the one who's made *me* happy. I want to tell them about the engagement.' Alice tried to protest but before she could stop him, he bellowed, 'One final thing. I've asked Alice to marry me.'

The room went silent. Clearly Dan's friends had not been expecting this. But then someone began to clap and everyone joined in.

Alice frowned. 'Dan, I told you I needed time for me and the girls to get used to the idea before announcing it.'

'Relax, darling, I told the girls when they arrived that I was going to announce it tonight. They told me to go ahead.' Dan beamed.

Before Alice could say anything else, there was a quiet cough at Dan's elbow and the event organizer shot him an apologetic smile. 'Excuse me, so sorry to interrupt, but I'd just like to check when you wish the food to be served, Mr Penfold.'

Dan kissed Alice once more, then headed towards the kitchen. Alice's brother, Kevin, came over to her. Squeezing her hand, he said, 'Calm down, it was going to come out soon anyway.'

'I know, but I don't like surprises. I'm worried about the girls.'

'They're fine. They really like Dan. Alice, smile, you're going to scare the guests.'

Alice laughed, letting go of the tension in her stomach. 'You're right. I guess I'm still getting used to the idea of marrying someone else.'

'You deserve to be happy. He's a good man. You have to look forward now.'

Alice's eyes filled with tears. 'Thanks, Kevin, you've been brilliant. I really do love Dan and, like he said, I'm going to take this second chance and embrace it.'

'Good for you,' he said. 'If only his brother was gay — I could get seriously used to this.' He waved his hand around at the plush furnishings and enormous chandeliers.

'Your prince will come,' Alice teased him.

'When? I'm not getting any younger. Older gay men are not in demand, especially the ones with no money!'

'If it can happen to me, it can happen to you.' Alice kissed her brother's cheek.

'By the way, you should probably say something, Alice. I overheard one of Dan's friends mutter that he hoped Dan was doing the right thing. They all seem nice enough, but I'd say the idea of him taking on a widow and two kids has raised a few eyebrows.'

Alice sighed. She and Dan had kept to themselves during their whirlwind romance so she didn't know his friends, but she did want them to like her. There were about twenty people gathered in the room, and she was doing her best to talk to each one. They seemed very nice, but it was all a bit intimidating. She decided her brother was right, that she needed to take the bull by the horns and say a few words.

Dan was walking towards her. As he came close she caught his hand and whispered, 'I'd like to say something too, if that's all right.'

He looked pleased. 'Of course, darling.'

Alice tapped the side of her glass for silence. The chatter died down. 'I'm sorry to string out the speeches, but I'd like to add something quickly. I never expected to be lucky enough to meet someone again, but then Dan came into my life and he's made me see that there is such a thing as a second chance. I –'

Alice was interrupted by Mrs Jenkins, Dan's housekeeper, who pressed her arm gently. She was holding a phone. 'I'm sorry, Alice,' she whispered, 'but there's a man on the phone who says he must talk to you urgently. An emergency. A Mr Jonathan Londis from the Foreign and Commonwealth Office.'

Alice excused herself, took the phone and walked out into the vast reception area.

'Hello?' Alice said, her voice sounding odd in the emptiness of the large hallway.

'Hello, Mrs Gregory, I'm calling you with some rather incredible news.' He sounded breathless. 'I have someone here who wants to say hello.'

Alice's heart began to beat very fast. Her mouth went dry. What was going on? Her hands were trembling uncontrollably. 'Hello – who is it?'

# PART I

# London, October 2012

*Alice*

Kevin locked up the surgery and handed Alice the keys.

'God, I'm tired today.' Alice yawned. 'It's been non-stop.'

'It's such a bitch being so popular,' Kevin said, grinning.

Alice smiled. 'I'm glad to be busy, but I'd just love a soak in the bath instead of a long evening wrestling with Jools about homework. And now Ben's invited David and Pippa for dinner tomorrow night, so I'll have to go to the shops on my way home.'

'Maybe Ben will come home early tomorrow and help cook for his friends.'

'Fat chance.' Alice sighed. 'I love David and Pippa, but dinner at nine on a Tuesday night just doesn't suit me. I'm always so tired after dealing with Jools.'

'You should have said no, then.'

Alice smiled at the idea. Kevin had never really grasped the concept of compromise in relationships. Which was probably why his never lasted very long. 'Ben was really keen to have them over and we do owe them. They're always inviting us to dinner parties in their house.'

'Get take-out and pretend you cooked. Problem solved.'

Alice shook her head. 'It'll be fine. I'll pop into M&S now on the way back. Don't mind me, I'm just being a grump.'

'Well, I'll think of you slaving over a hot stove as I'm flying into NYC.'

Alice punched his arm playfully. 'I hope you have a great

time, but don't go home with strange men. New York is dangerous.'

Kevin snorted. 'I'm planning on going home with as many strange men as will have me.'

Alice rolled her eyes. 'Like I said, have fun but be careful and safe too.'

'You'll miss me.'

'I always do when you go away, even for just a week.'

'I'm the best medical secretary around.'

'Yes, you are.' Alice kissed her brother. 'See you when you get back. Have fun.'

'I fully intend to!' Kevin winked at her. 'Now go home to your girls.'

Alice liked the fifteen-minute walk home, which allowed her to decompress. Some days being a GP was very hard – today, she'd been vomited on by a three-year-old with tonsillitis, shouted at by a patient with acute back pain and propositioned by a randy eighty-year-old man.

On days like this she envied Ben and his exciting job. He considered a general surgeon to be at a different echelon from a general practitioner. He never said it, he wouldn't dare, but she knew he thought it. He'd say things like 'I've had a hell of a day. I performed an inguinal hernia repair, a cholecystectomy, a cervical gland excision and two breast biopsies. How was your day?'

Sometimes she wanted to scream at him that (a) she had studied for almost as many years as he had and (b) she had chosen a job that allowed her to get home early for their children because someone had to be there. As a result, she not only ran a busy surgery but she also did the vast majority of the work involved in raising their two daughters. As she went into M&S, she felt a stab of envy for her husband's life:

hot-shot surgical job, no housework, setting up dinners without doing any of the organizing whatsoever. It must be nice to be Ben, she thought crossly.

Once she had decided on and bought the ingredients for dinner the next night, she walked quickly towards home. She wanted to get back in time to cook for the girls. Nora, her nanny, housekeeper and, at times, surrogate mother, was wonderful, but her cooking was very basic. When they were young it had been fine, but now the girls were a bit older, Alice was keen for them to try new things.

As she stepped into the hall of their Kensington mews home, she could hear Jools complaining: 'I'm not eating rice any more, Nora, only quinoa now.'

'Keenwa?' Nora snapped. 'Never heard of it.'

'It's kind of new. Gwyneth Paltrow eats it all the time and she's super-healthy. So can you please cook it for me?'

'Sure that one is like a toothpick. She needs a good feed. I bet you that keenwa is one of those new makey-up things. One of those scientist things that'll give you cancer in the end. Meat and two veg is what you need.'

Alice rounded the corner into the kitchen where fifteen-year-old Jools was looking very put out. She was pouting in the way Alice knew well – it generally preceded an outburst of one kind or another, which Nora wouldn't tolerate.

'I think quinoa is perfectly safe, Nora. Don't worry, I'll cook it for her. Why don't you head home?'

'I will so,' Nora said. 'Himself will be wanting his pork chops and potatoes. No keenwa for him!'

Alice laughed at the idea of Nora's husband, a retired plumber from Yorkshire, eating quinoa. They were a no-nonsense couple. Nora was from the deepest west of Ireland, with a sturdy farming background. When Alice had gone back to work after Jools was born, she had been delighted to find an Irish minder for her baby. Nora's kids had flown the nest and she wanted a nice job where she could earn some money. She had been there when Alice's parents had been killed in a car crash and had become a surrogate mother to Alice in many ways.

As Alice walked Nora to the door, her phone beeped. It was Ben: *Going for a cycle after work. C u about 9.*

Alice cursed. The selfish git. He had promised to help Jools with her homework tonight and now he was going for a bloody cycle. She could kill him!

'What is it?' Nora asked.

'Ben's going cycling after work. Again.'

'Sure aren't all men in their forties these days cycling around in tight shorts looking like right eejits. Don't worry, it's just a little mid-life crisis. Better his balls are tucked into the Lycra than into some young nurse.'

'Nora!'

'I'm just saying . . .'

Alice sighed. 'Let's hope it's not both!'

Nora slapped her arm gently. 'Stop that now. Ben is devoted to you and the girls. He's a good man, Alice. Let him off on his bike. This phase he's going through will wear off. He'll tire himself out eventually, or the Lycra will cut off his blood circulation. Either way, he'll get fed up.'

Alice laughed and waved Nora off. It had started to rain and she half hoped it might put Ben off cycling so he'd turn up before nine and do the homework shift.

When she went back into the kitchen, Jools was flicking through the Gwyneth Paltrow cookbook. Alice had bought it a few weeks previously in an effort to try different recipes and be more healthy generally. So far she'd only made one dish from it and she'd ended up eating a whole box of Maltesers afterwards, which had cancelled out her effort at healthy eating. Mind you, she liked looking at the pictures of Gwyneth and her beautiful children, sunlight kissing the tops of their heads.

Jools closed the book with a slap. 'So, we need to talk about my party.'

Alice smiled. Jools seemed to think turning sixteen deserved some kind of jubilee celebration.

'I know I said I wanted to be healthier,' Jools went on, 'but when it comes to my party, I want a chocolate bonanza. I want –'

'I would like,' Alice interrupted.

'Fine. I would like a chocolate cake, with Harry from One Direction on it, and a sleepover with my seven best friends – I've decided to invite Harriet, too, even though she's kind of a nerd but she's funny – and we're not watching some lame film. We're going to watch *The Texas Chainsaw Massacre* and I don't care what you say.'

Leaning over the table Alice said, 'Let me stop you right there. You will not be watching *The Texas Chainsaw Massacre* because it's really violent and frightening and is not suitable for you or your friends.'

Jools slammed her hand onto the marble countertop. 'I knew you'd say that. I knew you'd ruin my party. I'm going to ask Daddy – he'll let me.'

Of course he will, Alice thought. His giving in to Jools was the main issue that Ben and she argued about. Ben completely indulged Jools and it drove Alice nuts.

Alice reckoned it was because Jools was their firstborn, a girl and looked just like him. The moment Jools had been born, Ben had fallen head over heels in love with her. When he'd held her for the first time, he'd cried. The love in his eyes was overwhelming. Alice had known he'd be a great dad, but she'd also had the foresight to anticipate trouble ahead. A man so besotted with his daughter was going to be a walk-over when it came to discipline. Ben found it very hard to say no to Jools, so Alice had ended up with the role of 'bad cop'. Alice loved her daughter more than anything, but she didn't want her turning into a spoilt brat. She wanted her to know the value of things, to appreciate what she had and not to take everything for granted.

Holly had come along four years later and had been a dream child. Where Jools hadn't slept through the night until she was three, Holly had from ten weeks. Even as a baby Jools had demanded everyone's attention but Holly had always found something to occupy herself. Half the time Alice and Ben would forget Holly was even in the room. She was always so quiet.

Alice knew it was wrong to compare children, and that she shouldn't, but if she was being really honest, she found Jools very trying and Holly was just . . . well, easy.

Alice took a deep breath to calm herself. She didn't want to get into an argument with Jools. 'What do you want for birthday breakfast? You know you're allowed anything you like.'

Jools didn't hesitate. 'Pancakes filled with whipped cream and Nutella.'

'I really don't think you need cream on top of Nutella – you'll be sick.'

Jools eyeballed her mother. 'You said I could have anything I wanted.'

'Yes, but I thought you were trying to be more healthy.'

Jools snorted. 'I'm hardly going to have quinoa in my birthday pancakes.'

Alice decided to let this one go. 'Fine, but don't come crying to me if you throw up in school from sugar overload.'

'Don't worry, I'd never come crying to you. Daddy's the one I go to when I'm upset about anything.'

Alice tried not to show that she was hurt. She knew she was strict but she wasn't unsympathetic. Ben, on the other hand, was hardly ever home, these days, and when he was, he always sided with Jools. Alice was sick of being the bad cop. She needed Ben to help more. Lately, she had felt increasingly like a single parent.

'That was mean, Jools,' Holly said, as she came into the room, with a book. 'Mummy's just offered to make you a super-yummy breakfast. You should be grateful. There are nearly eight hundred and seventy million people in the world who don't have enough to eat. That's one in eight people.'

'Will you please shut up with your stupid facts? You're like a walking calculator.'

'Leave your sister alone,' Alice warned. 'You could do with a bit more fact-finding yourself – and a little less cheek,' she added.

'Yeah, like I want to be a nerd like Holly,' Jools snarled.

'Holly is not a nerd. She's a very clever girl.'

'Miss Robinson says I'm a joy to teach,' Holly defended herself.

'Good for her. I bet you are.' Alice kissed her.

'Nobody likes the teacher's pet, Holly. You'll end up with no friends.' Jools was unimpressed.

'She has lots of friends!' Alice said.

'Like who?' Jools asked.

'Jackie,' Holly said.

'Is she the geek with the big glasses?'

'Yes.'

'Seriously, Holly, you need to stop banging on about boring stuff and start making some cool friends before you totally blow it and end up being cast as a total nerd. I don't need my sister being the biggest loser in school.'

'I feel sorry for you, Jools.' Holly placed her book on the table. 'You care far too much about what other people think. Miss Robinson says you should be true to yourself and not worry about other people's opinions.'

'Miss Robinson is officially insane. Mum, you need to talk to her and stop her ruining kids' lives.'

Alice decided to step in. 'Okay, girls, let's try not to argue any more. I want us to have a nice time and not fight over dinner. Jools, I'll make you pancakes with Nutella and whipped cream for your birthday breakfast, but I'm only allowing you to eat two. I'll make big ones.'

'Three.'

'Two.'

'Three.'

'How about two and a half?' Holly suggested.

'Good idea,' Alice said.

'Fine,' Jools said.

'Yummy!' Holly enthused. 'I can't wait. Can I have two, Mummy?'

'Yes, pet.'

'Can I at least have a hot chocolate as well?' Jools asked.

Alice knew it was a case of picking your battles, and gave in. 'Okay.'

Jools almost smiled. 'Thanks.'

Alice went to the fridge to get a start on dinner while Jools and Holly did their homework at the kitchen table.

Alice spotted *Little Women* in front of Jools. 'Have you finished it yet?'

Jools flushed. 'No, not yet.'

'Aren't you supposed to be doing a summary of it for next week?'

'Yes, it's fine. I'll get it done.'

Alice frowned. Jools was a slow reader. She struggled with spelling. When she was seven, Alice and Ben had thought she was dyslexic but the tests said she wasn't. She was just a very bad speller. Alice had done everything in her power to get Jools to read more as she knew it would improve her spelling, but Jools didn't enjoy it and it was a constant battle to get her to read anything.

'No television tonight. I want you to read for an hour instead. You need to finish it, Jools. It's a brilliant book. You'll love it once you get into it.'

'That's what you said about those stupid *St Clare's* books with all those dorks at boarding-school having midnight feasts and playing lame stink-bomb tricks on their ridiculous French teacher. They were beyond boring.'

'If you'd read more than the first twenty pages, you would probably have enjoyed them.'

'I love those books, and the *Naughtiest Girl* ones,' Holly said. 'I'd like to go to boarding-school.'

Jools snorted. 'You should go to a boarding-school for geeks. You'd fit right in.'

'Stop it!' Alice snapped. 'Holly isn't a geek, she's clever and studious.'

'Yeah, and I'm thick,' Jools muttered.

'No, you aren't. You just need to concentrate your mind a bit more.'

'Yeah, right! It's okay, Mum, I know I'm rubbish at school

but I'm popular and good-looking so I'll be fine. You won't have to look after me. I'll marry some millionaire and live in LA.'

'I like looking after you and I hope you marry someone you love, regardless of the size of his wallet. Besides, I'd hate you to live in LA – it's too far away and it's full of vacuous people who've had too much plastic surgery.'

'Is "vacuous" a kind of Botox?'

Alice tried not to laugh. 'No.'

'Is it a type of filler?'

'How do you even know about these things?'

Jools shrugged. 'The Kardashians. They get it done and they look amazing.'

Alice frowned. 'I told you that I didn't want you watching that rubbish any more.'

'Then how come I caught you watching it last week?'

Alice had been caught red-handed, glued to *Keeping Up With the Kardashians* – it was her secret guilty pleasure. After dealing with patients' problems all day, she liked nothing better than to kick back and watch cheesy reality TV.

'I wanted to see if it was as bad as I thought.' Alice fudged the question.

'"Vacuous" means "not expressing intelligent thought".' Holly looked up from her dictionary.

'The Kardashians would be an excellent example of that,' Alice noted.

'I think they rock. Their life is so cool.'

'I want to be like Malala Yousafzai,' Holly said.

Alice paused. 'Well, yes, she is incredibly brave, but I'd rather you didn't get shot for your beliefs.'

Jools's mouth dropped open. 'OMG, is she the kid who got shot because she *wanted* to go to school? I thought it was a joke when Miss Kent told us about her. Then I presumed there was something wrong with her, like she was mentally ill or something. Why would anyone get on some stupid bus to go to school if they could stay at home? I actually said to Miss Kent that I wanted to go and live in Pakistan. It sounded awesome – no school for girls. How cool is that?'

Alice covered her eyes with her hand. 'What did Miss Kent say?'

'She was all red in the face and went on this crazy rant about women's rights and sufferagettes and equality and blah-blah-blah.'

Alice didn't know whether to laugh or cry.

It was Holly's turn to be incredulous. 'I'm actually embarrassed to be your sister right now. Malala Yousafzai is the bravest, most courageous girl in the world. She risked her life to get an education. You're just . . . just –'

'What? Dumb? Stupid?' Jools challenged her.

'Ignorant.'

'At least I knew Flo Rida was a rapper and not an actual place in America!'

'Florida *is* a place in America. It's one of the fifty states in America. He just took the name and cut it up,' Holly countered.

'Oh, my God, you're like an old woman who lives in the Dark Ages,' Jools shouted. 'You should read less and actually watch some TV so you know what's going on in the world.'

'Sure, because knowing Flo Rida is some loser who can't even sing is going to make my life so much better.'

'You might make some actual friends if you can talk to them about normal things.'

'You –'

Alice put a hand on each daughter's shoulder. 'Enough! Stop being so mean to each other. I always wanted a sister

17

and you're lucky to have each other. I hate seeing you guys fighting.'

'Kevin is kind of like a sister,' Jools said.

Holly giggled.

Alice grinned and went back to her cooking.

## *Ben*

Ben put his head down and hunched his shoulders against the driving rain. His legs were aching and his heart was pumping. He rode on. It felt good to push himself. He glanced at his watch: he was two minutes faster than last week. If he could keep it up for the final five miles, he'd beat his best time.

He pounded along the wet London streets, ignoring his ringing phone. It would be Alice, moaning at him for being late. She didn't get it. He needed to let off steam after a long day operating. She was lucky, really. Some of his colleagues went straight to the wine bar opposite the hospital and drank themselves into oblivion. Others shagged young nurses or interns.

But Ben preferred to cycle. Not that the idea of getting drunk or having hot sex with a young nurse wasn't appealing, but he was a married man and he took that seriously. Sure he'd been tempted over the years, but so far he had resisted.

He really wished Alice would back off and stop nagging him about cycling. She said it took up too much time and that it was dangerous. She said he spent enough time away from home at the hospital and didn't need to waste an extra six or seven hours a week cycling.

The problem was, her job was easy. Ben didn't want to belittle her, but it really was. She doled out antibiotics and listened to old people complain about aches and pains. It wasn't exactly cutting-edge. Alice was a very good GP and Ben was proud of how she had built up her practice, but she didn't understand the pressures of being a surgeon. Ben dealt with life and death. Granted, he did a lot of run-of-the-mill procedures too, but the complex operations always gave him a high. Occasionally they gave him a terrible low: a patient's death was never easy. Every patient he lost weighed heavily on his mind. People complained that surgeons got paid too much, but they had no idea of the toll a bad day could take on a person.

Thankfully the good days, of which there were many, made up for the bad ones. Ben loved the cut and thrust of the operating theatre. He loved the feeling of entering the 'zone', the place where you went when all noise was blocked out and it was just you and the body lying in front of you.

There was nothing like the rush of adrenalin when you were in the middle of a difficult surgery. Surgeons had a bad reputation. People accused them of having God complexes. Ben never felt like God, but saving someone's life was pretty fantastic. It was a high he'd never get tired of. That moment of elation, when he knew the patient was going to live because of his handiwork, was like a drug.

Alice couldn't understand. No one could. You had to be there. You had to witness it first-hand. Ben knew that he was at the top of his game right now and he wanted to do more. He wanted to challenge himself.

He looked up and saw David, wearing a bright green jacket, waiting for him, sheltering under a tree.

'I was hoping you'd cancel,' David said.

'No way. This is my release before going home to bedlam. Honestly, I think you and Pippa have it right – one child, who goes to boarding-school. Your home life must be bliss.'

David pushed his pedals and fell into rhythm with Ben. 'It

suits us, but come on, Ben, you adore your girls. You'd hate them to be away at boarding-school.'

Ben smiled. His friend was right. He would hate it if the girls were away. He loved seeing them, although lately it had become less fun. It was all homework and hormones, these days. Things had changed.

'Any more thoughts on applying for a job at Addenbrooke's?' David asked.

'I'm still thinking about it but haven't approached them yet. I'm very tempted. I want to push myself. I'm in a bit of a rut – I'm sick of doing appendectomies and hernia repairs.'

'Well, a major trauma centre like Addenbrooke's would certainly shake things up for you. But Cambridge isn't an easy commute,' David pointed out.

Ben wiped rain from his eyes. 'I know. Alice will go completely mad if I do get a job there, but I need more stimulation. I feel as if life is passing me by.'

'Well, be careful. Remember what happened to me when I had my mid-life blip two years ago? I almost lost Pippa.'

David had had a fling with one of the nurses at the private hospital where he worked and Pippa had found out. They had almost split up, but David had begged and pleaded and offered to go to marriage counselling, and things had settled down. Ben was glad they'd worked things out. They were good together. Pippa was a lovely woman and he would have hated to see them separate.

'You've got a good marriage,' David said. 'Don't rush into taking a job that might damage it. Pippa always says that you and Alice are the best couple we know because you still have fun together. All our other friends just bicker all the time.'

'We've been bickering a lot more recently, but I know what you mean. Alice is wonderful and I don't want to cause problems. Maybe I need to look for stimulation elsewhere.'

'As long as you don't look for it where I did,' David warned. 'Stay away from the nurses is my advice.'

Ben knew Alice would go nuts if he took a job in Cambridge. It would mean longer hours and many overnights at the trauma centre. Alice would never move. She had her thriving practice and the girls were settled at school. They'd only bought the house three years ago, Alice's dream home. It was just off Kensington High Street in a little courtyard of eight.

'I think turning forty-five has thrown me,' Ben admitted. David was the only person in the world he could say this to and not feel self-conscious. He knew his friend understood. 'I suddenly realized that more than half my life was over. Let's be honest here, I've only got ten more years at the top of my game, fifteen if I'm lucky.'

'But look at what you've achieved already,' David reminded him.

'There's so much more I want to learn and do. I suddenly feel as if a time-bomb's ticking loudly in my ear.'

'I do understand, but sometimes it's important to look at what you have instead of what you don't. Believe me, Ben, I made that mistake and almost lost my family.'

Ben arrived home soaking wet and exhausted. As he squelched through the hall in his wet socks towards the kitchen, he could hear Alice and Jools arguing.

'Come on, Jools, concentrate. It's ten past nine, you're tired and so am I. We need to get this finished.'

'I'm trying,' Jools snapped. 'I don't understand the stupid question!'

'It's not that difficult, darling. You just need to explain why Henry the Eighth split with Rome.'

'I don't care about boring old Henry the Eighth and his millions of wives. He was just a big, fat, greedy loser who married women to have babies with, and when they had girls, he killed them off. If you'd been married to him, you would have had your head chopped off.'

'If you could find a way to express that more eloquently, we'd be halfway there. Now, come on, why did Henry turn his back on Rome?'

'Because he wanted to marry Anne of Cleves.'

'No, not Anne of Cleves.'

'Fine. Catherine Something.'

'No, Jools, it was Anne Boleyn. We've been over this a million times.'

'Well, if he wasn't such a sleazebag and didn't marry so many women, I wouldn't be getting mixed up.'

Ben knew that this would end in yet another argument between his wife and daughter. They clashed constantly. Since Jools's hormones had kicked in, she had become more difficult to deal with, but Alice was too impatient with her. Ben found Jools trying too, but he was better at handling her. He came up with games to help her remember things. When it came to exams, Alice always begged him to help her study. He felt sorry for his elder daughter. It wasn't easy for her. Both he and Alice had sailed through school and Holly was always top of her class. Poor old Jools simply wasn't that academic. Ben just wanted her to be happy, get through school and do something she liked.

He and Alice were already putting money aside for both daughters to help them buy an apartment when they were older. Jools was very pretty and street-smart, and Ben reckoned she'd be fine. Holly was incredibly bright, but clueless about life. He worried more about her. He could see her spending her whole life with her head stuck in a book and waking up at forty, single, with no children and nothing but her work to keep her warm at night.

Alice told him he was being ridiculous: Holly would meet some like-minded brainbox and live happily ever after doing research or finding the cure for cancer. She worried all the time about Jools not having a career, taking a dead-end job, meeting the wrong type of boy and getting pregnant at eighteen.

'Hello, everyone. Having fun with the Tudors, I hear.' Ben kissed Jools's head.

'Ooh, you're all wet and gross.' She pulled away from him. Ben kissed his wife.

'You're soaking, Ben.' Alice wiped the rain from her cheek. 'Can you dry off and help Jools with her homework?'

'Give me five minutes for a very quick shower and I'll be straight back down.'

When Ben came out of the bathroom, Alice was sitting on the edge of the bed. 'Thank God you walked in when you did. I was about to shove the history book down her throat. She has the concentration span of a gnat!'

Ben pulled on a pair of jeans and a sweatshirt. 'I know, but you really must try to be more patient, darling.'

Alice tensed. 'That's easy for you to say, swanning in at nine o'clock. I've already spent almost two hours trying to help her with her homework, so please don't tell me I'm not being patient.'

Ben leant down and kissed her cheek. 'Don't blow a fuse. I know it's not easy. I'll take over and you can relax.'

'Sounds good to me.' Alice smiled.

He left Alice reading and went back down to Jools. When he walked into the kitchen, Jools had her back to him and was FaceTiming her friend Chloë. 'I know, right? He's totally hot,' she said.

'And he totally fancies you, Jools,' Chloë replied.

'No way!' Jools protested weakly.

Ben smiled. Jools was well aware that she was a good-looking girl.

'He so does. I bet you get together at Amelia's party.'

'Is he definitely going, then?' Jools was trying to sound nonchalant.

'Yes. He told Jeremy who told Alex who told Jude who told me.'

'Okay, well, that's cool.'

'What are you going to wear?'

Jools shrugged. 'I haven't really thought about it. Maybe my pink Topshop dress.'

'OMG, you should so wear that! It's amazing on you! Ollie will die when he sees you in it.'

Let's hope not, thought Ben. He didn't want his daughter causing anyone's demise.

'My mum thinks it's too short. My dad hasn't seen it. He'd go mental if he did. He's such a nerd – he thinks I should be wearing long skirts like those freaks who live in cults in America. You know, the ones where one man has, like, twenty wives and they all call each other "Sister". So weird.'

Ben coughed loudly. 'Exactly how short is this dress, Jools?'

Jools squealed and hung up. 'For God's sake, Daddy, you almost gave me a heart attack. How long have you been standing there?'

'Long enough to know some guy called Ollie likes you, you're getting together at Amelia's party and you're planning on wearing an obscenely short dress.'

Jools blushed. 'You shouldn't eavesdrop. It's rude.'

'You will not be going anywhere in a dress that's too short. You're a beautiful girl, Jools, and you don't need to show off all your flesh.'

'Please stop talking. You're so embarrassing.'

'I'm serious. I know you look at me and think, Old Man, but I was once a teenager and I didn't find the girl in the shortest dress the most attractive. It was the girl with the dress that actually covered her bottom and had the best smile that I went for.'

'Mum has a nice smile, when she uses it,' Jools said, doodling on her copybook.

'Mum has a fantastic smile. It lights up a room.'

Jools yawned, clearly bored with the conversation. Ben clapped his hands. 'Right, what have you got left to do?'

'I'm supposed to learn the first verse of this boring poem.' Jools handed Ben her book and pointed.

'Ah, "The Lady of Shalott" by Alfred, Lord Tennyson. I remember this one. Right, off you go.'

Jools's brow knitted in concentration. '"On each side of the river lies a field of long . . . grass"?'

'No, it's "On either side the river lie Long fields of barley and of rye, That clothe the wold and meet the sky."'

'Oh, yeah. Okay. "On each side" –'

'No, Jools, it's "On either side".'

'Okay. "On either side of the river lies fields of . . . of . . ."'

'"Long fields of barley and of rye".'

'"Long fields of barely any rye".'

'No, Jools, it's not "barely", it's "barley".'

She shrugged. 'It's the same.'

'No, it isn't. Barley is a grain and "barely" means "scarcely".'

'Fine, whatever.'

'Start from the beginning.' Ben glanced down at the

poem. There were nine lines to learn. This was going to take a while.

'"On each side of the river lies a field of barley and rye."'

'You're nearly there.' Ben was determined to be positive. 'You just need to add in a few words – "On either side the river lie Long fields of barley and of rye . . ."'

'That's what I said.'

'Not exactly. Okay, let's move on to the next line. We can get a rhythm going. '"That clothe the wold and meet the sky".'

'That closes the world and met the sky.'

'"Clothe".'

'Oh, "close".'

'No, the word is "clothe".'

'What?'

'"Clothe".'

'What does that even mean? Hello, it's just a made-up word.'

'No, Jools, it isn't. It means "to dress".'

'Dress the world? Is he a designer? Was he like Victoria Beckham back in the old days?'

'No. He was a poet. It's an expression.'

'Oh.' Jools looked disappointed. 'For a nano-second I thought he might actually be interesting.'

'He's one of the most famous poets in the history of the world.'

'Yeah, right. Well, he doesn't do it for me. This poem sucks.'

Ben took a deep breath. 'Come on, Jools, concentrate. You need to focus so you can learn the poem and not be here all night.'

'You sound just like Mum.'

'Well, she's right, you do need to concentrate a bit harder.

Okay, now don't get frustrated, we'll take it nice and slowly. Let's do the first three lines again.'

Thirty minutes later, they had got to line four. As Jools made yet another mistake, Ben lost it.

'For God's sake, Jools, will you please focus! It's not that hard. We're not even halfway through and you've got it wrong every single time.'

'It's not easy for me. I'm not bloody Holly with the freaky brain.'

'It's one verse of a poem, Jools! It's not a lot to remember and if you stopped looking around and getting up to fetch drinks and snacks, you might actually memorize it properly. This has nothing to do with your ability to learn and everything to do with your lack of focus. Now we are going to sit here until you memorize it, so I strongly recommend that you concentrate.'

'You're a tryant.'

'I think you mean "tyrant".'

'Whatever.'

Ben ended up bribing Jools. He told her that if she memorized the poem, he'd give her ten pounds. That made her concentrate and, after a further torturous twenty minutes, she kind of knew it. She tripped up here and there, but Ben had reached his limit. They called it a night, and when Jools was in her bedroom, ten pounds richer, Ben went up to Alice.

He handed his wife a glass of wine and took a large gulp from his own. Alice smirked at him. 'Did you have fun?'

Ben sat beside her on the bed and groaned. 'Christ, she's hard work. I'd forgotten how bad she is.'

Alice raised an eyebrow. Ben held up his hands. 'I know,

I'm sorry. I haven't helped her with her homework in a while and I'd genuinely forgotten what torture it is.'

'And exactly how "patient" were you?'

'I started off well, and then I lost my temper. You're a saint for doing that every night. Is it just me or is she getting worse?'

'The homework is getting more difficult and she's struggling to keep up.'

'Is she just . . . stupid?' Ben asked.

'No. She isn't interested. If you ask Jools to recite passages from the *Twilight* movies, she can do it, no problem. She just doesn't apply herself to schoolwork.'

'What are we going to do?'

'Keep helping her and encouraging her and –'

'Bribing her.'

'What?'

'I'm ashamed to say I bribed her.'

'Ben!'

'Alice, she was torturing me and poor Tennyson, who is definitely turning in his grave by the way. So I told her I'd give her a tenner if she'd just learn the bloody verse.'

'Did it work?'

'Not exactly. She's still reciting it with missing bits, but I couldn't listen to another word of it. She's ruined Tennyson for me for life.'

Alice began to laugh, such a happy, infectious sound. Ben loved it. He joined in, enjoying the release from his week's worries and having fun with his wife.

## Holly

Mummy and Jools are having a big fight because Jools lied about reading *Little Women*. Mummy gave it to her nineteen days ago and she never got past the first chapter. But she pretended she'd read it when she'd just watched the movie on her iPad. When Mummy asked her about the book, Jools said she thought it boring with a stupid end – Jo would never have gone off with Gabriel Byrne because he was way too old.

Mummy said that Jools was a liar for pretending she'd read the book. She said there was no one in the book called Gabriel Byrne. She said that Gabriel Byrne is a famous Irish actor.

Jools shouted that Mummy was mean and always trying to force her to be clever. She said she was sick of it and that Mummy should just leave her alone. Then she said something really mean and I saw Mummy's face go all red. Jools said that Gabriel Byrne wasn't famous at all, he was just a stupid old Irishman with a stupid accent like Mummy's. She said she wished Mummy had a normal voice and didn't pronounce words all wrong because it was embarrassing.

I stopped breathing for eight seconds because I was worried Mummy was going to be angry, but she actually just looked really sad. She said she was sorry that Jools found her so embarrassing and then she went upstairs.

Jools pretended she didn't care, but I knew she felt bad because she set the table for dinner, which she never does.

I went up to Mummy's bedroom. She was sitting on her bed doing deep breathing. I went up and gave her a hug. I told her I liked the way she talks. I said that I think her accent is lovely. It's very sing-songy.

Mummy hugged me very tight – a bit too tight. I counted to twenty and then I pulled away because I was having trouble breathing.

## Alice

Holly came into the kitchen and sat up at the counter. 'Mummy, I loved it.'

'What?' Alice put her phone down.

'*Little Women*. I read it and I adored it.'

Alice leant over and kissed her. 'You really are a wonder. I can't believe you've read it so quickly.'

Alice often wondered where Holly had come from. She and Ben were smart, but Holly was unique. Her mind never stopped working. She had been born a month premature and was still small for her age, but she was streets ahead of the other eleven-year-olds in her year. She was like a sponge that soaked up everything around her.

Alice worried that Holly didn't have enough fun. She was always reading or working things out in her mind. She wasn't very sporty, although she always tried her best, and she didn't seem interested in making jewellery, experimenting with make-up or listening to music, like Jools and her friends had when they were eleven.

Holly's pale blue eyes looked up at Alice. While Jools was sallow-skinned, like Ben, and had his thick dark hair and beautiful big brown eyes, Holly had Alice's strawberry blonde hair and light eyes, although Holly's eyes were so pale they were almost translucent. People often said she reminded them of the little girl in the movie *Atonement*.

Holly tapped Alice's arm. 'Mummy, did you know there are four hundred and forty-nine pages in the book. In chapter one there are . . .'

Alice knew that Holly was about to break the book down into chapter-by-chapter page counts, and while she was constantly astounded by her daughter's mind, sometimes Holly needed to be nudged in a different direction. The chapter page count would turn into a page word count and it could go on for hours. When she was five Holly had counted to a thousand – slowly – on the six-hour drive from London to Holyhead. Ben had described it as the ultimate form of torture. Thankfully, Jools had had her headphones on during the drive, which was the only reason Holly had survived in one piece.

'So, who was your favourite character?' Alice asked.

Holly stopped focusing on the word count. Pushing her long hair out of her eyes, she said, 'I think Jo is just wonderful. And Beth is so kind and sweet, but I was very sad when Amy stole Laurie away.'

'I totally agree. I always thought Jo and Laurie should have ended up together.'

'Professor Bhaer was nice and kind, but Laurie was fun and he was her best friend,' Holly said.

'And he was rich, young and fit.' Jools shuffled in. Then, raising her hands, she said, 'I know I didn't read it, but I do know the story.'

Alice took some mushrooms out of the fridge and began to chop them. 'Relationships are not about money or looks. They're about love, loyalty and respect.'

'And friendship, Mummy – you always say that Daddy's your best friend,' Holly reminded her.

'You're right, darling, he is.'

'Okay, fine, but being rich and handsome are not bad things either,' Jools said.

'No, but kindness and decency are much more important,' Alice replied. Jools was obsessed with fame and celebrity to an extent that sometimes worried Alice. She clearly wasn't going to thrive in academia, but Alice was concerned that she thought celebrity was some kind of a viable career.

'I love Marmee, too. She's so wise and gentle,' Holly gushed.

'And she never shouts,' Jools said, with a smirk, as she popped a grape into her mouth.

'That's because she has four daughters who do what they're told and don't give her cheek. Besides, I don't shout a lot.'

'Holly? Back me up! Does Mummy shout a lot?'

Holly's eyes grew wide. 'It depends on the situation.'

'Don't put Holly on the spot. I know I shout sometimes, but usually with good reason. Now, can you help me tidy up? David and Pippa are coming for dinner. They'll be here in half an hour and the place is a mess.'

'Where's Daddy?' Jools asked.

Alice gritted her teeth. 'Stuck in work yet again. Let's just hope he actually makes it in time to have dinner with the friends *he* invited over.'

'Mum, you need to take a deep breath,' Jools said. 'Daddy can't help being stuck at work. He's probably saving a life or something.'

Or just not bothering to come home and help, Alice thought darkly.

'We'll help you, Mummy,' Holly said, tidying up the books that were strewn all over the table.

'Thanks, girls – what would I do without you?'

Within half an hour the kitchen was tidy, candles were lit and dinner was cooking in the oven.

Ben strolled in at nine.

'Nice of you to turn up,' Alice snapped.

'Oh, God, don't start nagging again.'

'Don't invite your friends for dinner if you're not even going to be here!' Alice hissed.

'I'm here now and they haven't arrived,' Ben said, as the doorbell rang.

Alice glared at him and went to check on the food.

David and Pippa arrived full of good cheer, laden with wine and chocolates.

While Ben and David had a drink in the lounge and chatted to the girls, Pippa and Alice had a glass of wine in the kitchen.

'So, how are things? I haven't seen you for about six months,' Pippa said.

'Life is just so bloody busy all the time – I never seem to catch up with anyone,' Alice replied. It was true: she never saw her friends from medical school. The surgery, the girls and Ben took up all of her time.

'Oh, darling, I don't know how you do it.' Pippa sipped her wine. 'I barely have time to fit everything in and I don't work and William is away at school.'

Alice loved Pippa. Her life was so privileged and different from Alice's yet they got on really well. Pippa was kind, sweet and generous to a fault. Both she and David were from landed gentry. David's parents owned half of Berkshire and Pippa's half of Kent. They were a perfect match.

They lived in a huge house in Holland Park. When Alice was with them, she felt as if she was in an episode of

*Downton Abbey*. They actually had a housekeeper and a driver, and always had cocktails at seven, before dinner. Alice loved going there – it was always so civilized and calm, not to mention luxurious and elegant.

'Hold on a minute!' Alice gasped. 'Your bracelet nearly took my eye out. Is it new?'

Pippa wrinkled her nose. 'It's the guilt bracelet. David bought it for me last year, after his liaison with that nurse. I don't like wearing it – it's terribly showy – but David gets offended if I don't. Honestly, men are such children.'

Alice squeezed Pippa's hand. 'I think it's wonderful that you guys managed to work it out. I was relieved as well as glad because we get to keep you both as friends.'

Pippa smiled. 'It hasn't been easy, but I'm glad too. I do love him, you know, and he truly is sorry. He's much nicer to me now than before. I think it was a mid-life crisis, to be honest. He felt his youth slipping away and wanted one last fling. Mind you, if it happens again I've told David that Daddy has the best lawyer lined up for me, a total Rottweiler. That frightened him a bit, I can tell you.'

'Serves him right!' Alice said. 'To be honest,' she said, lowering her voice, 'I think Ben's having some kind of mid-life thing as well.'

'With a nurse?' Pippa was visibly shocked.

'No – at least, I don't think so.'

'Thank goodness, although I can't imagine Ben being unfaithful to you.'

'Never say never.'

'That's true – I never thought David would do it to me.' Pippa looked down at her bracelet. Glancing up, she asked, 'Are you having sex?'

'Yes.'

'Regular sex?'

'Yes.' Alice felt a bit awkward discussing it with Pippa. It wasn't a usual topic of conversation for them.

'Oh, good. Sorry, but I had to ask. My counsellor said part of our problem was that we weren't having sex. I just went off it a bit, darling, but I'm making more of an effort now and it's much better.'

'I honestly don't think Ben's having an affair. It's more of a restlessness with life. He seems to be unfulfilled in work. It's scaring me a bit, where it might lead.'

'Don't worry. All men have a wobble at this age. Ben adores you. I always say to David that you have such a good marriage. It's balanced because you both have jobs, you both earn money and you make each other laugh. I'm sure this is just a little distraction that he'll get over soon.'

'I hope so,' Alice said, as she lifted the beef bourguignon out of the oven.

Dinner was lovely. They drank too much wine and told funny stories of medical-school days and holidays, children and work. Alice felt the red wine relaxing her. She watched Ben as he told an amusing anecdote about their honeymoon. His eyes twinkled in the candlelight and she thought how handsome he was.

He caught her eye and winked at her. Alice's stomach fluttered. He still had it. He could still make her want to rip his clothes off – especially after a few glasses of wine.

As they waved David and Pippa off, Ben pinched her bum. He closed the door and spun her towards him. 'You look very hot tonight, Dr Gregory.'

Alice giggled. 'You look pretty sexy yourself, Doctor. Can I be examined, please?'

'I'll give you the full once-over.'

Laughing, Ben pulled Alice into the lounge and they fell

onto the couch, kissing and tugging each other's clothes off. Their bodies, so used to each other, came together in a familiar dance. As they lay side by side, half dressed in the moonlight, fingers loosely entwined, Alice knew that everything would be all right.

## *Alice*

Alice was lost in a book when the doorbell rang. Jools ran to open it and Alice heard her squeal, then a louder male squeal. She knew her brother's voice immediately.

'Happy birthday, Jools. I know it's a little early, but I just got in from New York and I was dying for you to see your present.' Kevin came into the kitchen carrying a large box tied with a huge red bow.

'Uncle Kevin!' Holly jumped off her stool and ran to hug him.

Kevin swung her into the air. 'How's my little Einstein? Are you still dazzling everyone with your brains?'

Holly blushed. 'Kind of.'

'Well, you inherited them from me,' he said, and Alice almost snapped the book closed on her finger.

'*I don't believe it!*' Jools screeched. 'You're the best ever! I love you.' She pushed Alice and Holly aside to reach Kevin.

'I am pretty awesome,' Kevin agreed, with a grin.

'What did you get?' Alice asked.

'Only the silver jeans from the new Kardashian collection and a pink Hollister hoodie!' Jools hugged the clothes to her chest.

'The hoodie is also new season,' Kevin added. 'Neither pieces will be in the shops here until January.'

Jools ripped off her school uniform and put on her new clothes.

'Wow, the jeans are very . . . shiny,' Alice said, trying to be diplomatic. Jools looked like she was applying for a job as an astronaut.

Kevin raised an eyebrow. 'They're of the moment and she looks fabulous.'

'OMG, I can't wait for my friends to see them! I'm going to wear them at the party on Saturday. I have to send Chloë a selfie – she's going to die of jealousy!' Jools rushed off to get her phone.

Kevin turned to Holly. 'And this is a little something for you.' He handed her a small blue box. She opened it to find a silver Tiffany bracelet with a silver heart that said *smart girls rock*. 'I got it engraved especially for you.'

Holly hugged Kevin. 'Wow! It's not even my birthday. Thank you! I love it.'

Holly went off to show Jools her present and Kevin sat up at the counter. 'Any chance of a glass of wine?'

'Absolutely.' Alice grabbed a bottle from the fridge, then handed it to her brother with the corkscrew. Kevin poured them both a large glass.

Alice clinked hers with her brother's. 'It's good to have you back. I missed you at work.'

Kevin smirked. 'I take it Karolina wasn't as good with the patients as I am?'

'She's a little too dour.'

'It's good to go away sometimes so your boss appreciates you more,' he teased, waving his glass at her.

'I do appreciate you. You're the best-paid medical secretary in London.'

'Not quite, but you're a good employer, although you can be a little bossy at times.'

'That's the older sister in me.'

'You can't help yourself.'

'So New York was good?'

Kevin sighed happily. 'Wild and wonderful and far too short. I need a holiday after it. God, the clubs there are just incredible, and the men are *so* hot.'

'Did you meet anyone?'

'I sure did.' Kevin chuckled into his wine. 'Lots of people.'

Alice raised her hand. 'Let's stop there, I don't need any more details. Thanks for bringing the presents for the girls – you spoil them.'

'I could see by your face that the jeans were a big hit.'

'Well, they're very in-your-face. Ben's going to have a seiz-ure when he sees them.'

Kevin rolled his eyes. 'Ben's a fashion bore. He thinks wearing a red jumper is cutting-edge.'

Alice laughed. Ben was a very conservative dresser but he always looked smart. Mind you, with his lovely tanned skin, he looked good in anything. Alice thought he looked even more handsome with his hair going grey. He had aged very well, better than she had. His wrinkles marked him out as distinguished. Hers made her look tired.

Alice was careful about what she ate, and she ran when she could – usually early mornings before the girls woke up or at weekends when Ben was home. She had kept her figure and her hair was thick and long, but her face had aged faster than she'd have liked. She hadn't ruled out Botox, but she knew Ben would go mad if she did it. He was dead set against it and he constantly told her she was gorgeous. He was good like that – he complimented her a lot.

Kevin leant back in the kitchen chair. 'So, how's Ben? Is he still having his Lycra-wearing, holy-shit-I'm-forty-five crisis?'

'Ssh.' Alice walked over and closed the kitchen door. 'Yes, he is. But in the last week he's been in better form, less restless.'

'He should be thanking his lucky stars for what he has – a gorgeous wife who earns lots of money, two beautiful daughters and a mews house in Kensington. It doesn't get much better than that. Take it from a single man living in a shoebox in Soho.'

'Don't you think you're a bit old for Soho?'

'Hello? I'm thirty-seven, not ninety. Besides, I like Soho – it's where all the hot young men are.'

'Maybe I should move there!'

'Don't tell me you're having a mid-life wobble too?'

Alice shook her head. 'Not yet. Women usually have them in their fifties, around the menopause.'

'Well, that's something to look forward to. When you turn fifty Ben should get a job in Glasgow and I can move in with you, a sad, lonely gay man who gardens all day.'

'Have you met anyone nice recently?' Alice asked, as she took dinner ingredients out of the fridge. She really hoped Kevin would meet a lovely guy and settle down. Although he had a very active social life, she knew he wanted to find someone special. He'd been partying hard since he moved to London fifteen years ago.

Alice had always worried about her little brother. She always known he was gay, but her parents hadn't had a clue. When Kevin had finally come out, aged twenty, their parents had decided it was only a phase and kept praying that Kevin would meet a nice girl who might change his mind. Alice's mother had lit hundreds of candles and said novenas for her son, but instead of meeting a nice girl, Kevin had moved to London and met lots of men.

They'd grown up in a small town twenty miles outside Dublin and Kevin was, literally, the only gay in the village. Well, the only one who admitted it. According to Kevin's gaydar, Mr O'Reilly, the butcher, was gay but didn't know it, as was Johnny Kane, who owned the hardware store.

It had been difficult for him, and Alice had always felt protective of him. When she'd moved to London to study medicine, Kevin was only twelve. Alice knew secondary school was going to be hard for him and it had been. Confused about his sexuality and wanting to conform to the 'norms' of small-town Ireland, Kevin had tried to go out with girls but always ended up as their best friend.

Alice was the only person he had opened up to and she had supported him as much as she could, in between studying and doing insane hours during her internship.

When Kevin moved to London and was free to be the man he wanted to be, they had seen lots of each other – Kevin had lived with Alice and Ben for the first three months while he got settled. When their parents had been killed in a car crash fourteen years ago, they had become even closer. They clung to each other – the only family they had left.

Jools and Holly loved Kevin because he was the indulgent uncle who gave them all the things that Alice would never buy. Jools also seemed to think it was cool to have a gay uncle. He was wonderful with the girls and they adored him.

Ben liked Kevin, but hated him camping it up. Kevin knew this and always went over the top just to wind him up. Alice wished he wouldn't. She wanted her husband and brother to be closer.

She threw some vegetables and chicken into the pan.

'Smells good,' Kevin said.

'Would you like to stay for dinner? The girls would love it and, to be honest, I could do with Jools being diluted. We're clashing all the time.'

'Just like you and Mum.'

'I didn't fight with her all the time.'

Kevin whooped. 'You were always at each other's throats. You only got on when you moved out.'

Alice tried to think back. Had she fought as much with her mother as Jools did with her? If she was honest, she had to admit that they'd clashed a lot. When Alice had moved to London at nineteen to study medicine, her relationship with her mother had got a whole lot better. With a bit of distance between them, they had become more like friends than mother and daughter.

Alice had been devastated when her parents died. It was such a shock. To become an orphan overnight at the age of thirty seemed as ridiculous as it was sad. Ben had been a rock, and Alice knew she wouldn't have got through those dark days without him.

Sometimes Alice wondered if her grief had affected Jools. Her little girl had been nearly two when the car crash had happened and Alice had been grief-stricken and very low for months afterwards. She worried that Jools had picked up on her sorrow. Days would go by when Alice hadn't got dressed or even washed. She hadn't left the house for weeks and cried all the time.

Kevin had reacted to the tragedy by going wild. He had partied hard, drunk too much and taken lots of drugs to try to obliterate the pain. Thankfully, they'd both come out the other side – Alice because of Ben, and Kevin because he did masses of therapy.

'What do you think I should do to help me stop fighting with Jools? What did Mum do that worked?' Alice asked her brother now.

He shrugged. 'I dunno. All I remember is a lot of slamming doors and you being grounded all the time. Mum was very strict with you, and you are equally, if not more so, tough on Jools.'

Alice sighed. 'It's because she struggles in school. I worry about her future. I was hoping she was dyslexic because then she could have got help and some exemptions from her exams. But she's just a bad speller and reader. I really need to help her keep up. I try so hard to get her to read, but she just won't do it.'

'Maybe you should back off a bit.'

'But if I do, she'll fall further behind.'

Kevin picked a piece of red pepper out of the wok and popped it into his mouth. 'It's hard for Jools, with Holly being so bright. She's always going to be the stupid one. I know how that feels. It was the same with us. You were the smart one and I was thick.'

'You weren't thick, just lazy.'

'I wasn't lazy, I just wasn't interested.' He grinned. 'But I turned out okay.'

Alice added some spices to the stir-fry. 'That's debatable! I just worry about Jools.'

'Well, stop worrying and give her a break . . . at least for the next few days. It's her birthday week, after all, and sweet sixteen on top of that. Anyway, she's so stunning she can always be a model. Problem solved.'

Alice added some noodles to the wok. 'She's five foot three, Kevin! Besides, I want her to go to college, have fun and get some kind of degree. But you're right, I do need to manage her better. I think from now on I'll get Ben to do her homework with her. He's so much more patient than I am, although even he has a breaking-point.'

'You're very calm with your patients.'

'I have to be. But after dealing with other people's issues

all day, I come home drained and the last thing I want to do is hours of sodding homework.'

'God, I do not miss schooldays at all. Whoever said they're the best days of your life was a delusional lunatic.'

'I actually liked school.'

Kevin groaned. 'That's because you had friends and were "normal". You didn't get called "steamer" and "arse bandit" on a regular basis.'

Alice was laughing.

'It's not funny!' Kevin cried. 'Mum kept asking me why they called me "steamer" and I had to say it was because I was a really fast runner – like a steam train.'

At that, they both burst out laughing.

'Oh, God,' Alice said, wiping tears from her eyes. 'Poor Mum. At least they were nice to you when you did come out.'

Kevin snorted. 'They weren't exactly thrilled.'

'They were just from a different generation, so it was hard for them initially, but they were supportive.'

'I know,' Kevin admitted. 'They were good. When I see how some of my friends were disowned and thrown out of home, I had it easy.'

Alice got five plates out of the cupboard. 'Our parents' generation had a very different upbringing. They lived in fear of the Church. It wasn't easy for them. We were lucky. We grew up questioning everything and having our own opinions from an early age.'

'Thank God for that.'

'Thank God for what?' Jools asked, as she walked in, still wearing her silver jeans and hoodie.

'I'm just telling your mum how lucky she is to have such a gorgeous and fabulous daughter,' Kevin said.

Jools's face lit up. 'Really?'

She was so beautiful and young and innocent. Alice

realized Kevin was right: she *was* too hard on her. She just didn't want her daughter to leave school with nothing.

'You're fabulous.' Alice smiled at her.

Jools pulled the sleeves of her hoodie over her hands. 'Okay, what are you about to tell me? Is my party cancelled? Am I in trouble for something?'

Alice went over and put her arms around her daughter. 'No. I just think you're wonderful and I don't tell you enough.'

Jools squirmed and wriggled away from her mother. 'Enough of the mushy stuff. What's for dinner?'

## Ben

Ben rushed his shower and hurried to get dressed so he wouldn't be late home again. But as he was about to leave the hospital, a nurse called after him to tell him that John Lester had phoned. 'He said it was important and asked you to call him back.'

Ben frowned. John Lester? What did he want? John Lester was a total maverick. He was always taking time out to go to conflict zones with Médecins Sans Frontières and other humanitarian organizations. The last Ben had heard, John was in Eritrea to train surgeons there.

Hang on! Maybe he wanted Ben to go with him on one of his trips. How exciting. Maybe this was his chance to do something stimulating. Ben had never done any humanitarian trips, mainly because of Alice. After her parents had been killed, she was a nervous wreck every time he left the house or if she couldn't locate the girls for more than five seconds. Thankfully, over the years her anxiety and panic had dissipated, but she still would not be happy to hear that Ben was off to some far-flung corner of the world.

Nonetheless, Ben felt a surge of excitement. Sure, it might mean the cold shoulder for a while, but if this call from John Lester turned out to be an opportunity to do something exhilarating, he was bloody well going to do it. Life was too short.

John picked up on the first ring. 'Ben?'

'I'm returning your call.'

'Good man. Right, I'll get straight to the point. I was due to fly to Eritrea on Wednesday to operate on the minister of health, Negasi Kidane. I met him when I was over there setting up a training programme. Anyway, I've broken my leg. Bloody nuisance. Slid on the steps outside the house yesterday morning. I can't go now but the poor man needs surgery. Bloody great tumour in the colon. Needs to come out. Can you fly to Eritrea on Wednesday? You'll need to stay for post-op care. I'd like you to take my intern, Declan, with you. He's Irish, a bit of a livewire, but huge potential. I think he'll go a long way.'

Ben's head was reeling. Eritrea on Wednesday! That gave him two days to clear his schedule and persuade Alice that it wasn't the worst idea in the world. His heart was racing. This was exactly what he'd been looking for – adventure, change, something new, exciting and challenging – and it had dropped out of the sky into his lap. It was meant to be. Nothing and no one would prevent him going.

'I'd love to go, John. Thanks for thinking of me.'

'Good man. I'm afraid I'm stuck at home, so could you pop over? I can talk you through Kidane's history and show you the X-rays. I'll get Declan to come, too, so you can get acquainted. We'll need to change the name on the ticket and I'll let the Eritreans know you're coming in my stead.'

Ben's heart was beating faster. 'No problem, John. I'm just getting onto my bike now. Can I call in on my way home?'

'Excellent! No time like the present. I'll call Declan right now. See you when you get here.'

John Lester hung up and Ben punched the air. Eritrea here I come, he thought. The timing couldn't have been more perfect – except for missing Jools's birthday. He knew the Cambridge post was going to cause too much trouble at home, with Alice and the girls. In any case, it would put a lot of extra pressure on Alice if he were away so much during the week. But this one-off opportunity would be great, and maybe others would come up once people heard he was prepared to travel for his work.

One or two of these interesting trips a year would keep him going. He made a mental note to get in touch with Médecins Sans Frontières when he got back. This was Fate. Ben strode purposefully towards the hospital entrance. He felt brighter, happier and more alive than he had in a very long time.

As he cycled towards John Lester's house, he was mentally organizing his schedule around the week he was going to need off. John had been clear about Ben staying to make sure that the minister's operation had gone smoothly and that there were no complications afterwards. On the off-chance that something did occur, Ben wanted enough time to deal with any post-op issues, however small. He wanted to prove himself on this mission. A week should be adequate to make sure the minister was recovering well.

Cycling home, Ben prepared himself for Alice's reaction to his Eritrean trip. He knew it wasn't going to be good. They'd been arguing quite a bit lately, partly because he'd been so restless and distracted, but he wished Alice didn't always have to react to everything as if it was the end of the world.

He climbed off his bike, removed his helmet, pulled out his key and took a deep breath.

He could hear voices in the kitchen. Damn! Kevin was here. Ben didn't want to say anything in front of Kevin because his brother-in-law always took Alice's side. It bothered Ben that Alice discussed so much with him. He felt that some things were private, such as their marriage. But since Kevin had gone to work for Alice two years ago it was even worse because they saw each other every day and talked about everything. Ben knew Alice complained about him to Kevin when she was fed up. He really didn't want to take on the two of them when he made his big announcement. But with only two days to departure, he couldn't be picky about timing – better to get it over and done with.

He squared his shoulders and opened the kitchen door. 'Hello, everyone,' he said, in an over-cheery voice.

He bent down to kiss Jools and Holly's cheeks and Alice's lips. Then he went to shake Kevin's hand. 'Welcome back. I hope New York was good.'

'It was fantastic, thanks. How are you?'

'I'm good. Great, actually.' Turning to Alice, he said, 'Darling, John Lester has asked me to go to Eritrea for a few days.'

Alice frowned. 'Eritrea?'

'Air-it-tray-on? Are you winding us up?' Kevin said, as Jools giggled.

'Eritrea is a country in Africa. It borders with Ethiopia,' Holly said.

'Thank you, Holly.' Ben ruffled her hair as he watched Alice's face.

'Ethiopia!' Alice's voice was shrill. 'Jesus, Ben.'

'It's fine. It's not dangerous.'

'The war with Ethiopia ended in 2000.'

Everyone stared at Holly.

'How in God's name do you know that?' Kevin wondered.

'Because she eats books,' Jools reminded him.

'I don't eat them, I read them. I read about it in the library when I finished my homework.'

'How long are you going for?' Kevin asked Ben.

'Oh, just a few days, a week at the most. I'm operating on the minister of health. It's fairly straightforward.'

Alice stood up abruptly. 'Ben, can I have a word in private, please? Kevin, can you make sure the girls finish their dinner.'

'Uh-oh, someone's in for a bollocking,' Jools drawled, as Alice nudged Ben out of the kitchen and into the lounge.

Alice closed the door and turned on Ben. 'Is this some kind of a joke? Are you trying to wind me up? Eritrea, Ben? Seriously?'

Ben knew it was vital that he remain calm and firm. 'Alice, it's perfectly safe. I'm flying in with John Lester's registrar – he's actually Irish. I'm going to operate – it's a fairly straightforward tumour in the colon – and then I'll stay for a couple of days to make sure the patient's on the mend before I fly home.'

'Eritrea is not safe. Anything could happen.'

'Alice, you'd hardly heard of Eritrea before now, so how do you know it's not safe?'

'Because it's beside bloody Ethiopia and, according to Holly, they had a war and what's to say it won't kick off again? Besides, Africa in general is not safe or stable. Anything could happen.'

Ben put his hands on his wife's shoulders. 'Alice, calm down. Don't make a big deal about nothing. It's a simple operation and I'll be back within the week.'

Alice shrugged him off. 'You're not going.'

'What?'

'You're not going. You're not allowed to put yourself at risk. You have a wife and two kids. You have responsibilities, Ben. You can't just decide to head off to dangerous places whenever you feel like it.'

Ben could feel anger creeping up from his stomach through his chest. 'Alice, I am going to Eritrea. I am fully aware of my responsibilities and I take them very seriously, but you won't stop me going on this trip.'

'Yes, I will.'

Ben gritted his teeth. 'No, you are not. I need this. I need to do something different. It's an opportunity to shake things up a bit.'

'Why do you need to shake things up? What's wrong with your life?'

Ben paced up and down. 'I'm a bit restless and this is a good opportunity to do something different. John told me he goes over and trains the surgeons there once a year. I'd like to do that with him in the future.'

Alice frowned. 'So you're planning on going to Africa once a year now?'

'I'm hoping to, yes. Africa or anywhere else where they need local surgeons to be trained.'

'Why?' Alice asked, her eyes filling.

'Because I just feel . . . I need something else.'

'Why aren't we enough for you?' Alice was crying now.

Ben felt bad. He went over and put his arms around her. 'You are, darling. You and the girls mean everything to me. This has nothing to do with you. I just feel the need to push myself a bit, shake things up work-wise.'

Alice wiped the tears from her face with her hands. 'I took a different path in my career so I could put our family first. I didn't plan to end up being a GP. I wanted to specialize in oncology. But it's what you do when you have kids. You give up certain goals to spend time with them. They'll be gone at eighteen.'

Ben sighed. 'I'm not asking a lot, Alice. A week here or there helping others isn't a big deal.'

'I just don't understand why you're so restless. It's freaking me out. We have everything we dreamt of. Why do you need more?'

Ben looked at his lovely wife. She was right: they had a beautiful home, two healthy daughters and good careers, but it just wasn't enough for him. He needed something else. He wanted more. Maybe he was selfish, but he couldn't help how he felt. His life seemed mundane and monotonous. He needed this trip.

'I can't really explain it. Maybe it's turning forty-five – I don't know. But this opportunity has come at the right time. I'm excited about it. I haven't felt that in a while.'

Alice rolled her eyes. 'I suppose a week in Eritrea is better than an affair.'

'It'll be totally safe. We'll be very well cared for. After all, we'll be operating on a senior government official.'

'Make sure you don't kill him.' Alice walked back towards the kitchen.

'I will.'

'Oh, and Ben?' Alice turned around. 'You can leave your mid-life crisis in Eritrea. I want a happy husband after this trip.'

# Ben

As Ben packed, Alice sat on the bed and watched him. 'Call me every day. I'll be worried.'

'I will. Listen, why don't we go on a trip when I get back? Christmas isn't too far off. We could go somewhere nice. How about Paris? I know it's your favourite place and we haven't been for so long.'

'That would be nice.'

'Paris, here we come!' Ben leant down to kiss her.

'Why are you talking about Paris? OMG, you're so gross. Stop kissing – it's embarrassing. Old people should never kiss.' Jools stood in the doorway, hands on hips, wearing her favourite bright pink tracksuit with 'Babe' emblazoned across the front in some kind of sparkly writing. It was appalling, but Kevin had bought it for her so Ben wasn't allowed to criticize.

No one was allowed to criticize Kevin, except Alice. Even when Kevin had got drunk and tried to shove his tongue down the throat of Clive Hetherington, a friend of Ben who was about as straight as it was possible to be, Ben hadn't been permitted to say anything. Alice said that 'poor Kevin' was having a hard time meeting a nice man and he was upset and confused. He wasn't confused: he was the horniest gay man Ben had ever met.

Alice said Kevin's 'enthusiasm' was because he'd grown

up suppressing his gayness and only come out when he'd moved to London so he had a lot of years to catch up on. Ben pointed out, reasonably, that he could do all the catching up he wanted, just not with his heterosexual friends. Kevin was, as it were, barking up the wrong tree. Alice said he was unsympathetic and needed to be kinder to him. Ben said no more, but decided to keep his friends away from his brother-in-law in future.

'I thought it would be nice for us to go on a family holiday. So when I get back from Eritrea, we'll fix up a trip to Paris.'

'I still can't believe you're missing my birthday,' Jools said.

Ben went over to his sulky-faced daughter. 'I promise to make it up to you with a huge present.'

'How huge?'

'Hugely huge.' Ben hugged his daughter. He felt brilliant. He couldn't wait to get on the plane. Everything looked brighter this morning. He must have been suffering from mild depression: he felt light and full of energy.

'Well, I'm amazing so I deserve a huge present. Besides, turning sixteen is a big deal. I can't wait for my party next weekend.'

'I'm so sorry, Jools, it looks like I'll miss that too.'

Jools rolled her eyes. 'I'm actually glad you're away for it. I'm having my seven best friends for a sleepover and I don't need you coming in and checking up on us every five minutes and saying really embarrassing things, like "One Direction rock."'

Ben grinned at her. At almost sixteen, Jools had already decided he was an embarrassment. It seemed like only yesterday when she'd climb onto his lap and ask him to read her stories.

'Don't be rude to your father or there'll be no sleep-over and no Paris.' Alice's arms were crossed and she was pacing.

'Relax, Mum, you don't have to jump down my throat. I know you're worried about Dad going to Erimea or what-ever it's called, but it'll be fine. You always make a big deal about everything.'

'Don't speak to me –'

Ben raised his hands. 'Ladies, can you please not argue? I have to go and I'd like to leave a peaceful house behind.'

'Fat chance,' Jools huffed. 'I wish I had a mother who wasn't always on my back. Charlotte's mum lets her have a Twitter account because she's normal, unlike you!'

'I told you, I had a young girl in my surgery who was trau-matized because she was receiving such vile threats on Twitter. There are bad men out there who prey on young girls like you,' Alice said.

'What do the bad men look like?' Holly had come into the room, eyes wide.

'Well, that's the whole point – you can't see them. They hide behind the anonymity of the computer so you don't know what they look like,' Alice explained.

'Oh, for goodness' sake, Mum, I know how to deal with dickheads.'

'Mind your language,' Alice barked.

'Fine, but I want a Twitter account. All my friends have them.'

'You're not getting one. And –'

'Sorry to interrupt,' Ben shouted, to be heard. 'I have to go now.' He bent to kiss Jools.

Then he gave Holly a bear hug – thankfully, she still allowed him to hug her.

'If you go for five days, you'll be gone for a hundred and twenty hours, or if it's six days, it'll be a hundred and forty-four hours,' Holly announced.

'You are a wonder.' Ben smiled at her.

'Daddy, I Googled Eritrea.' Holly pulled a piece of paper out of her pocket. Reading from it, she told them, 'The official languages are Tigrinya, English and Arabic. It has a population of six point one three million. A UN report estimated that about seventy per cent of Eritreans cannot meet their food needs on their own.'

Ben knew he had to stop her or she'd keep reading and he'd miss his flight. 'I'll take that and read it on the plane. Thank you, Holly.' He stuffed the paper into his suitcase.

'You're such a dork, seriously!' Jools said.

Holly shrugged. 'I was just helping Daddy to have information.'

'I really have to go. Be good for your mother.'

'If she lets me on Twitter, I'll be incredibly good.' Jools wasn't going to let this go. She could be exhaustingly tenacious when she wanted something, a trait she'd inherited from her mother, although Ben wasn't about to mention that now.

'Drop it, Jools, it's not happening,' Alice warned.

Ben leant over to give Alice a kiss. He murmured in her ear, 'Maybe we should let her have an account if all of her friends do. We can keep an eye on it.'

Jools's bionic ears picked it up. 'Yes! You see? Even Daddy agrees with me.'

Alice's eyes flashed. 'Thanks a lot, Ben. Bloody typical!

You always give in to her. You never back me up. I'm sick of it. Why don't you just stay in bloody Eritrea?'

Alice stormed out of the room. Ben sighed, headed for the front door and on to the airport.

Her final words were to haunt them both.

## Holly

Daddy has been away for fifty hours. He will be back in ninety hours unless he stays for an extra day. If he does, he'll be back in 114 hours.

Daddy didn't phone yesterday. He promised to phone every day. Mummy tried to phone him last night and again this morning. But he didn't call back.

Mummy said the Wi-Fi is obviously really bad. But how was he able to call on Wednesday? He sounded really happy when I talked to him then. He said Asmara, the capital of Eritrea, is beautiful and the people are really nice. He was being looked after very well – he and the other doctor, Declan, were taken to a nice restaurant by the minister's friends and ate yummy food.

He said Declan is really funny. He's Irish, like Mummy. Daddy said he's a bit high-spirited, but in a good way.

Daddy told us that he and Declan were going to visit a little clinic outside Asmara on Friday because the doctors over there need help learning how to do operations. Daddy is very kind. He likes to help people.

Daddy said Declan knew one of the Eritrean doctors in the clinic because he went there before, with John Lester. Daddy said he was looking forward to teaching them.

Mummy's face went a bit red when he said that, but she didn't get angry with him. I think she felt bad for shouting at him before he left.

But now he hasn't rung for thirty-eight hours and I know Mummy's worried. She keeps trying to call his phone and the hotel he's staying in, but there's no answer.

When I asked if she wanted me to make her toast because she hadn't had any breakfast, she shook her head. Her eyes went all watery and she looked like she was about to cry. It made my stomach hurt.

Mummy used to cry sometimes because she was sad about Granny and Grandpa. But now she really doesn't cry much at all. I can only remember her crying twice recently – once when Daddy shouted at her for being too hard on Jools. He said, 'You're making her feel like she's not good enough. It's cruel.'

Mummy locked herself in the bathroom and cried really hard when Daddy said that. I could hear her because the bathroom is next door to my bedroom.

The other time she cried was on Christmas Day last year when Granddad Harold said that Uncle Kevin was an embarrassment to the family. That time she was angry-crying. She shouted at Granddad and said that Kevin was her only family and he was never to be rude about him again.

I heard her arguing with Daddy later that night when Granddad had gone home. She said Granddad was 'out of order'. Daddy said that he shouldn't have said it but that Kevin was 'too much' sometimes.

Mummy said that Kevin was just sad because he was on his own and Christmas is lonely and that he had drunk too much wine and been a bit silly, but there was no need for Granddad to be so rude.

Daddy said that standing on the chair and singing 'On My Own' at the top of his voice and crying while we were all still eating was 'over the top'.

Mummy said it was a song that related to how he felt and

that he was allowed to do whatever he wanted when he was in her house.

Daddy said in a cross voice that it was 'our house' and that Granddad had been 'mortified' by Kevin, especially as Granddad's sister, Prudence, had been there to see it all.

Mummy said that Daddy's family were all 'stuffed shirts' and they should relax a bit and that it was better for Kevin to 'let it out' and not 'keep it in'.

I thought about what 'it' was for ages and I think she meant sadness.

I hate it when Mummy and Daddy fight because it makes me afraid that they'll get a divorce, like Laura's parents. She is super-sad because her parents live in different houses now. She said her Mummy has sad eyes all the time.

I asked her if they had loads of fights. Laura said her parents used to fight all the time and then they stopped and that was worse because they never really spoke to each other again.

I was glad to hear that because Mummy and Daddy don't have loads of arguments. They only fight a little bit and it's nearly always about Jools.

I love Jools because she's my sister, but she can be really mean sometimes. When I help her with her homework, she never really thanks me. She says I owe her because I got all the brains and it's not fair. But I think she's lucky because she's so beautiful. She looks like Selena Gomez but I'd never tell her that because her head would get too big.

Even though she pretends she doesn't know she's pretty, Jools is ALWAYS looking at herself in the mirror and taking selfies.

I hope Daddy calls soon. I think I'll make Mummy toast. It might cheer her up.

## Alice

Alice had felt bad for shouting at Ben before he left. She'd been glad when he called, but they hadn't had a chance to talk alone because the girls were there and insisted that he be put on loudspeaker. Alice barely got a word in. When he mentioned going to a clinic outside the city, she had felt her chest tighten. Why the hell did he want to go wandering about in a strange place?

Damn Declan whoever-he-was and John bloody Lester and their sodding do-gooder trips. Alice didn't want Ben going anywhere but the hotel and the hospital where he was operating on the minister. She'd already lost her parents — she didn't need to lose her husband too.

She had tried not to show any emotion because she didn't want the girls to worry. Well, Alice doubted Jools would even notice she was worried, but Holly would. Holly was a terrible worrier. Alice often wondered if that was why Holly was so studious. Reading and working out facts and figures seemed to calm her down. Alice found herself wishing she had such an effective coping mechanism. As it was, she thought about Ben constantly and couldn't shake the anxiety that had settled on her.

When Alice arrived at work on Friday morning, Kevin was waiting for her. He followed her into her room, handed her a strong coffee and closed the door.

'Brace yourself, we have thirty patients in today.'

Alice sighed. She hadn't slept well and she had been hoping for an easy schedule. Today all she wanted was someone to hold her hand and reassure her that Ben was all right. 'Who's first?' she said as she sipped her coffee.

'A new one. Miranda Langton refused to say what it was for. She said it was private and she wasn't going to discuss it with "the receptionist".'

'Yikes! Well, don't scratch her eyes out when she comes in.'

Kevin turned on his heel and, waving an arm in the air, said, 'Maybe just a little scratch.'

When Kevin brought Miranda in ten minutes later, he introduced her: 'Dr Gregory, this is Miranda Langton, date of birth July the eighth nineteen fifty-seven.'

'What?' spluttered Miranda.

'Sorry?' Kevin looked the picture of innocence.

'Excuse me, I was born in nineteen sixty-seven.'

'Oh, really?' Kevin raised his eyebrows in surprise. 'So you're not fifty-five, then?'

'Certainly not,' Miranda said, unable to look furious because of all the Botox she'd had.

'Wow.' Kevin tilted his head and winked at Alice, who suppressed a smile as her brother took himself and his revenge out of the room.

After back-to-back appointments all morning, Alice had a twenty-minute lunch break and tried repeatedly to call Ben. Once again his mobile went straight into voice-mail. She left another message: 'Ben, call me. I'm getting worried. I need to know that you're okay. Call me, please. I miss you.'

Kevin came in and handed her a latte from the coffee shop next door. 'Any word from Eritrea yet?' he asked.

Alice shook her head.

'He'll be fine,' Kevin said, picking at a salad. 'He's probably up the side of a mountain in some clinic in a cave with no service.'

Alice nodded. She wanted to believe him, but she couldn't help worrying.

'How's the birthday girl today?'

Alice took a sip of her coffee. 'Demanding! I made her pancakes with whipped cream and Nutella this morning.'

'How many did she eat?'

'Three.'

Kevin gasped. 'Think of the calories.'

'For goodness' sake, it was a special occasion.'

'It would take running a full marathon to burn that off.'

'Don't you dare mention calories to her. I don't want my girls worrying about their weight – it's dangerous.'

Kevin smoothed his fitted shirt. 'I know, but you don't want to be a fat teenager, believe me. The only kids who got bullied more than me at school were the fat ones.'

'Jools has a lovely figure.'

Kevin paused. 'Yes, she does, but teenagers can put on weight easily so I'm just saying she should be careful and lay off the Nutella pancakes.'

'You're just jealous. When was the last time you ate chocolate?'

'My body is a temple and, besides, fat gays don't get laid.'

Alice laughed. 'I sincerely hope you're going to have a slice of Jools's birthday cake tonight. I made it with Holly last night. Chocolate sponge.'

'I'll have a tiny bit, but only because it's Jools and I adore her. What present are you giving her by the way? Did you and Ben agree on the new iPhone?'

Alice nodded. 'I was against it, as you know, but Ben really wanted to treat her so we got her one. I'm going to give it to her tonight. I wish Ben was here, though. He deserves to see her face when she opens it. She's going to be thrilled.'

'I'll video it and we can send it to him,' Kevin offered.

Alice knew that if Ben didn't call tonight to wish his beloved daughter a happy birthday, something bad had definitely happened. She took a deep breath and crossed her fingers.

Alice and Holly lit the candles while Kevin distracted Jools. Then Alice turned out the lights and carried the cake to the table. Jools's eyes lit up.

'Ooh, chocolate sponge! My favourite! Thanks, Mum.'

She looked so beautiful, her face framed in the candlelight. Alice wanted to hug her but knew it would ruin the moment, so she just smiled. 'You're welcome, darling, and Holly deserves thanks too. She helped me.'

Jools looked across at her sister. 'Thanks, Holly. You can have a big slice, not as big as mine, obviously, as I'm the birthday girl, but almost as big.'

'Well, go on, then, make a wish,' Kevin urged.

Jools closed her eyes, inhaled and then, as she was about to blow and make a wish, Alice's phone rang.

'OMG, it's Daddy. I was just wishing he'd call and now he has!' Jools rushed to the phone and picked it up. 'Daddy? . . . Oh, sorry, I thought . . . Yes, she is, I'll get her now.' Jools handed the phone to Alice. 'It's someone called Jonathan Londis.'

Alice held the phone to her ear. 'Hello?'

'Hello, Mrs Gregory, it's Jonathan Londis here, from the Foreign and Commonwealth Office. I'm calling you from Eritrea.'

'Yes?' Alice felt a cold chill down her back. Why was the FCO calling her? Something was wrong.

'I'm afraid it's about your husband, Dr Ben Gregory.'

'What is it?' Alice whispered, her voice catching.

'The car he was travelling in was —'

'In an accident?' Alice interrupted. An accident was okay. An accident meant he was injured, but she'd help him recover. Jonathan Londis said nothing. The phone shook in Alice's hand. 'Is Ben all right? Tell me, is he all right?' Fear gripped her throat. Was Ben seriously injured? Maybe he'd just broken his leg or had concussion or something. She had to hope for the best. She clung to hope.

'Do you need me to come out and look after him?' she asked.

'I'm afraid it's rather more serious than that.'

Alice's whole body began to tremble. 'What do you mean? What . . .'

'I'm terribly sorry, Mrs Gregory, but the jeep your husband was travelling in hit a landmine.'

'I don't . . . I'm sorry, but what does . . . I . . .' Alice stumbled over her words as her mind tried to push away the dark thoughts engulfing her.

Jonathan Londis cleared his throat. 'I'm afraid it appears that your husband and his co-passenger, Declan Hayes, were killed instantly.'

'*Noooooo!*'

Alice's knees gave way. Jools screamed. Holly threw her arms around her mother as if to shield her from something that might come crashing out of the sky.

Although the girls didn't speak a word to each other, from their mother's scream, they understood. Their father wasn't coming home, ever.

# PART 2
# London and Eritrea

*Ben: ten hours earlier, Eritrea . . .*

Ben woke up and jumped out of bed. He threw back the thick curtains and looked out at the blue sky. He felt filled with energy. This trip had been like a shot of adrenalin in the arm. He was his old self, full of vigour and optimism, ready to take on the world.

So far Declan had been a great travel companion and colleague. He was enthusiastic, lively and knew his stuff. Ben was confident that he would be an asset in theatre when they operated.

The consultation with the minister had gone well. Ben had explained the transverse colectomy procedure to him and his wife. He had shown Negasi Kidane where he would make the cut in his abdomen to remove the middle part of the colon containing the tumour. He would also be taking out the lymph glands closest to the bowel, to check if any cancer cells had spread there, he said, then described how he would join the ends of the colon back together.

The minister seemed happy with the information and keen to get the operation over with. It was due to take place at nine o'clock on Saturday morning, which left today, Friday, free. Today Ben and Declan were going to a clinic outside Asmara, where Declan and John Lester had been on their last trip, to help train some local surgeons.

Ben was looking forward to it. Declan had organized a car

and was going to drive. He said it was about an hour outside the city.

Ben looked at his watch. It was only eight. They weren't due to leave until ten. He showered, then decided to go for a walk and grab breakfast at a café instead of in the hotel. He wanted to soak up some local atmosphere. He wandered down the palm-lined main street, Independence Avenue, watching the cafés setting up their tables and getting ready for the day ahead. He walked on to the old town square, where the imposing post-office building dominated everything. Ben's guidebook told him that Asmara had been colonized by Italy at the end of the nineteenth century and remained so until the Second World War. He could see the signs of Italian influence everywhere.

Apart from the architecture, there were lots of old Fiats parked on the roads. But most people in Asmara seemed to cycle. According to Declan, some of the surgeons in Eritrea only earned two dollars a day. He said the surgeons were very well educated but too bookish and had very little clinical focus, which was why John Lester had decided to help train them.

Ben wandered around for a while, then went to find the Casa degli Italiani, which the minister's wife had recommended. He walked through the imposing stone-pillared entrance onto a pretty terrace. Sitting there, sipping his coffee, he felt lighter than he had in ages.

He thought about Alice and the girls, doing the usual morning things at home, getting ready for school and work. He missed them, and feel guilty about Jools's birthday, but he was still glad to be out of that routine for a few days, to be in a new place, having new experiences. Would he be able to hold on to his energy and positivity once he was back in London? He wasn't sure. But things needed to change, he knew that now. He couldn't go back to living that humdrum life.

He would have to talk to Alice, explain to her how he was feeling, and between them they'd find a way to make their lives more meaningful and fulfilling. The girls were moving into new phases now, and it was time he and Alice did, too. He made himself a promise, sitting there in the sunshine, to try to be less distracted and spend more time at home when he got back, but also to have his own sense of purpose. If he could get Alice on-side, he knew they could have it all.

Ben glanced at his watch. Time to go. He paid the bill and headed back to the hotel. On his way he passed a jewellery shop. He glanced at the window and saw a gold necklace with the initial A on it. He decided to buy it for Alice. But when he went into the shop, he decided to buy three. Each necklace had an initial – A, J and H, one for each of the women in his life. The girls would be thrilled, and he hoped Alice would be too. He'd surprise them when he got home. Ben left the shop, delighted with his purchases.

Once back in the hotel, Ben tried to call home again, but his mobile still wouldn't work. He was about to ring Alice from the hotel phone when Declan knocked on his door and said they needed to get going. It would be best to call later anyway, when the girls were home from school.

Ben put the necklaces on his bed and grabbed a small backpack with a digital camera, wallet, laptop, mobile phone and his passport. He followed Declan down to the car.

The vehicle Declan had sourced was a very old, very battered Fiat, which he proceeded to drive like a maniac.

'Christ, where did you learn to drive?' Ben asked, clinging to the ceiling grab handle.

Declan grinned. 'My older brother taught me. He's a total nutter – he's written off four cars.'

'That's very reassuring,' Ben said. 'Don't you have to do driving tests in Ireland?'

'Technically, yes, but my uncle Tommy is one of the examiners, so I passed even though my three-point turn took about ten minutes and I knocked down a fella on a bike when I was coming out of the driving centre.' Declan roared with laughter.

'Perhaps I should drive?' Ben suggested, as Declan swerved to avoid knocking down yet another innocent cyclist.

Declan shook his head. 'Just relax. I'll get you there safely. I've never crashed.'

'Really?' Ben was shocked.

Declan lit a cigarette as he narrowly avoided an oncoming car. 'Well, not officially.'

'What does that mean?'

'It means I may have had a few bumps along the way, but not exactly owned up to them.'

'You mean you crashed and drove away?'

'In a way, yes.'

'But that's . . . completely . . . just . . . well, wrong.' Ben was taken aback.

'Keep your hair on, Ben. Where I grew up in Dublin rules weren't always obeyed.'

'What part of Dublin are you from? I've been there lots of times with my wife Alice – she grew up just outside the city.'

Declan flicked his cigarette out of the window. 'I doubt you ever went to my neighbourhood. I grew up in Ballymun. Six kids, three-bedroom flat, single dad.'

'What happened to your mother?' Ben asked.

'She fecked off with a Polish plumber and we never saw her again. My dad can't hear Poland mentioned without flying into a mad rage. He was disgusted when the European

74

Football Cup was held there. He even refused to watch the Irish team matches and he loves his football.'

'Gosh, I'm sorry to hear that. Did you ever hear from your mother again?'

'No. My sister Carol tracked her down when she was eighteen. She saved up for ages and we all gave her a few quid so she could fly to Poland. We told her she was mad, but she's an only girl and she really missed having a mother. When she got to my mother's house after travelling for thirteen hours, my mother opened the door, told her to feck off and slammed it shut in her face.'

'Your poor sister!'

'You don't know our Carol. Instead of falling down crying, she got a big rock and flung it through the front window where my mother's boyfriend was sitting watching telly. It nearly hit him too.'

Ben laughed. 'What did your mother do?'

Declan lit another cigarette. 'She came running out and shouted at Carol. But what she forgot was that Carol had sixteen years of pent-up anger and resentment rattling about inside her. So Carol walloped her across the face, told her she was a waste of space and left. The poor girl came back gutted, so we had a "funeral" to cheer her up. My brother Eddie made up a little coffin and we put our mother's photos into it and burnt it in the kitchen sink. Then we drank a load of booze and said, "Good riddance to the old hag." Carol felt better after that. Dad was thrilled that we all now knew what a complete cow our mother was.'

Ben was almost speechless. Declan's family sounded completely insane and yet there was something very touching about the way they had rallied around their sister. 'Did it help?' he asked.

'I think so. Carol hasn't mentioned her since.'

'How old were you when your mother left?'

'Four.'

'God, that's young. It must have been hard.'

Declan shrugged. 'I don't remember her at all. You can't miss what you don't recall. I think it was worse for Eddie. He was nine so he did remember. He went a bit mental when he was a teenager – mitching off school and shop-lifting and a bit of drugs, but Dad sorted him out. Dad's great. Raising five boys and a girl on your own with very little money isn't easy, but he did a good job.'

'He must be very proud of you,' Ben said.

'To be honest, he thinks it's mad that I've had to study for so long and still earn so little. I keep telling him that one day I'll be loaded. He's proud of all of us for keeping on the straight and narrow. We've all turned out grand. I'm nothing special.'

'John Lester rates you and he's a tough judge.'

'I enjoy it. I think growing up in a bad area actually helps. I don't get stressed easily and pressure doesn't bother me. When you grow up dodging drug-dealers and gangsters, surgery doesn't seem so daunting.'

Ben clung to the door handle as Declan swerved to avoid a woman on a donkey. They were going up into the mountains now and the road was a lot rougher. The car jerked about as Declan tried to avoid rocks and potholes.

'What about you? Where did you grow up?' Declan asked.

'London. My life has been very boring compared to yours. I'm an only child, went to a local school and then on to King's College to study medicine.'

'So you never really left London?' Declan asked.

'No, I didn't. I'd planned to go to America to do a couple of years there, but then I met Alice, married her and had children.'

'What have you got?'

'Two girls.'

'What age?'

'Jools turned sixteen today and Holly is eleven.'

'Teenage years!'

Ben chuckled. 'To be honest, Jools has been like a teenager since she was about eight.'

'Girls seem like a world of trouble. I hope I have boys – I know what to do with boys – but girls . . . They just wreck your head.'

Ben smiled. 'True, but they're also absolutely wonderful.'

'I can see you're smitten.'

'I take it you're not married yet.'

'No. I'm keeping it casual for the moment. I need to focus on work. I did have one serious girlfriend, but when she introduced me to her parents it didn't go too well. I wasn't quite . . . What shall we say? Son-in-law material. They were very posh and they kept talking about point-to-points. I thought they were on about trains and that they were train-spotters or something, so I told them how me and my brother Jason used to stand on the end of the platform and moon at the carriages as the trains pulled out.'

Ben imagined the faces of the 'posh' parents when they heard that story. 'I take it that didn't endear you to them.' He grinned at Declan.

Declan whooped. 'You can say that again. My leg was black and blue from Gwen kicking me under the table to shut me up. I knew after that weekend it was over. I'd never fit in. Pity, she was a lovely girl, but as my dad always said, there are plenty more fish in the sea. Mind you, he never got together with anyone after my mother left. Always said he was too busy working and raising us. I'd like him to meet someone. It'd be nice for him now we've all left home. The good thing is that all my brothers and Carol live near him and there are loads of grandkids, so he's hardly ever alone.'

'My mother died nineteen years ago. My father met someone else just a few years ago.'

'Do you like her?' Declan asked.

Ben thought about it. Did he like Helen? She was pleasant but cold. Ben's mother had been warm, loving, and had doted on him. She'd wanted more children, but Ben's birth had been complicated and she'd ended up having a hysterectomy.

Ben remembered how his mother's eyes had lit up when he walked into a room. Sometimes as a teenager it had been a little claustrophobic and he had felt smothered, but he'd known she couldn't help it. She had so much love to give and only one child to give it to. He was twenty-six when she received a diagnosis of ovarian cancer. Ten weeks later she was dead.

Ben had simply disappeared into studying and working while his father – a stalwart of the stiff-upper-lip generation – pretended everything was fine. Alice had been there to comfort Ben and she'd been wonderful. With Alice, he could cry and talk about how much he missed his mother.

Ben, in his naïveté, thought his father was actually fine. Until one day he'd come back early from the hospital. They'd sent him home after he'd cut his hand open with a scalpel. When he'd opened the front door, he'd heard a noise coming from the kitchen. He'd gone in through the open door and had seen his father sitting at the table, sobbing over his wedding photos.

Ben had never seen his father cry, not even at his mother's funeral. Everyone kept saying how brave Harold was, how strong. They said it was his army background. He had fought in the Falklands war and been awarded a medal for bravery.

Ben always thought his father was invincible. He knew his father loved him, but he had never been demonstrative. Like so many sons and fathers, there was a physical awkwardness between them.

The sound of his father's sobs ripped through Ben's heart. He froze. He didn't know what to do. Should he tiptoe by and leave him to grieve in peace, or should he go over and put an arm around him?

Taking a deep breath, Ben said, 'Dad?'

Harold's back went rigid. Ben approached his father tentatively and laid a hand on his shoulder. Looking at the photos, he said softly, 'I miss her too.'

His father nodded stiffly. He stood up, shrugging Ben's hand off, and wiped his eyes roughly, then packed away the photos. Still not facing his son, he said, 'Well, that's enough of that. I was tidying up and . . . well . . . there you are. Right, I'll just put them away.' He'd brushed past Ben and the moment was lost.

That was probably the closest they'd got to grieving together. One of the things Ben loved most about Alice was her freedom with her emotions. She didn't hide them or keep them in, she let them out. When something moved her, she cried, not like a Disney princess but in a loud, werewolf kind of way.

Strangely, though, when Alice's parents were killed, she hadn't cried that much. She'd got very low, and Ben had been really worried about her.

The tragedy had toughened Alice, though. She rarely cried at films any more. She was stronger and less emotional – except when it came to the girls: she worried about their whereabouts all the time. She liked to have her family close. Ben understood that, but sometimes it felt a little claustrophobic. If he didn't answer her phone calls quickly, she'd panic. She had got better over the years but still had a tendency to believe the worst was going to happen.

Thinking about her now, Ben felt bad about not calling that morning. He knew she'd be worried. He'd try to call her from the landline at the clinic.

'Ben?' Declan waved his hand in front of Ben's face.

'Sorry, I was miles away. Yes, I do like Helen. She's a nice lady and she looks after my father well.'

'You're lucky. I'd really like my dad to meet someone. He deserves a bit of love. We tried to set him up with a few local women, but it didn't work out. The first date was when Eddie lined up Marion from the bookie's, but it was a disaster. She's known as the local bike. She'd ride anything. Eddie said he was just trying to get Dad laid. But sure Dad wasn't able for her at all. When she pulled out a pair of handcuffs he locked himself into the toilet and called Eddie to come and get her out of the flat.'

Ben laughed. 'Maybe he should have started with someone a bit less . . . enthusiastic.'

Declan grinned. 'You English public-school boys, you make everything sound really nice and tasteful. I would have said "slutty" but you said "enthusiastic". I love it!'

'At least they teach us something for the astronomical fees they charge.'

'True. My school was the local national school. There were forty-three kids in my class. The main thing you learnt was how to survive the day without being punched in the face, having your lunch nicked or your head shoved down the toilet. Only four of us went on to college.'

'Why did you decide on medicine?' Ben asked.

'Because I wanted to save people and make the world a better place.'

'Right.'

Declan thumped Ben's arm. 'I'm joking. Our local doctor lived in the nicest house and drove the nicest car. I wanted that. Also, to be fair, I found the science subjects the easiest. What about you?'

Ben looked out of the window at the increasingly barren landscape as the car continued to climb. 'I actually did want to save people and make the world a better place.'

'Oh.' Declan looked sheepish.

Now it was Ben's turn to thump Declan's arm. 'Gotcha! *Casualty* was my mother's favourite show. I used to watch it with her all the time. I decided that I wanted to be the guy in the scrubs, saving lives and shagging pretty nurses.'

'How did that go for you?' Declan asked.

'Pretty well, until I met Alice.'

'What age were you then?'

'Twenty-five. She was a med student, too.'

'A gorgeous med student from Dublin. I need one of those.'

Ben smiled, turned his eyes back to the road – and screamed, '*Declan!*'

Fifty yards in front of them, a jeep was blocking the road. Four men dressed in army fatigues were standing beside it, pointing guns directly at them.

'Jesus Christ!' Declan slammed on the brakes.

Their car skidded to a halt in front of the jeep.

'Let me do the talking,' Declan said.

'What do they want? I have some money.' Ben reached for his bag, when a gun went off. His heart leapt.

'OUT! OUT!' the gunmen shouted, coming up to the car and yanking the doors open.

Ben and Declan were dragged out of the Fiat. Ben instinctively put his hands in the air. 'We're doctors,' he said.

'We're here to help your people,' Declan explained. 'We're going to the St Marco clinic. We're here to help,' he repeated.

The oldest man stepped forward. He was about forty, tall and broad. He had an air of authority about him. The other three were in their early twenties. They looked to him for instructions.

'I know who you are,' the leader said, in surprisingly good English. 'I know you are here to operate on Minister Kidane. But I need a doctor. My son is injured. You come with me to save my son.'

Two of the soldiers began to push them towards the jeep, while the other rifled through their bags. Ben saw him throwing their passports onto the ground beside the car. They took the money out of their wallets, then tossed them onto the ground, with Ben's camera and laptop.

'Hold on,' Ben said. 'Why can't you bring your son to the clinic? We can treat him there.'

The leader shook his head. 'You don't understand. If I bring my son to the clinic, he will be arrested. You come with us now.'

'After we've treated your son, will you let us go?' Ben asked. His mouth was dry and his heart was pounding, but his voice sounded calm.

The leader shrugged. 'If he survives, maybe.'

'Well, I'm not going.' Declan sat down on the road.

The leader shoved the butt of his rifle into Declan's chest. 'Get into the car or I will shoot you.'

'Fair enough,' Declan said, trying to seem unmoved, but as he stood, his legs buckled. Ben reached out to catch him.

'It's okay – we just need to stay calm.'

'Screw that! This is not an "unfortunate event", Ben, this is a "fucking disaster".'

Ben gripped Declan's arm. 'Getting yourself shot isn't going to help. Now shut up and stop antagonizing them.'

They were hustled into the jeep while the youngest of the men doused their Fiat in petrol and threw something into it. As they drove away they heard an explosion. They looked back to see their car engulfed in a ball of fire.

Declan looked at Ben. 'We're fucked,' he whispered.

## Holly

Daddy's dead. The man rang Mummy to tell her eight hours, twenty-six minutes and eight seconds ago.

Jools was blowing out her candles and the phone rang and Mummy fell down and Uncle Kevin spoke to the man and he said, 'Daddy's dead and so is the other man, Declan.'

Mummy didn't want us to know about the car exploding. She told us it was a car crash, but Jools and I heard her talking to Kevin later. They were in the kitchen and me and Jools were supposed to be getting ready for bed, but how could we? How could we just get ready for bed as if it was a normal day? We sat on the floor outside the kitchen door, listening.

Mummy kept crying and saying they thought it was a landmine and why was Daddy such a fool and why did he have to go off into the mountains to find some stupid clinic? Why couldn't he just have stayed in the hotel and let Declan go to the clinic by himself? She screamed and screamed about Daddy being selfish and a bad word that starts with B, and running away from us to find adventure. She cried and cried and said, 'Why weren't we enough? Why did he have to go chasing danger? Why . . . why . . . why?'

Then she shouted that there wasn't even a body to bury. Jools put her arms around me after that bit and we cried together. I cried quietly, but Jools cries like Mummy, very loudly.

Kevin heard her and came out. He pulled us into a big

hug. Mummy came out, too, and held us so tightly I could hardly breathe, but I didn't mind. It made me stop thinking about the pain in my head for a minute. I felt as if it was going to burst open and my brain was going to fall out.

Mummy and Kevin kept saying, 'It's going to be all right,' over and over again. But it isn't. It's the opposite of all right. It's all wrong.

Then Mummy's phone rang again and she had to talk to other people from the Foreign and Commonwealth Office for a long time. And then John Lester called and I could hear Mummy shouting, 'This is your fault! You sent him to Eritrea and now he's dead!'

I felt a bit sorry for John Lester because he didn't make Daddy go. Daddy wanted to go. I could see how happy he was when he talked about his trip. He was all smiley, like he used to be. So it was a bit mean of Mummy to shout at John Lester.

I said so to Kevin, but he said I wasn't to worry, that Mummy needed to shout a bit and that John Lester would understand. Then under his breath he said, 'Stupid bad-word-beginning-with-F do-good surgeon.' He didn't think I heard him say that, but I did.

Kevin helped me into my pyjamas and told me to try and sleep. He said he knew I probably wouldn't and that he'd check on me every twenty minutes. Jools came in and said she wanted to sleep with me. We cuddled up in my small bed and cried.

We couldn't sleep so I got up and Googled 'landmine'. One million three hundred and ten thousand results came up. I went to Wikipedia and read it out to Jools: 'A landmine is an explosive device, concealed under or on the ground and designed to destroy or disable enemy targets, ranging from combatants to vehicles and tanks, as they pass over or near the device.'

Jools put her hands over her ears and screamed at me to stop. She was sobbing into my pillow, covering it with tears and snot. She said I was never to say the word 'landmine' again.

I promised I wouldn't. Then I counted to twenty and asked her to give me my pillow so I could change the cover.

She said I was a freak to be worried about tears on a pillow when Daddy had just died. I said I wasn't worried about the tears, I was worried about the snot. Jools shouted that she didn't want to sleep with me because I was a lunatic and she went out, slamming my door behind her. Kevin came up. His eyes were all puffy and red. He asked me why Jools was shouting. When I told him what had happened, he smiled and said he would definitely have wanted to change the pillowcase too. He helped me find a clean one and then he went in to talk to Jools.

I went downstairs to see if Mummy was okay. I peeped in the kitchen door. She was kneeling on the floor, talking, I thought to herself, but then I realized she was talking to God and she was telling Him that He was cruel. I went over to her and put my arms around her.

She kissed my hands. I told her I loved her, then cried into her back. I think I might have put some snot there as well as tears. Then I felt even worse and cried harder.

Mummy pulled me around and sat me on her lap. 'It's okay, sweetheart. I'm here for you. Mummy's here.'

At twenty-six minutes past one I got into bed. Kevin tucked me in and told me that I had to try really hard to sleep, or I'd 'get sick'.

It's forty-seven minutes past two and I'm still awake. I think my heart is breaking. I just can't believe it – Daddy's dead. My daddy, my lovely daddy, who always told me I was special. Daddy, who hugged me and swung me around when

I did well at school. Daddy, who tickled me until I screamed. Daddy, who said I was the best thing that ever happened to him. Daddy, who said he loved me more than all the stars and the moon and the world and the universe. Daddy, who helped me build a replica of *Titanic* for my school project and I won first prize. Daddy, who said I could be prime minister of the UK and make the country a better place. Daddy, who made me feel special every day. My daddy. Gone.

## Alice

Alice woke up. Her eyes felt heavy and sore. She tried opening them, but the lids only moved a fraction. What was going on? She must have picked up conjunctivitis from a patient. She rubbed her eyes and they felt sore, but they opened. She turned to look at the clock and saw Jools lying beside her.

It hit her like a ton of bricks. BEN! She gasped for breath. NO no no no no no, God, please, no. It must have been a dream, just a bad dream. She closed her eyes. Maybe she was still dreaming. But the pain in her chest was suffocating.

She looked at Jools. Her daughter's face was red and puffy, and she was whimpering in her sleep. It all came toppling down on Alice. It was real. Ben was dead.

The events of the night before came flooding back. Clipped accents from the Foreign and Commonwealth Office telling her about probable landmines and passports found at the site of the explosion and Ben's wallet and how they would send his personal effects home to her but unfortunately there would be no body because of the magnitude of the explosion. There was no point in coming out: Eritrea was no place for a woman and two young girls, and Ben had been a 'good man' and a 'credit to her and to his profession' and on and on.

Alice knew Ben was a good man. He was a really good man, but he was also a selfish man, who had gone on a trip to assuage his mid-life crisis, and now he was dead and she was a . . . a . . . widow. Alice bit her lip and sobbed quietly into her pillow. She didn't want to wake Jools.

Her brain teemed with the questions that had been constantly whirling around in her head since that awful phone call. Why, Ben? Why? We had a good life, two beautiful girls and a lovely home. Why did you have to risk it all? Alice stuffed her pillow into her mouth to smother the sounds of her wailing, but her body was shaking uncontrollably.

Jools woke up. 'What's . . . where . . . why . . . Mum?' she stuttered, opening her bleary eyes.

Alice watched her daughter, dreading the moment when the awful realization kicked in. Jools blinked, looked around and then Alice saw it, the frown, the shake of the head, the eyes widening, and then the look of horror.

'MUM! Is it . . . did Dad . . . is . . . Oh, my God!'

Alice put her arms out and Jools fell into them. 'Nooooooo, Mummy, please say it isn't true. Please tell me I dreamt it.'

Alice held her in a tight embrace and rocked her. 'I'm sorry, pet, I'm so sorry.'

Jools cried as if her heart would break. Alice felt as if hers already had.

While Alice tried to comfort her, she could hear Kevin talking to Holly in the next room. He had slept in her room so he could be there for her if she woke up during the night.

'Kevin?' Alice heard Holly ask.

'Yes, angel?'

'Do you think Daddy's in Heaven?'

Alice knew that Kevin had forsaken all religion at a young age, but he knew the girls were being raised Catholic and was good enough to play along.

'I think he'd be the first man in the door. Your dad was a great person.'

Holly began to cry. 'Please don't say "was". Using the past tense makes me feel like it's all over.'

'I'm sorry, sweetie, your dad *is* a great man. Come here to me.'

Alice thanked God for her brother.

Jools pulled away. 'What are we going to do without Dad?'

Alice tucked Jools's hair behind her ears. 'We'll be all right. We have each other. I'm here for you, darling.'

Jools shook her head violently. 'No. Dad was my person. It's always been you and Holly, then me and Dad. Now I've got no one.' She began to sob.

Alice didn't think her heart could break any more. 'Jools, I love you, and if you'll let me, I'll be your person.'

'You can't just be someone's person. It's not a job, it's a feeling. Dad loved me the most and I knew it. I felt it all the time. We were really close. Like you and Holly have a connection, well, me and Dad had that, and now he's gone and I have no one.' Jools's shoulders shook and her face crumpled with grief.

'Come on, Jools, you have me. I love you so much.'

'You just don't get it.' Jools wiped her tears.

Alice did, though. She understood completely because Ben had been her 'person', too. He was her husband, lover, confidant and best friend.

She also knew what Jools meant about her connection with her dad. They did have a special bond, like Alice with Holly. Perhaps it was because Jools looked so like Ben, and Holly was so like her. Maybe the physical resemblance to a child drew you closer to each other, or perhaps it was personality. She'd have to try really hard to become Jools's person too.

She started by holding her elder daughter close to her. After a while, Jools's breathing calmed down and she pulled out of her mother's arms. 'Does Granddad know?' she asked.

Alice nodded. She had called Harold the night before. Telling her father-in-law that his only child, his pride and joy, was dead had been devastating.

Harold kept saying, 'There must be some mistake,' and 'This just isn't possible.' And then, as the reality sank in, he began to cough and splutter, then hung up abruptly, muttering about needing a moment. Later he'd sent a text: *Alice, I'll be up in London tomorrow to discuss arrangements. H*

Alice didn't want to see Harold. She couldn't cope with him. Even in the full of her health she found him difficult to manage. He was so cold and aloof. In the twenty years she'd been with Ben, he'd never once hugged or kissed her. Even when her parents had died and she'd been in pieces, when he'd called at the house he had merely shaken her hand in sympathy.

When Alice's mother was alive and Alice gave out about Harold being so cold, her mother always said that Harold was just from a different era when men didn't show emotion and weren't demonstrative. But Alice's father had been of the same generation and he'd hugged her all the time. In fact, he was very in touch with his emotions – he'd cried all the time, too. It was a family joke that every time he watched *This Is Your Life* he'd end up reaching for his handkerchief.

At her wedding, Alice's father had cried the whole way up the aisle. She'd had to hold him up and hand him over to her mother at the top of the church. Harold had been appalled. Alice could see his disapproving expression now as her father had walked her slowly to the altar, tears streaming down his face. She had been cross about Harold's obvious distaste. She'd wanted to shout, 'At least I know he loves me, at least I know he's happy for me, at least I know he cares.'

Ben said he didn't mind that his father was remote. He said his mother had made up for it. In fact, Ben suspected that his father had pulled back because his mother doted on him.

Alice was very sad to have known Ben's mum for such a short time. But she knew Ben's mum had liked her. She'd told her so. One night when Ben was getting ready and Alice was having a glass of wine with her, she had leant over and said, 'I'm so glad Ben met you. He should be with someone warm and loving.'

Alice had been thrilled. At that stage she was head over heels in love with him and knew she wanted to spend the rest of her life waking up beside him.

Ben was a perfect mix of his parents. Thankfully, his DNA had taken all of their good qualities and mixed them up to make a very special man. Ben had all of his mother's zest for life, her sense of fun and enthusiasm, with his father's drive and steeliness. It was an irresistible combination.

When Ben's mother had died, Ben had leant on Alice while his father grew more distant. Alice had tried to talk to Harold about his grief and to draw him out, but he had stonewalled her every time. Eventually, she had given up.

The other problem with Harold was that he was allergic to Kevin. He couldn't seem to handle him being openly gay, and for some reason Kevin, who was normally not that camp, turned into a caricature of himself in Harold's company.

Kevin said it was because Harold made him uncomfortable. 'I can't help myself. I become camper than a row of tents when that man is around,' he explained. 'He's so bloody disapproving. It just sends me into a tailspin.'

Alice had found it best to keep them apart as much as she could. The last time they'd been in the same room was on Christmas Day a year ago, when Harold had called Kevin an embarrassment. Kevin had been completely over the top, but Christmas was always hard for him because he was alone.

If it wasn't for Alice, he would have spent Christmas on his own – he had no parents, no partner, no kids. It was hard for him and made all the worse because he'd just been dumped by a guy he'd really liked.

Since that day, Alice had seen Harold only three times. She'd let Ben take the girls to visit him in Tunbridge Wells. The girls hated going because there was nothing to do, and Harold refused to allow them to watch television or eat sweets. His new wife, Helen, had eased things a little, but she was almost as cold as he was.

'Mummy.' Holly climbed into bed with her mother and sister, while Kevin went down to the kitchen to put on the kettle. She clung to Alice. 'I woke up and forgot.'

'I know, love, we all did.' Alice stroked Holly's tear-stained face.

'It's been twelve hours, seventeen minutes and, um . . . forty-six seconds since that man rang up.'

Jools groaned. 'For God's sake, Holly, will you stop bloody going on about the time? Who cares when it happened? It happened.' Jools began to cry again.

'Sssh now.' Alice rubbed Jools's back.

Holly's lip wobbled. 'Working out numbers helps to stop my head hurting. I can't do anything about my heart – it feels as if it was squashed by something heavy – but if I do num-bers my head hurts a bit less.' She burst into tears.

Kevin walked into the room bearing a tray laden with tea, orange juice and chocolate biscuits, to find all three in a hud-dle on the bed, crying uncontrollably.

He placed the tray down and said, gently but firmly, 'Come on, girls, I need you to drink some sugary tea or orange juice and eat a biscuit. The sugar will give you an energy boost. We need our strength today. Now, this cup of coffee is for your mother only.' Kevin handed Alice a cup and mouthed, 'Brandy.'

Alice drank the alcohol-laced coffee gratefully. She was going to need all the help she could find to get through today.

Kevin helped the girls get dressed while Alice had a shower. She stood under the water and cried her eyes out. She raged at God, life, Fate and Ben. She thumped the shower wall until her hands ached. When she got out, she curled up on the floor, unable to move.

Kevin came in and closed the door. 'Alice.' He pulled her to her feet. 'You can't do this. You can't fall apart. I know you want to – I know this is a complete nightmare – but the girls need you. Now come on. I'll help you every step of the way.'

He dressed her, putting her clothes on for her as if she was a little girl. Then he dried her hair and tried to put some make-up on her face. But Alice kept crying and the mascara kept running, so he gave up. 'Well, at least you're clean and you smell nice.'

Alice stood up and hugged him. 'Thank you.'

Kevin hugged her back. 'I'm here for you, sis.'

'Why did he do it, Kevin?' Alice started crying again.

'Alice, he was trying to help other doctors. It was a freak accident. It wasn't his fault.'

'Why did he have to go?'

'Because he was Ben.'

'I hate Ben.'

'No, you don't.'

'How am I going to live without him?' Alice cried.

Before Kevin could try to answer that impossible question, there was a knock on the front door. Alice heard Jools say, 'Hello, Granddad.'

'Shit, it's Harold. Already,' Alice whispered.

Kevin grasped his sister's hand. 'You can do this. Remember, he's heartbroken too.'

They went downstairs to the kitchen, where Jools, Holly

and Harold were sitting at the table. Holly was telling Harold how many hours, minutes and seconds had elapsed since the phone call from the Foreign and Commonwealth Office.

When Kevin and Alice walked in, Harold stood up. Alice was shocked. He had aged ten years overnight. He looked terrible. On impulse, Alice went over and put her arms around him. 'Oh, Harold,' she said.

He drew back. 'Was it your idea?' he said, eyes flashing.

'What?' Alice was confused.

'Eritrea! Was it your idea for him to go there?'

'No.'

'When I rang the Foreign and Commonwealth Office for details, they said Ben was with some Irishman. I presumed he was a friend of yours. Or his.' Harold jabbed his finger in Kevin's direction.

Alice's grief turned quickly to anger. How dare Harold accuse her of 'sending' Ben to Eritrea? She clenched her jaw to stop herself screaming at him. 'I've never met Declan. He was John Lester's registrar. He went to assist Ben during the operation. As a matter of fact, I totally disagreed with the trip and begged Ben not to go.'

'It's true. Ben planned the whole thing himself. Alice didn't know anything about it until he announced he was going. He wanted to go. He was very excited about the trip,' Kevin said, defending his sister.

Harold wouldn't even look at him. 'Please stay out of this,' he growled.

Alice could see Jools out of the corner of her eye. She was crying again. She needed to calm things down and take control of the situation. 'Harold, there's no need to be rude to my brother. I know you're upset. We all are. We're all in shock. No one is to blame. It was a horrible accident.'

'Bloody Africans, a law unto themselves. Never could control them. Dreadful lot, no morals,' Harold barked.

Holly's eyes widened. 'The Eritrean people have had a terrible history. They were colonized by the Italians and then had a long war with Ethiopia. They only got independence in 1992.'

'So what?' Jools shouted. 'It doesn't mean they had to plant landmines in the ground and blow up innocent people.'

Alice gasped. 'How did you —'

'Know about the landmine?' Jools cut across her mother. 'We heard you talking to Kevin. We know what happened, Mum. We know it wasn't a car crash. We know there's no bo-bo-body.' Jools began to wail.

Alice rushed over to comfort her.

'It's been fifteen hours, seventeen minutes and twelve seconds since the man rang,' Holly said, as tears streamed down her face.

Kevin pulled her in and hugged her.

Harold croaked, 'Forty-five years and nine months since he was born.'

Seventeen years and eight months since I said, 'I do', Alice thought, as she began to cry again.

## Ben

The soldiers pushed Ben and Declan onto the floor of the jeep and held guns to their backs. They drove for what seemed like hours, uphill and over very rough terrain. Ben's legs ached.

At first he tried to memorize the route, left, left, right, left . . . but soon it was a blur. He thought about Alice and the girls. He had to stay strong.

Declan kept asking the men where they were taking them. They repeatedly told him to be quiet. Ben whispered at him to shut up. He was only going to annoy them. But Declan was not to be deterred. When he asked for the third time, he got a rifle butt in the head. After that he was quiet.

They stopped abruptly. They were pushed out of the car. They were high up in the mountains. The land was arid and there was no sign of any life, just miles and miles of dusty, rocky mountainside. The men pushed Ben and Declan onward up the mountain, one man in front and two behind. The other man drove the jeep away, back down the mountain.

They were now walking on a narrow path that wound across the mountaintop. Declan was in front of Ben, who could see blood matting on the back of his head where he'd been hit. It was a small cut but, still, these men meant business. They'd have to be careful not to do anything to cause trouble for themselves.

Ben tried to remain calm. Every time he began to panic,

he thought of the girls – he had to stay alive for them. He'd operate on the leader's son and then, hopefully, they'd let them go. Ben prayed that he was able to save the boy's life. What if he was too far gone? What if the damage was irreparable? What if he got an infection and died? Ben doubted that the conditions for operating on anyone were going to be ideal in this remote place.

He plucked up the courage to approach the leader, who was walking directly in front of him. 'What are your son's injuries?'

'Bullets.'

'Can you tell me where?'

'Here.' The leader thumped his chest.

Now Ben was really worried. If it had been a leg or an arm, there was a good chance of survival, but gunshot wounds to the chest were a potential nightmare. The kid could be dead before they even got there. Then what would happen? Would they just shoot them? Ben somehow doubted they'd accompany them all the way back to their hotel, give them a pat on the back and let them go. Panic rose inside him and he struggled to stay in control.

He tried to focus on the patient. 'How old is your son?' he asked.

'Fifteen,' the man answered proudly. 'Very brave soldier. Now, hurry, hurry,' he said, urging Ben to walk faster. 'You need to save him. If he dies, it will be bad for you.' He gave Ben a dig in the back that shunted him forwards, so he was on Declan's heels.

'Fucking brilliant,' Declan hissed, under his breath. 'They want us to perform a miracle on a kid who's been shot in the chest. You need to tell the old man that we're doctors, not bloody magicians.'

'Keep your voice down,' Ben warned. 'I need you

conscious for the operation, not knocked out because you can't keep your mouth shut.'

'If the kid dies, we're dead men.'

'I'm aware of that, thank you. You're not helping.'

'How good a surgeon are you?'

'I'm good,' Ben said. It was true, but under these circumstances, who knew what might happen?

'I'd rather you'd said great. It would have been more reassuring.'

'We have to stay calm. Do not antagonize them in any way.'

'I don't have a death wish!' Declan said angrily.

'No, but you have a big mouth. Keep it shut.'

'One more thing,' Declan said, as he stumbled over the rocks.

'What?' Ben was getting frustrated.

'Ask him how long more to go.'

Ben raised his voice and asked the leader how much further they had to walk.

'Close now,' the man snapped. 'Hurry, hurry.'

Ten minutes later they rounded a corner and were met with the sight of about thirty tents. They were beige, so they blended in with the pale, dusty landscape of thorn trees and boulders. Women and children stared at them, while men wielding guns watched closely as they were rushed into a big tent to one side of the encampment.

Ben was surprised to see small children. It was like a makeshift village. He'd presumed it would be a soldiers' bivouac.

Inside the big tent was a 'hospital', with four men lying on stretchers made of tree branches and sheets. They were groaning softly. There was a dividing curtain, which was pulled back by one of the guards to reveal an 'operating theatre'. This consisted of a home-made wooden table with a bare bulb hanging over it, a bowl of water and some sheets on a low table in the corner. Another table was covered with suture kits, antibiotics, painkillers, two battery-powered head-lamps, scalpels, scissors, needles and a tourniquet. They'd clearly raided a clinic for medical supplies.

The fifteen-year-old boy was lying on the makeshift oper-ating table in a pool of his own blood. The leader went to his son and held his hand. He spoke gently to him, pointing to Ben and Declan, smiling and nodding.

'Looks like he's telling his kid we're going to save his life,' Declan whispered.

Ben looked at the large bloodstain on the front of the boy's shirt. 'We have to save him, no matter what. Even if we can keep him alive for a day or two, just long enough for us to persuade them that he's going to survive and they should let us go.'

'I don't think we're going anywhere until that kid is run-ning around playing football for the Eritrean national team. What the hell are we going to do?' Declan's voice shook.

Ben grasped his colleague's arm. 'We are going to do our job. Now, I need you to keep it together. I want full focus. We are going to save this boy's life.'

'I'm trying.'

'Try harder. I thought you came from a tough area of Dublin.'

'Living next door to a couple of drug-dealers and petty criminals hardly prepared me for lads holding Kalashnikovs in my face.'

'Get it together, Declan. Come on.'

While Declan composed himself, Ben blocked out his own fears and allowed himself to concentrate on his job. He asked everyone to leave the room, but the two soldiers with guns stayed, as did the father.

Ben was getting angry. 'If you want me to save your son,

you must leave. We never allow relatives to watch operations. It will upset you and you will distract me from my work. If you want to leave the gunmen, fine, but they are not allowed to say a word or make a move. I need complete silence and calm. One shake of my hand and your son could die.'

The leader reluctantly agreed, but said he'd sit outside the 'door'. Then he reminded Ben of the consequences of not saving his son, making a gun shape with his hand and pointing it at Ben's head.

Ben turned away from him. He picked up a pair of scissors and went to cut away the boy's shirt. The teenager had been hit twice in the right shoulder, an exit wound below the right nipple showing the path of one bullet.

Ben washed his hands carefully, scrubbed them and put on surgical gloves from the suture kit. Declan did the same and came over to look. The boy was gasping for breath. Ben tapped his chest with his fingers. On the right side, below the clavicle, it sounded normal, but when Ben tapped lower down he could hear a dull sound. *Thunk.*

'I suppose an X-ray is out of the question.' Declan half smiled, but Ben could see his hands were shaking.

'I'm pretty sure it didn't come with the suture kits. But I'm confident it's a left haemopneumothorax.'

Declan nodded. He'd heard it too.

Ben, now fully concentrated, felt with his fingers for the dip between the boy's fifth and sixth ribs. Declan, anticipating his needs, handed Ben a syringe of local anaesthetic, which Ben injected between the boy's ribs.

The boy's eyes snapped open and he cried out in pain. The leader came rushing in as the guards raised their Kalashnikovs. Ben raised his hand. 'Stop. Your son felt pain when the needle passed through the pleura – the membrane that lines the chest here.' Ben pointed to the exact spot. 'Now look.'

Ben pointed to the dark blood that was being sucked back into the syringe. 'Everything is under control. I need peace in my theatre, please.'

The leader spoke to his son, and left.

'Good thing he's not here for this bit,' Declan said, handing Ben a scalpel.

Ben cut through skin and muscle and the wound bubbled air. Declan handed him a tube, which Ben carefully inserted into the hole, then stitched it to the skin to prevent it being dislodged.

'Here it comes!' Declan said, as blood gushed out. The boy cried out in pain and coughed.

Again, his father came charging in and stared at the blood. His face fearful, he glared at Ben.

'STOP!' Ben shouted. Then he guided the man to his son's side and indicated that he should lean towards his son's chest. 'Listen to your son's breathing.'

The leader did so. With every gasp the boy was breathing more easily as the pressure left his chest. Declan connected the chest drain to a tube and then, using the bowl half filled with water, he placed the end of the tube in it to act as a simple one-way valve. With each exhalation, air and blood bubbled out of the submerged end of the tube and the lung started, little by little, to expand.

Ben peeled off his gloves and set them aside so they could be washed and reused.

'Your son will be fine. He needs antibiotics and painkillers. The lung will reinflate, then the drain can be removed. I'll show you how to do it. Then I want to leave.'

The leader smiled. 'Thank you for helping my son, but you will not be leaving until I am sure he is well. I also have more injured soldiers I need you to treat, Doctor. You're not going anywhere.'

'We had a deal. I save your son and you let me go,' Ben said, trying to stop his fear showing in his voice.

The leader laughed. 'I made no deal with you. You will stay here until I say you can go. You will stay here until I don't need you.'

Rage ripped through him. 'Fine. I have no intention of operating on anyone else. I helped your son and now I'm leaving.'

The leader put his big hand on Ben's chest, preventing him from moving past. He shouted some words to the two soldiers. One grabbed Declan and put his gun to Declan's head.

'If you refuse to help me, Doctor, I'm afraid your friend will have to die.'

'You bastard,' Ben cursed. 'Let him go.'

The leader ordered his man to stand down. Declan moved aside, white and shaking.

'War is hard. We do what we have to do to survive,' the leader said.

'What war?' Ben asked. 'Eritrea is independent. Who are you fighting?'

The leader's eyes narrowed. 'The Ethiopian scum who killed my parents and my brother. They say the land is on their side of the border, but it's my land and I won't stop until I get it back.'

'Once we've helped those soldiers out there, I want your word that you'll return us to Asmara.' Ben was desperate to get reassurances.

The leader laughed again. 'I spent a year in London studying English before I was called home when my village was attacked. You English are obsessed with your "word". Words mean nothing. Promises mean nothing. The only thing that matters is family and pride.'

'Exactly, and that's why we want to get back to our own families. So when we've helped the remaining wounded, I want you to let us go.'

'Save my men and then we will talk.'

'This is bullshit.' Declan found his voice. 'We need some kind of guarantee. Otherwise what's to say you won't shoot us when we've finished operating?'

The leader grinned at him. 'Nothing. As you say in England, "You're snookered." But if you do a good job, you will live. If not, you will die. That should be a good incentive.'

'Wanker,' Declan muttered.

The leader ordered his men to bring in the next patient, then left the room. The soldiers carried their friend in on a blood-soaked mattress.

As the two doctors bent over to examine the man, Declan whispered, 'Jesus, Ben, what are we going to do? These guys are total bandits.'

Ben shook his head. 'The important thing is to stay alive and try to figure it out as we go along.'

'Is that it?'

'What?'

'That's your solution?'

'Well, what's yours?' Ben snapped. 'Curse your way out of here?'

'We could use the scalpels.'

'A scalpel against a Kalashnikov? Seriously?'

'Okay, okay, it's not brilliant, but at least I'm thinking of ways to escape.'

'I've got two daughters and a wife. I'm not getting shot in some stupid escape attempt. Do you understand?'

The two men stared at each other, almost nose to nose, breathing hard. It was Declan who stepped back first. 'Okay, no need to rip my head off.'

Ben wanted to rip the head off every man in the room with his bare hands. He felt desperation and terror creeping in. What was going to happen to them? Would they be shot? Could he persuade the leader to let them go after they'd helped these wounded men?

Although Ben was usually an optimist, he had a sinking feeling that this situation was not going to end well. He had to stay strong, get out of there alive and back to his three girls. He had to. He'd do anything it took. Anything.

## *Holly*

I'm hiding in my wardrobe in the horrible black dress Kevin bought me. I hate it. Everything is ruined. Everything is just awful. My daddy is dead and we have his funeral today and I don't want to go.

I can hear Mummy crying every night through the wall. She never seems to sleep. Whenever I wake up – which is a lot because I keep having nightmares – she's crying. I go in to her most nights and sleep with her in her and Daddy's bed.

She looks so sad all the time. When she sees me or Jools, she puts on this fake smile and tries to be cheerful, but it's silly and she's really bad at it. We know her heart is broken. Our hearts are broken too.

I woke up at forty-three minutes past two last night and I heard Mummy crying. So I went in to her. Jools was already in the bed, asleep beside her. I cuddled into Mummy and she held me tight. We didn't say anything, just snuggled. There's nothing to say anyway. Daddy's dead and, as Jools says, 'Life sucks.'

It was nice all of us being together in the bed. It was less scary and lonely. I think I'll sleep with Mummy again tonight.

Granddad is here. He arrived this morning with Helen. They're all dressed in black too. Granddad looks really old now. It's as if someone smacked him over the head and squashed him. He keeps having to leave the room to 'blow his nose'. It's kind of silly because we all know he's crying.

Mummy said Granddad is a very private person and doesn't want to cry in front of anyone. We're all sad and we all miss Daddy, so he should just cry with us.

He's been up and down all week, helping Mummy organize the funeral. Well, he was supposed to be helping but he kind of took over and was very bossy.

Mummy's voice goes all stiff and sharp when Granddad's here. She's not like her normal self. She's sort of colder and more correct. Her voice sounds different. They had a fight about the readings at the funeral. Mummy wanted to have a poem read. It's beautiful – it's called 'Don't Cry For Me'. But Granddad said no poems, only proper readings from the Bible. Mummy said she'd really like the poem to be in the funeral mass but Granddad shouted, 'This is a solemn memorial service and we'll not have any of your Irish melodrama.'

I stopped breathing for six seconds. I didn't know what melodrama meant, but I knew it was bad. I looked it up later. It said 'overdramatic emotion or behaviour'. I think it was mean of Granddad to say that.

Mummy went very quiet and then she said, 'Fine, Harold, do what you want. We'll attend, of course, but the girls and I will have our own farewell.'

Granddad made a tutting sound, then Mummy left the room and I followed her. I saw her kick the wall and heard her say a really bad word. Mummy and Granddad haven't really spoken since.

Mummy told me and Jools that we'll have our own service, just us together, with lots of poems and music. And then we'll plant a beautiful tree and make it special.

Even though this has been the worst week of my life, one kind of amazing thing happened. It made me really happy but also really sad. It happened when Daddy's suitcase came home. A man from the Foreign and Commonwealth Office brought it to the door. Mummy opened it, and when she saw Daddy's clothes, she began to cry really hard.

Kevin had to hold her tight to calm her down. I opened the little pocket at the back of the suitcase and felt inside. I thought I might find Daddy's aftershave – I wanted to smell it, to remind me of him – but instead I found a little velvet bag. I opened it, and inside were three beautiful gold necklaces! One with an H, one with a J and one with an A.

When I held them up, everybody stopped talking. Mummy put her hand over her mouth and Jools just kept staring at them.

'Now you know how much he was thinking of you all,' Kevin said, in a wobbly voice, and we all began to cry again.

I will never, ever, ever, ever, ever, ever, ever take my necklace off. I feel as if Daddy is beside me now. I love this necklace so much. I'm so glad Daddy was thinking of us before . . . before the accident.

It's been one hundred and thirty-five hours, sixteen minutes and eight seconds since the phone call.

Mummy told us last night that Kevin's going to move in with us for a while. I'm glad because he is my favourite person after Mummy and Daddy. He always seems to know when I need a hug or when I need to be left alone.

I think it's good for Mummy too, because Kevin can help us to look after her. Even though Mummy is a doctor and looks after other people, she needs to be looked after now.

Every day I wake up and I forget, and then I remember and I feel sick. I keep thinking about Jo from *Little Women* and how she was so sad when Beth died, but then she started writing, and that's what I'm going to do. I'm going to write more and try to get all the sadness out.

I printed out the poem that Mummy wanted to read today at the funeral. I'm sticking it in here so I can read it when I feel sad. It's beautiful and it makes me cry, but it also makes me feel a tiny bit better. Daddy, I miss you so much.

### Don't Cry For Me

Don't cry for me now I have died, for I'm still here
    I'm by your side,
My body's gone but my soul is here, please don't
    shed another tear,
I am still here I'm all around, only my body lies
    in the ground.
I am the snowflake that kisses your nose,
I am the frost that nips your toes.
I am the sun, bringing you light,
I am the star, shining so bright.
I am the rain, refreshing the earth,
I am the laughter, I am the mirth.
I am the bird, up in the sky,
I am the cloud that's drifting by.
I am the thoughts inside your head,
While I'm still there, I can't be dead.

# Alice

Harold was a nightmare about the memorial service. He refused all of Alice's suggestions. She knew that if she didn't step back, they'd have a huge row and never speak again. In a way she would have welcomed that, but out of respect for Ben she bit her tongue and let her father-in-law walk all over her.

What really bothered Alice was the empty coffin: they had no body. When she had called Jonathan Londis at the Foreign and Commonwealth Office about Ben's remains, he had put her in touch with some senior person, who had told her that the local police in Eritrea had said that the force of the explosion had left no bodies 'as such' and that, unfortunately, there was nothing to return to them except Ben's personal items from the hotel, a charred passport and his wallet.

When she'd spoken to Harold about it, he was appalled that she would question the information she had received from the officials. He'd barked that 'The chaps in the FO know exactly what they're doing and you can't go about badgering them. Of course there are no remains. It was a great big bloody explosion.'

Alice shuddered every time she heard the word 'explosion'. She tried not to think about that part. The violence of Ben's last seconds on earth haunted her. She hated Harold for being so cold and formal. Why couldn't he just admit his heart was broken? Ben's death should have united them, but instead it was driving them even further apart.

Alice was devastated to be burying an empty coffin. It felt so soulless. She suggested putting some of Ben's favourite things inside it. Things to comfort him. The girls wanted to put in his favourite book, his favourite scarf, his spare stethoscope, a teddy bear and some photos. Harold told them it was absolutely out of the question. He said it wasn't the 'done thing'. Alice had wanted to punch him in the face.

She knew the memorial service would be stiff, cold and impersonal, just like Harold, so she decided to have her own ceremony at home where she and the girls could do whatever they wanted without Harold's disapproval.

Alice didn't remember much about the service. She'd let her mind wander off as the dark and depressing hymns and readings that Harold had chosen went on around her. This wasn't her farewell: she would do that with the girls, Kevin, Nora, David and Pippa on Sunday. Father Brendan, the local Catholic priest, had agreed to come to the house and say some prayers and they would read poems, and Jools wanted to play Ben's favourite song, Queen's 'Don't Stop Me Now', and everyone could say a few words and just remember.

Alice wanted the girls to be able to say what they wished, to say goodbye to Ben in their own way. This formal ceremony meant nothing to her.

Beside her, Jools fidgeted and Holly counted the words on the missal. Kevin sat stony-faced and rolled his eyes every time a new, even more depressing dirge was played on the ancient organ.

Ben wasn't in the coffin. Ben was in Eritrea, his ashes strewn around some dirt-track. When the girls were older, if

Eritrea was safe, Alice would take them there. She'd find the place where it had happened and they'd lay flowers. But for now she was going to keep Ben in her heart and mind. She fiddled with her gold necklace, twisting the A as she let her thoughts drift.

No one spoke about Ben. The priest droned on and on about his distinguished career as a surgeon and mentioned that he had a wife and two daughters. But he never spoke about the man Ben was – the wonderful, warm, funny, kind man he was. Alice dug her nails into her palms to stop herself standing up and screaming *'He wasn't just a bloody surgeon!'*

After the ceremony Ben's uncles and aunts shook her hand, some kissed her, one or two hugged her. She felt numb. It was as if she was looking down on herself from the highest branch of a tree. She felt as if she was playing a part – the grieving widow. She couldn't allow herself to feel. Not now, not here.

The only time she got emotional was when David and Pippa came up to her. She hadn't seen them since the news had broken. They'd left messages for her, but she hadn't been able to face talking to anyone. She didn't want to hear the words 'I'm so sorry' – they would make it all too real.

Like Holly, she didn't want anyone to talk about Ben in the past tense. She couldn't stand to hear 'He *was* a lovely man.' She wanted to keep him alive and in the present tense and somehow near her.

'Darling!' Pippa said, throwing her arms around Alice and clasping her tightly. 'We just can't believe it. We're so sorry.'

As Pippa turned to the girls, David came up and pulled Alice into a big bear hug. He was six foot six and as broad as he was tall. Alice felt safe and protected in his arms. 'Christ,

Alice,' he said, his voice breaking. 'Why Ben? Why did it have to be Ben?'

Alice began to cry: David got it. He understood how she felt. He was as confused and upset as she was. She knew how much David loved Ben. They'd been best friends since they'd met on their first day in medical school.

'Bloody Eritrea! I told him not to go. I told him John Lester was a maverick. It's all right for John to go off to Eritrea – he doesn't have kids and he's not married. I said it to Ben, "Don't go. If you want adventure, take up sky-diving." But he wouldn't listen. He was absolutely determined.'

'I begged him too,' Alice cried. 'Why did he have to be so stupid?'

David handed Alice a tissue. 'Ben always wanted to do more. He pushed himself harder than any of the rest of us, even when we were medical students. He was always striving for more. I was glad when he settled down and had kids – he seemed to mellow a bit – but in the last year I did notice that he seemed restless and keen to do something else. He was looking to challenge himself again.'

'Why weren't we enough?' Alice cried.

'Come on now,' David said. 'I didn't mean it like that. Ben adored you and the girls. He always said you were the best thing that ever happened to him. I suppose this was a kind of . . . well, a mid-life crisis thing. I see it all around me – colleagues volunteering for Médecins Sans Frontières or climbing Everest or misbehaving, like me.' David looked embarrassed.

Alice hugged him. 'You were such a good friend to Ben. Thanks for always being there for him. He always said you were the brother he never had.'

'I felt the same way.' David buried his face in Alice's shoulder and sobbed.

Alice rubbed his back, then shuddered as she heard Harold's voice behind her. 'David, good of you to come,' he said, sticking out his hand.

'Terribly sorry about Ben, Harold. Can't believe it.' David rubbed his tear-stained face.

'Yes, well, it's been a terrible shock for all of us. Still, best to hold our heads up high today.' Harold was clearly annoyed at David's display of emotion. Turning to Alice, he said, 'It's time to leave for the cemetery.'

'I'm coming, Harold, but I've decided I don't want the girls there, seeing the coffin being lowered into the ground.'

Harold frowned. 'They should be there. It will look most peculiar if they don't come.'

'I don't care how it looks.' Alice was doing her best to keep her voice even. 'It will upset them too much, and I know Holly will have nightmares about it.'

Harold opened his mouth to argue when David jumped in: 'Alice may have a point, Harold. It might be a bit traumatic for them. Why don't I come with you, Alice, then Pippa can take the girls back to our house for a bit?'

'Thanks, David, but Kevin can take them home,' Alice said.

'Kevin can go with them. Pippa would be delighted to have his company – she's been so upset since we heard about Ben.'

Harold muttered, 'Nonsense,' under his breath and went back to Helen.

Alice smiled weakly at David. 'You saved me there. Harold was going to try to bully me into bringing the girls.'

David put his hand on Alice's shoulder. 'Your idea to have a farewell ceremony at home is perfect. Ben would much prefer that. Poor Harold, he's just very old school. He looks shattered – it's a terrible thing to lose a child.'

Alice looked over at Harold. 'I tried to placate him, honestly, and I gave in to all his demands for this service, but I'm not traumatizing my girls just to keep up a show. I draw the line there.'

David patted her arm. 'Darling, of course. I understand completely. I'm on your side, believe me. I suppose I just understand Harold's type – my own father was like that.'

Alice squeezed his hand. 'Thank God you and Ben didn't inherit that awful stiff upper lip.'

When Alice told Kevin the plan for him to take the girls to Pippa's house, he was clearly relieved. She knew he'd be glad not to be at the graveside with Harold. She remembered the one time she'd brought Kevin to David and Pippa's house in Holland Park and he had spent the whole visit outside, flirting with their driver, who was from Brazil and very good-looking. She remembered Ben joking quietly to her that Kevin was like Lady Sybil from *Downton Abbey*, trying to shag the chauffeur. Now she smiled at the memory, but then pain hit her chest and she had to push it away. She kissed Jools and Holly goodbye, then steeled herself for the 'burial'.

A few days later, a small group gathered in the back garden at Alice and Ben's house. Nora was there, Kevin, David, Pippa, Alice and the girls, plus Father Brendan. They said a few prayers, then Father Brendan asked if anyone would like to read a poem or say a few words. Holly read 'Don't Cry For Me' . . . and everyone cried.

Pippa read Emily Dickinson's 'Because I Could Not Stop For Death'. David spoke about how much he missed Ben, but how lucky he felt to have been blessed with such a good, loyal and wonderful best friend. He had to stop then because he was overcome with emotion. Pippa reached out and took his hand.

Nora said Ben was the nicest employer she'd ever had and by far the handsomest, which made everyone smile.

Kevin tried to speak, but was crying too much.

Alice had written a letter. She put it in a little metal box, which she was going to bury under the cherry tree they were planting in the garden for Ben. It was too emotional to read out. Too painful. Too much.

Jools was last. Alice told her she didn't have to read anything if she didn't want to. She knew how much Jools hated reading aloud and she didn't want her to feel any pressure. But Jools said she had to. With trembling hands, she pulled out a piece of paper.

She took a deep breath:

'Daddy. You were my everything. My father, my friend, my supporter. You understood me like no one else. I am so glad that I have your eyes. I am so proud to be your daughter and so lucky to have been loved by you. I am so proud of you, Daddy. You're so handsome and clever and funny and brave and kind. You're like a bright light in our lives, and now that you're gone, it's all dark and lonely.

'I wish I'd told you I loved you more. I wish I'd hugged you more. I wish I'd laughed at your stupid jokes more. I wish you knew how much I loved you, because I did, Daddy. I loved you so much it hurt.

'Daddy, I don't know how I'm going to live without you, but I promise I will try to make you proud of me.'

Everyone was crying now – even Father Brendan had welled up. Alice hugged Jools tightly and whispered, 'He was proud of you every single day.'

David lifted the young cherry tree from the pot and placed it gently in the hole in the ground that he had dug earlier. Alice placed the box holding her letter beside it. Then everyone took turns to tip the soil back into the hole until the roots of the tree were covered and it was secure.

Nora passed around glasses of champagne and they raised a toast to Ben's life. Then Father Brendan said a final prayer, and that was it. Their goodbye was over. Ben's life was over. It was all done, and now, somehow, they had to find a way to keep going.

# Ben

Ben rolled over and felt a tug on his leg. The chain around his ankle clanked as he tried to get comfortable on his thin mattress. He opened his eyes and groaned silently. He was still there. In his dreams he had been at home with Alice and the girls, warm, safe, with his loved ones.

The reality, when he woke, hit him like a punch in the gut. He closed his eyes and tried not to panic. It couldn't last much longer. They wouldn't keep them there now. He had operated on all of the wounded. It was time for them to be released. Ben would ask to speak to the leader, Awate. He had to make him see that it was pointless to keep him and Declan there. He had to persuade Awate to let them go. He had to get the hell out.

He knew Alice and the girls would be panicking. When Ben thought of the anguish he was putting his family through, he felt physically sick. Did they believe he was dead? Would they know he'd been kidnapped? Did they think he'd just disappeared? Why the hell had he been so stupid as to come here? He cursed himself. He could hear Alice in his head, shouting, 'I told you not to go!'

'I'm sorry, Alice,' he whispered into the air. 'I'm so sorry.'

Beside him, Declan stirred. They were bound together by a long metal chain that wrapped around their ankles, then trailed out of their tent and wound around a tree. Two armed soldiers stood guard outside.

Declan rubbed his eyes. 'Feck it, we're still here. I dreamt I was back home. What day is it?' he asked.

'Thursday,' Ben replied.

'Nearly three weeks,' Declan said. 'Three weeks in this shithole with a bunch of lunatics fighting over some stupid bit of land. What the hell are we going to do?'

'I'll try to talk to Awate again today.' Ben sat up.

'Jesus, my leg,' Declan cried. 'Go slow, will you?'

'Sorry,' Ben said, and Declan sat up beside him, moving the chain with him. He lit a cigarette and offered Ben one.

Ben took it and inhaled deeply. He had taken up smoking on day ten. He'd asked Awate to let them go and Awate had refused. So Ben had asked him at least to let their families know they were alive. Awate had roared with laughter and told Ben not to be so stupid. 'Are you crazy? Do you think I will tell the world that I have two English doctors up here? We'd all be killed. You're my secret weapon, Ben. No one knows you're alive so no one will come looking. Just relax and keep helping me.'

When Ben had refused to operate on more soldiers, Awate had once again pointed a gun to Declan's head and threatened to shoot him. Ben and Declan had discussed it and said that, if it happened again, Ben was to stand his ground. 'But don't let him actually shoot me,' Declan said.

So the next time Ben had held his ground until Awate fired a bullet one inch to the right of Declan's ear. After that, he promised to continue operating. When Awate had left, Declan offered Ben a cigarette, which he had gratefully accepted. He needed something to calm his nerves. Lucky Strikes were the one thing the camp had in abundance. God only knew where they'd robbed them from. Declan had never asked, just accepted the packets gratefully.

'What the hell are we going to do?' Declan exhaled deeply,

a line of smoke floating into the hot air of their little tent. 'We can't escape with these bloody chains on us. We'll have to try to run during the day.'

'The problem with that is they'll easily follow us and catch or shoot us,' Ben said. 'We don't know the terrain. We haven't got a clue where we are.'

'What about getting hold of a phone?'

'The only person who has one is Awate and he always has it tucked into his belt.'

'Maybe you could bump into him and knock him over by accident, and when I'm helping him up, I could nick it,' Declan suggested.

'If I knocked him over, I'd be shot by at least three guards simultaneously. Awate is God to them.'

'Well, I'm not staying here another day. I'm going to make a break for it.'

'For God's sake, Declan, running off and getting shot is just stupid. We need a proper plan, one that will actually work. We need to gather information and plot our escape. I'm not getting killed and leaving my children fatherless on some impulsive, half-arsed scheme.'

'You've watched way too many of those war movies, Ben. We're not in the middle of a war, stuck in enemy territory with an army of people looking for us. We've been taken by a bunch of lunatics who don't give a damn about us and everyone we know thinks we're dead. These people have never heard of the Geneva Convention. They'll slit our throats as soon as we're no longer useful to them. We're going to have to get out of here ourselves and I'm not staying for one more day.'

Ben stubbed out his cigarette on the ground. 'Declan, please don't do anything stupid. I want to get home as much as you do, but we need to work out the best way to do it and not be killed.'

The tent flap was pulled back. The two doctors were given their breakfast and a new packet of cigarettes.

'Here we go again with the shitty *shiro*. Who the hell eats chickpea porridge?' Declan fumed.

'It's not that bad. You should have seen the food they served in the canteen at my school.' Ben ate hungrily.

'I thought you went to a posh place?'

'I did, but the food was awful.'

'After my mother fecked off on us, my da learnt to cook and then he taught us. I'm actually pretty good, if I say so myself. I love watching cookery programmes to relax. There are similarities between surgery and cooking. They're both about prepping, timing and the finishing touches.'

Ben grinned. 'I didn't have you down as a cookery-show watcher.'

'Love them, especially Nigella. For an older bird, she's hot. I definitely would.'

'Bit too busty for me. I'm a legs man.'

'I'm a take-it-any-way-I-can-get-it man.'

Ben chuckled.

'I tell you what, though,' Declan went on, 'birds love doctors. I've had a lot of patients coming on to me. I even had this one woman – she must have been about forty-five, good-looking, a MILF type . . . Anyway, she was rushed in for an appendectomy. The next day when I was checking her pulse she grabbed me and shoved her tongue in my ear.'

Ben laughed. 'What did you do?'

Declan puffed out a perfect smoke-ring. 'I'm a professional, so I extricated myself, but I got her number and met up with her when she was discharged. She was wild in the sack.' Declan ate some porridge and made a face. 'Do you have many patients coming on to you?'

'Some, but I've got quite good about setting boundaries.

In the early days I had a few close calls. I did have one woman who used to come in for consultations in a very short dress and make it obvious that she wasn't wearing any underwear.'

'Jesus, *Basic Instinct*!'

'Unfortunately she wasn't Sharon Stone. She was more like her older, larger, less attractive sister.'

'Don't beat around the bush, Ben. Just say she was a fat minger so you weren't tempted.'

They sat in silence for a minute.

'Do you think they'll let us go?' Declan asked.

Ben inhaled. 'We need to continue to be useful to them so that they keep us alive. And, in the meantime, figure out a way to escape.'

Declan lit another cigarette. Looking up at the roof of the tent, he said quietly, 'It's beginning to get to me.'

'Me too. But we have to stay strong and be clever about this. If we make them angry, they'll shoot us.'

'Don't worry,' Declan said grimly. 'I won't do anything stupid.'

The tent flap was pulled back and the big soldier who guarded them most of the time, Yonas, beckoned them to come out.

Later that morning, after checking their two remaining patients, they were sent to fetch water with some of the village women, under the watchful eye of Yonas and a younger man called Eyob. On their way, they passed women and men leading donkeys carrying big barrels of water. They also passed women who were almost bent double carrying heavy barrels on their backs, tied with rope.

'I guess having a donkey here is like having a car back home,' Declan said. 'That poor old woman looks like she's about to keel over from the weight of it. She's too old to be carrying that barrel.'

The woman stumbled. Declan and Ben went to help her. She smiled, revealing a mouthful of rotting teeth.

'Can I help her carry this back?' Declan asked Yonas.

Yonas's English wasn't particularly good, but he understood the basics. 'No, you help our womans, not other womans.'

'But she'll never make it – she's knackered. Look at the state of her! She's sweating and her legs are like toothpicks,' Declan objected.

Yonas shook his head. 'No helping. You come now.'

But Ben and Declan did help the woman. They tied the barrel on more securely and watched as she stumbled off up the mountain path.

'Do you think we could make a run for it now?' Ben asked. He'd been feeling increasingly desperate as the morning had progressed. He ached to see Alice and the girls.

Declan shook his head. 'Yonas or Eyob would shoot us. There's nowhere to hide here. The land's wide open.'

'What if we tackled him and grabbed the gun?' Ben whispered.

'Easy there, Tiger. I thought I was the mad one. If we tackle Yonas, Eyob would shoot us. He's got a mad glint in his eye. He reminds me of Mental Mickey on our road. You know by their eyes that they're unhinged. Now is not the time, trust me.'

Ben could feel his breath quickening. He began to gasp for air. Declan put his hands on his friend's shoulders. 'Deep breaths, mate, come on. It's okay. We'll get out of here. Just not now. Breathe in . . . and out.'

Ben's pulse began to slow and he stopped feeling as if he was going to have a heart attack. Declan was right: now was not the time. But when? When would they get out?

'No stopping. Move,' Yonas growled at them.

They walked for more than two hours over the dry, dusty mountains in the hot sun until they finally came to the water source. It was hidden between two huge rocks in a cave.

About eight women were bending down around the sandy, dusty water. They were scooping it up with plastic cups and tipping it into their large barrels.

Ben and Declan began to help the women they were with. Each had one drum. Each water drum held twenty litres of water.

The women smiled at the men and chattered among themselves. One of the younger ones, Feven, looked at the two doctors shyly from under her eyelashes. She was very beautiful. They had noticed her on the second day, when she came in to see how her brother was doing after his operation.

'She's a cracker,' Declan said, as he poured water into his barrel.

'She looks a bit like Whitney Houston.'

'No way! She's more like a tall Halle Berry. I think she's giving me the eye.' Declan winked at her and Feven immediately looked away, her cheeks flushed.

'She definitely likes me,' Declan said, with a cocky grin. 'See, Ben? Even in this God-forsaken place I can still pull the ladies.'

Ben looked anxiously over his shoulder to see if Yonas or Eyob had seen the exchange. Grabbing Declan's arm, he hissed, 'You can't flirt with the women here – you'll get us killed. The men would go mad if they thought you were eyeing them up. Stop it.'

Declan shook Ben's hand off. 'Relax – I was only having a bit of fun. Trying to distract myself for ten seconds from the shit we're in.'

'I know, but you have to be careful.'

They continued filling the water barrels in silence. When

they were finally full, Ben and Declan tied the barrels around their backs with rope and the four women did the same. Eyob and Yonas watched them, smoking.

'Hang on,' Ben said to Yonas. 'Aren't you going to help the women carry their water?'

Yonas threw his butt down and stamped it out. 'No. I am here to making sure you no escape. The womens carry the water every day.'

'But it's very heavy,' Ben said. 'You should help them.'

'You shut up and walk,' Eyob said.

'Drop it,' Declan muttered.

The two doctors followed the women up the steep mountain path, trying to keep up with the sure-footed gazelles.

'Jesus, it's heavy,' Declan moaned.

'How do they do this?' Ben panted, watching the women striding ahead.

'No wonder they're skinny. Who needs the gym?'

'How long more to go, do you reckon?' Ben asked.

'Only another hour or so,' Declan puffed. 'Look on the bright side, Ben. At least when we get back home we'll look fit.'

'And we'll have a tan,' Ben said.

'We'll be so hot, the women will be throwing their underwear at us during consultations.'

Ben laughed. He needed Declan. He needed his optimism and strength. He was grateful for one thing: that he hadn't been kidnapped on his own. That would have been a whole other kind of torture.

## Holly

Daddy's been gone for fifty-nine days, seven hours and forty-seven minutes. He left in October and now it's December. In one way it feels long but in another it feels like no time at all.

Mummy hardly speaks. Kevin said it's just her way of coping. 'I know she seems a bit detached but she's still here for you guys.'

I looked up the word 'detach' in the dictionary. Detach = disconnect, disengage, remove, separate, undo. It's exactly what Mummy is now. She's detached from everything. It's like she's there, as in her body is there, but her mind has gone somewhere else.

I hear her walking around at night. Sometimes I follow her. She just walks around the house touching things, like the photos of her and Daddy getting married or the painting he bought for her birthday. She mumbles to herself. I can't really make out what she's saying, but I've heard her say, 'Bad luck . . . follows me . . . I'm cursed . . . How can I do this alone? . . . Scared . . . Why, Ben, why?'

Every morning Kevin wakes her up, then pulls her out of bed and into the shower. I can hear him through the wall. He says, 'You have to get up for the girls.' He tells her that she can't 'fall apart' because me and Jools need her. He says if she stays in bed she'll never get up again. He says she has to 'face reality'. Then sometimes, when she starts crying, he soothes her – 'I'm here, sis,' and 'When they're in school, you can go back and pull the covers over your head.'

On the days when she just won't get up, it's kind of easier. When Mum's there, we all try extra hard to be 'normal', but it's so fake. When she's not there, Jools and I don't have to pretend. Kevin lets us cry or talk about Dad or just say nothing.

Kevin makes us breakfast now. He insists on giving us fresh fruit, yogurt and muesli. He says it's good for our brains and will give us beautiful bodies and beautiful skin. Jools said she already has beautiful skin. Kevin said that she's a teenager so she might get spots: she needs to stay away from processed food and to clean her face every night.

Jools said that Donna in her class has suddenly got loads of spots and a hairy lip and that she looks really ugly. She said it's because of Donna's raging hormones, and some teenagers get spots and a hairy lip.

I was a bit scared because I'd never heard about hairy lips and I didn't want to end up with a moustache.

Kevin said that Donna was unlucky and that some girls did get spots and hairy lips, but that there was lots of things you could do for the hairiness, like waxing or threading.

I asked what threading was and he said it was when they pull your hairs out with two pieces of string. I asked if it hurt, and Kevin said you have to suffer for beauty. He said he gets his eyebrows threaded, and that after the first few times, it was okay.

Jools said that Harry Upton told her she could still end up with a really hairy lip because she has tanned skin, and girls with tanned skin are hairier. Kevin said that Harry is a 'gobshite' who hasn't got a clue about anything. He said some girls with tanned skin are hairy and some aren't. He said that Jools won't get a big hairy lip because she doesn't have hairy

127

legs. He said the girls with hairy legs will most likely end up with hairy lips.

I checked my legs under the table and, thank goodness, they're not hairy.

Jools asked Kevin to write her another note for not doing her homework and Kevin said this was the last time. He said Daddy wouldn't be happy if Jools wasn't trying in school. Jools looked like she was going to cry and she said it wasn't fair because her homework was really hard and she didn't have Mummy or Daddy to help her with it, like she used to.

Kevin gave her a hug and said he was sorry, that he'd been so busy minding Mummy and us that he had forgotten about the homework. He said he'd ask Nora to come in for a few extra hours after school so he could help her. I said I'd help her too, but Jools shouted at me that I was just showing off and she didn't want a squirt in year six helping her with her year-eleven homework.

Kevin asked me if I was okay doing my homework on my own. I said yes. I didn't tell him that I got two spellings wrong last week. I'm still shocked. I never get spellings wrong. I was really upset and Miss Robinson said I wasn't to worry, that I'd had a big trauma. But I am worried. I'm worried that Daddy dying has affected my brain. I get muddled sometimes and the letters all jumble together. It's really bothering me because English is what I'm best at, along with maths, and it's my favourite subject.

Jools didn't tell Kevin about the trouble she's in at school. She hit Sally Geoff on the back of her legs with her hockey stick. Everyone was talking about it. Sally went around show-ing everyone the red marks and someone said her parents were really cross about it.

Jools told me that the headmistress, Mrs Kennedy, was very nice to her. She said Mrs Kennedy was very cross with

Sally when Jools told her that Sally had said Daddy wasn't a hero, like Jools was telling everyone. Sally said that Daddy was an idiot. She said everyone knew Eritrea was really dangerous and that Daddy was looking for trouble.

Jools said she was so angry, she just lashed out and hit Sally. She said she used all her strength because she wanted to hurt her.

'I wanted her to know what it feels like to be in pain,' Jools said. She was crying when she told me. 'I wanted that stupid, smug bitch to hurt like I do, all the time, every day.'

Jools was lucky that Mrs Kennedy was kind about it because Sally's dad is a judge and puts people in prison all the time. We decided not to tell Kevin about it. He's trying so hard to keep everything going at home and look after us all – he doesn't need to have to worry about Jools going to prison for violence.

Luckily, Mrs Kennedy took Jools's side and told Sally's parents that she wasn't going to bother Mummy with any of this nonsense and that both girls had to apologize to each other and that was the end of it.

Jools told me Sally's dad said it was a 'disgrace' and that 'Violence is unacceptable under any circumstances.' Mrs Kennedy said that the circumstances were 'tragic and extremely traumatic' and that she didn't want to hear any more about 'the matter'.

I'm really glad because I couldn't bear it if Jools went to prison. She's the only person I can talk to about Daddy. She's the only person who knows how bad the pain really is.

*Alice*

Alice stared at the department-store window. The elves were picking up brightly wrapped gifts and passing them to each other. Santa Claus sat in the corner, nodding deeply every thirty seconds. Mothers and children oohed and aahed at the display.

Christmas, thought Alice. How the hell could it be Christmas already? One minute she was a happily married mother and now she was a widow, staring down the barrel of a Christmas with no husband. She knew she had to go inside and buy presents for the girls, but her feet wouldn't move. It was as if her legs were made of lead. She stood staring but seeing nothing as people bustled by, full of Christmas cheer, bumping her with their shopping bags.

Alice loved Christmas. Since she'd had children it had become her favourite time of the year. She had loved the magic of seeing the girls waking up to stockings full of gifts and the wonder in their eyes as they opened the presents beside the fireplace.

Alice remembered five-year-old Jools shouting into the letterbox as she posted her letter to Santa, 'Thank you, Santa, you are a very kind man.'

This year Jools, who normally asked for a long list of presents, had asked for nothing. Holly had asked if maybe 'Santa could make the pain of losing Daddy a bit less awful'. Alice had held her tightly and tried very, very hard not to fall apart. The pain of Ben's death was still excruciating.

Every morning it took her breath away. She still wasn't sleeping. Kevin thought she should take tablets, but Alice was reluctant to do so. She didn't want to wake up groggy in the mornings. Kevin pointed out that she was like a zombie anyway and some pills might actually make her less groggy. What Alice really wanted to do was sleep for a year and wake up when the pain in her chest was bearable and she didn't feel like weeping all the time.

Kevin came out of Debenhams and handed her a bag.

'Jools's present is in here. I'll get Holly's tomorrow. Now, come on, stop staring into space – you'll scare the kids.'

Hooking his arm into his sister's, he drew her away from the window and towards home.

When they arrived at the front door, Kevin kissed her cheek. 'I'll see you tomorrow.'

Alice immediately felt panicked. 'What do you mean? Where are you going?'

Kevin tied his scarf around his neck. 'I've got a date.'

'But – but I need you to help me.'

'No, Alice, you don't. You need to be with your kids and stop hiding in bed or in the shower or pretending you're working on your computer. You need to sit down and talk to them. I've been with you every minute of every day for ten weeks. I need a night off.'

Alice blinked back tears. 'Of course. You're right. I just . . . Will you come in for ten minutes?'

Kevin shook his head. 'No. Nora's in there getting dinner ready. She'll be wanting to go home now. Alice, I love you and I'm here for you, but you need to stand on your own two feet. Your girls need their mum back. They're struggling and the only person who can make them feel better is you. Now I'm going. As I said, I have a very hot date and I'm badly in need of a drink.'

'But I —'

Kevin reached around her and opened the front door. 'You have to get it together, Alice. Tomorrow is your first day back at work and I need you to be alert and look like you're in control. You're only seeing eight patients. I'll make sure no one stays more than twenty minutes. I'm going to ease you back into it. But you have to try to engage with them, Alice. You need your job, you need the money. If you stare at your patients the way you're staring at me, they'll go to another GP.'

Alice bit her lip. 'I'm trying, Kevin.'

Kevin took her gloved hand in his. 'I know you are and I know I'm being harsh, but I'm doing it for you and the girls. I've done everything I can to hold it together, but your daughters need you, Alice. You have to come back to them. Jools is struggling really badly in school and I'm trying to help her but I can't figure out the maths. And Holly is like a lost puppy. She follows you around all the time but you barely even notice her. I'm sorry, but you have to snap out of it.'

Alice nodded, but inside she was screaming — *You don't know what it's like to lose the love of your life. You don't know what it's like to have your daughters' father blown up on some dirt road in Africa. You don't know what it's like to lose your best friend in the world, the person who understood you better than anyone else.* But she said none of it because she knew that, without Kevin, they wouldn't have made it. He had been wonderful and, deep down, Alice knew she'd been neglecting her children and her patients. She didn't want to face reality because reality was terrifying.

She threw her arms around her brother's neck. 'I'm sorry, Kevin. I know I've been sleep-walking these last weeks. It's just so hard. I promise to make more of an effort, and thank you. Really, thank you.'

'You're welcome and, let's not forget, you saved me when Mum and Dad died and I got lost in drink and drugs. I guess we're even.'

Alice watched her brother walk away. She knew he was right. She had checked out of life since Ben died. Having Kevin around had allowed her to fall to pieces. She took a deep breath and walked into the house.

Nora was waiting for her. She had her coat on. The girls were nowhere to be seen. 'There's a cottage pie in the oven. It's almost ready. Is Kevin not with you?'

'He's gone on a date,' Alice said.

'Good for him. He needs a night off. He's worn out looking after you all. He's a good man, that Kevin. To be honest, I always thought the gays were a bit self-centred, you know, because they don't have kids. Mind you, that Ricky Martin has children, but you know what I mean. Your Kevin is a very kind man. He's been keeping those girls going, but they need their mother, Alice. I know your heart is broken, but so are theirs.'

Alice frowned. Why was everyone telling her off? It wasn't as if she hadn't got out of bed since Ben had died. She had been with the girls every day. 'I don't think I've been a bad mother,' she said tightly.

'Don't get shirty with me, Alice. I'm only telling you the truth. I never said you'd been a bad mother. You've just been overwhelmed with your grief and wrapped up in your own world. I know you give the girls hugs and you try to put on a brave face, but you're not talking to them.'

'Yes, I am! I had a long conversation with Holly yesterday about the book she's reading.'

'What's the name of it?'

Alice thought. 'I . . . It's . . . I can't remember now but –'

'But nothing. That's the point. You're not present – they can't reach you. You need to talk to them about their father. They need to be able to cry and talk about how much they miss him. The poor things are trying to be brave for you, but their little hearts are crushed.'

'I'm trying, Nora.' Alice fought back tears. 'I just miss him so much.'

'I know, pet, I know you do. But I think you'll find if you really talk to the girls you'll feel closer to them and you'll help each other.' Nora handed Alice a tissue. 'Now, wipe your eyes. Go up there and tell them you want to know how they really feel. Jools is like a different girl – all the light has gone out in her. You need to try to get it back. Motherhood isn't easy, Alice. It's a lifetime commitment. Now, off you go.'

Nora shooed Alice up the stairs as she headed out of the door.

Alice stood outside Jools's bedroom door. She knocked gently.

'Piss off, Holly.'

'It's me,' Alice said. She turned the handle but the door was locked.

'Sorry, hold on a minute,' Jools called.

Alice could hear her daughter moving around inside. Jools opened the door looking a bit flushed.

'Why was it locked?' Alice asked.

'Because Holly keeps coming in and annoying me.'

'Are you all right?'

'I'm fine.'

Alice put her hand on her daughter's arm and looked into her eyes, Ben's eyes. 'No, I mean are you really all right?'

Jools flung herself down on her bed. 'Uhm, let me see – father blown up in landmine bomb, mother like a zombie, schoolwork a disaster . . . I've been better.'

'I'm sorry if I've been like a . . . zombie.' Alice flinched at the word. 'I've been wrapped up in my own grief and I haven't been there for you. I'm so sorry, Jools. I promise from now on I'll be a proper mother again.'

Jools shrugged. ''S okay, you don't have to beat yourself up.'

'You must really miss him – you were so close. He adored you, Jools. He thought you were just wonderful.'

Jools wrapped her arms around herself. 'I always felt he was the only person in the world who really got me,' she said, as tears formed in her eyes.

Alice went over and sat beside her. 'Jools, I think you're amazing too.'

'It's different. Daddy and I had a connection. I always felt so good when I was with him, like I was special. Now I just feel stupid and pointless.'

Alice threw her arms around her daughter. 'You are wonderful and special and beautiful.'

'And funny sometimes,' Holly said, appearing in the doorway.

Alice reached her arm out for Holly, who ran over and snuggled into her mother's side. 'I'm going to be here for you properly from now on. I promise.'

'I really missed you, Mummy,' Holly said, crying into Alice's shoulder.

'I know, sweetie, I'm so sorry. I missed Daddy so much I couldn't really function and it wasn't fair on you guys, or Kevin. But things are going to change now. I'll be stronger.'

They sat in comfortable silence, each lost in her own thoughts.

'Mum?' Jools said. 'What are we going to do about Christmas?'

'I'm going to spoil you rotten.'

'Does that mean I can have a new iPad?' Jools asked.

'No.'

'I preferred you when you were a zombie.'


The next morning, after dropping the girls off at school, Alice drove to the surgery for her first day back at work.

She was shaking when she walked through the door, but Kevin was waiting for her with a coffee and a croissant. She kissed him. 'Thank you – for absolutely everything. I talked to the girls last night – Jools and I even had a little argument. Everything is much more normal.'

'Brilliant! I'm delighted to hear that.'

'How was your date?'

Kevin smiled from ear to ear. 'Amazing, actually. Cocktails, dancing, laughter and sex.'

'That's about as good as it gets,' Alice said, with a grin.

'He's a really nice guy. I'm seeing him tomorrow. We're going to the movies.'

'Good for you.' Alice squeezed his arm.

'God, Alice, it is so good to see you . . . well . . . being more like yourself.'

Alice could feel the brittleness at the centre of her, which threatened to snap and shatter at any moment, leaving her helpless again. But she couldn't let Kevin see that. She managed a smile. 'I'm not sure how long it's going to last, so let's get to it.'

She sat in her consulting room, waiting for her first patient. Her legs were shaking under the desk, but she felt more clear-headed than she had in months. She was determined to try to get her life back on track. She had to. She had no choice. She was a single parent with bills to pay.

Kevin came in. 'First patient is Larry Johns. He says it's personal!'

'What?' Alice cried.

'He's coming in as a patient, I promise.'

'Are you sure?'

'Yes, I double-checked. He's not trying to foist new products on you.'

Larry Johns was a drugs rep who drove Alice nuts. He was very difficult to like. He was one of those very average-looking men whose mother told him he was God's gift to life every day and he believed it. He thought he was the hottest thing to walk the earth.

He came into the surgery regularly to promote new drugs and was always trying to take Alice out for lunch or a drink. She always said no, but Larry was not a man to give up easily. He had the skin of a rhinoceros. Eventually, Alice had instructed Kevin to block him from seeing her. Nowadays, when Larry strutted into the clinic, he got stonewalled by Kevin.

'It's my first day back – I thought you were going to ease me into it and I can't stand Larry,' Alice said. 'I bet you it's just his way of getting me to see him so he can try to force me to go out with him.'

Kevin held up his hand. 'I thought that might be the case, so I quizzed him but he assured me that it was medical. He said it's urgent and he sounded very distressed.'

'Okay, send him in.' Alice buttoned her cardigan and made sure her skirt was pulled down over her knees. Mind you, she thought, I look so awful, these days, not even Larry would try it on.

Kevin showed Larry to the door and Alice stood up to greet him. He looked worse than she did. Something was definitely wrong.

'Alice,' he said, walking towards her with his hand outstretched. Puzzled, Alice shook it. This wasn't Larry's normal style. 'I'm so sorry for your loss. Read it in the papers. Terrible thing to happen.'

Alice was so taken aback, she couldn't reply. She stood there with her mouth open, her hand still locked in his. She hadn't considered that patients would know about Ben and want to mention it. Yes, it had been in the papers, but it still felt so private. She had to fight the urge to wrench her hand away and run out of the consulting room, out of the surgery and hide under her duvet at home.

'Thank you, Larry,' she finally managed. 'Now, down to business. How can I help you?'

She lowered herself into her chair, her mind still reeling, but her face giving nothing away.

Larry sat down and leant forward across the desk. He smelt of stale cigarettes. Alice sat further back in her chair. Clearly the niceties were over.

'Well, the thing is, I had an encounter with a young lady from the office. You know how it is, Friday-night drinks and one thing leads to another. Anyway, she was all over me like a cheap suit, fancies the arse off me. They all do, and generally I try to let them down gently. I'm a married man, after all. But I'd had one too many and we shagged. Turns out the cow has chlamydia.'

'I see.' Alice had to fight the urge to smile.

'The thing is, if my wife finds out, she'll cut my dick off. She always said her heroine is that Lorena Bobbitt. You know – the one who cut her husband's off and threw it out the window when she found out he was cheating on her?'

Alice nodded and tried to keep a straight face. 'Well, Larry, the best thing for you to do is to make an appointment with the sexual-health clinic. I can give you their number.'

Larry shook his head. 'Are you having a laugh? I'm not going to the clap clinic. I Googled it and all I need is some azithromycin. It says on the Internet that one tablet will sort me out.'

'You need to be tested, Larry. Have you had any symptoms? Are you experiencing a burning sensation when you pass urine? Is there any milky discharge from your penis?'

Larry shuffled uncomfortably in his chair. 'Well, it does burn a bit when I pee. But I read about the tests they do on the Internet. I'm not having anyone – not even you, Alice – sticking anything up my dick to get samples. Just give me the tablets and give me one for my wife and all.'

'I'm sorry, Larry, but I can't prescribe anything for your wife. I'd need to see her first.'

'Are you mental? Do you think I'm bringing my wife in here? I told you, Doc, she'd cut it off if she found out. I've figured it all out. I'm going to crush the pill up and stick it in her coffee. Do you think the hot water would damage it?'

Was he clinically insane? Did he honestly think she was going to allow him to drug his wife secretly with pills she'd prescribed? Alice needed to nip this in the bud.

'Larry, drugging your wife without her permission is both unethical and illegal.'

'Come on, Alice, do you want to cause my marriage to break up and my dick to be cut off?'

I wouldn't mind cutting it off myself, thought Alice. 'I think the cheating might be the cause of your problems, not me.' Alice was actually enjoying watching Larry sweat it out. She felt almost human today. Maybe getting back to work had been a good idea. She needed this – it was a good distraction.

Larry threw his hands into the air. 'I knew you'd be like that. You women are all the same. Maybe you're not ready to be back at work. You're not on top of your game. I bet a male doctor would give me the pills.'

Alice chose to ignore the comment about her readiness to work. 'No doctor is going to allow you to drug your wife, Larry.'

'All right, then. How about you call her in for a smear? While you're rooting about down there, you could check for chlamydia.'

'I have no intention of calling your wife in or "rooting about" for anything.'

'Why are you being such a cow? I need those tablets and I need them now.'

Alice stood up. 'Well, then, you're going to have to look for them elsewhere.'

'Fine. I'll get them on the Internet.'

'Just remember that drugging someone without their consent is a crime.'

'You know what you need, you uptight bitch – a good shag.'

Larry stormed out and Kevin came rushing in. 'What happened?'

'Your plan to ease me back into it has failed. I've just been called an uptight bitch by my first patient.'

'Oh, God, I'm sorry, Alice.'

Alice smiled. 'Don't worry, it was extremely distracting. But do me a favour, put his name on your blacklist and don't ever let him through the door again. Right, who's next?'

## Ben: January 2013

Declan whistled under his breath. 'Christ, he's a mess.'

Ben rubbed his hand wearily across his face. 'We have to try to save him.'

'Let the bastard die.'

In front of them lay Eyob. He had been hit by a grenade. His right leg was barely recognizable as a human limb – a bloodied mash of bone and sinew.

'What about the Hippocratic oath?' Ben reminded Declan.

'To hell with it. The guy's a low-life scumbag and he deserves to die.'

'We're doctors. We have a duty to try to save him.'

'Don't start with your bullshit English duty. You know as well as I do that we should let him bleed out.'

Declan's face was flushed and his fists were clenched tightly. Ben needed to calm him down. He understood why Declan hated Eyob, but letting him die was not the answer. Yonas would be back soon to stand guard and Awate would be checking on them too.

Declan's breath was ragged as he clasped his left shoulder. It was the one that Eyob had dislocated. Ben knew that he was close to the edge. He had to stop his friend doing something stupid. Declan glared down at Eyob, hate radiating from his body.

\*

The fight had happened on New Year's Eve. As Ben and Declan prepared to ring in the new year sitting in their tent, chained to each other and the tree, Awate had come in and barked at Eyob to unchain them. He had insisted that the two doctors join the rest of the men for a drink. Devastated still to be prisoners as the new year dawned, they had been sitting in silence, lost in their thoughts, distraught to be away from loved ones with no end in sight to their captivity. So when Awate had offered them a drink, Declan had jumped up and proceeded to gulp down glass after glass of the local home-made brew, called *suwa*. Ben couldn't stomach the stuff – it was utterly foul and, besides, he was too depressed to drink. He wanted to weep every time he thought about Alice and the girls celebrating the new year without him. He ached to put his arms around his wife and daughters and hold them close. Once again he berated himself for leaving them – I'm a stupid, selfish, self-centred bastard, he thought, for the millionth time.

Declan, on the other hand, embraced the oblivion offered by the alcohol. He threw it back, claiming that it tasted like the *poitín* his granddad used to distil from potatoes. He drank like a man possessed, drowning out the darkness of his situation, pushing back the fear and rage that threatened to bring him down. When Ben tried to stop him, Declan brushed him off and drank with even more determination.

It ended up turning into a drinking competition between Declan and Eyob. They had never liked each other. Ever since Eyob had caught Declan winking at Feven, who, it turned out, was his cousin, he'd had it in for the Irishman. Any excuse he got, he'd shout at Declan, push him around and regularly shoved his gun in Declan's face.

Ben knew that the drinking game would end badly. Eyob

was young, nervy and unpredictable. After the seventh glass, Eyob said something to Awate.

'Eyob wants to fight you – like WWF, you know?' Awate translated.

Declan threw his head back and laughed. 'You mean this skinny prick wants to wrestle me? Bring it on.'

Ben stepped in and placed a warning hand on Declan's arm. 'Don't do it,' he urged. 'If you beat him, he'll make your life miserable. If you lose, you could get hurt.'

Declan pushed Ben aside. 'I grew up fighting on the streets. I'm going to nail this toe-rag.' He walked over and stood in front of Eyob. 'Come on, then! Show me what you've got.'

The two men faced each other, walking slowly in circles. Eyob was thin, but he was wiry and muscly. Declan was taller and very fit. All the water-carrying in recent weeks had made his arms taut and strong.

Word got out that there was a fight on and the women and children came over to watch.

Eyob threw the first punch, and Declan ducked. 'Ha, is that the best you can do?'

Declan swung at him, but missed. Ben held his breath. He prayed silently, 'Please, God, don't let him win, but don't let him get hurt either.'

Ben knew if Declan knocked Eyob down he would either get shot or badly beaten up afterwards. There was no way Eyob would allow the Irishman to embarrass him in front of his people.

Declan was too drunk: he was stumbling. So was Eyob, but less so. Eyob punched Declan right in the nose, and a cheer went up. Blood ran down Declan's face, but he just wiped it away and laughed in Eyob's face. Then he threw a dummy punch, which Eyob ducked to avoid, and when he came back up, Declan smashed him on the left cheek with a strong right-hander.

The crowd gasped as Eyob spun around and landed face down. Declan stood over him, gloating. 'That'll teach you, you son-of-a-bitch. Next time you point your fucking gun in my face, remember that you're just a pussy.'

'Declan!' Ben shouted, rushing over to drag him away. Was he mad? Did he have a death wish? It was bad enough that he'd knocked Eyob down – he didn't need to make him even angrier.

Ben tugged Declan's arm and pulled him in the direction of their tent, but Declan was yanked back. Ben spun around to see Fikru, Eyob's friend, holding Declan, while Eyob attacked him with the butt of his rifle.

'STOP!' Ben shouted. He looked for Awate, but the leader was watching the spectacle along with everyone else. Apparently they thought this was okay.

Ben grabbed Eyob from behind and pulled him away. Fikru let go of Declan to help his friend. Declan crumpled to the floor, clutching his stomach.

Ben screamed at Awate, 'You can't let him do this! It's obscene.'

Awate shrugged. 'Eyob needed to reaffirm his authority. It's over now.'

Ben was shaking. 'How the hell do you expect Declan to operate if he's injured? You promised that if we did what you asked there would be no violence.'

Awate put out his cigarette. 'Declan wanted to fight. Fighting is violent.'

'You have to let us go – we can't go on like this. I need to see my family. It's been nearly three months.'

Awate shook his head. 'Always so impatient. There is more

work for you to do here. We still have injured soldiers, pregnant women and sick children. You will stay.'

'When can we go?' Ben was on the verge of tears. 'When can I hold my children again? I can't do this, Awate, I can't do this any more. You have to let me go. I won't operate again. I won't help you. Keeping us here is inhumane.'

'You don't operate, I shoot Declan. He doesn't operate, I shoot you. You will stay until I say so, and you will work.'

'When? When will you say so? It's like torture not seeing my girls.'

Awate put his face close to Ben's and hissed, 'My daughter was killed by a landmine when she was eight years old. Don't talk to me about pain.'

'I'm sorry about that, but it's not my fault. Let us go. Please.'

'Enough!'

Awate barked an order to Yonas, who took Ben firmly by the arm and dragged him back to his tent. Declan was helped in by another soldier. Yonas chained them together in silence, then left.

Ben put his head into his hands and began to cry. He felt a hand on his shoulder.

'Hey, buddy, take it easy now,' Declan said gently. 'Anyway, I'm the one who should be crying. I think that bastard broke my collarbone, as well as a couple of ribs.'

Ben looked up at Declan's bloodied face. 'Sorry, bad day.'

'Every day here is a bad day. Come on, we'll get through this. We just have to stay strong.'

Ben stood up. 'Staying strong does not include challenging soldiers to fights. To use one of your own expressions, you're a gobshite. You could have been killed in there and I don't much like the idea of being stuck here alone. Next time, keep your big fat Irish mouth shut.'

'Yes, sir.' Declan tried to raise his arm in mock-salute, but winced in pain.

'Come on, let's have a look at you.'

Ben laid Declan back and unbuttoned his shirt. Declan's chest was a mass of red marks, bruises and cuts. Ben gently felt around for broken ribs.

'Right, three broken ribs and your left shoulder is out. I'll need to pop it back in.'

'Any chance of a drink first?' Declan asked.

'None, but on the positive side, you've had a lot already so the pain should be numbed a little. One . . . two . . . three.' Ben slammed his hand into Declan's shoulder, popping the socket back into place.

'*Chriiist* on a bike!' Declan howled. 'Whatever happened to a delicate touch?'

Ben smiled tiredly. 'Happy New Year. Now shut up and try to rest. It's going to hurt like hell in the morning, when the alcohol has worn off.' Ben cleaned Declan's bloody face and insisted that he sleep on both thin mattresses for comfort.

'I'm not taking yours.'

'Yes, you are. You'll need it tonight. You need as much padding as you can get.'

'There is no way I'm letting you sleep on the ground. I'm the idiot who got myself beaten up, I'll be fine.'

'Declan,' Ben snapped, 'this is a one-night-only offer. Now, shut up and take it.' Ben helped him to get settled on the two thin mattresses and covered him with a sheet. He lay down beside his friend on the straw mat and wrapped himself in a blanket, then tried to sleep, but Jools's face kept appearing before him – 'Where are you, Daddy? Please come home.'

Beside him, in the dark, Ben could hear Declan quietly crying.

Happy New Year.

Declan folded his arms and moved away from the operating table, where Eyob lay motionless. 'He bloody deserved it.'

'Declan, you have to assist me or you'll be shot,' Ben hissed.

As if on cue, Awate marched into the tent, looking tense. 'You have to save him. He is my wife's godson. He must be saved.'

Ben pulled on his surgical gloves. 'We will do everything we can, but he's very badly injured. Look – his lower leg has turned blue. I think he'll lose it.'

'Do your best or there will be consequences,' Awate threatened.

As he left, Yonas came in to stand guard. Ben bent down to have a closer look at the damage. Eyob's heel leg had been blown off and the tibia was splintered. 'Damn it, we'll have to amputate.'

Suddenly Declan was paying attention to the patient and his leg. 'Amputate? I've never done that. Maybe I will assist after all.'

'Be my guest.' Ben handed him the blade.

Ben administered ketamine anaesthesia. It was good for blocking pain, but Eyob would be confused and semi-wakeful throughout.

'Easy now, we don't want him to feel no pain,' Declan said.

Declan lifted the leg so Ben could fix the tourniquet at the top of the thigh. They then had to take flaps of skin and muscle long enough to cover the bone and form a stump. Declan made the front incision across the shin about eight inches below the kneecap, then drew the blade around the back of the calf in a downward curve through the skin and muscle. He was concentrating now and Ben needed his help. 'Right, we need to divide the nerves, cut them and dissect the arteries and veins.' Ben held up a blunt chisel. 'I'll scrape the periosteal membrane up so you can get a clean cut.'

Soon the only thing joining Eyob's leg to his body was the bare bone. Declan vigorously sawed through the fibia and then the much thicker tibia. 'This saw is blunt from over-use,' he complained.

'Keep going, you're nearly there,' Ben encouraged him.

Wiping sweat from his brow, Declan went back to it with renewed energy. The last bit of bone was finally separated and the leg fell into Ben's waiting hands.

Declan grinned. 'Hopalong won't be giving me trouble anytime soon.'

Eyob looked dazed and confused as he gazed at his leg on the floor. 'Don't worry, pal.' Declan patted him on the shoulder. 'It's only a leg. It could have been worse. Look on the bright side. You'll get more wear out of your socks.'

Ben stifled a laugh. 'You could take up karate for amputees – it's called partial arts.'

Declan snorted. 'You might need to change your name. You could be called Lee Ning.'

'Or Rocky,' Ben added.

'Balan Singh.' Declan had to pretend to cough he was laughing so much.

Eyob closed his eyes.

'Hey, Declan, what do you call a man with no arms and no legs sitting on your front porch?' Ben whispered.

'Matt. Hey, Ben, what do you call a man with no arms and no legs in a pool?'

'Bob.'

'What do you call a man with no arms and no legs in a pile of leaves?'

'I don't know that one,' Ben said.

'Russell!' Declan howled with laughter.

Both men cracked up, and once they'd started, they couldn't stop. Yonas came over and shouted at them, but it only made them laugh harder. Tears streamed down their faces as Yonas shouted at them to 'work'.

It was only when he cocked his rifle that they got back to their patient.

## Holly: March 2013

I said I thought we should think about getting a dog. Jools said I was trying to replace Daddy with an animal. She said lots of people do that. Apparently Laurie's dad bought her a dog when her mum left and went to live with the gardener.

Kevin said, 'He'd certainly be able to trim her bushes.' Jools laughed, but I didn't understand what was funny about it. I asked Kevin what he meant, but he just said that he was being silly and that I was too young to understand.

Kevin is excited at the moment because of this 'hot French-Moroccan guy' he's dating. When he talks about Axel, he looks so happy. He can't stop smiling.

Nora asked if he had a 'touch of the tar brush' in him. Kevin looked shocked and smacked her bum with a tea towel and then he said, yes, he did a bit, but only a light brush.

Jools and I looked at each other and shrugged. Sometimes Nora uses these really old Irish expressions that we don't understand. She says, 'May the road rise to meet you,' and when it's absolutely pouring with rain she says, 'It's a soft day.'

Daddy used to say that Nora 'put it on'. He said that Nora used those funny expressions because she was trying to hold on to her Irishness, like when Mummy called people 'eejits' and insisted that we watch the hurling final every year. When Kevin said that was ridiculous because Mummy had never even been to a hurling match and didn't know anything about it, she got cross and said it was part of her heritage and that she wanted her daughters to 'appreciate where they came from'.

Jools always said it was ridiculous because she was from London and it was a stupid game anyway. Who wants to run about waving a big stick in the air? Daddy laughed when she said it, but Mummy got very cross and said Jools was half Irish whether she liked it or not.

Sometimes I felt sorry for Mummy. She tried to make us like Irish things and listen to Irish music and stuff, but we just wanted to be like all the other girls in London. I tried to like Irish music, but I found it a bit samey. I prefer Lady Gaga and Rihanna.

Daddy has been gone almost six months – one hundred and seventy-three days and fourteen hours. Everyone kept saying it would get easier with time. That the pain would be less. But I still wake up every morning and feel as if there is a huge stone on my stomach. I find it hard to breathe. The first thing I do is take out my calculator and work out how long he's been dead because it calms me down.

Jools pretends she's okay about Daddy now, but I know she isn't. I heard her crying in her bedroom the other day, and when I peeped in, she was holding a photo of her and Daddy and she was kissing it.

I know she's worried about her GCSEs too, because for the first time in her life Jools is actually trying to study and she even asked for my help. I almost fainted with shock. She said she doesn't want to bother Mummy all the time so I need to fill in. I'm helping her as much as I can. Mummy did a study chart for her and I'm trying to get her to stick to it.

Mummy went out tonight. It's the first time since Daddy died. She's gone for dinner with David and Pippa. They've asked her loads of times, but she kept saying no. Kevin made her go this time. He said she couldn't stay locked inside for ever.

She wore a black dress that's too big for her. She's really skinny now. Jools got her a belt and helped her put it on. She looked better then. Jools also helped her to do her eye make-up. Mummy's hands were shaking. She was really nervous. Jools told her to take a deep breath. I held her hands while Jools did her eye shadow. Mummy said she knew she was being silly, but it was the first time she'd ever gone out with David and Pippa without Daddy. Jools turned away and pretended to look for a different colour eye shadow, but I knew she was trying not to cry because I was too.

Kevin, Jools and I waved Mummy off. She looked frightened. I ran out in my slippers to give her one last hug and told her I hoped she had a nice time. She squeezed me tight and said she'd try.

When Mummy left, Kevin's boyfriend came to watch a movie with us. I'd only met Axel once before and he seems very young. Kevin said he's twenty-six, but he looks younger and he acts younger.

Kevin said we had to watch a movie that was 'suitable' for me. So we watched *Mamma Mia!* but it was kind of annoying because Axel kept singing along and he really doesn't have a good singing voice. Kevin didn't seem to notice that Axel can't sing. He thinks everything Axel does is amazing. He looks at him with big melty eyes. When Jools told Axel to stop singing, he got really grumpy and said that she was rude and that he was quite famous in Morocco for his singing voice.

Jools said everyone in Morocco must be deaf. Kevin told her not to be rude. Jools said she wasn't being rude, just honest. Kevin said sometimes Jools was too honest and she should learn not to say everything that came into her head.

Jools said that Axel was being a 'drama queen' and that some-one needed to tell him he couldn't sing. She said she was being like Simon Cowell on *The X Factor* when he tells people not to give up their day jobs because singing is not for them.

Kevin said that Simon Cowell was no role model. Jools said that considering he was a zillionaire (which isn't a real number), she thought he was actually a very good role model.

Kevin said she should focus on role models who were kind as well as successful, like Bono. Jools said, 'Who's Bono?' and Kevin groaned. I know Bono is a really big Irish rock star who likes to help poor people. Then Axel shouted that he'd had enough of this 'boring talking' and he went home.

Kevin was cross with Jools and said she was selfish for being rude to his boyfriend and that she should have more respect. He said he'd tried so hard to be there for us and that he expected us to be polite to Axel. Jools's eyes welled up then and she said she was sorry. Kevin gave her a hug and it was all better and we watched the movie and ate popcorn.

I know it's mean, but I wish Kevin had never met Axel. It was better before, when Kevin was around all the time. Now he's always meeting Axel or else on the phone to him. You can see he's in love and it just makes me a bit sad because he's the one person I can talk to and now he's all detached, just like Mummy was.

I don't think Axel is the right person for Kevin. I said so to Mummy, but she said it was nice to see Kevin happy and that hopefully Axel wouldn't 'rip him off' like the last guy he went out with, who kept borrowing money for his 'sick grandmother in Sofia'. One day the guy said he was going to visit his grandmother in Moldova and never came back. Mummy said Kevin isn't very good at choosing the right per-son or at geography because Sofia is the capital of Bulgaria, so he was clearly lying the whole time and Kevin didn't notice.

I hope Axel doesn't take Kevin's money and that he's nice to him because Kevin deserves love. I hope Mummy had a nice time tonight. She seems so sad all the time and I want her to be happy.

I hope the pain in my tummy goes away soon. It hurts so much whenever I think of Daddy, which is at least thirty times a day.

## Alice: France, July 2013

Alice put down her book. She couldn't concentrate. She hadn't read a novel since Ben's death. Before he died she'd read at least a book a week, but since October she'd found she couldn't concentrate properly on reading. The words twisted and slipped away and she would end up reading the same paragraph over and over without taking anything in.

To her right Jools, eyes closed, lay basking in the hot French sun, although she had insisted on wearing a rash vest for the first time ever. Alice had thought it odd, but Jools said she didn't want to end up with a wrinkly chest. Still, her face and legs were getting browner by the minute. To her left, huddled under the parasol, Holly was lost in her book.

In front of them, going redder by the second, was Kevin. He was wearing a teeny tiny pair of Speedos and was determinedly sunbathing, despite his milky skin.

Alice reapplied sun-cream to her legs, adjusted her hat and lay back in her lounger. Around them, families were enjoying the warm sun and playing in the big crashing waves. Alice had chosen St-Jean-de-Luz because it was somewhere they had never been with Ben. She couldn't face going back to Biarritz, where they had spent the last four summers. She had decided to go somewhere new and different.

She couldn't bear the thought of walking by restaurants they had eaten in or lying on beaches where they had gone together as a family. It would have been too painful for all of them. When she had told the girls they were going somewhere new, they had looked relieved. They, too, had obviously been dreading the memories of their dad in Biarritz.

Alice picked up her book in an effort to read.

'The guys were so much hotter in Biarritz,' Jools moaned, from behind her sunglasses.

'You need to look to the right,' Kevin said. 'That lifeguard is seriously fit.'

'I thought you only had eyes for Axel.' Jools smirked at her uncle.

'You know the saying, honey – just because you're on a diet doesn't mean you can't check out the menu.'

'He is good-looking.' Jools pulled her glasses down to have a closer look.

'He's also about twenty and you're still only sixteen. I'd prefer you to focus more on your school work and less on boys,' Alice said.

Jools threw her hands into the air. 'You promised you wouldn't nag me on this holiday! You said you were proud of me for trying so hard with my GCSEs, remember?'

'I'm not nagging, just saying you need to focus really hard on your studies for the two final years at school. I know this has been a really difficult year. You needed help and I haven't been helping you enough. I'm sorry. I promise I'm going to be there for you in September.'

'Oh, God, Mum, you're not going to be on my case every night, are you?'

'Yes, I am.'

'Why can't you just accept that I'm not good at school work but I'm street-wise and that's even better and I've got choose-pa.'

'I think you mean chutzpah,' Alice corrected her.

'That's what I said.'

'Chutzpah isn't going to get you into college,' Alice warned her daughter.

Jools groaned. 'Mum, you'll soon have to face the fact that I'm not going to make it to college. Holly can go to Oxford and find the cure for clipstick fibrosis and cancer and win one of those Nobel prizes.'

Alice groaned and Holly gasped. 'Seriously, Jools, you're so embarrassing. It's cystic fibrosis.'

'Whatever, Einstein. Why don't you go back to your boring book and leave me alone?'

'It's not boring. It's actually really interesting. It's about this hobbit called Bilbo Baggins who lives in his hobbit house until the wizard Gandalf chooses him to take part in an adventure.'

'OMG, Holly, you're actually putting me into a coma here!' Jools exclaimed.

Ignoring her, Holly continued. 'J. R. R. Tolkien is one of the most respected writers ever. He wrote *The Lord of the Rings* trilogy, which I'm going to read next.'

Jools rubbed sun-cream onto her legs. 'Whatever. Good luck with that because I can tell you now that if you go on about books like this next year you'll have zero friends.'

'My friends like to read. They don't spend all day taking selfies, like yours do.'

'The difference between you and me, Holly, is that I actually have fun with my friends. We don't sit around talking about books, like sad old women. Next thing you'll be setting up one of those boring book clubs.'

'I was thinking of doing it next year.'

'OMG, Mum, please stop her. She's going to be an outcast.'

'Stop it, Jools. Holly can do whatever she wants.' Alice was sick of the girls bickering, which they did non-stop, these days.

'Fine. If you want your daughter to be the biggest geek in school, that's your problem, but I'm disowning her. She'll ruin my reputation.'

'Why don't you stop moaning and take another selfie? You haven't taken one for at least ten seconds,' Holly snapped.

Kevin rolled over onto his stomach. 'Okay, kittens, let's not scratch each other's eyes out. Who wants ice-cream? I'm going to walk by the hot lifeguard to get some.'

Jools jumped up. 'I'll come.'

While they went off across the sand, Holly turned to Alice. 'Mummy?'

'Yes, pet.'

'What are we going to do for Daddy's birthday?'

Alice caught her breath. No one had mentioned it, so she hadn't been sure that the girls would remember. She'd been kind of hoping they wouldn't. Ben's birthday was in two days' time. He would have been forty-six. Alice remembered how last year they'd had a late picnic on the beach in Antibes. After eating cheese and bread and salami and olives, the girls had gone into the sea while Ben and Alice had shared a chilled bottle of champagne, toasting each other and their two beautiful daughters.

Ben had seemed happy, the most relaxed Alice had seen him all that year. The holiday had done them good. He was away from work, cycling and the distractions that pulled him away from her. They had got on well, laughed together and had a lot of sex. She'd felt close to him, closer than she had in months. But as soon as they landed in Heathrow, he'd been off again – gone from her physically and emotionally.

Alice really missed him. It was wonderful that Kevin had agreed to join them for the first week of their holiday. The days were bearable because they were busy doing things and the beautiful scenery helped. But at night Alice desperately missed having Ben beside her. She missed drinking wine on the balcony, when the girls had gone to bed, and chatting about life, old times and their hopes for their daughters' future. She missed laughing with him about funny things the girls had done or said. She missed dinners out in restaurants as a family, their perfect family of four. Now they were just three, with a big hole where the fourth had been.

Kevin was leaving the next day, so they would be alone for Ben's birthday. Alice preferred it that way. They could cry and talk about Ben as much as they wanted. Kevin deserved to be at home with Axel, having fun. He had been so generous to them all. It was time for him to live his own life.

When the holiday was over, Alice was going to talk to Kevin about moving out of the house. He stayed with Axel three or four nights a week anyway, and it was time for him to move on. Although she wanted him to stay because he was such a big help with the girls, she knew it wasn't fair. She had to let Kevin go.

Alice needed to come to terms with the fact that she was going to be a single mother for the rest of her life. Even if she did meet someone else he would not be the girls' father. Alice was their only parent and she had to take full responsibility and stop leaning on Kevin. She still had Nora to help her and she was lucky that she could organize her work to suit their school schedule. She had to face up to her new life.

But Alice felt panic rising in her chest every time she thought about the long, lonely road ahead. Since Ben had died, she'd gone alone to all their concerts, sports days and parent-teacher meetings. And it hurt, really hurt. It was so lonely.

The school had been very kind and the teachers had been

patient with Jools, trying to help her as much as they could – and, to be fair, Jools had tried to study harder this year – but she had struggled and Alice should have helped her. But the thought of having to sit with her doing hours of homework every night had made Alice want to weep. She had barely the energy to get out of bed and go to work. But she had no choice. She was the only person who could help Jools over the next two years, which were very important.

Holly's teacher said she was doing very well, still ahead of the other children in all subjects, but she did mention the obsession with her calculator.

'Holly's always checking the time and calculating hours. It seems to be a nervous tic she's developed since her father's death,' Miss Robinson had said.

'I know it's a little obsessive, but it keeps her calm. I'm sure she'll stop soon,' Alice said. 'I don't want to take the calculator away – she finds it a comfort.'

'Of course. I'm just concerned that it's halting her progress in maths because she's not doing her calculations herself. She insists on using the calculator, which does give her an unfair advantage over the other children and won't help her learn.'

Alice had promised to try to wean Holly off the calculator during the summer, but it hadn't been going very well. Whenever she mentioned it, Holly freaked.

Ben would have known how to deal with it. Alice lay awake at night fretting about being a lone parent. She cried when she thought of being at their weddings alone. She would proudly walk them up the aisle, of course she would, but, God, it would be so lonely.

Was this it? Was this really it? A lifetime of being solo, of doing everything on her own? The only alternative path was if she met someone, but the thought of being with another man just made her feel really tired and slightly nauseous.

The idea of having to get to know another man was exhausting. All the hours of talking and explaining who you were and telling them your life story, it just made her feel weary. As for sex! The idea of having sex with someone she barely knew gave her the shivers. Ben understood her – he knew everything about her. It was easy.

Of course they'd had their ups and downs, but they loved each other, they were best friends. Alice couldn't imagine having another person in her life like Ben. You only get really lucky in love once.

She knew that Harold meeting Helen had changed his life and made him happier – well, as happy as Harold was capable of being. Maybe she would meet someone in a few years when she didn't feel like crying all the time, but then she'd have to introduce them to the girls and they'd hate him because he wasn't Ben.

Besides, who'd want a widow with two daughters who now had to take sleeping tablets every night to stop her mind exploding with all the anger and sorrow that constantly threatened to overwhelm her? She wasn't exactly a great catch. But when she thought about spending the next twenty or thirty years alone, she felt utter dread.

Alice sat on the balcony, wrapped in a blanket, watching the sunrise. 'Happy birthday, Ben,' she whispered, into the early-morning breeze. 'I miss you.' She allowed herself to have a long cry and then she went to have a shower. When she was dressed and feeling calmer, she went in to the girls. They were already awake. She took one look at their red eyes and threw her arms around them. 'I know. It's awful.'

'I miss him so much,' Jools sobbed.

'Why did God have to take him away?' Holly sniffed.

Jools pulled back and took something from under her pillow. It was a present, all wrapped in paper. 'I bought him a jumper. I know it's stupid because he's dead, but I didn't want to have nothing.'

Alice kissed her cheek. 'That's lovely, darling.'

'I bought him something too,' Holly said, producing a small box tied with a bow. 'It's only a key-ring but it's an Arsenal one.'

'That's very thoughtful.' Alice choked back tears. 'Well, what would you like to do? We can have a cry and then go to the beach, or we can stay here and close the curtains and watch DVDs and eat chocolate, or we can go for a walk and stop at that café that does the huge ice-creams with chocolate sauce and whipped cream.'

'I'd like to go to mass and pray for Daddy, then come back and snuggle up, watch movies, eat chocolate and then maybe go to the ice-cream place later,' Holly said.

'Mass? Seriously?' Jools was not impressed with this plan.

Alice looked at Jools and shook her head very slightly.

Jools put an arm around her sister. 'Okay, Holly, let's do that. We can light a candle for Dad.'

The three Gregory ladies headed off to the local church, hand in hand. Together, a new team, a new family, a smaller broken one, but still a family.

## Ben: September 2013

Eyob sat with his gun on his lap, glaring at Declan as he examined the tiny girl's abdomen. Feven was holding the child's hand, crying silently.

Declan cursed under his breath. Dehab was in a bad way. 'Why the hell didn't they bring her in sooner?' He shook his head.

Feven, who was watching Declan's face closely for signs of hope, began to wail.

Ben placed a reassuring hand on her shoulder. 'It's all right. We'll do our best to save her.'

Although she hadn't understood what Ben had said, Feven took comfort from the tone of his voice and his half-smile. He guided her out of the tent and indicated for her to wait, then went back in to examine the little mite.

Her eyes were sunken and her skin was sagging from lack of fluids. 'Jesus Christ, it'll be a miracle if this child survives,' Declan raged. 'They can't wait this long. What's wrong with these people?'

Yonas coughed, and the two doctors looked at him.

'The women not want to come to doctor,' Yonas said.

'Why not?' Ben asked.

'They afraid.'

'But we can help,' Ben replied.

'Women think if child comes here, he die.'

'But we're doctors.'

Yonas shrugged. 'Women afraid, not trusting you.'

'I'll have to talk to Awate about that,' Ben said. 'In the meantime, we need to find a vein.'

'I've looked, none viable. We'll have to find one on her scalp.' Declan took out a scalpel and held it to Dehab's head. Eyob roared and cocked his rifle. Feven came rushing in and screamed.

'STOP!' Ben shouted. 'We're looking for a vein to rehydrate.' He looked to Yonas for help, but the guard didn't understand.

Ben gestured for them to gather around the operating table. Eyob hobbled over on his wooden crutches.

Ben showed them his arm and indicated a vein. He pointed to Dehab's arms and the lack of veins. Then he showed them the vein under Dehab's hair where Declan was about to shave it so they could insert a needle and hydrate the child.

Feven nodded. She understood. Declan indicated for her to shave her daughter's head but she refused. She patted his hand and smiled.

Eyob bristled, and as he limped past Declan, he rammed his crutch on Declan's foot. Declan's face reddened with rage.

'Let's get on, shall we?' Ben said firmly to Declan, before there was trouble.

Declan gently shaved a small section of soft hair from Dehab's temple, then placed a rubber band around her head as a makeshift tourniquet. Feven stood beside him, watching. Declan showed her the vein. Feven nodded, then left the tent again.

'It's not much thicker than a thread, but hopefully I can cannulate,' Ben said as he advanced the needle with tiny probings. 'Got it!' he said, as a strand of dark blood curled back into the plastic tube.

Declan taped the drip in place and counted the drops as they fell through the clear chamber to make sure the flow-rate wasn't too fast or too slow. Then he lifted the listless child and placed her on a mattress on the floor in the next tent and hung the drip bag on an overhead wire. Dehab lay beside five other children who were also suffering from gastroenteritis.

Having settled her, Declan came back in and removed his surgical gloves, which he washed carefully.

'I'll have to get Awate to talk to everyone about being extra vigilant about hand-washing and drinking clean water. We need to stop this spreading,' Ben said, as he dried his hands. 'We're running out of saline. We'll have to teach the women how to make their own solution.'

'What is it again? One teaspoon of salt and eight of sugar?' Declan asked.

'Actually, it's only half a teaspoon of salt and eight tea-spoons of sugar per litre of cool boiled water.'

'I'll go and talk to Feven and see if I can explain it to her.'

Ben frowned. 'Declan, let me do it.'

'I'm not going to do anything stupid, just talk to her,' Declan whispered back.

'Eyob doesn't need to be provoked. You know how pro-tective he is about her.'

'He's just a one-legged wanker who can't get laid.'

'He's a one-legged wanker with a gun.'

'Relax, Ben, I won't get myself shot. I'm not going to try to shag her, although I am tempted.'

'Don't even think about it.'

'I can't help it.'

'If you don't get yourself shot, you can sleep with every woman you meet when we get out of this shit-hole.'

'Will we get out?' Declan was suddenly serious.

'We have to,' Ben said, looking down at his hands. 'We just have to.'

Later that night, Ben and Declan were playing chess. The chess set had been a gift from Awate when they had saved Eyob's life.

Eyob had been a lot less grateful when he'd woken up with only one leg. He had freaked out and accused Ben and Declan of trying to kill him, but Awate had shouted at him and told him that the only reason he was alive was because of the surgeons' skill. He'd made Eyob thank them.

'He's about as happy as a turkey on Christmas Eve,' Declan had muttered.

Since the amputation, Eyob had been even more aggressive and edgy than before. Ben hated him guarding them: Eyob made him nervous.

'I'm too tired to play.' Declan rolled onto his side.

Ben blew out the candle. 'It's late – we should get some sleep. I think we'll have more gastro cases tomorrow, unfortunately.'

'I hope I don't get it. I hate the trots.'

'We should take care not to,' Ben said. 'We need to keep our strength up.'

Beside him, Declan tossed and turned on his mattress. In the dark he groaned. 'Jesus, I'm so horny I'd nearly ride you!'

'Thanks all the same, but I'd rather you didn't.'

'I can understand how fellas in prison for years and years end up together.'

'Think of all the gorgeous women you'll have sex with when we get out of here.'

'I'm telling you, Ben, when I get back to London I'm going to ride every woman I meet and then I'm going to find an Alice and get married and have a shedload of kids.'

Ben went quiet. Declan was dreaming of meeting 'an Alice' and Ben had one and he'd blown it. He'd ruined everything by being selfish. He swore for the millionth time that if he got out of there, he'd be more attentive to his family, more loving, more present, and put their needs first.

'Ben?' Declan said. 'I know you're going down the if-only road. I can sense it. Stop, it won't do you any good.'

'Why was I such a stupid, selfish idiot?' Ben cried.

Declan reached for his hand and held it. 'Don't worry – I'm not coming on to you. Ben, listen to me. You did something you wanted to do. It's not a crime. What happened to us was just sheer bad luck. That's all. When you get home, you can tell Alice how much you love her and how sorry you are. But feeling guilty all the time in here will kill you.'

'She's just so –'

'Perfect. I know – you've only said it a thousand times.'

'What was I looking for? I had it all. And now . . . my girls are nearly a year older . . . Christ, Declan, do you think they'll have forgotten me?'

'Don't be mad. Kids never forget their parents.'

'Do you think Alice will have moved on? She's really pretty and I bet lots of men are moving in on her.'

'Jesus, stop torturing yourself. Don't even think about that.'

Ben exhaled deeply. 'She thinks I'm dead. Why wouldn't she move on? I wouldn't blame her – she deserves someone better.'

Declan lit a cigarette and handed it to Ben. 'That's enough self-pity. Alice loves you. Think about it. Would you have moved on in less than a year if you'd thought she was dead? No way. I bet you she's looking at a photo of you right now and missing you . . . or she's on her back being banged by some beefy bloke called Brad that she met at the gym.'

Ben thumped his arm and gave him a crooked smile.

'Knock, knock.'

'I'm not playing.'

'Come on, Ben, it'll distract you.'

'They're ridiculous kids' jokes.'

'I know, but cheesy can be funny. Knock, knock.'

'Who's there?'

'Anee.'

'Anee who?'

'Anee one you like!'

Despite himself, Ben laughed. 'How do you know so many of these silly jokes?'

'Because they made Da laugh when my ma left. We used to say them to him to make him smile. It worked, so we kept going. Between us all, we had loads of them. Knock, knock.'

'Who's there?'

'A herd.'

'A herd who?'

'A herd you were home, so I came over.'

Ben chuckled. 'If the surgery doesn't work out, you could become a really bad comedian.'

'I'll be too busy having all the sex with all the women to do that, remember?'

'In between the sex.'

'In between the sex I'll be eating steak and drinking champagne and living every second of every day.'

'Oh, God, what I'd give for a steak right now.'

'After I get home I'll never eat a chickpea or lentil again as long as I live,' Declan declared.

'I look forward to using cutlery and sitting in an actual chair.'

'I'm dreaming of long hot showers, soft mattresses and

sleeping without a chain on my ankles or a sweaty bloke by my side.'

'You're not so fragrant yourself,' Ben said. 'In fact, my first gift to you when we get out of here will be a large can of Lynx.'

'My da wears that,' Declan said, and Ben instantly regretted saying it because he could see in Declan's eyes that he was being pulled back into the past, and it was dangerous to spend too much time there. He knew that from experience. 'He always puts on way too much. You can smell him before you see him. He's a gas man, always in a good mood. Even when things were really tough he was sunny-side-up. His favourite expression is "Sure it could be worse". It used to drive us all mental. When Darren found out his fiancée was shagging someone else, Da said to him, "Sure it could have been worse, you could have been married." Darren went mental and started punching the wall in frustration. But Da was right. I wonder what he'd say to me now? I think he'd be stumped to find a positive spin on this.' Declan's voice broke and his body began to shake.

Ben gripped his hand. 'Come on, mate, it *could* be worse. I mean, Christ, you could be chained to John Lester.'

Declan's sobs turned to laughs, then back to sobs. Ben held his hand and waited for the darkness to pass.

## Holly: October 2013

Three hundred and sixty-five days. Twelve months. One year. One whole year since Daddy died. Mummy asked us what we wanted to do. She wanted to treat Jools because it's her seventeenth birthday. But Jools said she just wanted to go back to bed and sleep through the day. I said I'd do whatever Mummy wanted to do. She looked so sad and so tired.

While we were trying to decide, Kevin arrived with coffees and *pains au chocolat*, muffins and smoothies. He gave Jools her present, but she just put it beside the ones from me and Mummy and said she'd open them tomorrow because today doesn't feel like a birthday.

I wasn't hungry, but just having Kevin in the house made us all feel a bit better. He fussed over us, making us eat and distracting us with funny stories about Axel. Kevin said that Axel has decided he's not going to be a singer, he's going to be a chef. Kevin said that Axel can barely boil water, but he doesn't want to crush his dreams.

Mummy said it was lucky Axel had a rich father who could fund his son's madcap ideas. Kevin said Axel is working his way through one of Nigella's cookbooks, and when he comes home he is usually greeted with burnt fish, charred meat or soggy vegetables. He has to eat it because Axel stands in front of him in his chef's coat – he loves to have the proper outfit for whatever he's doing, Kevin says – and waits for Kevin to comment.

'What do you say?' Jools asked.

'At first I told him it was lovely but perhaps a tiny bit over-cooked, and then he shouted at me in French for ten minutes. So now I just say everything is *formidable*.'

'But that's ridiculous! You're lying to him. He'll never get a job as a chef. You need to stop lying.'

'Jools, I'm not going out with Axel for his gastronomic aptitude.'

'But that's just it,' Jools said. 'Axel's gastronomic attitude is a total pain.'

Mummy looked at me and winked. We tried not to laugh. It was nice to have something to smile about, even if it was about Jools being a bit silly with her words.

Kevin just kept talking about Axel's disastrous meals and making us laugh. When we'd cleared up the breakfast things, he took Mummy upstairs and made her put on a nice dress, then told me and Jools to do the same.

When Mummy came into my bedroom, I told her she looked lovely. She didn't really. The dress was too big for her. She's lost even more weight and her eyes are so sad. Some-times when I see how pale and tired Mummy looks, I feel a really bad pain in my heart. What would happen to us if she died? Would Kevin look after us? I couldn't bear it if Mummy died. I honestly don't think I could survive it.

I went over, hugged her really tight and tried not to cry, but I couldn't stop the tears. I told her how much I loved her and then she started crying, too. Kevin came in and told us both off. He said we were going to drown in tears in this house and that we needed to start living again. He said we'd done all the horrible first things – first birthdays without Daddy and first Christmas – and all the awful days where we missed him so much and that, hopefully, this year, it wouldn't be quite so awful.

That's what the lady said in the grief-counselling session Mummy took us to. But none of us liked her and we didn't go back. She kept talking about Daddy as if she knew him, but she didn't. I know Mummy took us because she wanted to help us to deal with our sadness, but Jools and I both said we hated it and that we didn't want to talk to a stranger about Daddy.

Mummy said okay, but that we had to talk to her about Daddy when we were sad and not to worry about upsetting her. She said we had to let our grief out, or it would make us ill inside.

I talk to Daddy all the time. I look at his picture and talk to him. Sometimes I actually think he talks back. When I close my eyes, I can hear his voice. Like the other day, when I didn't know what to do about Simon. He's always calling me a 'swot' and a 'freak' and I try to ignore him, but he just keeps saying it and some of the others laugh and I feel really bad. I told Daddy about it and I could hear him saying, 'You have to stand up to him.'

I was really scared, but the next day when Simon called me a 'swot' I told him I'd rather be a swot than always coming bottom, like he does. He just laughed, but I felt a bit better.

I'm not sure if Simon would have stopped being mean after that. I'm not the sort of girl who can frighten people – but then Jools heard about it from Simon's cousin, Jeremy, who is in her year. So Jools and her friend Lance, who is in year twelve too, and captain of the rugby team, went up to Simon the next day, pushed him up against a locker and told him that if he ever even looked sideways at me again, Lance would use him as a human rugby ball. So now Simon leaves me alone.

I worry about Jools, though. She doesn't talk about Daddy

enough. Mummy tries to get her to talk about him, but Jools just keeps saying she's fine. Mummy and she are fighting a lot because Mummy is helping Jools with her homework every night and it's always a battle. Mummy tries really hard not to get annoyed, but Jools is annoying. She's not trying. She said she's worn out with all the studying she did for her GCSEs. She did better than any of us thought she would but not exactly brilliantly – although she did get an A star in art. She said her mind needs a break and she'll work harder when the next lot of exams are coming up. She doesn't seem to care that she's at the bottom of her year.

Mummy is trying to get her to read more – she even said she'd pay her for every book she finished, but Jools refuses. I heard Mummy telling Kevin that she was worried Jools would end up stacking shelves in Tesco.

Kevin said there were worse things she could be doing, like 'swinging around a pole in a dodgy nightclub in Soho'. Mummy didn't think it was funny. She actually just looked really worried.

When we were all dressed, Kevin took us to a fancy restaurant called Le Toit. I don't think I've ever seen Kevin eat so much. He ordered all of the side dishes, including the creamy potatoes, which he never usually does because he's always watching his weight. He said he was starving because of all the awful food Axel was cooking, which he had to spit into his napkin when Axel wasn't looking.

We had a nice time and then we went home and Mummy took us out to the garden where Daddy's cherry tree was growing and she asked us all to talk to Daddy. That's when things got really sad. Jools totally lost it. She said, 'I needed you, Dad, and you left me. I hate you for going to Eritrea. I HATE YOU.' Then she ran inside and locked herself in her bedroom, and even when Mummy said she could watch

*Keeping Up With the Kardashians* and eat a whole box of Celebrations she wouldn't come out.

Mummy then said she had a headache and would I mind if she had a little lie-down. I said it was fine and that I might do the same. Mummy said I could come and snuggle up in her bed, but I knew she wanted to cry and she wouldn't in front of me, so I said I'd rather just go to my own room. That wasn't true.

After about an hour I went to check on Mummy and she was fast asleep, surrounded by tissues. I could see the light on in Jools's bedroom, so I knocked on her door. She didn't answer. I went in. I wish I hadn't. It was awful. I feel sick every time I think about it. I don't know what to do. She made me swear I wouldn't tell Mummy or Kevin or anyone.

But it's serious. She said she's only done it once or twice, but the scars were all the way up her arms. When I went in, she was in the middle of cutting herself with a razor and there was blood dripping down her arm into the black towel she had underneath. Her face looked really weird – like she was in pain but also happy.

I'm really scared now.

*Alice: December 2013*

Alice sat with her handbag on her lap, twisting the strap around her hands.

'Thank you for coming, Mrs Gregory. I know that your family has suffered greatly in the last year and we've turned a blind eye to a number of misdemeanours in Jools's case, but I'm afraid I can't let this go.'

'What exactly did she do?' Alice asked.

Mrs Kennedy clasped her hands together. 'She rang the school switchboard and said there was a bomb in the science lab.'

'What?' Alice was shocked. How could Jools do a thing like that?

'Obviously we had to evacuate the building until we were able to establish that it was a hoax.'

'Are you sure it was Jools?'

Mrs Kennedy pursed her lips. 'Yes. We called the mobile number back and Jools answered.'

How could Jools be so stupid? 'Did she say why she did it?'

'Apparently she was trying to avoid doing a test.'

She must have been really desperate to get out of it. Alice felt sorry for her daughter and furious with her in equal measure. 'She's finding it difficult to keep up. I'm helping her as much as I can, but her father . . . well . . . he was better at it, more patient, than I am.'

'Perhaps you should consider hiring a tutor to help,'

Mrs Kennedy suggested. 'After all, the next two years are important.'

Alice nodded. 'I was planning to do that. It's just . . . I didn't want to push her too much because she's been so upset and I knew she'd hate having a teacher coming to the house to do extra work. I'll sort it out this week. I should have done it before now. I just . . . It's been . . .'

Mrs Kennedy reached over and patted Alice's hand. 'You've had a terrible shock. We understand. I just want the best for Jools and it's time she had some extra tuition. She's a bright, lively girl. She just needs her energy channelled in the right direction.'

Alice smiled. 'That's what Ben used to say. How's Holly getting on?'

Mrs Kennedy smiled. 'She's a pleasure to have in the school. Such a serious and studious girl. As I mentioned to you earlier in the year, we have noticed that Holly has been a little withdrawn but her year head, Miss Long, assures me that she is doing very well in her work and has a nice little group of friends.'

Alice sighed and loosened her grip on the strap of her handbag. 'That's good to hear. I worry about them so much. I'm trying to make things as normal as possible.'

'They are two lovely girls and you are doing an excellent job. I think the extra tuition will help Jools immeasurably and take some of the pressure from your shoulders. I'm sorry to have called you in, but it was a serious incident.'

Alice nodded. 'I understand. Thank you. I promise it won't happen again.' She stood up and shook Mrs Kennedy's hand. As she walked through the quiet school corridors, she saw classrooms full of children working. She peeped in at Holly's class. Her daughter was writing, a frown of concentration on her sweet face. Along the next corridor she saw Jools's class. Jools was using her ruler to flick balls of paper at the girl in front of her.

Chalk and cheese, thought Alice. She'd have to have a serious talk with Jools after school. She dreaded it. Ben had been so much better at dealing with her. Alice always ended up saying the wrong thing or just losing her temper. But this was serious. Imagine calling the school to say there was a bomb! Mrs Kennedy could have excluded her. Alice was going to have to be firm. No more dancing around Jools's feelings. This was unacceptable and she'd have to be punished.

Alice knew what would bother Jools most: confiscation of her phone. She knew her daughter would freak and make her life miserable, but she was going to do it. Enough was enough.

When Alice got home from work, Nora was taking a roast chicken out of the oven.

'Perfect timing,' Nora said, as she put the chicken on the island. 'The girls are upstairs doing their homework.'

'Thanks, Nora.' Alice took off her coat. 'I was called to the school today.'

'Jools?'

Alice nodded, and filled her in on the 'incident'. Nora threw back her head and laughed.

'It's not funny.'

'You have to hand it to her, she's original.'

'She could have been kicked out of the school!'

'Well, she wasn't. Lookit, Alice, the poor divil doesn't know what she wants or where she's going. All teenagers are a nightmare. My lot drove me wild and turned my hair grey.

And that poor child had her dad die in the middle of all those swirling hormones. It's a wonder she isn't stone mad.'

Alice sat down on a stool and rested her chin on her hands. 'But she has to behave or she'll land herself in big trouble.'

'Go easy, Alice. She's fragile, that one. She pretends to be all big and bold, but she's a ball of mush. She misses Ben more than anyone. Holly's stronger.'

Alice rubbed her eyes. She felt exhausted. She'd stopped taking the sleeping tablets because she was afraid of becoming addicted to them, but that meant she was back to fitful sleep and wakeful nights.

'It's not easy, Alice, I know. But you'll be fine. What you need is a good ride.'

'*What?*' Alice's head snapped up.

Nora swatted her with a tea towel. 'Don't look so shocked. I'm sixty, not ninety, and I know what a woman needs. You need to have a one-night stand with some handsome fella, no strings attached. It'll do you the world of good, wake your body up.'

'Jesus, Nora, I couldn't even think of being with another man.'

'Nonsense. Just drink a few glasses of vodka, close your eyes and get on with it. It'll break the cycle.'

'What cycle?'

'The misery cycle.'

Alice felt herself flushing. 'I couldn't. I can't even bear the thought of being with someone else. It feels wrong – as if I was being unfaithful or something.'

'He's dead, Alice. He hasn't gone on a holiday. He's not coming back. You need to start living. You're a young woman – you need to get out there and start smiling at men instead of going about like a ghost.'

'But it's only been a year.' Alice was shocked at Nora's

advice. In one way it felt as if it was only yesterday that Ben was there, beside her. On the other hand, she sometimes felt as if she'd been on her own for ever.

'It's been fourteen months now and you need to have some fun and feel like a person again. You've spent the last year looking after those girls. Now it's time to look after yourself. The first thing you need to do is go shopping. Your clothes are all falling off you. Get yourself some nice new outfits and put on some lipstick and go out and find yourself a strapping young lad to give you a night of passion. You don't want it to dry up.'

'Nora!' Alice was not comfortable having this conversation.

'I'm right and you know it. Now, I'd best be off before Himself runs off with the young one next door. I've seen him lusting at her over the hedge.' Nora put on her coat and headed for the door. 'Remember now, don't be too hard on Jools.'

Alice was reeling from Nora's pep talk, so she went to pour herself a glass of wine to calm down after an eventful and revealing day – Jools causing a bomb scare and Nora telling her to get laid by a stranger. As Alice drank her wine, her eye caught a picture of her and Ben at a fancy-dress party. They'd gone as Bacon and Eggs – Ben was the bacon and Alice was the fried egg. They looked utterly ridiculous and extremely happy.

Could she sleep with another man? It was so long since she'd had sex with anyone but Ben. She wasn't even sure if she'd be any good at it. She and Ben had had their own rhythm. They knew each other's bodies so well, so intimately. Alice didn't even particularly like her body. Her boobs were saggy from her years of breast-feeding plus gravity; her stomach and thighs had stretch marks that looked like train tracks. Even if she wanted to have a one-night stand, she wouldn't be able to find anyone to have sex with. Could you hire someone? Maybe she could get sex lessons.

Her phone rang. It was Kevin.

'Can women like me hire a man to have sex with?'

'How many Xanax have you taken?'

'Seriously, is there an escort service for sad women in their forties?'

'Okay, you're not slurring your words, you don't sound out of it, what the hell is going on?'

'Nora told me I needed to have sex.'

'Go, Nora!'

'I'm not going to. I can think of nothing worse. But is there a service for women like me?'

'Honey, this is London. There's something for everyone.'

'Nice men, not seedy, smelly, nasty, rotten men.'

'You don't need to go to an escort service. Believe me, this is a big city. There are plenty of very nice, hot, fragrant, fit men.'

'Nora said I should go for a younger man with no strings attached.'

'Nora's a dark horse.'

'How do you meet someone like that?'

'Tinder.'

'What's Tinder?'

'Alice, seriously, get with the program.'

'What is it?' Alice repeated. She was beginning to realize how clueless she was about everything.

'It's an app for matchmaking.'

'How does it work?'

'You sign up, then other users can check out your Facebook profile so they can see what you look like and how old you are. The app will pair up potential candidates who are most likely to be a good match, based on where you are and if you have mutual friends or common interests.'

'That's it? You see a photo and their age – which they can lie about – and then you meet them? It sounds mad and probably dangerous.'

'There are some downsides. I hooked up with a guy recently. In his headshot he looked very handsome, but when I met him he was tiny and really fat.'

'Never mind short and fat, what if he's a psychopath?'

Kevin sighed. 'I use it all the time and I've never had any problem.'

'I don't understand how you can be in a relationship that isn't monogamous. How can it not cause problems? I would have been insanely jealous if Ben had been with another woman.'

'I'm not into monogamy and nor is Axel. It works for us.'

'Do you think Jools is on the Tinder?'

'God, Alice, please don't call it "the Tinder". You sound so old.'

'Okay, Tinder then.'

'No, she isn't. I checked. She's too young. It's aimed at eighteen and over. I'd say Nora might be, though, the dirty old thing.'

'Nora can barely use her ancient Nokia mobile phone. I doubt somehow she's meeting up with strangers on Tinder.'

'I dunno. After the advice she gave you, she just might be.'

'Anyway, it's not something I need to know about.'

'Maybe not now, but in time you'll come around to it. We all have needs.'

'Time! Time heals all wounds. In time I'll feel better. All time does is crawl slowly by and remind me of how shit everything is and how bad a parent I am.' Alice opened the fridge and poured herself another glass of wine.

'I forgot – you had that meeting. Go on, what did Mrs Kennedy say about Jools?'

Alice drank deeply. 'Your niece made a hoax bomb-scare call to get out of doing a test.'

Kevin hooted down the phone. 'Genius.'

'Why does everyone think this is funny? Nora laughed too. It's very serious, Kevin. Mrs Kennedy wasn't remotely amused.'

'Give Jools a break. She was obviously terrified about failing the test. I know how that feels. I remember faking chickenpox before a history exam.'

Alice had a flashback to Kevin lying in bed with white make-up all over his face and spots painted on with red marker. She laughed. 'I'd forgotten that. You looked ridiculous. You could smell the stuff from a mile away.'

'I was desperate. But Mum let me off. She pretended she bought the story and she allowed me to stay at home. I knew she knew I was faking and she knew I knew she knew, but she still let me off.'

'So what are you saying? I should let this thing with Jools go? The whole school was evacuated until they figured out that it was Jools's mobile. Which they did by just ringing the number, by the way. No fear of our Jools becoming a criminal mastermind. That's something, at least.'

Kevin laughed. 'I'm saying you shouldn't go in there all fired up and start giving out. Talk to her, let her tell you why she did it. She's just a confused teenager who's lost the most important person in her life.'

'Jesus, Kevin, I have feelings, you know.'

'Oh, come on, she loves you too, but we both know that Ben was her hero.'

I've lost the most important person in my life too, Alice wanted to shout. But no one was listening.

'Okay. Well, I'd better go up to her.'

'Good luck – and if you need me to pop over later, I can.'

'Thanks.'

Alice downed the rest of her wine and went upstairs to talk to Jools.

## Ben: February 2014

Ben was dreaming about Alice. He was walking towards her, arms outstretched, but just as he got close, she turned to dust and vanished.

'Ben! Ben!' Someone was shaking him.

Ben's eyes snapped open. It was Yonas. 'You come, you come now.'

Beside him, Declan sat up. 'What's going on?'

'My wife, she sick. Baby coming.' Yonas looked wild-eyed with worry. He unlocked the chains with shaking hands.

Ben stood up and put his hand on Yonas's shoulder. 'It's okay, we'll help her.'

Yonas ushered the two men into the operating theatre where his wife, Segen, was hunched on a chair.

Ben and Declan brought her over to the table. She whimpered as she rolled onto her back. Ben examined her abdomen. He couldn't feel the baby moving or hear a foetal heartbeat with his stethoscope.

'Damn, we're going to have to do a C-section.'

'Do we have enough anaesthetic?' Declan asked.

'Awate brought some yesterday. Apparently they raided the clinic in Asmara again.'

'Are they planning another attack?' Declan asked.

Ben nodded. 'He wanted to stock up because he knows there'll be lots of injuries.'

'What the hell is wrong with them?' Declan fumed. 'It's a shitty piece of barren land and they're causing mayhem over it.'

'It's not about the land. It's about ownership and rights.'

'I'm Irish, Ben. I grew up with people bombing each other over rights. I just don't think this crappy land is worth it. Awate'd be better off packing up and taking his clan to a decent place where they could run a little farm, or down to Asmara and open a business or something. This is bullshit. We're stuck here because of a stupid, pointless fight. We'll never get away.'

Segen groaned, and Yonas barked at them, 'You help!'

While Declan administered the anaesthetic, Ben tried to explain that they had to do a Caesarean. Yonas didn't understand, but he placed a hand on Ben's arm. 'You good man, Ben. You good doctor.'

Ben asked Yonas to stand outside, which he reluctantly agreed to do. Before he left, he kissed his wife and tried to soothe her fears. He stood outside, his back to the tent, praying.

As soon as Segen was unconscious, Ben performed an internal examination. 'Her cervix is only partially dilated, and look.' He held up his bloodied glove. 'We need to get this baby out now. I'm pretty sure there's an anterior tear.' He picked up the scalpel.

'There's no time for neat incisions, hurry,' Declan urged.

Ben cut Segen's abdomen in a vertical midline incision below the umbilicus. Time was their enemy. The pregnant uterus bulged forward into the wound.

They could see free blood in the abdomen. The baby was under Ben's hands. He reached in and lifted it out. It was covered with a slippery mess of blood and meconium. He handed it to Declan, who wiped the baby's face and the inside of his mouth with a towel while Ben clamped and cut the umbilical cord.

'Shit, I think he's inhaled the meconium. It's like bloody tar.' Declan bent down, placed his mouth over the baby's and started breathing very gently into it. He pulled back. Nothing.

He did it again and this time the baby's chest rose. 'Yes!' He punched the air with his fist.

Ben grinned and turned back to Segen. 'I have to deliver the placenta or she'll bleed out.'

Thankfully, the placenta came away easily. 'Christ.' Ben cursed under his breath as dark blood filled the abdomen. He wiped sweat from his brow with the top of his sleeve.

'Bad?' Declan asked.

'It's like a bloody dam. We have to save her,' Ben said. 'Yonas is a decent man – he treats us with respect.'

While Declan worked on the baby, Ben packed Segen's abdomen with swabs to stem the bleeding. 'I need your help, mate.'

'Just give me another minute to stabilize this little fella's breathing and I'll be over to you.'

Two minutes later, Yonas came back in, concerned for his wife. The soldier gasped when he saw all the blood. Trying to distract him from Segen, Declan called him over to the corner to see his son.

'It's a boy.' Declan smiled. 'He was having trouble breathing, but he's okay now. Keep an eye on him and let me know if anything changes. I need to help Ben with Segen.' Declan handed the infant to his father, who cradled him in his arms.

'She is okay?' Yonas asked, looking over to where his wife lay, blocked by Ben.

'We're doing everything we can.' Declan patted him on the back and urged him to focus on his son.

'I need you,' Ben called to Declan, who rushed over.

While Declan swabbed the blood from Segen's abdomen, Ben whispered that they had to do a hysterectomy.

'Are you going to do a subtotal one?'

Ben nodded. 'I have no choice. We have to save her.'

'Do it and I'll close her up,' Declan said.

Ben frowned in concentration as he began the surgery. When it was finally over, Declan checked Segen's pulse for the umpteenth time. 'It's still very weak,' he whispered.

Ben handed him a hand pump. Declan placed it over her face and began to squeeze the bag rhythmically, willing her to live.

Ben raised her feet into the air to help blood-flow, then hooked her up with intravenous fluids that contained vital antibiotics. Finally he went to check on the baby. His pulse was still very weak, but he was alive and breathing by himself. 'Congratulations, Dad!' he said to Yonas, who couldn't stop smiling at his son.

Yonas looked at Segen and his face clouded.

'She's okay,' Ben said. 'She's still very weak, but we're doing everything we can. Bring the baby to her.'

Yonas followed Ben to where Segen was now lying. They had moved her to a mattress in the 'recovery room'. Declan was kneeling beside her, taking her pulse.

Yonas lay down beside his sleeping wife and placed the baby on her chest. The baby gurgled and began to breathe in rhythm with his mother. Yonas whispered to Segen and stroked her thin, drawn face.

Ben and Declan stayed with them all night, taking it in turns to check on Segen and the baby while Yonas slept beside them, protecting them.

*

As the sun rose, the two men stepped out for a cigarette.

'We could take Yonas's gun and go,' Declan said.

'It's wedged under his arm – he'd wake up. Besides, how would we get past the two soldiers standing right over there?' Ben pointed to the guards at the entrance to the camp.

'We could threaten them with Yonas's gun.'

'They'd shoot us.'

'Not if we shot them first.'

'That would wake everyone up and they'd all shoot us.'

'Fuck you, Ben, you always think of reasons for us to fail.' Declan threw his cigarette on the dusty ground and stamped on it.

Ben rounded on him. 'I just don't want to bloody die, okay? My need to survive is stronger. I will get out of here, but not in a body bag. I want to see my kids again. I fucked up by coming to this bloody country in the first place. I'm not going to get myself killed. I'm going to go home and be a good father, a good husband and a good man. A better man. A much better man.' His voice cracked.

Declan's face softened. 'You are a good man. If it wasn't for you, I'd have been shot at least six times.'

'Well, there's no bloody way I could stick this on my own. We'll get out of here, Declan, but we have to be patient. We can't just run for it. We have no idea where we are, and even if we made it to the nearest village, they'd hand us straight back to Awate. Everyone's terrified of him.'

Ben reached his arms around his back to stretch it out. He was stiff and sore from sitting up all night with the patients. 'We'll never get out of here without someone local helping us or persuading Awate to let us go. We have to keep developing relationships and try to persuade them that holding us here is cruel and inhumane.'

'Awate's a heartless prick. All he cares about is his stupid patch of land. Maybe Yonas would help us now that we've saved his wife and kid,' Declan suggested.

'He's Awate's cousin, so I doubt it. Mind you, he's by far the most decent of the soldiers, and if Segen and the baby don't develop an infection and recover well, he'll owe us. We should work on that.'

'Let's get in there and show him how dedicated we are,' Declan said, turning to go back into the tent.

*Holly: May 2014*

Mummy's gone to a dinner party. She was going to wear her navy dress, but Jools made her get changed. She said Mummy had to stop looking so dull all the time and ordered her to put on her lovely red dress. Jools wanted Mummy to wear red lipstick too, but Mummy put her foot down. She said it would be 'too much'. But she did look pretty.

She was listening to music while she was getting ready. Not sad music, like she normally does, but happy music, like she used to when she and Daddy were getting ready to go to a party. She was listening to Madonna's 'Into The Groove', which she always used to play before Daddy died. Daddy used to joke that it was a cheesy song, but he always smiled when Mummy danced around to it. They used to dance to it together and do silly moves to make me and Jools laugh.

Jools says Madonna is 'really lame' and a 'saddo' because she tries to be cool when she's just an old woman who should put some clothes on and stop trying to bend her legs over her head.

Jools came into my room and sat beside me on my bed, listening to Mummy singing along to the song. She squeezed my hand. 'She seems almost happy,' she whispered.

'It's lovely to hear her singing,' I said, almost afraid to break the spell. 'Well done for making her wear the red one.'

'She needs to go out and have fun. I know we think she's really old, but she isn't. Chloë's mum is fifty and she's getting married again.'

My stomach did a flip when Jools said that. I don't want Mummy to get married to another man. That would be so weird and awful and . . . well . . . wrong.

Jools looked at me. 'Don't get all freaked out. Mum's not going to marry anyone, but she might meet someone else. She's not bad-looking and she's nice when she wants to be. Besides, it's lonely for her, Holly. She's always on her own.'

'But she's got us.'

'We'll be gone soon and she'll be alone in the house.'

'I won't leave her. I'll stay here and look after her.'

'Holly, you're going to get a scholarship to some amazing university full of geeks. You'll fit right in and be so happy with all your nerd friends that you won't want to come home. You'll want to read boring books and discuss the meaning of poems until the sun comes up, while normal students are getting drunk and shagging. Anyway, Mum would never let you stay with her. She'll want you to go and live your life.'

'I just don't want her to stop loving Daddy.'

'She won't. But it's selfish of you to want her never to have a life or meet another man.'

'I'm not selfish, Jools, I just don't want anyone trying to replace Daddy. He's irreplaceable.'

'Nobody will ever replace him,' Jools said fiercely. 'No one. But I don't want Mum to end up on her own for the rest of her life either.'

Jools is right, but I can't bear the idea of another man sleeping in Mummy's bed where Daddy used to be. It makes me feel sick.

After Mummy went out, Jools went into her bedroom to get ready. She was going to a party at Lance's house. Kevin was coming to be with me and make sure Jools came home at midnight.

I asked if I could sit in her room while she got ready. She

was excited about the party and in a good mood, so she said yes. She took her clothes into her little bathroom to get changed but she didn't close the door fully and I saw her in the mirror.

I screamed. Her stomach was covered with cuts.

Jools spun around. 'Shit!'

'Oh, my God, Jools, what are you doing? You told me you'd stopped.'

Jools pulled a long-sleeved top over her head and came to sit beside me. 'Calm down.'

'Why are you doing it? You're going to die,' I said, and I started crying. I couldn't help it. 'You promised you'd stop.'

Jools hugged her stomach. 'I'm trying to. I really am. I had stopped, but then I just had a day where I really missed Dad and I cut again. I've had a bad few weeks. But I'm going to stop. I promise.'

After the first time I'd found her cutting, I Googled it to try to understand. It's called self-harming and the people who do it said that it made them feel better. They said it was like letting out all the bottled-up feelings: each time they cut their bodies, they felt like they were in control again.

'I tried it,' I said, showing her the small, faded scar on my arm.

'What?' Jools spun around to face me.

'I wanted to see if it made me feel better, but it hurt and I still felt sad.'

Jools's face was bright red. 'Don't you ever do that again. You're an idiot for trying it.'

'What about you?' I shouted. 'You're doing it all the time.'

'I *am* an idiot. Remember? I'm the stupid one, the thick one. I do dumb things all the time.'

'You're not stupid, but cutting yourself is. Jools, if you don't stop, I'm telling Mummy.'

Jools put her face close to mine. 'Don't even think about it. I will kill you if you tell her. You'll just upset her. I'm going to stop.'

'You have to, Jools. You're ruining yourself and your beautiful skin. What if you cut too deep and die? I can't bear it.' Now I was crying hard. Jools leant over, hugged me and promised over and over again to stop.

I'm not sure if I believe her, but I'm going to keep a close watch.

Jools put on a very short mini and sky-high heels. She looked so gorgeous. Everyone in school fancies Jools, except Lance. He's totally in love with his girlfriend, Hayley. I know Jools likes Lance, but she pretends she doesn't. Jools hates Hayley for two reasons: first, because she's a do-gooder, and second, because she's really smart.

Kevin arrived and came upstairs to join us. He sat beside me on the bed. He knew about Lance and Hayley, but he didn't know about the self-harm. 'So, will Hayley be there tonight?' he asked Jools, as he winked at me.

'Yes, but she's going to be late because she's giving hot soup to the homeless or something. She's such a pain.'

'What a bitch! Imagine – feeding homeless people.' Kevin grinned.

Jools turned around, waving her mascara. 'She's trying to be some kind of modern-day saint. I mean, who's she kidding? Those people do not want some crappy watery soup. They'd much rather a burger or a stew or something that'll actually fill them up.'

'They'd be happy with any food. They're homeless, Jools,' I pointed out.

'I wouldn't eat vegetable soup if you paid me. I'd rather starve. Besides, Hayley is such a Debbie Downer – she's always talking about these homeless people and how they used to live in normal houses but then they lost their job or whatever and they ended up under a bridge. She loves making everyone feel really depressed.'

'Lance obviously likes her charitable side.' Kevin loved winding Jools up.

Jools frowned. 'Lance just has a big heart. He really wanted to have a fun party, but Hayley made him feel guilty so now we all have to give money tonight – there's going to be a collection box for the homeless in the hall.'

'I think that's lovely,' I said.

'You would!' Jools said. 'Why can't she just go and be a do-gooder nun and join one of those convents where you can't speak? She thinks she's like Mother What'shername anyway. You know, the little wrinkly dwarf woman who went around India in a tea towel.'

'Oh, my God, do you mean Mother Teresa?' Mother Teresa is one of my absolute heroines. 'She was a saint.'

'Whatever. At least she didn't hog the captain of the rugby team. At least she went off to India and did her holy stuff by herself. I wish Hayley would bugger off somewhere far away and feed those people her rotten soup.'

'You've such a big heart,' Kevin said, and he was laughing. It was funny.

'Holy Joes should not go out with hot rugby guys. They should either be married to their job or married to another do-gooder who wears socks and sandals and wants to talk about misery and death and hunger all the time. Lance is far too cool for her.'

'Maybe you should go with her on a soup run. You might actually like it. Giving back to people can be very fulfilling,' Kevin suggested, and winked at me again.

Jools stared at him. 'What would you know? You're not exactly saving lives.'

'Actually, I help your mother help sick people. So, in a way, I do charity work every day.'

'I don't mean to be harsh, Kevin, but it's a bit different from going around feeding starving people,' I pointed out.

Kevin bristled. 'Whose side are you on, Holly?'

Jools clipped in her hair extensions. 'The point is, Hayley is a bore and I'm fabulous, and I just don't understand why Lance doesn't see it.'

Kevin sighed loudly. 'Welcome to the world of unrequited love.'

'Did you and Axel break up?' I asked.

'No, but David Gandy will never be mine.'

'Who's he?'

Jools groaned. 'Seriously, Holly, stop reading boring books about the olden days. David Gandy is the hottest model ever.'

Kevin nodded. '*Soooooo* very hot.'

'Yes, but, Kevin, he's out of your league and he's straight. Lance is not out of my league. To be honest, he should be chasing me. I'm going to get to the party early while Mother Tessa —'

'Mother Teresa,' I said.

'Whatever. I'm going to get there early so I can work on him while Hayley is feeding everyone who lives under a bridge.'

I felt bad for Hayley. She was a good person and Jools wanted to steal her boyfriend.

'Why don't you go for someone who doesn't have a girl-friend?' I asked her.

Kevin patted my hand. 'Because we all want what we can't have. Forbidden fruit and all that.'

He had a point. I wanted Daddy back and that was never going to happen.

## *Alice: May 2014*

Pippa came into the hall, then flung open her arms to embrace Alice. 'Darling, I'm so glad you came. And you look gorgeous, like your old self. Getting out a bit more suits you.'

'Thanks, I almost didn't come.' Alice smiled, trying to hide how nervous she still was. Since Ben had died, she'd only been out with Pippa and David on their own, not to a dinner party with other people.

Pippa handed her a glass of champagne. 'Drink that. It'll help with your nerves. Now, as I said to you on the phone, it's just six friends for dinner. No pressure and no fuss.'

Alice knocked back the champagne. David came out to them, carrying another glass.

'Ah, I see Pippa's ahead of me. Here, you might need another.' David handed Alice the glass and kissed her warmly on the cheek. 'I know it's difficult for you, but we're so glad you came. It is important for you to get out a bit and . . . well . . .'

'Move on?'

'No!' David was flustered. 'I don't mean that . . . I just want to make sure you're all right and I . . . Well, I can only imagine how difficult it is for you and the girls. I miss Ben awfully myself.' He looked down at his shoes.

Alice put the two glasses on the side-table and hugged him.

'Stop it.' Pippa flapped about beside them. 'No tears

tonight. For goodness' sake, David, we're supposed to be cheering Alice up.'

'Sorry.' David wiped his eyes while Pippa dabbed delicately at Alice's with a tissue, making sure not to ruin her make-up.

'There,' she said. 'Now, you two, no more crying. Deep breaths.'

David smiled at his wife and regained his composure. 'Has Pippa told you who's here? It's just us, you, of course, my sister Ruby, her husband Norman and our neighbour, Dan.'

'Dan?' Alice frowned. 'Oh, God, is this a blind date? Are you setting me up? Guys, come on!'

'No!' David assured her.

'Absolutely not, darling,' Pippa said. 'Dan moved in next door a few months ago. He seems awfully nice. He's a self-made chap, very dynamic, very successful and good fun. We wanted to invite him and thought it would be a good way to make up numbers.'

'And you're sitting beside me so I'll look after you,' David said, leading Alice into the vast drawing room.

Alice was introduced and gave Dan a cursory glance. She was embarrassed and annoyed. She didn't want to be partnered with someone, even if it was just to 'make up numbers'. What the hell was wrong with uneven numbers anyway? Why did people always feel they had to have a round number at dinner parties?

They sat down and David was wonderful, keeping the conversation going and being incredibly attentive to Alice. After the starter and a large glass of white wine, she began to relax. Dan had been talking to Ruby most of the time and it was only when the main course arrived that he turned to Alice.

'So, what's your story then, Alice?' he asked, his eyes smiling at her.

Alice felt David freeze beside her. 'Well, my husband got blown up by a landmine in Eritrea eighteen months ago. So I'm a widow with two daughters. That's my story.'

Dan didn't flinch. He looked directly into her eyes. Alice noticed how blue they were. 'Well, that makes an interesting change from "I'm a lawyer" or "I'm an accountant."'

Alice laughed. She hadn't meant to, but it was the way he said it. He was so relaxed, not awkward at all. She'd expected him to blush or stutter or apologize or just be mortified, but he wasn't and she liked it. It was refreshing. 'What about you, Dan?'

'My wife left ten years ago and moved to Argentina with her tennis coach. I've got one daughter who's twenty-three.'

'Did she take your daughter with her?'

Dan's jaw set. 'No, just a lot of my money.'

'Gosh, that's cold.'

Dan grinned. 'I can think of a lot of other ways to describe it, but cold is more polite.'

Alice decided to be direct too. 'Did you ever meet anyone else?'

A slow smile spread across Dan's face. 'Oh, a few, but none that I became attached to.'

Alice felt something in her stomach. A flutter? A twitter? Some kind of movement that she hadn't felt in a long time. She smiled back at Dan. She liked him. She liked his honesty. She liked his eyes and she liked his smile too. 'Do you think you're too choosy?' she asked.

'No. I'm old enough to know what I like and young enough not to settle for second best.'

Alice laughed. 'I like that.'

'So what do you do when you're not being a mum?'

'I'm a GP.'

Dan raised an eyebrow. 'Good-looking and smart. I like that.'

'You?'

'I'm in property.'

'Sounds vague.'

'I buy rundown buildings – hotels, office blocks, that kind of thing – do them up and sell them on.'

'Do you buy all over the world or just the UK?'

'All over. I've just bought an apartment block in New York. How do you manage to juggle work and be Mum?'

Alice was surprised by this. No man had ever asked her how she did it all. 'I just do. I don't know if I'm doing a very good job, I just muddle through each day, I guess.'

'I remember when my wife left, how difficult it was trying to keep my eye on Stella and work. It's not easy. I admire you.'

Alice was warming to Dan. He got it. 'I admire you too. Being a single dad can't be easy.'

'I got lucky with Stella. She's fantastic.'

'I hope my girls turn out all right. It's been hard on them.'

Dan lowered his voice. 'It's hard on you too. How are you doing?'

Alice felt comfortable with him. His wife had left him alone with a child. He knew what it was like. She didn't pretend. 'I have good days and bad days. More good than bad now, thank God. The girls are still shattered, but they've definitely been less fragile in the last few months.'

'Don't worry. They'll be okay. Kids are amazingly resilient. Stella went a bit wobbly at first, but then she got through it and she's really great now.'

'What does she do?'

'She works in an art gallery. She was never very good at school – then again, neither was I. But she's doing well and enjoying it.'

Alice nodded. 'That's all I want, for the girls to be happy. Jools, my seventeen-year-old, isn't academic and I do worry about her.'

'What's she good at? What does she like doing?'

'She's obsessed with art and fashion.'

'Then send her to art college or help her get a job in the art world. Parents get obsessed with their kids going to university. You have to let them follow their passions, or they'll be miserable. Stella wasn't cut out for the academic life, so I let that ambition go and we talked about what she'd be happy to get up and do every day. Turns out it's being around artists and art exhibitions. And she's bloody good at it too, so it was definitely the best choice.'

Alice thought this over. It was true that she and Ben had always wanted the girls to go to university. It was their dream for them. But it wasn't Jools's dream. Dan was right: happiness should come first. Maybe Jools should go to art college and follow her passion.

Alice smiled. 'She picked out my outfit tonight.'

Dan drank Alice in with his eyes. 'She has very good taste.'

They were interrupted by Norman asking Dan about a big new hotel his company had just bought in central London. Dan told them about his plans for the revamp and Alice sat back watching him. He was very animated when he talked about work, full of energy and life. Alice felt more alive just by sitting close to him.

When they were having coffee, Dan leant in towards her. 'Do you do many house calls as a GP?' he asked.

'Not many, but some.'

'If I called and asked you to come to my house because I had a very serious issue, would you come?' He smiled.

'Probably not.'

'Why?'

'Too soon.'

Dan shook his head. 'It's all about baby steps, Alice. I remember from my own experience that everything seems very daunting, but once you dip your toe in the water, it's less so.'

'Coming out tonight was a big step for me.'

'How's it going?'

Alice smiled. 'Pretty well, actually.'

'So how about another step. How about coffee?'

Alice paused. She liked him. He was nice and he knew what it was like to lose someone you love. He wasn't pushy, just encouraging. She felt safe with him. It was strange: she didn't know him but she felt very comfortable in his company. And, if she was being honest, she found him very attractive.

'I'll throw in a muffin too,' he said with a smile.

'Okay.'

'Where do you work?'

'West Kensington.'

'How about tomorrow, at one, the Royal George Hotel?'

Alice felt a bit flustered. Tomorrow? It was a bit soon.

Dan placed his hand gently on her arm. 'If we don't make an arrangement to meet now, you'll start to overthink it and say no. It's just a coffee, Alice.'

Alice took a deep breath and said, 'Tomorrow at one.'

The next day, Kevin commented on what she was wearing. She'd got changed three times and opted for a plain black dress with a chunky necklace and very high heels that flattered her legs. 'You look nice. I haven't seen you wear heels in ages. How was last night?'

'Fine, nothing special,' Alice said, keen to avoid a

conversation about it. She didn't want to admit she was going for coffee with a strange man. She was hassled about it and had decided to cancel when she woke up, but she didn't have Dan's number and she didn't want to have to call Pippa for it because then it would become a 'thing'. And it most certainly was not a 'thing'. She'd just go and meet him, stay for ten minutes and make it clear she wasn't ready for any of this. It was too soon. It felt wrong. She felt guilty but also, surprisingly, excited and nervous. No, it was too soon. She was being silly. She was just flattered by the attention. She'd go because it was rude not to turn up, but that was it.

The ten-minute walk from the surgery to the hotel felt like ten hours. Alice dragged her feet and kept berating herself for having agreed to it at all. Her shoes hurt and her feet throbbed. By the time she turned the corner to the hotel, she was in a grump. This whole thing was ridiculous.

But when she reached the hotel, the uniformed doorman opened the door for her and she was immediately greeted by the manager. 'Dr Gregory?' he asked. 'Mr Penfold is waiting for you in the morning room. Please follow me.'

Alice was taken aback. Forgetting her sore feet, she followed the manager through the marble foyer into a lovely bright room, tastefully decorated in pale blue and cream. Dan was standing at the window, talking on his phone. He turned to her and mouthed, 'Sorry!'

The manager led Alice to a table that was set for two with lunch. In fact, it looked like lunch for a small army – there was a large variety of dishes, more than the two of them could possibly eat.

As Dan wrapped up his phone call, Alice studied him. He was attractive in a rugged, sexy kind of way. Very different from Ben's tall, handsome good looks. Dan was smaller, stockier, but very fit and healthy-looking. His hair was grey but cut into a short manly style. Just as she remembered from the night before, he radiated energy and dynamism.

He snapped his phone shut and walked over to her, kissing her gently on the cheek. 'I'm sorry about that. One of our hotels had a flood and the manager is not handling it well. How are you?'

Alice had been so distracted by the food, the setting and Dan that she'd forgotten her nerves. 'I'm fine, thank you, but we seem to have very different definitions of coffee.'

Dan grinned. 'I didn't know what you liked, so I ordered plenty.'

'I take it this is one of your hotels?'

'Yes. Do you like it?'

'It's lovely. I've passed it lots of times but there was always scaffolding up. Have you just finished doing it up?'

'Three weeks ago,' Dan said proudly.

'You've done a wonderful job. It was very rundown before and now it's stunning.'

'Thank you, I'm really glad you like it.'

Dan sat down beside Alice and poured her some water. It was nice. It was comfortable. Alice smiled inwardly. She felt like an individual for the first time in so long. She wasn't a mum or a doctor – worrying about the girls, work, finances, timetables or patients – she was a woman being spoilt by a man, and it felt really, really nice.

Dan was in the middle of telling Alice about his hilarious childhood growing up in the East End when her phone rang. It was Kevin.

'Where are you? It's two thirty. There are three patients waiting for you.'

'Oh, my God!' Alice looked at her watch. 'I'm on my way.'

She stood up and grabbed her coat and bag. 'I have to run. I had no idea it was so late. I was . . . I was . . .'

'Having a good time?' Dan suggested, helping her into her coat.

Alice smiled. 'Yes. I was having a lovely time. Thank you.'

'It was my pleasure. I had a nice time too. Lenny, my driver, will run you back to your surgery.'

'No, it's fine.'

Dan put his hands on her shoulders and leant in from behind. 'I insist. I kept you here so it's my fault you're late.'

Alice could smell his aftershave and felt the slight stubble of his chin on her cheek and his breath in her ear. Her heart began to race. She felt her body coming back to life. She bent her head to stop Dan seeing her blush. She felt like a teenager. It was so silly . . . and yet very real.

Dan led her out of a side door, where a black Mercedes with tinted windows and a uniformed driver were waiting. He kissed her cheek. 'I really enjoyed today. May I call you?'

Alice was going to say no – it was too soon – but she stopped herself. She wanted to see Dan again. She had really enjoyed being with him. It was fun and kind of exciting. It was lovely to be treated and looked after. She'd been drowning under responsibility and decision-making for so long.

She kissed his cheek and whispered, 'Yes.'

*Ben: June 2014*

Declan wiped the sweat from Ben's face with a cool cloth. He gently lifted his head and tried to get him to drink some water, but Ben retched and spat it out.

'Come on, Ben, you have to drink a little,' Declan pleaded.

'I'm trying but I just – Oh, *nooo.*' Ben tried to hobble to the corner of the tent but the chain prevented him. He grabbed a bowl, closing his eyes with shame and mortification, and crouched over it, his insides falling into it. 'I'm sorry, mate,' he said. 'It's out of my control.' Sweat was pouring down his face.

Declan patted him on the back. 'It's nothing. Let me deal with it.'

Declan took the stinking bowl and shouted for the guard, Nebay, who flung back the tent flap and glared at them. Declan shoved the putrid bowl in his face. 'We need to be unchained. Ben has to get outside to shit and I need to get fluids to hydrate him.'

Nebay shouted, 'No outside.'

'He's sick, you stupid dickhead. I need to get medicine.' Declan pointed to the tent where they operated and kept the medicine.

'No outside.' Nebay cocked his gun and pointed it at Declan.

Declan gestured at the bowl. 'What the hell am I supposed to do with this?'

'You stay.'

'I want to speak to Awate,' Declan said.

They heard a shuffling and Eyob appeared at the door. Taking in the scene, he shook his head. 'Awate is sleeping. You stay here.'

'For Christ's sake, he's sick, Eyob. He's sick – he can't shit in here all night.'

Eyob shrugged. 'You shut up. You no shout me.'

'For God's sake,' Declan said, losing his temper. 'You can't treat Ben like this after all he's done for you lot and your families.'

'You shut up!' Eyob shoved his gun into Declan's face.

'Stop, please. Stop,' Ben croaked.

Declan was shaking with rage and Ben was terrified he was going to attack Eyob. 'Declan, it's okay.'

'No, it fucking isn't.' Declan's eyes glistened with tears. 'They can't treat you like this.'

'You can go, Eyob, it's fine,' Ben said.

'You shut up now,' Eyob warned Declan, and retreated from the stench of the tent.

'Bastards,' Declan spat.

'It's okay, don't get . . . Ooooh . . .' Ben soiled himself.

Declan cleaned him up, using the water jug they had and a T-shirt.

'I'm so sorry. This is above and beyond,' Ben said, as sweat dripped down his face and body.

Declan rolled him onto the clean side of the mattress. 'Hey, I've seen a lot worse than this.'

'It's humiliating,' Ben said.

'They're treating you like an animal and I'm going to see Awate tomorrow, Ben. This is not okay.'

'No, it really isn't. You're right, we have to make a stand. Oh, God . . .'

Ben was ill all night, and by the next morning they had no

206

clean clothes, both mattresses were badly soiled and the tent stank.

When Yonas came to unchain them and bring them their breakfast, he was shocked by what he found. Declan filled him in as best he could and Yonas helped Declan to carry Ben to the operating tent. Ben was weak and had a high temperature.

Declan washed him properly and set him down on a clean sheet with a large bucket by his side. He tried to get him to drink some water but, again, Ben couldn't hold anything down.

Declan stayed by his side, cleaning him up and changing his sheet every few hours. Ben was getting weaker by the minute.

'If the surgery doesn't work out, you'd make a damn good nurse,' Ben muttered.

'I wiped an arse or two in my early days, but yours is an ugly sight.'

'At least it's not hairy like yours.'

'I've had no complaints about my arse.'

'Alice always said she liked mine. She said it was pert.'

'Alice needs to go to Specsavers.'

'Alice has impeccable taste.'

'I can't wait to meet Alice and compare notes on sharing a room with you.'

'You'll love her, she's –'

'Gorgeous, smart, funny, kind and thoughtful. Yeah, I know, you've only told me a trillion times.'

Ben smiled weakly. 'She really is.'

'I know, Benji, I know. Now come on, try to drink a little water.'

Once again, Ben retched.

'When you get over this, we're going to need to fatten you up. From now on I'm telling Awate we need meat. Feck the vegetarian shit. The soldiers all get meat but we don't. It's bullshit. We need a better diet.'

'Stop talking about food.' Ben clutched his stomach, was sick again and then fell into a fitful sleep.

When Ben woke up, Segen was kneeling beside him, mopping the sweat from his brow. Unable to speak English, she smiled at him and patted his head. Yonas sat on his other side, clearly concerned.

Ben smiled at her and said, 'Thank you.' As another crippling cramp overcame him, Declan stormed into the tent, followed by Awate.

Segen and Yonas jumped up as their leader stood over Ben, examining him with his eyes.

'You can see he's in a bad way and I want to hook him up to a saline drip,' Declan said.

'We don't have much left. I need it for the soldiers. We will wait until tomorrow and see how he is. Ben is a strong man. He will fight this, I am sure.' Leaning down towards Ben, he said, 'You will be okay, Ben.'

'He's not a strong man. He's a weakened man because of the shit food you give us. We've both lost tons of weight, and if you want us to continue saving your soldiers' lives, you need to feed us properly.'

'You are treated well here,' Awate snapped. 'You should not complain.'

'Fine, but if we faint during a surgery, don't blame us, blame the fucking lentils,' Declan retorted angrily.

Ben raised his hand to calm Declan down.

'Ben will be okay,' Awate repeated.

'He'd better be, because if anything happens to him, I'll kill you.'

Awate glared at him. 'You should be careful, Mr Irish. Threatening me is a very dangerous thing to do.'

'He's had no sleep, Awate. He's stressed and tired. Let it go,' Ben said. 'Now can you all please stop talking? I need some rest.'

Five days later, Ben was still barely able to hold down water and was very weak. Declan never left his side. Ben woke up one night to find Declan kneeling beside him, whispering, 'When I despair, I remember that all through history the way of truth and love has always won. There have been tyrants and murderers, and for a time, they can seem invincible, but in the end, they always fall, always.'

Ben smiled. 'That's very powerful.'

Declan looked up, surprised. 'I thought you were asleep.'

'Is it Gandhi?'

'Yes. My da used to quote it all the time. Whenever anything bad happened, which was quite often in our house, Da would sit us down and make us say it.'

'He sounds like an amazing man. I'm looking forward to having a pint with him in Dublin.'

Declan looked at his friend. Ben's cheekbones now jutted out through his emaciated face. Declan began to cry.

'Hey, it's going to be okay. Come on now.'

'Just get better, you bastard. You are not leaving me alone with these freaks.'

'If anything does happen, you make sure you get out of here alive. I want Alice and the girls to get my letters. You know where they're hidden. Promise me, Declan?' Ben tried to lift his head, but he was too weak.

'I promise. Now shut up and drink some water.'

Ben tried, but once again his stomach heaved and he vomited instantly.

Declan wiped Ben's brow with a cool cloth and held his hand as Ben drifted into fitful sleep.

## Holly: June 2014

Mummy has a boyfriend. I feel very strange about it. I'm happy for her, but I'm also really sad. His name is Dan and she's been out with him four times. She hasn't said much about him, but she seems much happier already.

Jools decided to ask her about him because she wanted to know what was going on. We both do. Jools is calmer about it than me. She says Mummy deserves to have a life, but I'm scared she'll forget Daddy. Jools said I'm being ridiculous, but she looked sad when I said it.

When Mummy came home after she'd been to the cinema with Dan, we were still up, chatting to Kevin. 'How was your date, Mum?' Jools asked.

'Fine, thanks.' She looked away.

'When are we going to meet him?' Jools wanted to know.

'Well . . . I . . .' Mummy looked at me and I tried really hard not to go all red, but I couldn't help it.

'I want you to be happy, Mummy. Really I do.' But my voice was a bit wobbly.

Mummy came over to me and pulled me into a hug. I hugged her back.

'I'll always, always, always love your dad. He was the best man in the world and he gave me you two.'

I felt calmer then because I knew she wasn't forgetting him.

'Kevin said that Dan is super-rich and lives in a mansion in Holland Park,' Jools said.

Mummy glared at Kevin. 'Did he? Well, none of that matters. Dan is a nice, kind person and that's what's important.'

'Does he know you have two fabulous daughters?' Jools asked.

'Of course he does. I talk about you all the time. You're my pride and joy.'

'Don't talk about them too much – you don't want to scare him off.' Kevin winked at us.

'Actually, Dan has a daughter too, Stella. She's twenty-three.'

'Is he, like, really old?' Jools asked.

'He's fifty-two.' I could see Mummy felt a bit strange talking about him. She was sort of wriggling about in her chair.

Kevin said it was time for him to go, and I heard Mummy scolding him in the hall. 'Why on earth did you tell them Dan was rich? I don't want them to know anything about him. We've only been out four times.'

'The girls aren't stupid, Alice. They can see that you're happier. They're worried about it. They need you to talk to them. Did you see Holly's face when you reassured her that you'd never forget Ben? She almost passed out with relief. She was scared that Dan was going to take his place or something.'

'But it's only been four dates!'

'I know, but for them it's not about Dan or how many times you've gone out with him. It's that they can see you're moving on with your life. You're coming out of your limbo and moving forward. It's frightening for them – they're worried that you're moving on from their dad too.'

Mummy's voice got all shaky and she said, 'How can I forget Ben? Jesus, Kevin, he was my whole life. I've been to Hell and back. I'm just having fun and Dan is . . . He's lovely and he treats me so well and he's so nice to me and I like it. I like feeling like a person again and I like feeling alive again. But I'll dump him tomorrow if the girls want me to. I'd never go out with someone if it made them unhappy. Never.'

'Hey, now, calm down. They just needed you to talk about it and tell them that you'd never forget Ben, which you did. It was all you needed to say. It's fine, Alice.'

'I'd never put a man before my girls. You know that, Kevin. Do you really think it's okay? The girls are my priority, nothing and no one else.'

Jools pushed past me and walked out to the hall. 'Mum, stop freaking out. We're fine. We want you to have a life. We know you love Dad and us, but sitting around being sad all the time isn't good for you. Go out with Dan – seriously, go for it.'

'You weren't supposed to hear this conversation but thank you, darling.' Mummy hugged Jools, then saw me over her shoulder. 'Are you really okay about this, Holly? I don't ever have to see him again if you're not. Your happiness is all I care about.'

I went over and put my arms around Mummy and Jools. 'I am, Mummy, I promise. I know Daddy will always be here.' I pointed to her heart and Mummy blinked back tears.

## Alice: July 2014

Dan wanted to meet the girls, and Alice agreed so he wouldn't seem like some big shadow looming at the edge of their lives. She checked with the girls first, then accepted his invitation to lunch. She felt it would be easier if the meeting took place somewhere else. She didn't want to bring Dan into their home just yet. She worried that if he called round, the girls might feel more pressure to like him. This way, they could get to know him on neutral territory. It was still very early in the relationship and Alice didn't want them to think things were serious. They weren't serious – they hadn't even had sex yet. She kept putting it off.

But they had kissed, and it had been wonderful. After their fourth date, outside the cinema, she'd been talking about the movie when Dan had just leant in and kissed her. Alice had felt her whole body melt. She didn't want the kiss to end. They stood on Kensington High Street, in front of all the people leaving the cinema, and snogged like teenagers.

When Alice had eventually pulled back, Dan had groaned. 'Don't stop.'

Alice giggled. 'I need air. I can only breathe through my nose for so long.'

Dan pulled her in and buried his face in her hair. 'Please tell me you're coming back to my place for some really great sex.'

Alice shook her head. She wasn't ready for sex. Her body

was – in fact, her body was screaming out for sex with Dan right now. But her mind wasn't. She kept thinking about Ben. How could she have sex with someone else? What about Ben? Yes, he was dead, but still . . . It would feel wrong, weird, guilty.

Besides, she was scared. She hadn't had sex with another man for so many years. What if she was bad at it? Sex with Ben had always been good. Their bodies knew each other – they knew how to turn each other on. What if she was terrible at it with Dan?

'Is there any point in me begging?' Dan asked.

'Sorry, just not ready yet,' Alice muttered into his shoulder.

Dan pulled her head back gently and looked into her eyes. 'Hey, it's all right, I understand. Can I kiss you again, though?'

Alice put her hands up and pulled him in for another long, sensual kiss.

Kevin called in an hour before the lunch with Dan to help calm everyone's nerves. Nora was busy cleaning the kitchen, and when Kevin walked in, she pointed to the ceiling and said, 'That one's up to ninety about the big introduction. You'd better go up there and work your magic on her.'

Kevin grinned. 'Well, isn't it great she's met someone?'

'I'm happy for her – sure it's lovely to see her smile again. I just hope he's a good man. She'll be hard pressed to find someone as good as Ben. He was a true gentleman.'

'You're right, Nora,' Kevin said. 'But Dan seems nice, and so far it's going well.'

'Sure it's early days. You can't know a fella this quick.'

'True. How are the girls?'

'Grand. Holly seems a bit worried but sure that poor child would worry about the grass growing. Poor little mite. I told her it was only a bit of lunch and she wasn't to be getting herself into a knot about it.'

'You always know the right thing to say. You've been so great through all this.'

Nora blushed and wagged a finger at him. 'Now don't you go using your flattery on me. I have the measure of you.'

Kevin laughed. 'Better than anyone, Nora.'

Nora looked around quickly to check no one was coming, then went over to her handbag and took out a Sunday supplement.

'What's this?' Kevin said, curious.

'I saw it in my local café and put it in my bag,' she said quietly. 'Look! It's the multi-millionaire himself, in all his glory.'

Kevin grabbed the magazine. 'Wow, a profile on Dan.' He scanned through it quickly. 'Anything interesting?'

'Self-made, wife ditched him for her tennis coach, one kid and a lot of jetting about the world buying things. Needs a good woman to make him settle down, I'd say.'

Kevin smiled. Nora was always hard to impress.

'Mind you, I wouldn't want to get on the wrong side of him,' she added. 'Sounds like he's got to where he is by being a bit cut-throat when he needed to be.'

'Really?' Kevin was intrigued. 'Well, I suppose you don't make it in business like he has without breaking a few rules.'

'Exactly,' Nora said. 'I just hope he's not going to hurt our Alice. If he does, he'll have me to answer to.'

'We'll keep an eye on her. Will you leave the article here so I can read it when they're gone?' Kevin said.

Nora nodded. 'You get her out the door and then we'll have a nice cup of tea and a good read.'

'You're on,' Kevin said, then headed upstairs to see how Alice was getting on.

Alice, as Nora had said, was wound up and stressed out at the thought of the two families meeting. Kevin sat on the edge of the bath, trying to calm her down.

'What if they hate him?' she asked, for the tenth time.

Kevin sighed. 'They won't. You said he's a great guy.'

Alice wiped her lipstick off and rummaged around in her bag for a different colour. 'He is great, but he's not Ben.'

'The girls know that, Alice. They're not stupid.'

Alice smacked her lips together, then wiped off the second lipstick. 'I'm just worried. It seems too soon. We've only been seeing each other for six weeks.'

'The girls can see that he means something to you. It's obvious, Alice. You're all glowy and skittish.'

'Skittish?'

'Yes. You're constantly smiling, full of fun and just happy. Even the patients have noticed. You're like the old Alice and we're all glad for you.'

Alice turned to face him. Twisting a tissue between her hands, she said, 'I'm beginning to feel like the old me again and it's really nice, but every time I catch myself being happy, I feel guilty.'

Kevin stood up and went over to her. 'Alice, you deserve to be happy. No one wants you to be sad for the next forty years. The girls want you to be happy too. Stop feeling guilty and enjoy it. You've had a rotten time so embrace the good stuff when it happens.'

'Do you really think the girls are okay about meeting Dan?'

'Yes! They want to and it'll stop it being this big deal. It'll normalize things. They just need to see that he's nice and that he's not trying to take you away or replace their dad.'

'He'll never replace Ben. Nor would he want to. Dan understands what it's like to lose someone. I think he'll be good with the girls because he has a daughter he adores.' Alice tied her hair up, then took it down again. 'God, I hope they like him.'

'I'm sure they will. What's not to like? He's a multi-millionaire who seems to be obsessed with you, judging by the amount of calls you get every day and the gigantic bouquets of flowers that are constantly being delivered to the surgery.'

Alice smiled. 'Dan does everything in super-size. Even the restaurant today – it's really upmarket. I asked him to book somewhere casual, but he insisted that we go to La Gourmande. He wants to treat us all. He's very generous.'

'So kick back and enjoy letting someone look after you.'

'I find it hard to let go. I'm so used to doing everything that it seems strange not to have to make decisions. I'm turning into a control freak – I was actually a bit annoyed that he ignored my advice about going casual. But I must say, it is nice to have someone doing lovely things for you.'

'It sounds like Heaven. I wish Axel was more like Dan. I'd love to be taken care of. His father has cut his allowance off, so now I'm supporting him. I've realized he's actually lazy and has no interest in getting a real job. He just wants to do endless courses and keeps coming up with ridiculous new careers he wants to try. He came home last night and announced he wants to be a fitness instructor. The guy is so lazy, he barely gets out of bed.'

'Maybe it's time to have "the talk",' Alice suggested. Kevin had been giving out about Axel daily for the last three months. Their relationship was clearly over and Alice was glad. Axel wasn't good enough for Kevin. Her brother deserved better. She desperately wanted him to meet a good man who would really love him and be there for him.

Kevin picked up the nail scissors and trimmed a stray bit

of his designer stubble. 'I know I should break up with him but I don't have the energy. I will soon, though. All we do is argue and sex is non-existent.'

'A bit like me and Dan!' Alice smiled.

'You're going to have to get on your back soon.' Kevin wagged a finger at her. 'A man like Dan isn't going to be happy holding hands and snogging for much longer.'

Alice covered her face with her hands. 'I'm just not there yet. But I do find him very sexy. I actually want to have sex with him, I'm just scared. I haven't had sex with anyone but Ben in so long.'

'Sex is sex. Just get drunk and put that man out of his misery. Don't let him go, Alice. He's been such a positive force in your life. Besides, I've got used to the lovely flowers in the surgery and seeing you smile again.'

Kevin was right. Alice knew he was. It was just a matter of being brave and taking the plunge.

# Holly: July 2014

Mummy was very nervous about us meeting Dan for lunch. She kept saying, 'If you don't like him, I'll never see him again,' and 'He's never going to replace your dad,' and 'He's really just a friend . . .'

Eventually Jools lost her temper and shouted, 'Will you just relax? It'll be fine.'

But, really, we were all nervous – even Jools was jittery. Mummy told us that Dan's daughter, Stella, was coming. Mummy hadn't met Stella before, so I think she was worried about that too.

When we arrived at the restaurant they were waiting for us. I hadn't realized I was holding my breath until Jools nudged me. 'Breathe or you'll pass out.'

I let out a big puff of air.

'He's not nearly as good-looking as Dad,' Jools whispered.

Dan isn't handsome like Daddy. He's smaller, but he does have nice blue eyes.

'Stella looks cool,' she mumbled.

She did, in the kind of way that Jools loves. She had lots of really chunky jewellery and her hair was held up by chopsticks in a messy kind of way.

We all shook hands and a waiter showed us to our table.

'Sorry about the restaurant,' Stella said. She poked her dad playfully in the ribs. 'Dad picked it. I told him it was far too stuffy. We should have gone somewhere with a bit more atmosphere.'

Dan held up his hands and smiled. 'Guilty as charged. Sorry, girls, I wanted to book somewhere nice, but Stella says I got it all wrong.'

'Have you eaten at the Shark's Fin?' Stella asked Jools and me.

'No, but I really want to. Is it amazing?' Jools asked.

'It's the best sushi in London. You have to go – you'll love it. My friend is the manager, I can get you a table, if you like.'

'Cool.' Jools's eyes were really wide and she was smiling.

Stella and Jools chatted all the time. We sat at a round table. Stella was between me and Jools. 'So we girls can chat,' she said. I didn't really know what to say so I just listened.

Stella told Jools all about the art gallery she worked at, then pulled up some photos on her phone of the artists they showcased.

'Call in anytime – you can see whose work we're exhibiting.'

'Seriously?'

'Sure. I'll give you my number so you can just text when you're free.'

'Wow, thanks.'

I think Jools was a bit in love with Stella. I liked her too – she was really warm and friendly – but I was distracted by the way Dan was looking at Mummy. You could see he really liked her. His eyes were all gooey when he talked to her.

Mummy wasn't relaxed – she was really jumpy and knocked over a glass of water. I watched as Dan put his hand on Mummy's and whispered, 'Alice, darling, it's okay.'

I felt a bit hot and sick when he called her 'darling'. It just felt strange to hear another man call her that. Jools's hand squeezed mine under the table. I felt better then, calmer.

Dan was very friendly. He asked me and Jools about school and what we wanted to do when we left. I said I wanted to be a surgeon like Daddy and everyone went very still. But Dan just smiled and said that that sounded like a great idea: surgeons were very special people.

Jools said she wanted to be an artist. 'I'm sure Mum's told you I'm not very academic, so I don't think university is an option for me.'

'The only thing your mum's told me about you is how proud she is of you,' Dan said.

Jools went a bit red and looked pleased.

'Besides, I wasn't academic either. In fact, I left school when I was sixteen because I failed all of my exams.'

Jools perked up when she heard that. She asked him how he became so rich if he was stupid.

Mummy went all red in the face and said, 'Jools, don't be rude,' but Dan didn't seem to mind. He laughed and said he was a good businessman and that he'd always been good with numbers. He'd left school, got a job, then bought a tiny flat, done it up and sold it for a profit, and that was what he'd been doing ever since.

'And if it makes you feel better, I wasn't great in school either. I could have tried harder, but all I've ever been interested in is art,' Stella said. 'Dad was great. He never pushed me – he always said, "Follow your passion and you'll be successful." I was never good enough to produce my own work, but I enjoy selling other people's. I just love being involved in that whole world.'

'Wow.' Jools looked at Dan. 'That's pretty cool. Did you hear that, Mum?'

Mummy nodded. 'Dan's made me think differently about it. I think he's right, that you should follow your passion. So maybe you should look at going to art college or getting an internship at a gallery.'

Jools almost fell off her chair. 'Really?'

Mummy smiled. 'Yes.'

'You should come and hang out where I work. I'll introduce you to lots of people,' Stella said.

'OMG, this is the best day ever. Thank you!'

Jools was so happy, and I felt really glad for her. I know it bothers her that she's not good in school, but now it looked like she'd be able to do something after she finishes next year that she loves. Dan and Stella were super-nice.

When we were leaving, I saw Mummy reaching for Dan's hand. He turned and kissed her on the lips. I felt a bit funny inside – it was strange to see Mummy kissing a man who wasn't Daddy.

But I liked Dan. He was nice and kind, and he asked me about school and was interested in all of us . . . but most of all in Mummy.

When we got home, Jools Googled him. Until we met him, Mummy had refused to tell us his surname. Kevin had said he was rich, but Jools started screaming when she saw that he had a property portfolio worth £600 million.

I don't care about his money. I just care that he's nice and that he loves Mummy. You can see that he really does. And Mummy is all smiley. It's as if a big weight has been lifted from her. She's funny and relaxed and just . . . well, happy.

## Alice: July 2014

Alice looked at herself in the huge bathroom mirror. Her face was flushed with alcohol and adrenalin. 'You can do this. Just take a deep breath, close your eyes and do it. It's like riding a bike.'

She squeezed a bit of toothpaste onto her index finger and began to haphazardly brush her teeth. She rinsed her mouth, counted to three, turned the big brass lock and opened the door.

Dan was standing, sipping a glass of red wine. He handed Alice a glass.

'Nervous?'

She smiled gratefully for his understanding. 'Very. I feel like a teenager. You'd swear I'd never had sex before.'

'It's not easy after being married to someone for a long time. After my wife left me, it took me almost a year to have sex with someone else. The first time is the hardest. After that it's like –'

'Riding a bike?'

Dan smiled. 'I was going to say it's like a familiar jacket but with new buttons.'

Alice laughed. 'I've never heard it described like that before.'

Dan pressed a remote control and some music came on – 'I Want Your Sex' by George Michael.

'Jesus, Dan, you don't have to spell it out. Subtlety is always a good approach.' Alice giggled.

Dan reddened. 'Sorry.' He pressed a button. 'All I Wanna Do Is Make Love To You' came on.

He pressed it again. 'Tonight's The Night'.

Alice's laughter grew louder.

Dan pressed more buttons. 'Damn. I've no idea how this ridiculously complicated music system works. Stella made a playlist for me. She said I should use it on a night when some-one special came back to the house and I'm afraid I've never tried it before.'

'How long ago did she make it?' Alice asked.

Dan smiled. 'About nine months ago.'

'No one special's been up here in all that time?' Alice raised an eyebrow. She hoped it looked sexy, not squinty.

Dan winked. 'No one . . . special.'

'It feels like a honey trap. The wine, the music, the flattery . . .'

Dan threw the remote control onto the couch and moved towards her. 'I only want to trap the queen bee. And so far she has proven very evasive.'

Alice took a swig of her wine. Her heart was racing. 'I'm here now.'

'After six bouquets of flowers, five lunches, four dinners and three films. I find I'm usually more irresistible.'

'I've always been choosy.'

'The best things are worth waiting for.'

Alice winced. 'I'm not sure how brilliant this is going to be. I'm good at sex – I mean I was with Ben and before – but now . . . I'm not sure . . . I hope . . . but I –'

Dan took Alice's face in his hands and kissed her. It was soft at first and then she opened her mouth and let him in. It was deep and sexy. She could smell his aftershave and feel his light stubble rubbing against her chin. A groan of pleasure and longing came from deep within her.

Alice let herself go. She sank her body into Dan's and he responded.

Within minutes her dress was on the floor, and she was lying back on his four-poster bed impatiently pulling Dan's trousers off. Within seconds he was inside her and she wrapped her legs around him willing him to be closer, to go deeper, to consume her.

'Wow!' Dan fell back on the bed, panting. 'You're quite the tiger.'

'How were the new buttons? Did you like them?'

'I loved them!' He grinned.

Alice smiled back at him. Dan leant over and kissed her softly on the lips. Something about the gentle gesture triggered it – a tide of emotion hurtled through her body and exploded in her chest. Alice cried out and began to sob.

Dan didn't ask. He knew. He understood. He held her and rocked her, rubbing her back and telling her over and over again that it was 'going to be all right'.

When Alice had calmed down enough to speak, she wiped her face with the tissue Dan handed her. Then she apologized.

'Was I that bad?' he asked.

'No, it was bloody brilliant. I think that's the problem. I didn't think the sex was going to be any good.'

'Thanks a lot!'

Alice gave him a watery smile. 'I thought I'd never be able to let go with anyone else. But it felt so good to be with a man, and then I felt guilty for enjoying it and . . . Oh, God . . . I don't know what I'm supposed to feel.'

Dan tucked a strand of her hair behind her ear. 'Forget everyone and everything else and tell me . . . what do you feel?'

Alice bit her lip. 'I feel alive.'

'Is that so bad?'

'I'm not sure. How are widows supposed to feel the first time they have sex with someone else? I'm new to this.'

'I've never been widowed, or is it widowered? Anyway, I don't know how you're supposed to feel, but I think if you feel alive, that's a good thing.'

'It felt so good, so raw, so real.'

'Yes, it did!'

'Was it okay for you, though? Did I rush things a bit too much?'

Dan put his hand under her chin and raised her face. 'Darling Alice, it was pretty mind-blowing. If you feel up to it, I'd really like seconds.'

Alice threw her arms around his neck and kissed him.

When Alice came down to breakfast the next morning, Kevin glanced up and did a double-take. 'Someone got laid last night!'

'Sssh,' Alice said, panicked.

'I'm whispering, the door is closed and the girls are in the lounge watching TV. So . . .' Kevin beamed at his sister '. . . gory details, please.'

Alice blushed and covered her face with her hands. 'I feel so upside-down.'

'Was it good?'

'Amazing.'

'Wow!'

'I know, but that's just it, I feel guilty even saying it. Is it wrong to like being with someone else? Is it betraying Ben and the girls? It feels too soon.'

'It's been almost two years, Alice. You're allowed to live and have fun and have a life.'

'I keep wondering how I would feel if Ben was having sex with someone twenty-one months after I'd died.'

Kevin spread jam on his spelt bread. 'I'm sorry to be the one to tell you this, but I reckon Ben and ninety-nine per cent of red-blooded men would have had sex a lot earlier than that.'

'Do you really think so?'

'I know so. Anyway, tell me about it.'

Alice sipped her coffee. 'It was just lovely. He's lovely. He's so . . . nice and sexy too.'

'And *loooaded*, which always helps.'

Alice frowned. 'I don't care about the size of his wallet.'

'Just the size of his package!'

Alice giggled. 'Stop! You're like a teenager.'

'You'll have to introduce me to him now that you've consummated your relationship.'

'Three times,' Alice said, with a grin.

'Go, Alice!'

Alice closed her eyes, savouring the memories. It had been hard leaving Dan's bed in the middle of the night, but she'd wanted to be home when the girls woke up. They still had to come first, even if she was in a tailspin with all these exciting new experiences.

Jools walked into the kitchen, followed by Holly.

'I'm hungry.' Holly went to get some cereal.

'Ask Jools about Lance,' Kevin said, with a wicked grin. Jools shot him a look and stuck out her tongue at him.

'How's Lance?' Alice asked.

'He's great.' Jools smiled like the cat that got the cream. 'He's totally over Saint Hayley and is totally into me. I must say we make a very hot couple. Everyone says so.'

'Poor Hayley, she looks sad,' Holly said.

'It'll give her more time to feed the homeless and save the lepers or whatever she wants to do.'

'Jools!' Alice was not impressed.

'What? She's always banging on about wanting to help others, so now she has more time to do it.'

'Heartbreak isn't easy,' Alice pointed out.

Jools scowled. 'My father was blown up by a landmine – I know all about heartbreak. Shit happens and you just have to get over it.'

They all stared at her.

'Well, she has a point,' Kevin said finally, breaking the silence.

'Do you really like this boy?' Alice asked.

'Yes, totally.'

'No, she doesn't,' Holly piped up. 'Now she's got him, she doesn't even really want him. She said he's boring.'

'Seriously? After all that work, you finally get him and he's dull?' Kevin was incredulous.

'He isn't! He just sometimes goes on about rugby too much and he made me watch some documentary called *The Incontinent Truth* by some bore called Alf Gore. It was *soooo* boring. I kept having to pinch myself to stay awake.'

Alice shook her head. Jools was impossible. For months all they'd heard about was Lance this and Lance that, but now she was going out with him, she was bored. How would she manage life? Work? Marriage? Motherhood?

'It's one of the best documentaries ever made. Al Gore really made people realize the dangers that society faces from climate change,' Holly said.

'OMG, I've already sat through it. I don't need another lecture on it.'

'Holly's right, it is very informative,' Alice said, even

though she hadn't watched it either. She'd gone to see it with Ben but as they were about to go into the cinema, they'd looked at each other and both said, 'Pub.'

'So, are you going to dump him for being dull and making you watch dreary programmes?' Kevin asked.

Jools popped a raspberry into her mouth. 'No. I still like him, it's just not as exciting as I thought it would be. But we work well as a couple. We look perfect together. Chloë said we're like Victoria and David Beckham because Lance is brilliant at rugby and I'm really into fashion.'

Kevin sprinkled sugar on his grapefruit. 'There's a difference between being into fashion and being a hugely successful fashion designer.'

Jools flicked her hair. 'Yes, well, I've decided that I'm going to go to art college and become a designer. Dan told Mum that people should follow their passions. Well, now she agrees!'

'Good for you.' Kevin beamed at her. 'And good for you,' he said to Alice, giving her a thumbs-up.

'You should see her sketchbook. She's really talented,' Alice said. 'I've spoken to her art teacher and she said Jools should think about applying to art colleges next year because it's what she's best at.'

'Good for you, Jools. Can I see the sketchbook?' Kevin asked.

'Sure.' Jools ran off to get it.

'I've decided I'm going to be a surgeon like Daddy,' Holly told Kevin.

'Good for you, Brainiac,' Kevin replied, kissing her forehead.

While Holly told Kevin, in excruciating detail, what type of medicine she was planning to specialize in, Alice went up to check on Jools, who was taking a long time coming back.

When she approached her bedroom, she could hear sobbing. Alice went in and found Jools lying on her bed, crying.

'Hey, sweetheart, what's wrong? Did Holly upset you?'

'No. I'm fine. I'm just having a moment. It's just that I wish I could show my stuff to Dad. I know he'd be proud of me and make me feel better about doing so badly in my other subjects.'

'Oh, Jools, I know you miss him. But I'm proud of you, really proud of you. The way you've handled things since your dad died has been incredible. You've been so good to Holly and so caring and kind to me. I wouldn't have got through it without you. Dad would be so proud of how wonderful you've been.'

Jools pulled her sleeves over her hands. 'Thanks, Mum. I've really tried to be helpful.'

'You've been a rock, Jools. You're the one who's held us together. I couldn't be prouder of you or love you more.' Alice's voice shook with emotion.

Jools smiled. 'Don't get all weepy. I'm fine.'

'If it's too much for you to see me dating another man, I can stop. It's no problem. You and Holly are my priority. Nothing else matters.'

Jools wiped her nose with a tissue. 'No, Mum. I'm glad you've met Dan. I don't want you to end up alone. I want you to have someone to look after you when Holly and I leave home. Harriet's mum is divorced and all she does is drink and smoke and shout at Harriet about how men are all bastards. I do not want you to turn out like that.'

'Poor Harriet.'

'It's grim at her house. Dad would have wanted you to be happy. He loved your smile – he always said that. You've got me and Holly through the storm, now go and have some fun.'

Alice kissed Jools's forehead. 'Now I feel like the daughter. You're a very special girl, Jools.'

They heard Kevin hissing up the stairs, 'For the love of God, will you please come down? Holly's torturing me here with minute details of the operations she's going to perform. I'll take the documentary on saving the planet any day over this.'

Jools and Alice laughed.

## Ben: September 2014

Declan put his face up close to Ben's and roared, 'Ten more! Now, come on, you can do it.'

Ben gritted his teeth and pushed up with all of his might. His whole body was shaking, but he was determined to reach his goal. The pain in his arms was excruciating but he kept going.

'. . . and ten. Yes!' Declan punched the air. 'Well done, mate.'

Ben lay on the ground gasping for air, sweat pouring down his face. 'You're going to kill me,' he groaned.

'Nope, I'm going to get you into tip-top shape. You were skin and bone after that bout of gastro. Now you're almost as well built as me.'

Ben looked at his arms: they were almost back to normal. The gastroenteritis had left him weak for ages. He'd been frightened by it. He'd felt death very close by. Declan had literally dragged him back to life – he'd never forget his friend's devotion and kindness. 'You're a bloody slave driver,' he said, grinning.

'I might give up surgery and open a gym when I get back to London. Imagine all those fit birds coming to me for one-on-one sessions in their tight Lycra gear . . . Ooh.'

Ben laughed. 'I'm not sure you'd be able to concentrate on the fitness.'

'God, I need to get laid badly. The first woman I meet

when I get out of here is getting it. I don't care what she looks like. I just need sex!'

'I know how you feel.'

'Lucky Alice.' Declan winked. 'She's in for a good time.'

Ben smiled and closed his eyes, remembering for the millionth time the last night of passion they'd had. He could see Alice's naked body, feel her skin, smell her hair . . . God, he missed her. The nights were the worst – he ached for her. He longed to touch her, talk to her, laugh with her.

'Hey.' Declan nudged him. 'Up you get. We have to teach Segen, Feven and Almaz wound management and suturing.'

'I'm going to try to persuade Awate to let us teach basic surgical procedures to Yonas. He wants to learn – he's keen.'

Declan rolled his eyes. 'Jesus, Ben, let it go. Awate says no every time. You're just going to wind him up.'

'If we can teach Yonas how to look after the men, we're no longer needed.'

'When are you going to get it into your thick head? They're not going to let us go, Ben. If we're no longer useful, they'll shoot us and bury us in this God-forsaken place.'

'They might let us go if we help them to help themselves.'

'Awate doesn't want Yonas to learn. You've asked him fifty times. The only way we're going to get out of here is by escaping.'

Ben sighed. They would soon have been there two years. He couldn't bear the idea of spending a third year in captivity. Every time he thought about it he had a panic attack. They were getting worse and wearing him down. They came over him at night, when darkness fell and his mind wandered. During the day he could control his thinking by keeping busy, but at night his demons reared up and ate him alive.

Declan paced the room, like a caged tiger. 'I get the feeling they're gearing up for another attack. That's the time to go. When the men are off fighting and there are only a few lads left here to guard us. We could overpower them, take their guns and go while the others are fighting. I think it's the best shot we have.'

Ben nodded. 'You're right.'

Declan looked shocked. 'What? You're not going to try to talk me out of it? You're not going to tell me all the things that could go wrong or how we don't know where we are or where to run to?'

Ben shook his head. 'I can't do this any more. Jools turns eighteen next month. I can't miss another birthday. I'd rather die than stay here.'

Declan came over and clasped his shoulders. 'That's exactly the way I feel. Let's do it, Ben. Let's get the hell out of here.'

Segen handed Biniam to Ben. He sat him on his lap and sang 'Incy Wincy Spider' to the little boy, who stared at him with his huge brown eyes, giggling hysterically when Ben tickled him under the chin.

To their left, in the shade of a tree, the older children were attending school. The teacher leant his blackboard against the trunk of the tree.

Biniam and Ben had a special bond. Ben had monitored Biniam very closely for the first few months of his life. He was small and slow to grow, but in the last three months he had thrived. He looked healthy now. He was underweight, as all the children were, but he was full of energy and curiosity.

Biniam held up his arms and Ben cuddled him, the baby's soft cheek against his. Feelings of anguish and love poured through him. He remembered Jools and Holly at this baby age. He would sit them on his lap, sing silly songs to them and pull faces to make them laugh. He ached to hold his girls again.

Holly was thirteen now, a teenager already, and Jools almost eighteen. God, he'd missed so much. Had they changed? He knew they would have. Losing their father at such a young age would have changed them, too. He hoped they were all right. He had faith in Alice. She would be there for them, helping them with their grief, watching over them like the mother hen she was.

But what about Alice? Who was she leaning on? He supposed Kevin would have been a rock to her. Thank God she had him. Ben tried not to let his mind go to that other place, but it did: had Alice met someone else? Had she moved on?

He wondered if the situation were reversed, if he thought she was dead, would he have moved on by now? How long would it take to get over the death of someone you loved? Ben rubbed his eyes to push away thoughts of Alice with another man.

Alice was so loyal and loving. She'd been so proud and protective of their little family. After her parents had died, she had become obsessed with family, closeness and being together. She'd done such a great job, creating a lovely home and raising two beautiful and very special girls – Ben should have told her so more often. He should have praised her more. He should have been more present. He had been a selfish git.

'If I . . . No. When I get home, I'll be the best bloody husband and father in the world. Please, God, just get me home alive,' he prayed.

Biniam wriggled in his lap. Ben threw him up in the air and caught him. Biniam screeched with glee. Yonas walked by and laughed. He came and sat beside Ben. Biniam held his hands out to his father. Ben passed him over and Yonas took his son onto his knee. 'He's doing really well,' Ben said. 'He's a healthy boy.'

'Healthy, yes.' Yonas smiled. 'You good man, Doctor Ben. You help me and Segen and Biniam.'

'You're lucky you have your family beside you. I have two daughters I want to see. I haven't seen them in almost two years. I am very sad, Yonas.'

Yonas said nothing. Segen watched them from where she was cooking.

Ben paused. 'Maybe one day you can help me to see my children again.'

Yonas averted his eyes. 'Awate is leader. He say you stay.'

Ben put a hand on Yonas's arm. 'I need to see my children. I need to see my wife.'

Segen said something to Yonas. He replied to her, shaking his head. 'Awate is leader,' he repeated.

Ben stood up slowly. 'I saved your wife and your baby, Yonas. Don't forget that.'

As he walked away, he heard Segen and Yonas arguing with each other.

Ben was approaching the operating theatre to help Declan scrub it down in their constant battle to keep it as clean and hygienic as possible when he heard a blood-curdling scream. He spun around to see Nebay hurtling towards him carrying his son, who was bleeding profusely.

Declan came running out and they rushed to Nebay. The boy had stepped on a landmine.

'Come on, let's get him inside. Quickly.' Ben led Nebay to the tent and helped him lay the boy on the operating table.

Nebay kissed his son's face and spoke to him in reassuring tones. Ben glanced up at Declan, who was biting his lower lip as he cut through the boy's trousers.

Nebay's wife came running into the room and shrieked when she saw her son. Ben tried to hide the gap where the boy's legs used to be. Yonas came in to see if he could help. Ben indicated that he had to get Nebay and his wife out so they could work on the boy.

Yonas understood and talked to them softly, asking them to wait outside. The bleeding was profuse. No matter how hard they tried, they couldn't save the child. The injuries were too severe. They tried stemming the blood-flow, but it was like trying to stop a dam with a plaster.

'He's gone,' Ben said quietly. 'There was nothing we could do.'

'To hell with this.' Declan cursed as he slipped on the blood-soaked floor. 'I can't do this any more. It's so depressing. He was just a little kid. He had his whole life ahead of him. And now he's dead because of some stupid fight about land.'

Ben tried to clean the boy up as best he could before he told the parents.

'What future do these kids have?' Declan ranted. 'Living in this hell-hole. If it doesn't rain soon, they'll all die of hunger anyway. If it does rain, they'll probably get diarrhoea and die, and if that doesn't kill them, malaria or a landmine will. Christ, I thought I had it tough growing up in inner-city Dublin. It was a walk in the park compared to this. I complained about beans on toast! What a naïve wanker I was. I'm going to give my da the biggest hug when I see him. I might even kiss his feet for what he did for me.' Declan snapped off his surgical gloves and threw them into the bowl. 'They're just innocent kids.'

Ben mopped up the blood. 'It's senseless.'

'I've decided when I get back I'm going to specialize in paediatrics. Seeing the kids here, it just breaks my heart.' Declan began to cry.

Ben went over and put an arm around him. 'It's been a bad day, but think of the kids we've saved. Think of the eight babies we've delivered safely since we got here.'

Declan roughly wiped his eyes. 'I know, but look at him. He was a lovely little lad. I used to see him playing football with an old rag tied up. He's just an innocent child, blown to shreds. When you get home, don't let your daughters out of your sight. Cherish them.'

'I will. I do.' Ben choked up.

'Shit! Sorry, Ben. I didn't mean to set you off.'

'It's just so hard sometimes.'

Declan squeezed his arm. 'Come on, mate. Let's get this little man cleaned up and talk to his parents.'

They walked back to their tent to the sounds of a mother and father screaming in grief.

When Yonas had chained them up for the night, they lay back on their mattresses.

'Knock, knock,' Declan said.

Ben shook his head, but Declan wasn't taking no for an answer.

'Come on, Ben, it'll distract us. I need this. We need this. Knock, knock.'

'Who's fucking there, then?'

'Noah.'

'Noah who?'

'Noah good place we can get something to eat?'

This time Ben could only raise the ghost of a smile. They were silent for a while, lying side by side, each trying to let the day's blackness roll away from him.

'We're agreed. We're not staying here for Christmas?' Declan asked, his voice hushed.

'Agreed. I can't do this any more. We have to at least try, even if we die in the process.'

'Now all we need is to wait for an opportunity.'

Ben rolled onto his side, the heavy chain clanking. He closed his eyes and tried to picture Jools and Holly. The really frightening thing was that he couldn't see their faces clearly any more. He could picture Alice perfectly, but the girls were fading and it was terrifying. He began to gasp for breath. He scratched at his neck, gasping, gulping . . . His throat was closing over.

Declan pulled him up and bent him forward. 'Easy, Ben, easy. Breathe in and out. Follow me, in and out.'

Slowly, Ben's breathing eased and the panic subsided.

'They're getting worse,' Declan said. 'I'm going to ask Awate to nick some Valium.'

'No,' Ben said. 'I don't want him to know. It makes me look weak.'

'It makes you look human,' Declan snapped.

'I can't remember their faces properly,' Ben whispered.

'Describe them – go on. Start with their hair, and the rest'll come back to you. I'm here, mate, I'm here.'

Ben closed his eyes and described his daughters. As he spoke, he began to remember the details, the little things he'd forgotten – Jools's beauty spot under her right ear and Holly's small scar where she'd hit her head falling off her bike. Ben talked and talked until his heart stopped thudding and he could see the girls clearly, his beautiful daughters, his pride and joy. So close but yet so far.

*Holly: September 2014*

Mummy was like Taz the Tasmanian Devil, rushing about cleaning the house, checking the oven and rearranging the flowers.

I escaped upstairs to get away from her. She was so wound up. I found Jools in her room, sitting on the windowsill, smoking out of the window.

'I wish you'd stop smoking. It'll kill you. Every year, over a hundred thousand smokers in the UK die from smoking-related causes.'

'I swear to God, Holly, if you start spouting on about death rates from smoking, I'll flick hot ash on you.'

'There's no need to be so grumpy.'

Jools took a deep drag. 'I'm not. I'm just . . . well . . . He's coming into our house. Dad's house. It feels . . .'

'Weird,' I said. It felt more than weird: it felt like Daddy was being put in a box and hidden away.

Tonight was the first time Dan had come to the house for dinner and Mummy was all hyper about it. It was a big deal having him at our house to have dinner at the table Daddy used to sit at.

'Is Stella coming?' Jools asked.

I shook my head. 'No. I wish she was but there's an opening at her gallery tonight.'

'Do you think he'll sit in Dad's chair?' Jools asked.

'He'd better not. I'm planning on sitting there.' Kevin

walked in, with a glass of wine. 'I've left Marco Pierre White's insane twin sister in the kitchen, bashing pots and pans around. I told her not to worry about the cooking. Dan's so in love with her, he wouldn't care what she gave him to eat.'

'Dan looks at Mum the way Lance looks at me,' Jools said. 'It gets boring after a while. Mind you, it would be less boring if Lance was a millionaire.'

'How is Lance?' Kevin asked.

'Annoying. I'm going to break up with him next week. I can't take it any more. He keeps giving me articles to read on Africa and stuff.'

'I take it these aren't articles about African fashion,' Kevin said, teasing her as usual.

Jools put out her cigarette. 'No, they're all about disease and misery. I'm sorry, but I don't want to read that stuff. I've had enough misery with Dad dying. I don't want to read about kids dying because they didn't have a mosquito net. I've been bitten loads of times by mosquitoes and I'm still alive.'

'Mosquitoes in Africa infect children with malaria!' I said. It was just incredible the way Jools was so clueless about the world. She lived in her Jools bubble. Sometimes I wanted to shake her and make her see.

'Well, yesterday we went for a coffee. Lance insisted we meet in this "save the world" coffee shop where you have to buy coffee made in Africa, which is just awful. I much prefer Carlito's – it has nice Italian coffee and they serve it in really cool mugs and the guys that work there are all Italian and really fit. Anyway, Lance made me go there and it was full of people in very uncool clothes and T-shirts that said "One Planet, One Chance" and "Hunger Bites. Bite Back" – another said "Kids Aren't Made To Be Soldiers". What does that even mean? You have to be, like, eighteen to join the army.'

'I don't think they were talking about the British Army,' I pointed out. 'I think it was about boy soldiers in Sierra Leone and places like that.'

Jools twisted her hair up. 'Well, I don't know about Sarah Leon, but the coffee was rotten and the cakes were all gluten-free and gross. I couldn't eat the muffin I ordered. It was disgusting. Then Lance gave me a lecture on wasting food and this other guy went off on a rant about how we throw away seven million tons of food a year blah-blah-blah . . .'

My blood was boiling. 'It's not blah-blah-blah, Jools, it's a really serious issue. If we all stopped wasting food, the benefit to the planet would be the equivalent of taking one in four cars off the road.'

'OMG, Holly, I don't need to hear it all twice. Anyway, I said to the guy, "If your food tasted nice, I wouldn't be throwing it away."'

'You are so rude!' I said.

'No, Holly, I'm honest.'

'How did the guy react?' Kevin was grinning, I think he actually liked it when Jools was being naughty.

'He said I was the first person not to like it, which I knew was a big fat lie because it tasted like cardboard. Then he and Lance started talking about food waste and how greedy Westerners are and how we need to save Africa from famine . . . and it was so boring that I started yawning and then Lance got all embarrassed and the guy said, "I'm sorry I'm boring you. Most people are actually interested in what's going on in Africa."'

'What did you say to that?' Kevin asked.

Jools twisted a strand of hair. 'I said, "Well, I don't like talking about Africa because it's where my father was blown up by a landmine."'

'I'd say that shut him up,' Kevin said.

Jools grinned. 'You should have seen his smug, do-gooder face. He went from treating me like a complete fool to fawning all over me and giving me free cups of revolting coffee and asking me all about "the incident".'

'He sounds like an idiot!' I snapped.

'He was. But then Lance got all jealous because his lame friend was suddenly so interested in me.'

'Poor Lance. I feel sorry for him. He's far too nice for you,' Kevin said.

Jools sighed dramatically. 'I need someone more challenging. It's all too easy with Lance and, besides, he should really be with another do-gooder. I'm just not interested.'

'You're so mean, Jools. You made him fall for you and leave Hayley, who was interested in all those things, and now you're dumping him. And by the way, Kevin, being too nice is not a bad thing.'

Kevin held up his hands. 'I know it isn't, but Jools needs to be with someone strong who can manage her and stand up to her.'

'What about me?' I asked.

Kevin hugged me. 'You need the nicest man in the world.'

'Actually, Holly, you should go to that place and hang out. It's right up your street. Full of nerdy geeks reading books and talking about "serious issues". They even had a poster of that girl, Majella Yousifuzzy or whatever her name is, the one you love.'

'Malala Yousafzai.'

'Yeah, her, and I'm sorry, Holly, but she's clearly brain-damaged. The poster said, "I believe the gun has no power." She got shot in the head and nearly died. Hello? I think the gun does have power.'

I stood up, my fists curled into balls. She made me so angry, more than anyone else could. 'Do not speak ill of Malala. She's a hero. You're just an empty vessel.'

Jools went to light another cigarette, but Kevin snatched it out of her hand. 'I may be an empty whatever, but at least I'm not going around telling people that guns aren't dangerous. She's completely insane.'

I could feel my face burning. Kevin reached over and took my hand. 'Come on, girls, you can't be fighting in front of Dan. Calm down and behave yourselves.'

The dinner was fine because Dan, Jools and Kevin kept chatting, but Mummy was quiet and so was I. Kevin sat in Daddy's chair and Dan sat in the one that was always spare. Dan kept saying everything was wonderful and the food was delicious. At one point he went over to the counter to open some wine and I saw him giving Mummy a kiss and a hug. She leant her head against his chest and smiled at what he whispered to her. She looked young and pretty and I felt glad for her.

I want her to be happy and Dan is really nice. He'll never, ever, ever replace Daddy, but at least he's good and kind.

At the end of the dinner, Dan said he wanted to ask us a favour. He asked if it was okay if he took Mummy to Venice in two weeks' time. He'd obviously arranged it with Kevin already, because Kevin said he was free and would move in with us. Jools and I both said it was fine. Jools said Mummy needed a nice break and that Dan should spoil her and book a really fancy hotel.

Dan said he had booked the Aman Canal Grande and he hoped that would do. Kevin almost choked on his wine. 'That's where George Clooney got married! It's incredible.'

Dan said he was very grateful to us for lending him Mummy for the weekend and that he had a surprise for us to say thank you: he'd arranged for Stella to pick us up and take us to dinner at the Chiltern Firehouse.

Jools started hyperventilating because it's where all the celebrities eat and apparently it's almost impossible to get a table there. Dan is incredibly generous. He always plans everything and tries to make everyone happy.

It seems to be getting serious with Mummy and Dan. I think she's in love.

*Alice: October 2014*

Alice tried to concentrate on what Laura Jones was saying, but her mind kept drifting back to the night before and the great sex with Dan. He was so strong and solid, and she felt so safe with him. He made her feel so special and beautiful that sometimes she had to pinch herself to check this was actually her reality. Everything with Dan was easy. He was decisive, knew his mind, organized absolutely everything and swept her off her feet with his big romantic gestures.

'So what do you think, Doctor? Doctor?'

'Sorry, Mrs Jones, I think a course of antibiotics is wise. We need to clear up this chest infection.' Alice typed up a prescription and handed it to the patient.

Two minutes later, Kevin came in. He closed the door and sat down opposite her. 'You've got a ten-minute break. The next patient just cancelled and the one after hasn't arrived yet. Mrs Jones was just saying how well you look. She asked me if you were "seeing someone".'

Alice smiled. 'Is it that obvious?'

'The beaming smile, the shining eyes, the glowing complexion from all the sex . . . Yes, I'd say it's very obvious.'

Alice blushed. 'He's just so . . .'

'Perfect?'

'Well, yes. He just makes everything so easy. I never have to organize anything. He does it all. He completely spoils me.

He picks me up and takes me to all these amazing restaurants and fancy parties and hotels.'

Kevin sighed. 'You're making me jealous. Axel can barely afford to pay for a glass of wine.'

Alice leant back in her chair. 'Stella told me last week that she's really glad he met me. She said he'd dated lots of women, but none of them ever stuck. She said Dan's really happy and that it's down to me. Wasn't that a lovely thing to say?'

'God, Alice, that's great.'

'I told her Dan had saved my life. I think he did. He made me look forward instead of back. I can't believe I was lucky enough to meet him.'

'You deserved a bit of luck.'

'Do you think the girls are okay with it all? They've been so positive to my face, but are they really fine with the fact that we're a proper couple now?'

Kevin nodded. 'They really like him and they adore Stella, especially Jools. They see how happy Dan makes you. And he's good with them. He never tries too hard or overdoes it, he's just himself.'

'And you?'

'Honey, if he had a gay twin brother, I'd marry him in the morning.'

Alice got up and paced the room. 'Sometimes, when I'm on my own at night, I feel guilty. It's as if I'm forgetting Ben or casting him aside or something.'

Kevin came to stand beside her at the window. 'You're not forgetting him. You'll never forget him. He was your first love and you had two amazing children together. You're just living. You can either stand still and be miserable for ever, or move on. I figured that out after Mum and Dad died.

I wallowed in my grief for ages until I realized it wasn't going to bring them back. Life is about sinking or swimming. You have to swim if you don't want to drown.'

Alice sniffed, wiping a tear from her cheek. 'You're right. I just wish I could have told Ben I loved him before he left. I wish we'd never had that stupid fight. I still miss him so much. Whenever anything happens with the girls, I yearn to tell him. He'd be so proud of them.'

Kevin put his arm around his sister. 'He'd be proud of you too.'

Alice rested her head on his shoulder. 'Life never turns out the way you think it will. It's full of surprises.'

Dan opened the door of the car, helped her out and pointed to the private jet.

'Are you serious?'

He looked into her eyes. 'I've never been more serious.'

'We're going to Venice in a private jet?'

'Yes, and this is only the beginning. I have lots of treats in store.'

Alice hugged him. 'You are wonderful. Thank you for coming into my life.'

Dan held her face in his hands. 'Thank you for making me so happy.' He kissed her.

'Have you ever had sex on a plane?'

'Are you offering?' Dan asked.

'I might be.'

'Dessert before lunch?' He smiled.

'I was thinking of it more as an appetite enhancer.' Alice grinned, took his hand and ran towards the plane.

Dan poured Alice another glass of champagne.

'I'll be drunk soon. Are you trying to take advantage of me?'

'Absolutely.'

Alice sat back and took in the view from the balcony. Here she was, in Venice, at the most incredible hotel, drinking champagne with a man she loved. Yes, Alice thought, I really do love him. He makes me happy.

Alice reached out her hand and held Dan's. 'I love you.'

A wide smile spread across his face. 'Well, that's good to hear.'

He leant over and Alice thought he was going to kiss her but instead he bent down. She heard him exhale loudly.

'Are you all right? Did you drop something?' Alice knelt beside him, looking at the floor.

'What are you doing? Sit back down, for God's sake,' Dan snapped.

Alice was taken aback by his tone. 'I was only trying to help – I know your knee is sore from overdoing it in the gym.'

'You're not bloody helping.'

'What's wrong – Oh, Jesus!'

Dan was holding up a ring . . . a huge ring . . . the biggest diamond ring Alice had ever seen.

'"Oh, Jesus" good, or "Oh, Jesus" bad?' Dan asked.

Alice's hands were covering her mouth. She was shaking. She didn't know whether to laugh or cry or scream.

'Alice, my knee is killing me, give me an answer, quick.'

Alice had a flashback to Ben proposing to her at dusk on the Pont des Arts in Paris. He'd been wearing a tuxedo he'd borrowed from David. It was too big for him, but he had looked so handsome. They were so young and in love. Life had been so full of possibility and adventure . . .

'Alice!' Dan was getting annoyed.

Alice looked down at Dan, the man who had saved her, and said, 'Yes.'

'Thank God for that.' Dan smiled as he got back up. He slipped the ring on Alice's finger. It fitted perfectly.

'How did you know my size?'

'Stella. Remember a few weeks ago when she tried on your ring? She was checking out your size for me.'

'My God, Dan, you really think of everything. It's beautiful.' Alice gazed at the rock now resting on her hand. If she was being honest, it was too big for her liking, but it was certainly stunning.

'This is only the beginning, Alice. I want to make your life perfect. I want you give to up work and move in with me – there's plenty of room for the girls. I'll look after you all. You need never worry about anything again. We'll be together and happy and there's so much we can do – travel, five-star hotels, all sorts. We'll have a really good life. I want to give that to you.'

Give up work? Move in? She loved work and she loved her house. Dan seemed to be taking over her life. Her head was spinning with the suddenness of it all, and the weight of his expectations.

Dan kissed her hand. 'We'll go to Barbados for Christmas – we can get married out there on the beach –'

'Dan.' Alice interrupted his flow. 'I love you and I do want to marry you, but can we have a long engagement? It's a lot to get used to and I want to ease the girls into it.'

Dan seemed a bit crestfallen. 'If that's what you'd like, but the sooner the better, as far as I'm concerned. No point wasting time at our age.'

Alice leant over and kissed him. 'I'm sorry. I'm really happy and, yes, I do want to marry you. I just need some time to take it all in. It's all happened so fast and it's been wonderful, but there's no need to rush the wedding, is there? I'm not going anywhere. I'm right where I want to be.'

Dan pulled Alice onto his knee and they were soon consummating their engagement.

The next morning, on the way to the airport, Alice asked Dan if they could put off telling anyone outside the immediate family about the engagement.

He frowned. 'Why? You haven't changed your mind, have you?'

'God, no! I just want to ease the girls into it, then let the news settle with them before telling anyone else. It's a very big deal and I don't want them to feel rushed.'

'I'm not a patient man, Alice. You know me, I like to get on with things. I don't see why we have to wait. We love each other, we get on with each other's kids, what's the problem?'

Alice looked out of the window of the water taxi at the beautiful Venetian buildings. 'It's going to mean a big adjustment for the girls and I want them to feel completely happy with everything.'

Dan sighed. 'All right, but let's not stretch it out too far. I want you to be my wife as soon as possible. The girls will be fine about it. I know they will. You'll see. I'm always right.'

Alice looked down at her enormous ring. She wasn't so sure the girls were going to be thrilled about it. Getting married was very final: it was saying goodbye to Ben for ever.

## Holly: October 2014

Jools kept squealing every time she saw a celebrity. It was kind of embarrassing. Stella was really nice about it, even though she did tell Jools to shush a few times, especially when she shouted, 'Look at Cara Delevingne's eyebrows!'

Stella ordered champagne and poured Jools a glass. She ordered me a non-alcoholic cocktail, which came in a fancy glass and tasted delicious.

'OMG, this is so cool!' Jools sighed happily. 'Drinking champagne in the Chiltern Firehouse surrounded by stars. Wait until I tell my friends. I'm going to ask if I can get a selfie with Cara.'

Stella grabbed Jools's arm as she tried to stand up. 'No. Sorry, Jools, but you can't ask her. People come here to chill out and be with their friends. They don't want to be asked for photos. Just sit back and enjoy it.'

Jools nodded. 'You're right. I'm being so uncool. Sorry, I'm just really excited. Oooh, look, there's Alexa Chung.'

Stella grinned. 'So, guys, I think it's getting serious with my dad and your mum.'

'Yeah, totally,' Jools said, but she wasn't listening: she was looking Alexa Chung up and down.

'Are you okay about it, Holly?' Stella asked.

I shrugged. 'It's nice for Mummy to have someone to look after her and be kind to her, but it feels a bit strange sometimes.'

Jools stopped staring at celebrities and listened in.

'I know what you mean,' Stella said. 'The first relationship Dad had after Mum left us was weird for me. It was as if Dad was trying to replace her or something. I was stupidly still hoping Mum would come back.'

'Do you have any contact with her?' Jools asked.

Stella's jaw set. 'No. I cut her off a few years ago. She's the most selfish person in the world. Besides, I don't need her. I have Dad. He's always been there for me. Alice is the first woman he's dated that I really like. Maybe it's because I'm older and have my own life, but I wouldn't mind at all if they got married.'

'Married?' Jools frowned.

My stomach clenched. Did Stella think they were going to be married? So soon?

Stella nodded. 'Dad's ready to get married again and he really loves your mum.'

'But what about our dad?' I said. It popped out. I didn't mean it to . . . it just did.

Stella reached out and held my hand. 'I know my mum is still technically alive, but she died for me a long time ago. So I do know how hard it is to lose a parent. But once you accept it, it makes it easier, I promise. Your dad is gone, sweetie, and he isn't coming back. You have to let go.'

I looked down at my food and felt sick. I knew she was right – it was just so hard.

Jools held my other hand and squeezed it. I knew she was feeling sad too. The thought of Mummy marrying someone else was really strange.

'It could be great,' Stella said, trying to cheer us up. 'I've always wanted sisters. I hate being an only child. Think about it, girls, we could do fun stuff like this all the time.'

'Really?' Jools's eyes lit up.

'Absolutely, and my dad has homes all over the world – we could go to Barbados and Dubai and New York and have great times. Honestly, girls, it'll be fantastic.'

Jools jumped up and down in her seat. 'Wow! I've always wanted to go to New York . . .'

As they chatted and planned trips abroad, I sank back in my chair. I didn't want everything to change. There had been so much change already. Would we have to move house? Would we always be travelling? I don't like the sun – I hate being too hot. My head began to ache. I wanted to go home and think about it all, work it out in my mind, calmly in the quiet of my bedroom.

The next evening, Kevin cooked dinner for me, Jools and Stella. When we were having dessert, the front door opened and we heard Mummy's voice. I ran out to see her. She held me really tight.

'I know it's only been two days but I missed you,' I said.

She kissed the top of my head.

I felt myself relax. It was going to be fine. Dan was making her happy, not taking her away.

As she went to hug Jools, I saw Kevin's eyes widen. He was staring at Mummy's hand. I looked down – she was wearing the biggest diamond I'd ever seen.

When I looked up Stella was watching me. I tried to keep my face calm while my mind raced. It was happening. They were getting married. Then Jools spotted it.

'Oh. My. *Gooooood!*' she shouted. 'Mum?'

Mum went red. 'Well, yes, I do have something to tell you.'

'It's bigger than Kim Kardashian's!' Jools pulled Mummy's hand up.

'Well, I wanted something to show the world how I feel about this woman,' Dan said, beaming.

Mummy seemed embarrassed about the size of the diamond. I much prefer the engagement ring Daddy gave her, which she'd been wearing on her other hand since he died.

Kevin, Stella and Jools all hugged Mummy and Dan and me. When Mummy hugged me again, she whispered, 'Don't worry. Nothing will change for a while.'

Then the doorbell rang. It was Pippa and David arriving with flowers and champagne.

'Congratulations!' they called, as they came in.

'But how did you know?' Mummy asked. She looked a bit shocked.

'Dan rang us this morning and asked us to come and celebrate,' Pippa said.

I saw David hugging Mummy. They both had tears in their eyes. 'I'm really happy for you, Alice. You deserve this.'

I could see Mummy was too emotional to speak. She just nodded and smiled.

Then Dan tapped his glass for silence. He said he wanted to say a few words. 'Thank you all for being so enthusiastic about our announcement. I'm so delighted to be making this amazing woman my wife. And you girls,' he said, pointing to me and Jools, 'are a very welcome addition to my family. You're the sisters Stella never had. I know we're all going to be very happy living together in Holland Park.'

Mummy said quickly, 'But we won't be moving for a while. We're going to take it slowly. We all need to get used to the idea.' Looking directly at me and Jools, she said, 'Nothing will happen until you're both ready.'

Jools said, 'Can we pack now?' and everyone laughed.

'That's my girl,' Dan said. 'The sooner the better, as I keep telling Alice. I'm hoping we could maybe even get married this Christmas in Barbados. I know the exact spot. I can have it arranged in no time. How do you all feel about Christmas in Barbados?'

Mummy frowned. 'Dan, we discussed this. We might not be getting married for a while. We all need to take a breath and let the news settle.'

'Why wait?' Dan threw his hands into the air. 'We're all going to be so happy! Why put it off?'

'Slow down, Dad, you'll scare them.' Stella rolled her eyes at me and Jools. 'They're not employees you can boss around. Give everyone some breathing space.'

Dan sighed. 'All right, I'll back off. I'm sorry, everyone – I'm just really keen to start our lives together.'

'I'll go to Barbados anytime you like – tanned, toned men in Speedos are right up my street!' Kevin said, making us all laugh.

Then David said how lovely it would be to have us living next door and that we could call in anytime.

Pippa said she'd be so happy to have us close by because she'd always wanted a daughter and now she gets two surrogate ones, plus Stella.

Later, when everyone was chatting, Pippa came over to me and took me outside to Daddy's tree. 'Are you all right, Holly, darling?' she asked.

'I'm fine. I'm glad for Mummy.'

Pippa rubbed my hands in hers to keep them warm. 'Dan is a very nice man. But I know this can't be easy. I know how much David misses Ben. He lost his best friend and he still finds it very difficult, so I can only imagine how much harder it is for you having lost your dad. If you're upset or want to talk about anything, I'm here for you.'

We watched Mummy and Dan hugging through the kitchen window. From the outside looking in, you'd never know there had been so much sadness in that kitchen.

'Honestly, Pippa, I'm really glad Mummy has Dan. He's great.'

I could feel someone watching me. Mummy was peering out of the window at me. I smiled at her and gave her a thumbs-up. She smiled and mouthed, 'I love you.'

I turned back to the cherry tree and prayed silently that wherever Daddy was – Heaven, the afterlife – he was safe and happy.

*Alice: 26 October 2014*

Alice tapped gently on the bedroom door. She pushed it open and found Jools sobbing into her pillow. She put the tray down and went over to sit on the bed. 'Hey, there, don't cry, it's your birthday.'

'I wish Dad was here. Eighteen is a really big deal and he's not here and he's never going to be here for any of my birthdays. Why did he have to die on my birthday? It sucks.'

Alice wiped Jools's face with a napkin. 'I know it hurts, pet. It's rotten that Dad died on your birthday, but I'm going to try to make it a special day for you. Come downstairs when you're ready. I have presents for you.'

Alice went back to the kitchen and, with Holly's help, put the final touches to the decorations. Five minutes later, Jools came down in her pyjamas. When she opened the kitchen door she was greeted with huge displays of balloons and *Happy Birthday* banners, flowers and a table filled with all her favourite food.

'Wow,' she said, peeping through an enormous bunch of balloons. 'This is great.'

'Come and sit down.' Alice led her to a chair they had transformed into a birthday throne.

Holly placed a crown on her sister's head. 'I think we got every single chocolaty thing that you love.'

'Yum,' Jools said, eyeing up the treats and taking a bite out of a mini-chocolate muffin.

'Here are your presents,' Holly said, handing her sister a big bag laden with packages. 'Mummy got you seventeen little ones and one big one.'

Jools ripped open the big one first. She looked up at her mother, dumbfounded. 'Are you serious?'

'What is it?' Holly asked.

'Only the coolest tablet in the world! The Samsung Galaxy Tab S.'

'Wow.'

'You deserve it. Eighteen is a big deal,' Alice said.

Jools flung her arms around her mother. 'Thank you, Mum – this is amazing. I never thought you'd buy it for me.'

'I wanted to treat you. Your last two birthdays have been awful because of Dad, so I wanted to make this one better.'

'That's why I've decided to celebrate my birthday a day later from next year on. I was thinking of doing it the day before, but then I thought, no, because we'll all still be dreading the next day. So, from next year on, the day after Dad's anniversary will be my birthday.'

Alice smiled. 'That's a brilliant idea. It means we have something to look forward to the day after.'

Jools took a bite of *pain au chocolat*. 'But I have to say, Mum, this is actually turning out to be a good birthday. When I woke up I was dreading it. I just wanted to stay in bed and cry, but the balloons and the presents and the chocolate have all made it really nice. Thanks.'

'You're welcome, sweetheart.'

Holly handed Jools a present. It was an envelope. Jools tore it open and looked inside. She read out loud: 'You have given three goats to a family in Africa.' She frowned. 'Is this a joke?'

Holly and Alice burst out laughing. 'Yes. Here's your other present.'

Holly handed her a Topshop bag. Inside Jools found a sweatshirt with a sequined cat on the front.

'Cool! I love it. Thanks, Holly.'

'Kevin helped me choose it.'

'This is from Dan.' Alice handed Jools another envelope.

'OMG! It's two hours with a personal shopper in Selfridges!'

'I thought it was too much but he insisted on spoiling you for your eighteenth birthday. Stella fixed it for him – she knew you'd love it. She's picking you up at ten.'

Jools jumped up and down. 'This is the best birthday ever!'

Alice beamed at her happy daughter. It was so lovely to see her smiling on her birthday. The last two had been so awful. Things were definitely getting better. This year would be a new chapter in their lives, a happy one.

'OMG, I have to FaceTime Chloë and tell her.' Jools ran off to talk to her friend.

Alice put the kettle on to make herself a strong cup of coffee. She'd been up early to decorate the kitchen and wrap all the presents and she needed some caffeine.

'Mummy?' Holly said.

'Yes, pet.'

'Sometimes I can't remember Daddy's face properly.'

Alice put down her cup and went over to her. 'That's why we have photos and videos to remind us.'

'But how can you forget your own dad?' Holly's eyes filled.

'You haven't forgotten him, sweetheart. You just can't remember details.'

'But he's my dad! I can't remember what his voice sounds like either. I'm scared that I'm going to only remember him by photos.'

Alice hugged her daughter. 'You'll never forget him. He's in here.' She pointed to Holly's heart. 'Dad is half of you.

He's in your DNA. He helped to make you the wonderful person you are.'

Holly blinked back the tears. 'I think he's becoming a memory and not a real person now.'

'Dad will always be real. He was a brilliant father and husband and we were lucky to have him.'

'I wish I could have had him for longer. When Katie goes on about her dad being a pain, I want to shout at her and tell her how lucky she is to have a dad.'

'Oh, Holly, I'm sorry.'

'I'm fine, Mummy, honestly. It's just today is a sad day.'

'I'm here for you, darling. Talk to me anytime.'

Holly wrapped her arms around her mother. 'I know, Mummy, and you've been brilliant. I'm glad you met Dan. He's really nice and he looks after you. You need looking after.'

It was Alice's turn to well up. 'Thank you.'

When Jools came back, her mother and sister were in each other's arms. 'No no no no no. No one is allowed to cry on my birthday. This is going to be a happy day. Dad would want us to be happy. Now, come on, let's go out to the tree and toast me being eighteen with Dad, and then I'm going to shop till I drop!'

Alice took her coffee and the girls took a glass of juice each and they went out to the cherry tree. They stood under the orange and red leaves and toasted Ben.

Her daughters had come a long way in two years, she thought. They were battered, bruised and scarred, but strong and resilient too. For the first time since Ben died, she knew it was going to be all right. They'd survived the worst and happiness was possible again.

*Ben: November 2014*

They waited for the first casualties to arrive. The attack had been planned for weeks and every able-bodied person was involved – women and men. It was a night-time attack, a final push to regain the land.

Declan looked at Ben.

Ben's heart was pounding.

'The first chance we get, we go,' Declan whispered.

Soon the tent was full of injured people. The two doctors patched up the ones they could and laid the fatally wounded outside, covered with sheets.

It was pandemonium. People were running in and out, screaming, shouting, crying . . .

Ben and Declan worked through the night until early morning when an eerie silence fell over the camp.

The casualty count was high. The mission had failed. The remaining soldiers returned home defeated and depleted.

Through the calm, Yonas came staggering into the tent with someone on his shoulder. He laid him down. It was Awate, with a gaping hole in his chest.

'He's fucked,' Declan said.

Ben searched for a pulse. There was none. 'I'm sorry, Yonas, he's dead.'

Yonas covered his face with his hands.

Declan looked at Ben and nodded.

Ben put his hand on Yonas's shoulder. 'He's dead, and you have to help us,' he whispered.

Yonas looked up.

Ben tightened his grip on the soldier's arm. 'Yonas, we saved your wife and your son. You have to let us go. We need to see our families. You have to help us.'

'We can't stay here another day. If you don't let us go, we'll kill ourselves,' Declan said.

Yonas peeled Ben's fingers from his arm. He said something to the soldier who was guarding the tent, then indicated that Ben and Declan should follow him.

They went to his hut. Yonas spoke to Segen, who nodded and went to fetch a bag. She quickly packed it with water and food.

Ben's breathing was ragged: a panic attack was coming on. Was this it? Were they finally going to be free?

Yonas took the bag and told the two men to follow him. They walked on in the half-dark in silence. After about thirty minutes, as the sun began to rise, Yonas stopped and handed them the bag.

'You go down and you find village. Ask for Nasih. You give him this.' Yonas handed them a note. 'He help you get to Asmara.'

Ben held out his hand. Yonas shook it. 'Thank you.'

Declan tried to speak, but no words came out. He clapped Yonas on the back.

'You good men. You good doctors. You go now.'

They didn't have to be told twice. Ben and Declan walked away, stumbling over rocks, exhausted, kept going now by pure adrenalin. They didn't speak – they daren't. They were too afraid to jinx it.

They were going home. They were going to see their families.

Ben felt as if his head would explode. He tried to suppress hope, excitement, anticipation and fear – fear of being taken back, fear of not making it. He gritted his teeth and walked faster – towards the light, towards home, towards happiness.

## *Holly: November 2014*

Dan's house is really enormous. I know Jools thinks it's amazing, but I prefer ours. It's much more cosy. Mummy said we don't have to move in with Dan until we're ready. I don't really want to move at all. I like things the way they are. I like it just being me, Jools and Mummy at home. I'm really happy that Mummy met Dan and I want her to be with him, but I'm worried that if we move in with him, he'll want Mummy's attention all the time and take her on trips away every week.

Dan is super-nice, though – he gave me and Jools diamond bracelets. Mummy was a bit shocked and said it was too much, but Jools put hers on straight away. I kind of agree with Mummy and, besides, the only jewellery I want to wear is Daddy's H necklace.

Jools said she can't wait to live in Dan's house. It has a gym and a cinema. She wants to invite all her friends over and have parties. But I hate the thought of leaving our home.

Mummy asked us to be on our best behaviour at the party because we were going to be meeting Dan's friends. There were seventeen people there when we arrived and everyone was very friendly, but I did hear one man saying, 'I don't know why, with all the women he could have had, he picked a widow with two teenagers. Has he lost his mind?'

The woman he was talking to said, 'You know Dan. He's always trying to save something or someone. He needs a project.'

I thought that was a bit mean. Mummy doesn't need to be saved: she has us. I felt a bit cross so I went over to the corner and sat in one of the window seats. David came over to me. I love David and Pippa – they make me feel close to Daddy.

'Are you all right, Holly? Is it all a bit overwhelming for you?'

'No, I'm fine. I just thought I'd sit here and keep out of the way.'

'It must feel a bit strange, having your mum engaged to someone else. I even find it a bit strange myself. I keep thinking back to when Ben and Alice got engaged. We all went to the pub and drank too much beer.'

'Were they very happy?'

David smiled. 'Incredibly happy. Your dad was head over heels in love with Alice. They were great together.'

'Do you still miss him a lot?'

David nodded. 'You?'

I nodded, too, feeling like I might cry.

'Listen, darling, if you ever want to talk about your dad or look at my photos of him from our university days, pop around anytime.'

'Thank you.'

'And I'm sorry if I made you sad. Tonight's supposed to be a celebration. Dan's a good man and your mum deserves to be happy. She's a very special lady.'

'I know. I am glad about it. I was just –'

'Having a moment?'

I nodded again. David kissed my head. 'Me too.'

Stella and Jools came over to us. 'We've been looking for you,' Stella said. 'Here, I thought you might like this.' She handed me a bowl full of chocolates. 'I opened one of the boxes a guest brought. They're delicious.'

I smiled at her, even though I knew I couldn't eat any-thing. 'Thanks.'

Jools bent down. 'You okay?'

'Fine. Just watching everyone.'

Jools patted my arm. 'I know it's all a bit strange.'

'It's strange for me too,' Stella said. 'But we're lucky that Dad and Alice met each other. Look how happy they are.'

We saw Dan say something that made Mummy laugh. He put his hand up to her face and she held it.

The woman who organized the party went to Dan and asked him something, then Kevin whispered to Mummy. She tapped her glass and said she wanted to say a few words. But in the middle of her speech, Dan's housekeeper, Mrs Jen-kins, walked over to Mummy and said something to her. Mummy dashed out of the room. When she came back in, she looked sick.

Dan had his back to Mummy so he didn't see her face, but Kevin rushed over to her and she whispered something in his ear. Kevin went white. Something was wrong. Jools was looking at art on Stella's iPad. I grabbed her arm.

'Ouch – what?'

'Come now.' I knew something bad had happened. My heart was pounding.

'What's wrong?' Stella asked.

'Nothing, I just feel a bit sick.'

We went over to Mummy and Kevin. Mummy looked as if she'd seen a ghost. She was shaking. When she saw me, she hugged me really tightly and started to cry. I felt very scared.

'Out. Now.' Kevin pushed us all into the hall.

'What's wrong?' Jools asked Mummy. 'Are you having second thoughts? Do you have cold feet?'

Mummy shook her head. Kevin ushered us into the library. He locked the door.

Mummy looked at Kevin. They were both crying.

'Mum, what is going on? You're starting to freak me out!' Jools's voice shook.

'I have some news. I've just found out that . . . well . . . it's . . . it's your dad.' Mummy was falling over her words. She sounded really strange. My heart kept on pounding. What could she have found out about Dad?

'What about him?' Jools asked.

I stopped breathing. Something was wrong. But he was dead. What could be worse? I tried not to cry.

'He's alive. Your dad isn't dead. He's alive.' Mummy was crying so much it was hard to understand her.

Jools screamed, but I couldn't say anything. I didn't understand. How? How could a dead person be alive? What was she talking about?

'He wasn't killed. He was kidnapped. He's been in Eritrea all the time. He's coming home,' Mummy said, through her tears.

Jools kept screaming. Kevin squeezed her in a big hug and said over and over again, 'It's okay.' Eventually she started to calm down and stop making so much noise.

Mummy went over to Dan's big desk and handed us all tissues from the box there. I hadn't realized I was crying.

Alive? I couldn't take it in.

'But how?' I asked. My voice sounded so small and far away. It was as if I wasn't really inside my own body.

Mummy turned to me and held my hand. 'I don't know all the details. The Foreign and Commonwealth Office just called and said he's in the British Embassy in Asmara. They're flying him home tomorrow.'

'Asmara is the capital of Eritrea,' I said.

'Are they sure it's him?' Jools asked.

'Yes. I spoke to him.'

'You heard his voice?' I was shaking again.

Mummy had stopped crying and smiled. 'Yes. He said, "Hi, Alice, it's Ben. I'm alive." And then he said he couldn't wait to see you both. He said he loves us all very much and he'll never leave our side again.'

Jools fell into a chair, put her hands over her face and started crying, her shoulders shaking.

Oh, God. Was this real? Was I dreaming? I pinched myself. No, I was awake. I sat down, too. I needed to get things straight in my mind. Everything was all muddled up. 'We'll see him tomorrow? We'll see Daddy tomorrow?' I wanted to know that I'd understood what was going on.

'Yes, pet, you will.' Mummy hugged me.

'Can we talk to him now?' Jools managed to ask.

'They said he had to see the doctor and be debriefed, but they'd get him to call later.'

There was a loud knock on the door. We all looked around.

'Alice? Darling, is everything all right?'

It was Dan. We froze. Mummy's hand flew up to her mouth. Her diamond ring flashed.

Kevin took charge. He went over to the door and talked loudly through it. 'Sorry, Dan, the girls are just having a wobble. They're a little overwhelmed. They just need a few minutes.'

'Are they all right? Is Alice all right?'

'She's fine. Everyone's fine – it's just an emotional day. We need a minute to calm things down.'

'I'll check back in a few minutes.'

Kevin leant against the door and exhaled loudly.

Mummy collapsed into a big leather chair. 'Oh, my God, what am I going to do?'

Jools was staring at Mummy in a weird way. 'What do you mean? Just tell him Dad's home and you can't marry him.'

Mummy looked shocked. 'I can't just . . . I need to . . . The Foreign and Commonwealth Office said I mustn't tell a soul yet.'

Kevin paced the room. 'We need to buy some time. Tell Dan that Holly's freaking out about the engagement and you have to take her home.'

But Mummy wasn't listening. She was twisting the diamond ring around her finger, staring into the fire.

Kevin bent down beside her. 'Alice, we have to get out of here and go home. You need space. You need to get your head around this. It's a huge shock.'

Mummy nodded.

Knock on the door again.

Kevin cursed.

'Alice, sweetie, it's Pippa. Are you all right? Dan's worried about you.'

Kevin pulled Mummy to her feet. 'I'll talk to her, but I need you to hold it together while we get out of here. You can fall apart at home.'

Mummy looked at Jools and me and held out her arms. We rushed to her side and held on to her.

Kevin went to the door. He opened it a fraction. 'Sorry, Pippa, Holly's having a bit of a panic attack. The whole night has been too much for her. We have to take her home immediately. Can you help us slip out? Alice doesn't want a fuss.'

'Oh, the poor darling. Why don't I take Holly to our house? I can look after her there. It means Alice can stay on and celebrate. It'd be a shame for her to miss her own engagement party.'

Kevin remained calm. 'Thanks, Pippa, but Holly's really very upset. She needs her mother tonight. The best thing is for us to get her home.'

'I understand. I'll grab your coats and have my driver take you.'

'Could you explain it to Dan for us?'

'Well I . . . Of course, if you want me to . . . but he might want to speak to Alice.'

'Please, Pippa, she's upset about Holly. She just wants to get out of here with minimum fuss.'

'No problem. Leave it with me.' Pippa ran off to get the coats and Kevin shut the door.

'Look, guys, I know this has been the kind of shock that could kill a person, but I need you to walk out of here now and straight down the steps into Pippa's car.'

We held hands as we stepped into the hall. Pippa handed us our coats and gave me a hug. 'Oh, sweetie, I know this is hard for you, but Dan is just wonderful and he makes your mummy so happy.'

David came over to me and crouched down. 'I feel responsible for upsetting you. I shouldn't have talked to you about Ben tonight. I'm an idiot. I'm so sorry, Holly.' He swept me up in a big hug and I could feel everything building up in my chest. I hated lying to him and making him feel bad. I felt awful.

'It's not your fault, David. You've always been wonderful to us,' Mummy said. 'I . . . Something has . . . I can't . . . I'll call you tomorrow and explain properly. I have to go. Please, we have to go home now.'

'Sorry, of course.' David stepped out of the way. 'I'll phone later to see how Holly's doing.'

Mummy and Kevin grabbed me and pulled me down the steps towards the waiting car.

Out of the corner of my eye I could see Dan walking quickly towards the front door.

'Alice?'

We stopped dead.

Dan looked worried. 'What's happening?'

Mummy couldn't look him in the eye. 'It's . . . it's . . .'

'It's Holly,' Jools said, pushing between Dan and Mummy. 'She's freaking out.'

Dan looked hurt. He came over to me. 'Holly, I thought you were all right about this. You told me you were happy I was marrying your mum. What's wrong? Can I help?'

Dan's face was all sad and I couldn't take any more. First David, now Dan, everyone looking at me. And Daddy alive. And we couldn't say anything. I opened my mouth to say sorry and a howl came out.

Dan stepped back in shock. Mummy pulled me close. 'I'm sorry, Dan. She's just upset. I need to get her home now.'

David came down and took Dan's arm. 'I'm to blame. I spoke to her about her father earlier. I'm so sorry.'

Pippa held Dan's other arm. 'Come on, you need to get back to your guests. Let Alice take Holly home.'

Dan shrugged helplessly. 'All right. Alice darling, I'll call you later.' He leant over to kiss Mummy, but she turned her head and he ended up kissing her ear instead of her lips.

'Let's go!' Jools pulled Mummy and me down the steps and into the car.

I lay on Mummy's lap, crying the whole way home.

# PART 3
# London, 2014-2015

*Alice*

Alice stared at the ceiling. Ben. Alive. Not dead. Coming home. Arriving soon. She wasn't a widow. Her husband was going to be home in two hours.

What the hell was she going to do? She felt happy and sad, terrified and worried. So incredibly, shakily worried. Would he have changed? He sounded the same, but how would she feel when she saw him? What if she didn't love him any more? Would he have post-traumatic stress? What if he had been tortured and his body was scarred, or worse? What if he was a different person, like a stranger? What if . . .

Her phone beeped. It was Dan again. He had called twice and sent three texts. She couldn't talk to him. He'd know by her voice that something was very wrong. Alice wished she could tell him. She wished Dan was beside her now, putting his arms around her, telling her that everything was going to be all right, protecting her.

Oh, God, what was she going to do? Dan would know what to do. He always knew what to do. He was brilliant at giving her advice and solving problems. But then, she thought, this was one problem he really couldn't help her with. How can you tell the man you're supposed to marry that your husband has come back to life? How do you tell the man you love that the man you used to love is about to walk through the door?

But things with Ben couldn't just go back to normal, could

they? Everything was different. Alice was different. She'd changed. She was stronger now, more independent. She'd spent two years working on herself, making herself stronger, more steely, managing the girls and the finances and life. It had been so difficult, but she'd done it.

Was Ben just going to walk through the door and back into their lives as if nothing had happened? As if those two long years didn't matter?

Would he be sleeping in her bed tonight? Alice's stomach churned. She was scared, nervous and full of dread. She loved Dan. But she did love Ben . . . She had loved Ben. Could she just switch back? Her head throbbed.

Jools came tumbling into the room and jumped up and down on Alice's bed. 'Come on, Mum, get up. Get dressed. Let's go and see Dad!'

'He's not landing for another two hours. They're sending a car for us at ten.'

'I'm too excited to sleep. I'm so happy. I just can't believe it! Dad's alive! Oh, Mum, it's like a dream.'

Alice smiled at her daughter. It was lovely to see Jools so happy. It was wonderful for the girls to have their dad home. She was so pleased for them, but she was worried that he would struggle to adjust to 'normal life'.

Holly came in and sat down beside Alice while Jools continued to bounce.

'How are you feeling, pet?' Alice asked.

'Happy but nervous.'

'Nervous? About what?' Jools crash-landed on the bed.

Holly picked at the duvet cover. 'Well, I'm scared Daddy might have had a terrible time and have PTS.'

'What's PTS?'

'Post-traumatic stress disorder,' Alice said.

'What – like soldiers get?' Jools asked.

Alice nodded.

Jools sat down. 'But he sounded completely fine on the phone, just like Dad. No different. Not all crazy in the head or confused. He's fine. He's the same. It was so strange because when I heard his voice I felt as if he hadn't been gone long at all. God, it was so incredible to talk to him.'

Alice crossed her fingers under the duvet. She hoped Jools was right. Ben certainly had sounded 'normal'. But there was no way he couldn't be affected by two years in captivity.

Alice's phone beeped again. Jools shouted, 'It's Dad!' and grabbed it to read the message. Her face fell. 'Oh, no, it's Dan.'

'Have you told him about Daddy?' Holly asked.

'No.'

'You have to tell him,' Jools said. 'He needs to know Dad's home and that you can't marry him now.'

'It's not quite that simple,' Alice said.

'Yes, it is.' Jools handed Alice her phone. 'Here, call him. Tell him about Dad.'

Alice placed the phone on her bedside locker. 'I'll do it later.'

'Poor Dan. He's going to be heartbroken,' Holly said. 'And Stella.'

Jools crossed her arms and scowled at Alice. 'He'll be fine. He's got his work and Stella and . . . Well, he'll just have to get over it because Dad's back. End of.'

Alice felt sick, but she stayed still and said nothing.

'Do you think Daddy will look the same?' Holly asked.

'He said he's thinner. I asked him to send me a selfie, but the boring old farts at the embassy said he wasn't allowed to,' Jools answered.

Holly hugged her knees to her chest. 'It's a miracle. A real-life miracle.'

'You'll have to take that off,' Jools said, pointing to Alice's engagement ring.

Alice took it off and placed it carefully in the Cartier box beside her bed. She then pulled her gold necklace with the A out of a drawer and put it on. She had stopped wearing it after Dan had proposed. It just didn't seem right to have Ben around her neck and be engaged to someone else.

The necklace felt like a weight on her chest. She could feel her heart racing.

'Will you give Dan back the ring?' Holly asked.

Alice nodded, not trusting herself to speak. Her hand looked so bare now.

'She has to. She can't let Dad see it. How do you think he'd feel if he found out Mum was engaged? I've been thinking about it, Mum. We mustn't let Dad find out about Dan. It would really hurt him.'

'We can't lie. David and Pippa know too,' Alice said.

'We have to.' Jools was adamant. 'It's not fair for Dad to come home and think we've all moved on without him.' Her voice cracked. 'He'd be heartbroken.'

'Dan's going to be heartbroken too,' Holly said quietly.

'Yes, but Dad is our dad. Dan is just a person.'

Alice had been thinking the exact same thing. How the hell was she going to tell Ben that she had almost married someone else? Should she lie? Wasn't that the wrong thing to do? He was probably going to be very fragile and emotionally fraught when he got back and she couldn't just land that on him. But what if David said something or Pippa let it slip? She didn't want him to hear it from anyone else, but it was a terrible thing to have to admit to him. Jools was right: they shouldn't say anything. Not now anyway, perhaps not ever.

Alice wanted to scream. Just when she'd found happiness and moved on, Ben had turned up alive. She felt torn in two.

She loved Dan and couldn't bear to tell him it was over. She didn't want it to be over. She wanted to run to him right now.

'Okay, shower time.' Alice rushed into her bathroom before she broke down. It wouldn't do to have a panic attack in front of the girls. On what should have been such a happy day, she just felt sick and terrified.

She heard the front door open and slam. Then Kevin's voice called up the stairs: 'Anyone here ready for the reunion of their lives?'

Jools squealed, 'Yes!' and Alice felt her whole body start to shake.

'Where's your mum?' Kevin asked.

'Bathroom,' Holly said. 'And we need to get showered as well.'

'Off you go,' said Kevin. 'I'll wait here for her.'

Alice heard the two girls run to their rooms, then silence. From the other side of the door Kevin said, 'I'm right here, Alice. I'll be here when you come out.'

Alice turned on the shower so he wouldn't hear her crying.

Kevin pulled three dresses out of her wardrobe. 'This one, I think,' he said, holding up the baby blue one. 'It brings out your eyes.'

'That's Ben's favourite.' Alice had thought it wasn't possible to cry any more, but tears fell down her cheeks, hot and salty. Her eyes were sore from weeping.

Kevin went over and locked the bedroom door. 'You're afraid you won't feel the same way about him?'

'Yes,' Alice sobbed. 'What if I don't love him, Kevin? I let Ben go. I moved on. I love Dan. I genuinely do. I know that makes me a really bad person, but I can't just un-love Dan.'

Kevin handed her a tissue. 'You're not a bad person. You

were so sad and so full of grief I thought you were going to have a nervous breakdown, but you dug deep and, instead of going off the rails entirely, you pulled yourself up and began to live again. There is absolutely no shame in that.'

Alice blew her nose. 'But what am I going to say to Ben? What's going to happen? Are we just going to come home and live as if the last two years weren't real? The only person I want to see right now is Dan.' Alice slumped onto her bed.

'Have you spoken to him since last night?' Kevin asked.

'No, I don't know what to say, but he keeps calling and texting.'

'You have to say something or else he'll come here and then you're in real trouble.'

'What am I supposed to tell him?' Alice said weakly.

Kevin picked up her phone and handed it to her. 'Just text, *Really sorry, having bit of family crisis, will call as soon as I can.*'

Alice tried to type but her hands were shaking, so Kevin did it for her. 'God, Kevin, I really want to talk to him.'

Kevin put his hands on her shoulders. 'I know you do, but you can't, Alice. Not today. You have to focus on the girls and Ben now.'

Alice decided not to wear the blue dress. It felt wrong. She felt as if she was letting Dan down by wearing Ben's favourite dress. Her head was so muddled she thought it was going to burst. In the end she chose a simple black dress that she liked and felt comfortable in, then sat down to do her make-up. By the time she had finished, she looked better – tired, older and a bit weary, perhaps, but not too bad.

Once Alice was ready, she nodded at Kevin and he unlocked the door. A few minutes later the girls came in all dressed up. Jools was wearing tight black trousers and a silver top with black detail, and Holly was in a lovely red and navy tweed mini-dress.

Kevin stood in front of them and told them to stand together for a photo. 'It's a momentous occasion so we need to mark it.'

Alice put her arms around her two girls. The three *amigos*. Soon to be four again. Holly huddled close to her mother, while Jools hopped from one foot to the other, desperate to see her dad.

The bell rang. 'It's the car!' Jools tore downstairs to open the door.

Alice stood frozen to the spot.

'Oh. Hi, Granddad.'

'Oh, Christ, it's Harold!' Kevin hissed. 'I'd forgotten all about him.'

'Why did he come here? I told him to meet us at the airport,' Alice said.

'Guilt, because he hasn't contacted you in so long,' Kevin said.

Holly went downstairs to greet the grandfather she hadn't seen for nearly a year.

Alice and Kevin could hear Harold's voice booming, 'Incredible . . . wonderful . . . can't believe it . . .'

'I really don't want to see him,' Alice said fiercely. 'The mean old bastard never even rang the girls on their birthdays.'

Kevin put on his jacket. 'He's Ben's dad. You're just going to have to suck it up.'

As they left the room Alice's phone beeped. *I hope ur okay. Call me. I'm sure I can help. I love you. D x*

It took all of her strength to put the phone into her bag and not call him.

As she walked downstairs, Harold beamed at her for the first time in all the years she'd known him. 'Wonderful day. What a thing to happen.'

Alice forced a smile. 'Yes, it is. It's wonderful.'

'I can't quite believe I'll be seeing my boy in a few hours,' Harold marvelled.

'It's so exciting!' Jools did a little skip.

'We must be careful to keep our emotions in check, though. He'll have had a difficult time. It's important that you stay strong and don't upset him.'

Alice gritted her teeth. 'They'll react however their hearts tell them to, Harold.'

Harold scowled. 'Ben will need a calm environment to come home to. He'll be pretty shaken, I imagine. He'll require peace and quiet to readjust.'

Before Alice could tell Harold just what she thought of his wretched advice, David and Pippa rushed through the door.

Alice had called David late the night before to tell him and he had cried down the phone.

He ran past Harold, picked Alice up and swung her around. 'I haven't slept a wink. I can't believe it. I'm beside myself. I just can't believe he's alive. It truly is a miracle. What an incredible man he is. Surviving and escaping. That's Ben, though. He's an amazing person.'

'Put her down, David, you'll crush her,' Pippa scolded.

Alice managed to whisper in David's ear, 'Not a word about Dan.' He looked surprised for a moment, then nodded quickly. Thank goodness he understood. Alice couldn't bear the thought of Harold finding out about Dan – he would never forgive or forget it. Even more than Ben, they had to keep news of Dan and the engagement from Harold.

David turned to the girls and hugged them both. He shook hands with Harold and clapped him on the back. Then the two men congratulated each other on the 'miracle'.

'Are you all right, darling?' Pippa whispered to Alice, as she embraced her.

Alice held on to her, glad of the support. 'I'm not sure. I think I'm in shock.'

Pippa squeezed her tight. 'I'm sure you are. It's hard to take in.'

'How was Dan last night?' Alice whispered.

'A bit worried that Holly's "breakdown" will make you change your mind. He's desperate to talk to you. He called me this morning to ask if I'd spoken to you. I lied and said no and told him I thought you'd need a day or two to sort things out.'

'I feel sick about it all,' Alice said, trying not to cry.

'I know. It's so wonderful about Ben, but Dan's going to be crushed.'

'I love him, Pippa.'

'Oh, darling, I know. I could see how happy you were last night.'

'The girls don't want Ben to find out, not yet anyway. So will you guys keep it quiet? I need to get my head straight.'

'Of course. We actually discussed it last night. David said it's up to you to decide what to do. He'll say nothing about it.'

'Thanks. I will tell Ben, just not now, not for a while.'

Jools shouted, 'The car's here, Mum. Let's go!'

When they arrived at the airport, they were brought into a private room full of people drinking champagne and talking loudly.

As soon as Alice walked in a big man in a 'Welcome home' T-shirt enveloped her in a hug. 'You must be Alice. Isn't this the best day ever?'

Alice nodded politely.

'I'm Declan's da, Billy. We spoke on the phone after it happened. Do you remember?'

Alice had a vague memory of it, but she had been in the throes of grief and shock and it was all very hazy. 'Yes, of course. How are you?'

'Feckin' ecstatic! Can you believe it, Alice? Our lads were alive all this time. I'm going to kill that Declan when he gets off the plane. I had hair before this happened.' He grinned and patted his bald head.

'I'm Jools.' She proffered a hand.

'Come here to me, you little beauty.' Billy hugged her, then Holly, Kevin, David, Pippa and even Harold, much to the older man's dismay. 'Now come and meet my mad lot.' Billy introduced his five children plus their spouses and children. Forty-one people in all.

Alice was glad of the company and the crowd. It was easier to disappear among all those people and it was distracting too.

A few minutes later Billy came back over and handed her a glass of champagne. 'Get that down your neck. You look like you need it. I thought I was going to have a heart attack myself when I heard the news yesterday. We all flew over on the six a.m. flight this morning. None of us slept a wink. It's just magic.'

'Yes, yes, it is.'

Billy patted her back. 'I can see you're overwhelmed, love, and I understand. It's like they've risen from the dead or something. We're all in shock. When I spoke to Declan last night, I thought my heart would burst. He sounded just like himself. You know?'

'Yes, I do.' Alice smiled, Billy's enthusiasm was infectious.

'Declan told me your Ben was brilliant to him out there. I think they helped each other through it.'

Alice hadn't spoken to Ben about Declan because he'd been too busy asking about the girls.

'It's just going to be brilliant to see them and get back to normal. It must have been very hard for you and your girls.'

Alice gulped some champagne. 'Yes, it was. But for you too. I mean, losing a son is just as bad.'

'I thought I'd die of a broken heart. I was just talking to Harold about it, but he kept banging on about "all in the past" and "onwards and upwards". He's a cold, uptight git, if you don't mind my saying.'

Alice threw her head back and laughed. 'I couldn't agree more.'

'Seriously, who ate his dessert? You'd swear nothing had happened. He's going to pretend Ben was never away. That's not right. My Eddie is married to Marie over there talking to your girls. Well, Marie loves reading them psychology books and she said we need to let Declan talk about it and get it off his chest. Pretending like it never happened is what they used to do in the world wars and that's why so many soldiers were so messed up. They came home from being on a battlefield, watching their friends getting their heads blown off, and their wives offered them a cup of tea and a cucumber sandwich! Feckin' mad, that is. Maybe that's what happened to Harold.'

'Maybe.'

'Or he's just a dickhead. No offence.'

'None taken.'

'So, what are you going to say to Ben?'

Alice hadn't thought about that. 'I don't know.'

'I'm going to tell Declan that if he ever gets on a plane again, I'll shoot it down myself, and that Manchester United are having a terrible season.'

What would Alice tell Ben? How could she even begin to fill in the last two years? She started to panic again.

'Take a sip of champagne. I can see your nerves going. So, how did a nice Irish girl like you end up with an English surgeon?'

Alice paused, then said honestly, 'Love. Ben was the most perfect man I'd ever met.'

'I thought my wife was perfect when I married her, but then she fecked off with a Polish plumber so I realized she wasn't so perfect after all.'

'Sorry to hear that.'

'Shit happens. You get over it and move on.'

'Yes, you do.'

'You don't realize how strong you are.'

'Absolutely.'

'Life has to go on.'

'I agree.'

'Otherwise you'd never get out of bed.'

'I know.'

'The key is to look to the future and away from the past.'

'Yes.'

'And you have to look for happiness again and take it.'

'Exactly. That's what I did and now I'm engaged to some-one else.'

'Jesus Christ!' Billy's eyes almost popped out of his head.

Alice's hand flew to her mouth. 'Jesus – sorry. I don't know why I said that. Oh, my God, I think I'm going mad. I'm just so . . . so . . .'

Billy pulled her over to the corner of the room, took the champagne from her and handed her a tissue. 'Right, no more booze for you. Look, love, you need to keep that info on the QT. The media are going to be all over this story. Two doctors presumed dead come back home? It's going to be a zoo when it gets out. You can't tell anyone about the other man. And if I was you, I certainly wouldn't be telling Ben anytime soon. You need to let the poor man recover from his ordeal first.'

Alice looked up. 'I know. I am. I will. I'm not a bad person. I thought Ben was dead. I met Dan six months ago and he . . . after all the grief and loneliness, he swept me off my feet. I loved Ben more than anything, but he was gone. He was dead.'

'Hold on now, I'm not judging you, love, I'm just giving you advice. You need to wait a bit before dropping that bombshell on your Ben.'

'I'll have to break up with Dan.' Alice was crying again.

'Oh, Jesus, don't cry. I can't handle women crying. This is supposed to be a happy day.'

'I'm so stressed I think my head is literally going to spin off.'

Billy shook her gently. 'Your long-lost husband is going to walk through that door any minute now, and you need to be smiling and acting happy. I don't know about this Dan fella, but I do know that you'll be savaged if the press gets wind of this. And if you don't look the part of the happy wife, it'll only encourage them to start sniffing around.' Billy took her hand. 'Come on, love, shoulders back and smile. I'm here, beside you. Here we go.'

Alice clasped the stranger's hand and held her breath . . .

## Ben

Declan ran down the steps and kissed the ground. 'We're home, Benji! We made it.' He threw himself on Ben and they hugged.

A man in a dark suit greeted them. 'Welcome home. I'm Quentin Jones of the Foreign and Commonwealth Office. We're very glad to have you back, gentlemen.'

'We're very glad to be home.' Ben shook Quentin's hand. 'It's been a rocky ride.'

'Yes, indeed, terrible thing to happen. I understand you've been debriefed already at the embassy in Eritrea. I'll need to go through some details with you later on but, for now, if you'll follow me, your families are waiting for you.'

Ben grabbed Declan's arm. He felt faint with excitement. For more than two years he'd prayed and dreamt of this moment and now it was happening. He was home. He was going to see his family. He swallowed the emotion that was threatening to swamp him.

Declan patted his arm. 'Don't lose it. Don't cry all over them – you'll freak them out. Just walk in there and say, "I love you and I'll never leave you again." '

Ben exhaled deeply. 'Thanks, mate.'

Declan playfully punched his shoulder. 'It's been one hell of a rollercoaster. I couldn't have done it without you. You saved my life more than once and my sanity on a daily basis. You're one hell of a guy. I . . .' His voice broke.

Ben put his arm around Declan. 'Hey, I feel the same way. You saved me out there, you crazy Irish bastard.'

Declan grinned. 'Who should I shag first? Eva Longoria or Beyoncé?'

'Why not have a threesome?'

'You're a genius.'

Quentin Jones paused in front of two large iron doors. 'You go through these doors and into the room on the right where your families are gathered. Are you ready?'

Declan and Ben looked at each other and laughed. Pushing past Quentin, they rushed towards the door.

Everything went still.

She was standing there. It was as if a light was shining on her.

'Alice, my Alice,' Ben gasped, and beside her was another woman. 'My Jools, my precious Jools, all grown-up,' and then, 'Holly, beautiful, gentle Holly.'

Ben tried to control himself, but when Jools screamed, 'Daddy!' and flung her arms around him, he lost it.

Holly and Jools clung to him. He held them tight and they all cried. Alice stood beside them, looking lost. Ben reached out a hand to her and pulled her in. He tried to kiss her but only got the corner of her mouth because Jools moved.

'Welcome home,' Alice said. She had to shout as there was pandemonium going on, with Declan's family whooping and cheering and crying.

'I'm sorry, Alice, I'm so sorry,' Ben said, and Alice began to cry.

Ben managed to find a space between the two girls and stepped forward to hold his wife. He inhaled her scent. 'Alice, my Alice.' He breathed deeply, drinking her in.

'Hello, son,' Harold said, from behind Alice.

Ben opened his eyes. 'Dad!' He let go of Alice and reached out to his father. They hugged awkwardly.

Harold's eyes were moist when he looked at his son. 'Good to have you home safely. Rotten lot those Eritreans, unruly, simply feral.'

'Yes.' Ben nodded.

'Still, you're back now. All in the past.'

The past? He'd barely landed. Did his father really think he could wipe out the last two years in two minutes? Ben pushed the angry thoughts to the back of his mind.

'Ben!' David threw his arms around his best friend.

'Oh, David, it's so good to see you.'

'Let me in.' Pippa laughed, and nudged her husband aside so she could hug Ben too.

'Dad, did you miss us?' Jools clutched Ben's arm as David and Pippa stood back.

'Oh, darling, more than you can ever know.' Ben held her to him again.

'Daddy, look, we're wearing your necklaces.' Holly showed him her H.

'Oh, my God, you got them.'

'Yes, and I never took it off. Ever,' Holly assured him.

Ben kissed her beautiful face. 'I missed you so, so much.'

'Never leave us again,' Jools said. 'Never.'

'Never.' Ben caught them in his arms.

'You look the same, Daddy,' Holly said. 'I was worried you'd be different.'

'Well, he's thinner,' Jools said.

'You both look so grown-up. I can't believe how much you've changed.'

'But we're the same inside,' Holly said. 'Well, a bit sadder, but the same.'

Ben winced.

'Shut up, Holly!' Jools snapped.

'Oh, it's okay, Daddy. I'm not sad any more.' Holly was upset.

'I promise I'll make it up to you both. We're going to be together all the time now.'

'Good!' Holly said.

Declan tapped Alice on the shoulder. 'The beautiful Alice, I presume?'

She smiled. 'Yes. And you must be Declan.'

Declan kissed her cheek. He leant in and said, 'Your husband is the best man I ever met. He's a hero to me. And I can tell you, he loves you more than anything in the world.'

'Wow. Well . . . that's lovely to hear . . . thank you.' Alice stumbled over her words, trying not to let emotion overwhelm her again. 'How are you doing?'

'I'm okay, thanks. But once I've had a few pints of Guinness and got laid, I'll be great.'

Ben moved over to them. 'Stay away from my wife, you.' He grinned and put an arm around Alice's shoulders.

'Don't worry, Benji. I'm not going to try it on with Alice.'

'Benji?'

'Declan's annoying nickname for me,' Ben explained.

'I see,' Alice said. 'What was your nickname for him?'

'Mostly Ben just called me the MIB – Mad Irish Bastard.' Declan grinned.

'Can you believe I've had to sleep beside this reprobate for two years?' Ben said.

'Sounds cosy.' Alice smiled.

'I'm happy to hand him back to you, Alice,' Declan said. 'You can sleep with him now and put up with his smelly feet. I'm going to find myself a supermodel.'

Alice felt her stomach sink. The idea of sleeping with Ben terrified her. She longed for Dan's protective arms around her. *Stop it!* she shouted inwardly. *Your husband is home. Stop thinking about Dan.*

Billy came thundering over and flung his arms around Ben. 'How the hell are you? I'm Billy.'

Ben laughed. 'I've heard an awful lot about you, Billy.'

Billy kissed him on both cheeks. 'Thank you for looking after my lad. He told me how brilliant you were to him. We're for ever indebted to you. Christ, I'm just over the moon to have you home.' Billy wiped tears from his face.

'Jesus, Da, stop crying, you're killing me,' Declan said.

'I can't help it, you little shit. I thought you were dead.'

Declan held his father's hand. 'I'm back now, Da. Back to torment you.'

'If I even hear of you looking at a picture of Africa I'll kneecap you, do you understand?'

'Calm down.' Declan patted his father's arm.

'I'm serious. You are never to go anywhere but the UK and Ireland.'

Two men came over and introduced themselves as Declan's brothers, Sean and Eddie.

'You gave us some fright, you bastard,' Eddie said, thumping Declan on the back.

'Poor Da lost all his hair. You'll have to pay for one of them hair transplants for him,' Sean said.

'Don't worry, Da. I'll get you a nice thatch.'

'Maybe we could grow marijuana on it.' Eddie snorted.

'Or a herb garden,' Alice said.

'I love a bird with a sense of humour. I'm taking her home to Dublin,' Sean said, linking his arm through Alice's.

'I don't think so. She's all mine.' Ben drew Alice closer to him. She crossed her arms and glanced at the girls.

'Did you hear Declan's plan for the next few weeks?' Eddie asked Sean.

'No?'

'Tell him, Declan.'

'I'm going to ride every bird I meet and then I'm going to find an Alice and get married and have a shedload of kids.'

Billy coughed and Alice was blushing.

'Not a bad plan,' Sean said. Then, shouting over his shoulder, he said, 'Here, Collette, I'm going to hang out with Declan for the next few months. You look after the kids and the garage, okay?'

'In your dreams, Sean. I heard about Declan's plan. The only thing you'll be riding is the baseball bat I'll shove up your arse.'

Declan roared with laughter. 'I told you, Ben, they're all mad.'

Ben grinned. 'I feel as if I know them already. Declan talked about you – a lot!'

Holly and Jools came over. 'Have my family been talking at you?' Declan asked. 'I bet you didn't get a word in.'

The girls smiled. 'They're lovely and so funny,' Jools said.

'They swear an awful lot,' Holly said.

'We all do. It's feckin' shocking,' Billy said, and Holly giggled.

Declan hugged them both. 'Girls, your dad bored me to death every day about you. He kept going on and on about how wonderful you are, how beautiful you are, how incredible you are . . . and you know what? I didn't believe him until now. You're a pair of stunners.'

'Thanks,' Jools said, while Holly went red.

Quentin Jones approached them. 'Sorry to interrupt, but the media have got hold of the story. Someone leaked it, so it's all going to be a bit quicker than we wanted for you. They're clamouring for a press conference, as you can imagine. Do you think you'd be up to doing one in about an hour? We'll be there to manage any awkward questions.

I think it would be wise as you might have some chance of them leaving you alone if you speak to them now. Otherwise they'll just camp outside your homes until you do.'

Ben looked at Declan. They'd talked about this last night. The embassy had told them their story would cause a big fuss. After discussing it, they'd decided to do one press conference, give the whole story, then never speak to another journalist again. With a bit of luck, some other news would crop up and interest in them would blow over quickly.

'They'd like to see you with your wife,' Quentin went on. 'How would you feel about photos including Alice?'

'No way,' Ben said quickly. 'Declan and I will be interviewed, but our families are to be left out of it. That'll be the deal.'

'Very well.' Quentin nodded. 'I completely understand. We've prepared a press statement, asking for privacy so you and your families can readjust. We'll stress that you want your families left out of all publicity. Hopefully, that wish will be respected.'

Alice breathed a sigh of relief. The last thing she needed was Dan's friends seeing her in the morning papers, smiling on her husband's arm. Her head ached with the web of deceit she was caught up in now.

'Wait! Will there be TV?' Jools asked.

'Yes,' Quentin said.

'Is Dad, like, going to be famous?' Jools's eyes lit up.

'No,' Ben said sharply. 'Declan and I have agreed to do one press conference to get the media off our backs and that is it. End of story, end of journalists.'

'I don't want the girls near any of this attention,' Alice said.

'Why not? Why can't I be on TV?' Jools complained.

'Because it's not appropriate.' Alice was firm.

'Dad?'

'Mum's right. We need to protect you. It'll just be Declan and me.'

Jools pouted.

Ben smiled. 'Just like old times with Jools,' he whispered. Alice didn't smile – she seemed miles away.

'Alice?'

'Sorry – what?'

Before Ben could speak, Quentin asked them all to get ready as a car was waiting to take them to the Savoy Hotel for the press conference.

Jools and Holly each held one of Ben's hands while Alice followed behind, staring at her phone.

## *Holly*

Today was the best day EVER. Daddy came home. He looked the same but different. He is thinner and older, but the same really.

When he walked through the door he stopped like he was in shock or something. He just kept staring at Mummy and me and Jools. We were staring back, and then we all hugged and it was just so amazing.

Granddad seemed really happy too – except he's not very good at showing it. I think he was a bit awkward because everyone was crying, even David and Daddy. Declan's family, who are very loud and a bit scary, were all crying, too, and shouting and jumping up and down.

Mummy always says Granddad isn't good at showing his emotions. She says he's 'a cold fish'. But I think he probably felt a bit worse today because he hasn't seen Mummy or us since last Christmas, when he told Mummy that Daddy was too good for her and that he should have married a nice English girl who would have kept him at home and out of danger.

It was wrong of him to say it and I was proud of Mummy because she kept her cool. She didn't shout, she just asked him to leave the house. She hadn't spoken to him again until yesterday, when she called him to tell him about Daddy being alive.

I'm sure things will be fine again between them now Daddy's back. I texted Kevin to tell him how great Daddy looks. He was waiting for us at home with a big surprise tea for Daddy. Jools and I stayed up late last night, decorating the house. We didn't have any 'welcome home' banners or balloons, but we found lots of *Happy Birthday* ones left over from Jools's eighteenth so we used them instead.

Daddy and Declan did their interview at the Savoy Hotel. We stayed in a big suite with Declan's family and watched it all on the TV.

Mummy was on her phone when the interview started. I went out to get her, but she was crying really hard and saying, 'I love you too. I don't know what to do. I'm freaking out. I'm sorry.'

I knew then that she was talking to Dan and I felt sick. I knew she'd have to tell Dan and talk to him, but when she said, 'I love you,' it made me scared. She needs to love Daddy now.

She looked up and saw me. She jumped and then said she'd follow me in, and when she did, her eyes were really red and her hands were shaking. I felt sorry for her. It's all so confusing. I held her hand and she clung on tight.

There were so many people waiting to hear Daddy's story – loads of cameras were flashing the whole time. It was so weird to see him sitting at a long table with a huge micro-phone in front of him. But he didn't look a bit scared. He and Declan even made the people laugh, even though they were telling them how awful it was. Daddy was actually chained up every night. I nearly started crying when he said that.

Daddy was just brilliant, and all the journalists laughed when Declan said he wanted to have lots of sex with lots of women. He really is a bit mad, but in a good way.

When one journalist asked Daddy what had kept him going through the dark times, Daddy looked into the camera and said, 'Dreaming of being back with my beautiful wife and two incredible daughters.'

Declan's family, Pippa and David all cheered and Jools and I cried. Mummy just looked really sad. Billy, Declan's dad, leant over and said into her ear, 'He really loves you. It'll all be fine.' Mummy gave him a little smile, but it wasn't a happy one.

I knew she was thinking about Dan, but I blocked him from my mind. Today should be about Daddy and only Daddy.

Another journalist asked them if they had been treated badly or tortured. It went really quiet in the room except for Declan's brother, Sean, who cursed under his breath.

Daddy and Declan looked at each other and then Daddy said, 'We weren't tortured. We were treated reasonably well. They had to keep us in relatively good health so we could operate. But there were certainly some very dark moments.'

Then Declan said, 'Being away from your family and loved ones is a form of torture.'

Daddy nodded and looked like he was going to cry, but he didn't. Then they were asked if they wanted revenge on their captors.

Daddy said, 'Revenge would achieve nothing. The leader of the camp was killed in battle, which is how we managed to escape. There were some good people in the camp. But the best person was this man here.' Daddy put his arm around Declan. 'He is the brother I never had.'

Declan looked down, and then he said, 'Ben saved my life and my sanity almost every day. If it wasn't for him, I don't think I would have made it.'

That made me cry because you can see that they're so close and really love each other. Billy was sobbing beside me. He was holding Jools's hand and she was crying too.

When it was over, the journalists all stood up and clapped. We cheered.

I felt really tired then, and I was glad it was time to go home. We all said goodbye to Declan's family. They were flying home to Dublin with Declan to have a big party.

The hotel staff were really nice. They knew we didn't want to be photographed or anything so they got the journalists into a room for refreshments, then took us quickly to a back entrance and had a taxi waiting to take us home.

When Daddy and Declan said goodbye to each other, they hugged for a long time. Declan said, 'I'll miss you, Benji.'

I'd never heard anyone call Daddy 'Benji' before and it sounded funny.

Daddy said, 'Me too. Call me.'

'I will.'

'Ah, for Jesus' sake, will you come on? Haven't you spent enough time together?' Sean laughed at them.

'Are you not sick of him?' Eddie said. 'I shared a room with him growing up and he drove me mental.'

'He had his moments,' Daddy said, and gave Declan one last hug.

We walked down the corridor together. Daddy was holding Mummy's hand, but then her phone beeped so she let us walk on and started texting.

When we got home, Kevin was standing on the doorstep holding a big bunch of pink birthday balloons. Daddy said, 'I see nothing's changed, then.'

Mummy got cross and said, 'Kevin saved all our lives. He was our rock.'

Then I explained about the balloons being left over from Jools's birthday decorations and Daddy said he was so sorry he'd missed it. Jools said it was okay, but that he owed her a 'seriously big present'.

Kevin gave Daddy a hug and Daddy said, 'Thank you so much for looking after my three girls.'

Kevin was all pleased and Mummy smiled a real smile.

Then we went inside and Daddy stopped and looked around and walked really slowly through the house, as if it was his first time.

When he opened the kitchen door, and saw the decorations and the table full of all of his most favourite food, his eyes got watery.

He sat down in his chair – the same one he always sat in – and laid his head on the table.

Mummy went over and put her arms around him. 'Welcome back.'

Daddy smiled. 'I've dreamt of this so many times. I just can't believe it's true. God, I love you guys so much.'

'We love you too,' Jools said.

Mummy's phone beeped. Jools glared at her. 'Put it on silent. It's interrupting us.'

Mummy went over to her bag and switched off her phone. I was glad she did because I didn't want to be reminded of Dan.

We had a lovely dinner. Jools did most of the talking, filling Daddy in on school and boyfriends and her life. When Daddy asked me, I just gave him a short summary, but Mummy told him about the award I'd won for Best Essay and he said he was really proud.

When Jools asked Daddy about Eritrea, my stomach went all funny. You could see he didn't really want to talk about it. He didn't say much. He just said it had been very hard because he missed us terribly and that he had worked as a doctor there and tried to help people, that Declan had been a great friend and that he'd never leave us again.

That was the best part, because of the way he said it. He

looked into our eyes and said it like it was a promise. I totally believed him and it made me feel safe and warm inside.

It was when we were clearing up that he noticed it. 'That's new,' he said, pointing to the cherry tree in the back garden.

Jools grabbed my arm. Mummy went over and put her hand on Daddy's shoulder. 'It's a tree we planted when we heard you had . . . well . . . that you were gone.'

Daddy stopped moving. 'Oh. I see. Well . . . it's beautiful.'

We all went to bed at the same time because none of us had slept the night before and we were super-tired.

After brushing my teeth I came downstairs to get a glass of water and I heard Mummy and Kevin whispering at the front door.

'Telling Dan was so hard, but I had to before he saw it on the news.'

'What did he say?' Kevin asked.

'He said he loves me, and that he'll wait for me.'

I wished I hadn't heard that.

## Alice

Alice sent Dan a quick text, *I'll call you when I can talk XXXX*, then turned off her phone.

She drank a very large glass of wine, took a deep breath and went upstairs. Ben was sitting on their bed, waiting for her.

Alice busied herself with taking off her shoes and earrings. What would happen now? Would Ben want to have sex with her? Would he be able? Could she? Oh, God.

'You're so beautiful,' Ben said, coming up behind her and putting his arms around her.

Alice tried to keep her body relaxed, but she was incredibly tense.

'I've been waiting to hold you in my arms for so long. God, Alice, I missed you so much.'

Alice was afraid to speak. She thought she might cry. Ben turned her around to look at him. He leant in to kiss her.

'Let's turn the light off, shall we?' Alice said, trying to buy time and hoping against hope that if it was dark it would be less strange and uncomfortable.

'Do you mind if we don't? I want to look at you.' Ben's pupils were dilated and Alice could feel his erection digging into her thigh.

Ben kissed her hard. He began to tug at her dress, pulling it so roughly that Alice was afraid it would rip. He spun her around and yanked down the zip. The dress fell to the floor.

Alice kicked it away from her ankles and watched as Ben tugged off his shirt and trousers.

When Alice saw her husband's body, she tried not to gasp. He was so much thinner than she'd thought. His clothes had disguised his weight loss. His ribs jutted out.

Ben grabbed her and pulled her onto the bed. He was like a man possessed. He kissed her forcefully, shoving his tongue far into her mouth, then climbed on top of her. She could feel his urgency. He yanked her legs apart and entered her, pushing himself deep inside her. Alice tried not to cry out in pain. Ben grunted as he drove deeper and deeper. Alice tried to find a rhythm, but Ben kept thrusting until he cried out and collapsed on top of her.

Alice bit her lip to stop herself crying. Who was this man? She felt as if she'd just had sex with a total stranger.

Ben lay like a dead weight on top of her, his head buried in her shoulder, weeping. All Alice wanted to do was run into the shower and wash him away.

She lay still, waiting for him to move. After a few minutes he pulled his head back and looked at her, his face wet with tears. 'Sorry if I was a bit eager. I've waited a long time for that. I just can't believe I'm free and here. I'm with you.' He started crying again and kissed her. 'I love you so much, Alice.'

Alice pasted a smile on her face and kissed him gently on the lips. She moved her body and Ben rolled off her. Then she got up and went into the bathroom.

There, she ran the taps, sat on the floor and screamed silently into a towel. What was she going to do? He was her husband. She had to stay with him, but all she wanted to do was run to Dan and have him put his arms around her and protect her. She wanted to be shielded from this.

It wasn't fair. She'd spent two years getting over Ben and

minding the girls, and just when her life was good again, he'd come back, different and damaged, and she had to drop everything and start all over again.

Was she a terrible person? He was Ben, her Ben. Her wonderful husband was alive. This should be the best day of her life, but it wasn't. It was awful. She felt dirty and sick and sad – deeply sad.

'Everything all right?' Ben pushed the door open. Alice jumped up, wrapped the towel around herself and splashed water on her face.

'Sorry, just a bit emotional,' she said.

Ben, who was still naked – God, she wished he'd put on some clothes – came over and put his arms around her. 'I know, me too. It's a lot to take in.'

Alice moved away from him and walked back into the bedroom. She found her pyjamas, which she put on. 'Do you mind if we sleep now? I'm exhausted and I'm sure you are too.'

'If you like,' Ben said, and climbed in beside her. Alice rolled away from him and closed her eyes, praying for sleep to take her away from reality.

She woke with a start and looked at the clock. It was two a.m. She turned slowly to see if Ben was asleep. He was lying on his back with his eyes wide open.

'Can't sleep. Too much adrenalin,' he said.

'I think I'll get a glass of water.' Alice began to get up.

'No, let me get it for you. Stay there.' Ben got up, put on his boxer shorts and went downstairs. Alice's head was throbbing.

Ben appeared at the door with two glasses of water and a packet of cigarettes. 'Do you mind if I smoke? I'll do it by the window.'

Alice was surprised. Ben had always been very anti-smoking. Seeing her face, he said, 'A bad habit I picked up from Declan. Smoking got us through some horrible nights.'

Alice sat up and cuddled her knees as Ben smoked his cigarette. Standing with the moonlight on his face and the shadows hiding his thin frame, he looked more like her old Ben.

'Was it awful?' she asked.

Ben paused. 'Yes, but not because we were badly treated – compared to most kidnap victims we were treated quite well. They wanted to keep us in good health so we could operate. But the mental torture of not seeing you and the girls was acute. I knew when they blew up the car that you'd think we were dead and I found that very difficult to deal with.'

'We got the call on Jools's birthday.'

'Christ.' Ben rubbed his eyes.

'It's all right now,' Alice soothed him. 'She's got you and her birthday back.'

Ben lit another cigarette. 'How are they?'

Alice fiddled with one of her pyjama buttons. 'They're fine.'

'Really?'

'Yes. The first year was awful – they were devastated – but this last year has been better. And now you're back.'

'Jools has grown up so much. She's a woman!' Ben said. 'She's so beautiful. She must have boys queuing up.'

Alice smiled. 'They are.'

'And Holly! My little girl is not so little.'

'She's taller, but she's still the same,' Alice said. 'She's probably a bit stronger and less naïve, but she's still very sweet and gentle. I keep waiting for her hormones to kick in. Maybe when she turns fourteen next year it'll all go crazy.'

Ben stubbed out his cigarette on the windowsill. 'I'm so

sorry I left you, Alice. I've thought about it so much. I was a selfish bastard for going. I think I was having some kind of midlife crisis. I don't know what it was, really, but I can see how self-centred I'd become. I didn't appreciate what I had. I didn't understand how incredibly lucky I was. But I do now. I really, really do.' Ben's voice broke.

Alice didn't hesitate. She went to him and took him in her arms. He cried into her shoulder and repeated over and over, 'I'm sorry, Alice, I'm so sorry.'

Alice rubbed his back. 'It's okay. Everything's okay.'

They stood like that at the window until Ben's sobs subsided. Then they fell into bed, spent after the roller-coaster day.

Ben slept but had nightmares. He tossed and turned and muttered and cried out in his sleep. Beside him, Alice lay awake, watching his distress and wondering what lay ahead.

'Rise and shine, sleepyheads!' Jools shouted.

Alice peeled open one eye. She felt as if she'd slept for just a few minutes.

Ben woke with a jolt and fell out of bed. He scrambled up, eyes wide. 'What the . . .' He looked around in confusion. 'Where – Oh, Christ . . . Is it? Am I really . . .'

'It's okay, Dad, you're home.'

Ben turned to her. 'Oh, my God, I am. I really am. Oh, thank God. I thought I was dreaming.' He covered his face with his hands.

Jools looked at Alice, her eyes full of tears. She went over to her father and gently laid a hand on his shoulder. 'Dad, you're home now. You're safe.'

Ben drew her close and Jools rested her head against his chest.

'Thank God it's real. Thank God,' Ben said.

Holly came in and sat on the bed beside Alice. 'Is Daddy all right?' she whispered.

'He's just emotional because he's so happy to be home.'

'What are we going to do today?' Holly asked.

Alice had no idea. What do you do when your dead husband walks back into your life? What's a 'normal' thing to do? 'Why don't you ask Daddy what he'd like to do?'

Ben loosened his grip on Jools. Alice could see that she was thrown by Ben's outburst. They were used to him being strong and never showing emotion. But this Ben was different. He'd changed . . . They'd all changed.

Ben went to the window and lit a cigarette.

'Daddy!' Holly was shocked.

Ben frowned. 'What?'

'You're smoking.'

'It's fine,' Alice said.

'No, it isn't. It can kill you.'

'I'm sorry, darling. It's a habit I picked up. I'll give them up soon, but I really need one now.' Ben's hands were shaking as he tried to light the cigarette.

Jools took the matches from him and lit it for him. Ben inhaled deeply.

'But, Daddy, we've only just got you back, you can't smoke and then die of lung cancer.'

'For God's sake, Holly, shut up,' Jools snapped. 'He's been stuck in a hell-hole for two years. If he wants a bloody cigarette, let him have it.'

Holly's lip wobbled. Alice took her hand and gave it a gentle squeeze. There was silence as Ben smoked.

Alice needed to take control. 'Holly was just wondering what you'd like to do today, Ben.'

'Oh. Well . . . uhm . . . I don't know. All I really want to do is be with you guys.'

They heard the front door slamming. They all jumped.

'So where is he?' a voice called. 'I've come to see if he's really risen from the dead.'

'Nora?' Alice shouted.

'Where are you?' Nora asked.

'We're all up in Mum's bedroom,' Holly bellowed.

'Mum and Dad's,' Jools corrected her.

'Sorry.' Holly blushed.

There was a tap on the door. 'Are you decent?'

Ben was only wearing pyjama bottoms. Alice handed him a bathrobe and opened the door.

Nora stood there, holding a bag full of fresh croissants. She hugged Alice, then moved towards Ben. 'Let's have a look at you,' she said, hands on hips. 'Mother of Jesus, you're a toothpick. What did they feed you over there at all?' She swiped away tears.

'A lot of chickpeas and lentils,' Ben said, with a smile. 'It's good to see you, Nora.' He bent down to kiss her.

'Well, get these pastries into you. You need feeding and minding.'

'That sounds good to me.'

'It's lucky for you that you have four women to do it, so.'

'Very lucky.' Ben bit a large piece of croissant and groaned with pleasure. 'Oh God, thank you, Nora. This tastes fantastic.'

'I see you're the big story of the day. It's all over the papers. Look.' Nora chucked the *Daily Mail* onto the bed. The front-cover headline read: 'Miracle Surgeons Back From The Dead'.

'Wow, Dad, you're famous.' Jools read the article. '"Surgeon Ben Gregory left behind two daughters, Julia and Holly." What? They misspelt my name. That's so annoying. I'm going to have to ring them and tell them it's "Jools".'

Alice grabbed her arm. 'Don't go near them.'

Nora grabbed the other. 'Listen to your mother, Jools. They're a nasty lot. All they want is gossip about your family to splash all over the papers. Tell them nothing. If they can't get any information, they'll leave you alone quicker.'

'Calm down, you two. I won't ring.' Jools pouted.

'How've you been, Nora?' Ben asked.

'Better than you, I imagine. You don't look bad considering, thin but not sick. I hope you've learnt your lesson and won't be going on any more crazy trips to Africa.'

'I can promise you that I will never be going to Eritrea again.'

'Or anywhere else,' Jools added.

'Or anywhere else,' Ben said solemnly.

'Stay here and focus on your lovely family.'

'I will, Nora, I promise.'

'Right, well, I'll tidy up, put the kettle on and leave you to it. I only came to see if you needed anything and check if it really was Ben. Now I've seen you, I know you're all right. I'll put some breakfast out and leave you in peace.'

They followed Nora down to the kitchen. Ben tripped on a step. 'Oops, not used to stairs any more.'

Holly looked at Alice, her eyes full of fear. Alice was sure her own eyes were reflecting the same emotion.

# Ben

Ben threw the remote control across the room. It smashed against the wall. He had no idea how things worked. The new television was impossible. He went into the kitchen to make himself a cup of coffee. Alice had a fancy new coffee machine. Jools had made him a cappuccino yesterday.

Ben stared at the buttons and tried to figure it out, but he couldn't concentrate properly. He felt exhausted. All he wanted to do was lie down and sleep but he couldn't because every dream brought him back to Eritrea, to the darkness. He wanted to be here, in the present, in the light.

He pushed a few buttons, then gave up and boiled the kettle for a cup of tea. His phone rang. It was Declan.

'Howzit going, Benji?'

Ben smiled. 'Good to hear your voice, mate, although you sound rough.'

'I'm dying of a hangover. My cousin had another welcome-home party for me last night. I think it's my tenth. I tell you what, our little sojourn in Eritrea has made me a very cheap date. After two pints I'm hammered.'

'Sounds like fun.'

'What have you been up to?'

'Oh, you know, just getting used to being at home and spending time with the girls, although they went back to school a few days ago. Alice didn't want them to miss too much.'

'How's Alice?'

Ben stirred his tea. 'She's good.'

'Ben,' Declan said, 'it's me.'

Ben sat down in his old seat at the kitchen table. 'She's different. She's tougher and she seems distracted all the time. I know she's had to be strong to get through the last two years, but I can't find her. You know, I can't find my old Alice.'

'Give her time, Ben. It's only been two weeks. Don't forget, she thought you were dead. She mourned you. It's going to take a while for her to get used to you being back.'

'You're right. I suppose I just thought she'd be the same.' Ben didn't tell Declan that Alice had been avoiding sex with him. After the first night, she had started coming to bed late, and when he reached for her, she said she was tired. It hurt. It really hurt that his wife didn't want to have sex with him. On the two occasions they had had sex, it was as if she was somewhere else. She insisted on turning the lights off and closed her eyes. She seemed to want to get it over with.

Ben wanted her. He yearned to be intimate with her and to feel her naked body against his. She obviously didn't feel the same. He was trying to be patient, but he was worried and frightened by her detachment.

'How are the girls?' Declan asked.

'Jools is great, the same but a little wiser and kinder. Holly is still a little guarded with me. I think she's worried I'm going to disappear again. She's begun to relax a bit in the last few days, though. She's always been a worrier and I've made that side of her worse by giving her so much to worry about.'

'Stop it. No beating yourself up. Remember, we agreed that we weren't going to let those bastards steal our future. They took two years but they're not allowed to take any more. You can't change the past. You have to live in the present, Ben.'

'I'm trying. How are you sleeping?'

'Shite. I'm waking up with nightmares all the time but, Jesus, the relief when I remember I'm home. I cry every time.'

Ben smiled. 'Yes, I know that feeling.'

'Mind you, I haven't been alone since I got back. I'm a superstar in Dublin. There are birds throwing themselves at me. It's a pity you're married, Ben. I'm telling you, coming back from the dead is very good for your sex life.'

'Different one every night?'

'Pretty much. I'm doing what I said I'd do. I'm riding every bird I meet. I have to send them home early, though, because of the nightmares. The first girl stayed the night and the poor thing nearly had a heart attack when I woke up screaming and roaring.'

'Has the hospital been in touch about going back to work?'

'Yeah.'

'What are you going to do?' Ben asked.

'I dunno, Benji. I can barely decide whether I want to shag a blonde or a brunette. I'm in no fit state to go back to work yet. I told them I needed time to "consider my options". To be honest, I might stay in Dublin. It's nice being back.'

'I see.' Ben was disappointed. He wanted Declan to come back to London so they could see each other regularly. He knew it was selfish of him, but he missed his friend terribly.

As if reading his mind, Declan said, 'My family keep slagging me. They think we have a bromance. Apparently I say "Ben says" or "Ben thinks" all the time. Sean says we're like conjoined twins. They all think it's hilarious, but I do miss talking to you whenever I want. When something happens I turn around to tell you, but you're not there.'

Ben smiled. 'Same here. It's because we're the only people

in the world who understand. God, Declan, it's harder than I thought.'

'I knew it was going to be harder for you because you left a wife and kids behind.'

'I just wish Alice would open up to me. She's not angry or sad or hurt, she's just numb. I can't get through to her. What if she's moved on?'

'Ah, now, come on. She was crying her eyes out when she saw you in the airport. She loves you. Actually, my da asked about her. He seems to have taken a shine to your Alice. He was wondering how things were going with you both and I just told him that you said she seemed different. Da said, "Tell Ben to be patient and to talk to her about old times and remind her of how happy you were together and all that."'

'It's good advice. Thank Billy for me.'

'Why don't you come over to Dublin? It'd do you good to have a change of scenery. Come over and stay with me.'

'I can't leave now. I've only just come back.'

'Well, if it all gets a bit too much, hop on a plane and come, even just for a night.'

'Thanks, I will.'

'What are you going to do about work?'

Ben lit a cigarette. 'I don't know. I'm not sure if I'm ready to go back, but I think I'll go mad if I don't do something. I can't sit around the house all day. Alice went back to work two days ago, so it's a bit quiet and lonely here. I've got a meeting with Nathan Meadows next Monday. I think I will go back – it'll be a good distraction and good for the girls to see me back to normal.'

'Well, take it easy. Get your confidence back with some appendectomies before you launch into the open-heart surgeries.'

Ben laughed. 'Don't worry, I plan to start slowly. And now I'd better let you go.'

'Okay, mate. I'll talk to you very soon.'

The phone went dead and Ben went out into the garden with his cigarette. He stared at the cherry tree. He knew it had been planted as a loving symbol, but he hated it. Every time he looked at it, it reminded him of all that he had lost.

Ben stirred in his sleep and opened his eyes. Jools was staring down at him. She was waving something.

He sat up. 'Sorry, I must have nodded off.'

'You're exhausted, Dad, you need more sleep. By the way, was this you?' She held up the black pieces of the TV remote control.

'I couldn't work it out and got a bit frustrated.'

Jools sat down beside him and pieced it back together. 'It's not broken. And, don't worry, it took Mum ages to figure out the TV, too.'

Ben scratched his stubbly chin. 'I feel ridiculous. I'm usually good with new technology, but for some reason I can't get the hang of that television.'

Jools patted his hand. 'You're just out of practice. If I'd spent two years in a tent eating lentils, I'd be hopeless too. Mind you, I'd be super-skinny, which would be cool.'

Ben smiled. 'You're perfect, Jools. No one wants to be skinny – it's unhealthy.'

Jools rolled her eyes. 'Newsflash, Dad. Every girl in the world wants to be skinny. Clothes look better on you when you're tiny. My problem is chocolate. I just love it.' Jools pinched a very small bit of flesh that hung over her school uniform skirt.

'You're gorgeous, just like your old man.'

Jools grinned. 'I'm so glad you're back. It's nice to have someone who looks like me in the house again.'

'You're so like my mother, it's incredible,' Ben said.

'I'm glad you didn't say I looked like Granddad,' Jools joked.

Ben seized the opportunity to find out why there was so much tension between Alice and his father. When he'd asked Alice, she'd just muttered something about a disagreement and said that they'd had a little cooling-off time but nothing serious. They'd never got on particularly well, but now you could feel the tension when they were in the same room.

'What happened between Mum and Granddad?'

Jools twirled a strand of her long hair between her fingers. 'Well, last Christmas, Granddad and Mum were talking about you and he said that Mum shouldn't have let you go to Eritrea. Mum said she'd begged you not to go and Granddad said she obviously didn't do a very good job of it. So Mum got cross and said, "Ben is very strong-minded, like you. If he wants to do something, there is no stopping him, and if you thought it was such a bad idea, why didn't you try to stop him instead of sitting on the sidelines and blaming me?" So then Granddad got all red in the face and said that if his son had been happy at home, he'd never have gone looking for adventure elsewhere and that he should have married a nice English girl who would have kept him at home and out of danger.'

Ben was shocked. No wonder Alice was cool with his father. How could Harold have said something so harsh? Sometimes he didn't understand his father at all. Why would he alienate Alice and the girls?

'Mum handled it really well. She didn't lose it, or freak out, she just asked him to leave. We didn't see him again until you came back. I kind of felt sorry for him. I mean, I know what he said was horrible, but he was just sad and depressed and lashing out. Mum said if he apologized she'd be okay, but he never did.'

'Sometimes my father can be very foolish and stubborn. Poor Alice, she didn't need that.'

'It was kind of horrible, especially as it was Christmas Day and we were all trying to pretend everything was fine. But after Granddad left, Mum said that the pretending was over and we went out to the tree and had a good cry, then snuggled up under our duvets and watched movies and ate sweets.'

Ben shuddered as he imagined them crying on Christmas Day. He had done that to them. He had caused them so much pain. He reached over and pulled Jools to him. 'I'm sorry, Jools. I'm so sorry for everything I put you through. I promise to try to make it up to you.'

Jools shrugged. 'It wasn't your fault you got kidnapped. That was just really bad luck. Anyway, it's over now and everything's back to normal. By the way, I'm a total celeb in school.'

'Really?'

'Totally. Everyone is talking about you and your amazing escape and how brave you are and the girls think you're really hot – for a dad – and the boys think you're a hero. It's kind of cool, actually.'

'I'm glad I've raised your "cool" status in school.'

Jools flicked the television on. 'My "cool" status was already sky high. You've just made me more intreeking.'

Ben laughed. He had sorely missed Jools and her mispronunciation. It was wonderful to hear it again. 'Do you need help with your homework?' he asked.

'Does Victoria Beckham eat lettuce? Of course I do. But can we just watch one episode of *Keeping Up With the Kardashians* first?'

Ben was happy enough to put off having to do Jools's homework with her. He still felt very tired. A kind of tiredness he hadn't felt in captivity, a tiredness deep in his bones.

The programme started. A lot of girls with long black hair and far too much make-up were sitting around eating.

'You'd better fill me in. What's going on and who are these people?'

'The Kardashians are like the American royal family.'

'Really? Who's their father? Some politician?'

'No, Kim, Khloé, Kourtney and Rob's dad was a lawyer. He defended some crazy sports guy who killed his wife but then he got off because his gloves were too small or something.'

'O. J. Simpson?'

'Yeah, I think that's his name. Anyway, his lawyer, Robert Kardashian, was their father, but Kendall and Kylie's dad is Bruce Jenner. He was in the Olympics or something, I don't really know – he wants to be a woman now. They all have the same mother, Kris, and she's a momager.'

'A what?' Ben was finding it difficult to keep up.

'Momager – you know, a mum who is also a manager.'

'What does she manage?'

'Duh, their careers.'

'What do they do?'

'Well, lots of stuff, like photo shoots and opening night-clubs and they have a clothes line and they do make-up and Robert does socks.'

Ben watched as one of the dark-haired sisters shouted at a guy called Scott for drinking too much.

'Who's Scott?'

'He's married to Kourtney and they have three kids, but he has a drink problem.'

'Are the other sisters married?'

317

'Kim is married to Kanye West and they're called Kimye now. She was married to this other guy called Kris, but it only lasted about five weeks. Khloé was married to this guy called Lamar. But she married him after nine days and he has loads of problems with drugs and stuff, so that's over. Kendall and Kylie are too young to be married. Kendall is nearly the same age as me and she's like a really successful model now, making zillions.'

'Is her mother her manager, too?'

'Yes, but I think Kim's jealous because Kris is spending a lot of time momaging Kendall.'

Ben was having trouble following it all. 'What about the brother, where's he? Busy making socks?'

'No. Poor Robert has issues with his weight. He's really fat and he won't go on the TV. They've put him into therapy and all of that, but he keeps eating. Khloé feels guilty because she thinks it might be because of Lamar and his drugs, but Kim just thinks he should get over his issues and stop shoving doughnuts into his face.'

'What does his momager think?'

'She was crying about it, but she's getting divorced from Bruce so she's got a lot going on. I'm not sure what's going to happen now because I think Bruce and his sons from his first marriage will be axed from the show. They're kind of boring, to be honest. All they do is surf and play with their dogs.'

'There are more of them?'

'Yes, Brody and Brandon are on the show as well, but Bruce also has two other kids that aren't really in the show – Casey and Burt.'

'Is Kris their momager too?'

'No! They have a different mother. They don't really get on with Kris. They feel she stole their dad and that he spends way too much time with the Kardashians and Kendall and Kylie and not enough with them.'

'So who is their mother?'

'I don't know. She's never in the show. I doubt Kris would let her – she's very controlling.'

Ben began to laugh. 'This is ridiculous.'

Jools frowned. 'No, it's brilliant.'

Ben put a cushion over his face and groaned loudly. 'Jools, I've been watching for twenty minutes and nothing has happened. They've eaten, shouted at the guy with a drink problem, driven around in their cars and eaten again.'

'They do seem to eat a lot. I don't know where they put the food.'

'In their backsides,' Ben said.

Jools giggled. 'They're famous for their big bums.'

'They seem to be famous for nothing else.'

The door opened and Holly walked in. 'Hi. Oh, my God, Jools, please tell me you're not making Dad watch *Keeping Up With the Kardashians*. You'll make him want to go back to Eritrea.'

'Holly!' Jools was shocked.

Holly's hand flew to her mouth. 'God, sorry, I didn't mean that.'

Ben laughed. 'It's funny. You don't have to tiptoe around me. Besides, Holly, I'm glad somebody else thinks this programme is nonsense.'

'They're completely vacuous and shallow,' Holly said.

'They're not shallow. Kim wanted to adopt a child from an orphanage.' Jools defended her TV friends.

'And did she? Did she adopt her?' Holly challenged.

'No, because Kris said Kanye might not be too happy if Kim came home from holiday with some random orphan.'

'She's ridiculous – they all are,' Holly fumed.

'Well, you think Angelina Jolie's great and she adopted kids,' Jools countered.

Holly's eyes were wide. 'Yes, because she actually did adopt them and is bringing them up as her own. Not to mention her work for the UN, which got her appointed as special envoy of the UN High Commission for Refugees.'

'Well, I prefer Kim. She's less annoying.'

Holly threw her hands into the air. 'She's the most annoying person in the universe.'

Ben stood up and turned off the television. 'Okay, girls, please stop arguing. Let's go and have something to eat.'

As Ben walked ahead into the kitchen, his two daughters continued to bicker. He smiled to himself. He'd missed this.

# *Holly*

Daddy can't sleep. I hear him walking around the house at night. He seems very restless. He wanted to go back to work, but they said he should take a bit more time off and come back after Christmas.

He seems a bit lost, like he doesn't know what to do, and he looks so tired. Most of the time when I come in from school, he's asleep on the couch.

He's going for walks now and sometimes he's out for hours. He went on a big walk a few nights ago and didn't come back for ages. Jools kept calling his phone, but he had it off. We all began to panic. Mummy tried to keep us calm, but I could see she was worried too.

When he finally came home, Jools ran out and threw herself on top of him. She was sobbing. I tried not to cry, but when I saw him I did a bit. I was just so relieved.

Poor Daddy looked really sad and kept saying he was sorry.

Mummy shouted at him for being so 'bloody thoughtless'. She said we'd been through 'enough shit' and he was never to go out without his phone on again.

Things with Mummy and Daddy are not the same. Mummy works late a lot and seems stressed. She doesn't look happy and I've heard her crying in her bedroom when Daddy's downstairs or gone for a walk.

I also heard her on the phone to Dan. I know I shouldn't listen at her bedroom door, but I'm scared. I want to know what's going on. She was supposed to break up with him and be with Daddy. She was crying and kept saying, 'I wish things were different. I miss you.'

But why does she wish things were different? Daddy coming home is a miracle, we should all be so, so happy, but instead it's like everyone is scared all the time. Except Jools: she seems really happy and isn't nervous around Daddy. I still feel a bit strange with him. Kevin said it's completely normal and it'll just take a while to get used to Daddy being back because it was a big shock.

Stella sent me a text and I knew she sent it to Jools, too. When I asked her about it her face went all red, her eyes teared up and she shouted, 'We can't be friends with Stella now. It's not fair to Daddy.'

Stella's text said: *I'm so happy for you guys that your dad is okay. You must be so happy. I miss you two. If you'd like to hang out together, please just call me. I'd love to see you again – when you feel ready.*

I had no idea what to say back to her. The whole situation is so confusing. Stella's great and she was becoming like a sister. But Jools is right: we can't see her any more because it's disloyal to Daddy. I just wrote back: *Thank you.*

People in school keep saying it's a miracle and we must be so happy to be back together again . . . to have our family back . . . to be 'back to normal'. But nothing is the same. We're different people. Daddy's quieter than before and he's jumpy – if you slam a door, he literally jumps out of his seat. The other day a car backfired in front of us when we were driving and Daddy was in the passenger seat and he dived under the dashboard, head first.

I looked up the symptoms of PTS and Daddy has quite a few of them. Difficulty falling or staying asleep. Difficulty concentrating. Feeling jumpy and easily startled. I spoke to Mummy about it and she said that Daddy is seeing a specialist in post-traumatic stress disorder and that I'm not to worry.

Mummy looked sad when I talked to her about it. She said that Daddy would take a while to get 'back to himself'. She said that we had to be patient and try to help him readjust.

Mummy is looking after Daddy well. She's being very kind and caring, but something's missing. She's not relaxed around him. When we're all together it's okay because we chat about general things, but Mummy is hardly ever alone with Daddy. I'm scared she's still in love with Dan. I hope I'm wrong, because Daddy is her husband and she should love him more, even if she did think he was dead. Sometimes I wish Mummy would just tell Daddy about Dan. Then there wouldn't be any more secrets. But I don't think Daddy is strong enough to hear any bad news.

Kevin isn't calling in much. I rang him and asked him why. He said he wants to 'give us space'. But there seems to be too much space. I miss Kevin being around. Mummy's lucky because she still sees him at work every day.

I think Daddy was a bit surprised when Mummy went back to work so soon. He'd only been home a week, but Mummy said, 'We need an income.' Daddy didn't say anything else after that.

I tried to talk to Jools about my worries, but she told me to shut up. She said she didn't want to hear anything bad: Daddy was alive and everything was going to be fine.

Jools seems to be enjoying all the attention we're getting at school. I hate it. People keep asking me about Daddy and what it was like 'over there'. The boys are especially interested. Bradley asked me if Daddy was tortured! I told him not to be so rude and stop asking annoying questions. Bradley said it wasn't rude and maybe Daddy had been turned and was now a spy for the Eritreans, like the guy in *Homeland*.

I've never watched *Homeland* so I asked Jools about it. She said Bradley was a 'complete and utter moron' and I should ignore him.

The next day, Jools came to find me at break time. I pointed out Bradley. She marched over and grabbed him by his blazer. 'Stop asking my sister stupid questions about our father, you little twerp. He's a hero.'

'He could be a spy.'

'For who? The Eritreynons? What the hell would he be spying on? Their lentils? Their mountains? You really are a total moron. My father is not spying on anyone, and if he ever heard what you were saying about him, he'd probably use all of his pent-up anger at being kidnapped for two years to beat the crap out of you.'

'It's Eritreans.'

'Excuse me?' Jools glared at him.

'You said Eritreynons.'

Bradley must have a death wish, I thought.

Jools put her face very close to his. 'Are you seriously correcting me?'

'Yes. You mispronounced it.'

'Do you not know how school works? Younger people bow down to older ones. They do not annoy, irritate or bug them. Now, if you want to survive this school year, you'd better zip your fat mouth shut.'

'I'm not afraid of you. My cousin's in your year and he said you're thick.'

'She is not!' I shouted.

Jools went red but remained calm. 'I may not be the brightest, but I'm the best-looking. Unlike you, who looks like a weasel with acne. The only way you're ever going to have sex in your sad little life is with an electronic device. Now go away. You're so ugly that looking at you is hurting my eyes.'

Bradley scurried off. Jools turned to me. 'Eritreynons, right?'

I shook my head. 'Eritreans.'

Jools shrugged. 'It sounds the same to me.'

When I came home from school today, Daddy was looking at old photos. I didn't know if I should go in to him or not. He was sitting on the floor surrounded by albums and boxes. When I'm on my own with him, I never really know what to say. I decided to leave him, but he looked up and saw me.

'Hey, Holly, how was school?'

'Okay.'

'I found all these photos. It's incredible to think how small you were.' Daddy held up a picture of me as a baby. Mummy's holding me and Daddy has his arm around her. They both look so happy.

I felt my throat catch. 'Wow,' was all I could say.

'They were great times,' Daddy said. 'Really great times.'

I stood at the door, wondering whether to sit down. Daddy put down the photo. I could see one sticking out from under the couch. I bent down to pick it up. 'Here's another.' It was Mummy and Daddy on their wedding day.

Daddy reached for it. His face sort of crumpled when he saw what it was. He coughed and muttered that he needed to go out for a cigarette. He promised he'd give up. He's smoking so much, I'm afraid we'll have to go through losing him all over again.

I climbed the stairs to my room to do my homework. I had an essay to write. The theme was: 'If someone hurts you, can you forgive and forget?' I knew the answer already. I was living with it – you can forgive, but you can never forget.

# *Alice*

Alice had a full day ahead. Patients were queuing to come in before the Christmas holidays began and she closed her surgery for ten days. Usually she looked forward to her Christmas break, but this year she was dreading it.

Spending time with Ben was a huge strain. She was trying really hard to make everything nice and normal. She wanted him to settle back in, but it was impossible to erase the last two harrowing years.

He was different. She was different. They had had sex the night before. She couldn't refuse him again. She'd brushed him off four times over the previous two weeks. She had insisted on turning out the lights and it had been easier in the dark, but it still felt wrong. The passion was gone. It was mechanical, emotionless. She didn't feel the same. She'd closed her eyes and pictured Dan.

Alice switched on her computer and tried not to think about Dan. She was meeting him after work to give him back his ring. She was looking forward to it and dreading it in equal measure. She couldn't wait to see him, but knew it would be goodbye and felt sick at the thought of not having him in her life.

Kevin came in with a coffee. 'You look like you need it. Still not sleeping?'

Alice thanked him, sipped and put the cup down. 'Last night was a bad one. I'm seeing Dan tonight.'

'Give me one more look at that spectacular ring?' Kevin asked.

They gazed down at the sparkling diamond in the box. 'Wow, it really is beautiful.'

Alice nodded.

'Hard to give him up. He's a good man.'

She felt a lump rising in her throat.

'It seems really twisted that the miracle of Ben being alive means that you have to give up someone you love,' Kevin added.

'It's just so much harder than I thought.' Alice began to cry. 'I don't know if Ben and I will ever get back to where we were. I'm not sure I even love him any more. I feel like such a bad person and I'm trying, I swear.'

Kevin hugged her. 'I know you are, but the psychiatrist told you it would take a long time for everything to settle. There's no quick result with something like this.'

'But what if I don't ever feel the same?'

'Maybe you should keep the ring, just in case,' Kevin said.

'No, I have to let Dan go. It's the right thing to do.' Alice wiped her face. 'But I love him. We've been texting a lot – I've been too afraid to speak to him. I know if I hear his voice, I'll crack up. I'm so dying to see him today and be with him. But it's to say goodbye and I just can't bear it. I hate this. I can't help loving Dan. He's been so wonderful to me and the girls and . . .' Alice was sobbing.

'Oh, God, Alice, I feel for you, I really do. Maybe you should tell Ben about Dan. Be honest, and tell him you need time to think things over.'

Alice shook her head. 'I can't. He's too fragile. His night-mares are terrifying. And he has this really sad look in his eyes all the time. I know it's guilt. He knows that he caused us a huge amount of pain and it's eating him up. How can

I add to his anguish by telling him I'm in love with someone else? I just can't do it.'

'Can you really let Dan go, though? I mean, you're engaged to the man. It wasn't just some fling.'

'I have to give my marriage a chance for the girls' sake. I don't honestly think we'll make it, but I have to try, even if that means giving up the man I love.'

Kevin held her as she wept into his shoulder. 'My God, I really don't know what to say, Alice.'

Alice took a very deep breath. 'I have to pull myself together. Distract me with patients.'

Kevin looked at his book. 'First up is —'

They heard a primal wail from the waiting room. They rushed out. A very large girl was bent double, screaming in agony. She was holding her stomach in one hand and a break-fast roll in the other.

Alice and Kevin helped her into Alice's consulting room. She sat down, stopped yelling and took a large bite of her roll.

Kevin went to take it from her. 'I'll mind that for you. You really shouldn't be eating in here.'

'No way, mate. I'm starving.' The girl took another bite.

'A few salads wouldn't go amiss,' Kevin muttered, as he left the room.

Alice asked the girl her name, age and address. Kelly was seventeen and lived in a block of flats about three miles from the surgery – Alice knew the address well. It was a rough area and quite a few of her patients were from there.

As Alice took down Kelly's details, the teenager polished off her roll, stinking out Alice's room.

'Okay, Kelly, when did these stomach pains start? Have you vomited or had loose stools?'

'Loose stools? What's that?'

Alice decided to be more direct. 'Diarrhoea. Runny poos.'

'Jesus, no. Just pains. My mum thinks I'm constipated. I tried to shit it out, but nothing happened.'

Kelly's face suddenly crumpled and she bent over in agony. She began to scream again and arch her back. 'This must be some bloody massive dump,' she cried out.

Alice thought the poor girl must have a twisted bowel. She needed to examine her, but there was no way she could move her at the moment. Poor Kelly was writhing in pain on the floor.

Alice came around her desk, crouched and pulled up the girl's big jumper.

'Oh!' she exclaimed.

'I know I'm a fat bitch. I just can't stop eating,' Kelly puffed.

Alice smiled. 'No, Kelly, you're not fat, you're in labour.'

'What's that, then? Some kind of stomach thing?'

Alice looked at her. Was she joking? 'Kelly, your baby's coming.'

'What baby?'

'The one inside you.'

'I ain't got no baby in there. What you talkin' about? Are you mental?'

Before Alice could answer, the next contraction started and Kelly crushed Alice's hand as she screamed.

Alice could feel adrenalin rushing through her veins. This baby was coming fast. She'd delivered babies during her training, but it was a long time ago. She had to give Kelly an internal examination and find out if there was time to get her to the local hospital.

When the contraction subsided, she discovered that Kelly was eight or nine centimetres dilated. Damn, she'd never make it to hospital. Alice called Kevin.

He rushed in. 'What's going on?'

'Kelly's in labour and I need you to call an ambulance, then stay here and help me.'

'Alice, you know I'm not good with blood.' Kevin was shaking his head, backing away from the writhing patient.

'I need you,' Alice snapped.

'I ain't 'avin' no baby. I ain't up the pole.'

'Kelly,' Alice said firmly, 'you are pregnant and the baby wants to come out now.'

'No way.'

'Do you have a boyfriend? Someone we can call?'

'No, I ain't got no one.'

'Well, you must have had sex with someone to get pregnant. You're not the Virgin Mary.' Kevin was rapidly losing patience.

'Kevin!' Alice glared at him.

Kelly frowned in concentration. 'I did have sex with this local lad, José or Juan or somefink, when I were in Magaluf. But that was ages ago and I was so pissed I didn't think it counted.'

'Sex is sex, honey, drunk or not,' Kevin said, holding her hand. She crushed it during another contraction.

'Didn't you suspect anything when your stomach swelled up?' Alice asked. She listened for the baby's heartbeat – it was steady.

'Nah. I just thought it was all the burgers and crisps I was eatin'. I was mad for them all the time so I got fat. I used to be a size ten.'

Kevin raised his eyebrow. 'Seriously?'

'I swear. I was really thin before this. But no matter how much I ate, I wanted more, so I got fat.'

'Didn't you feel the baby kicking?' Kevin asked.

'Is that what it was?' Kelly smiled. 'I thought it was me stomach going mental because of all the food.'

'Food doesn't kick, unless you eat a live goat,' Kevin explained.

'Is there anyone you'd like us to call? Is your mum around?' Alice asked.

'Yeah, she is. But she's going to get a bit of a shock. I told her I was popping out to get sausages.'

Kevin threw his head back and laughed. Alice tried to remain professional but couldn't help joining in. Even Kelly was laughing.

'Can you imagine? Hello, Mum, I got them sausages for you and, guess what, I got a baby and all.'

They all laughed until Kelly had another contraction.

'How long did the ambulance say?' Alice asked Kevin.

'Ten to fifteen minutes.'

Alice examined Kelly again. Her cervix was fully dilated. The baby was coming. 'Kevin, go to the cupboard and get me a sterile delivery pack. We have a few emergency ones. Then grab a towel and get back here. Oh, and explain to the other patients that we're going to be delayed today.'

Alice washed her hands and put on sterile gloves. Kevin came back in and Alice told Kelly to do as she said. 'Try not to push until I tell you.'

'I want one of them injections that makes you not feel anything,' Kelly demanded.

Alice shook her head. 'It's far too late for that. Right, now push.'

Kelly let out a blood-curdling scream and the baby's head appeared.

'Kevin, I need you,' Alice ordered.

'Really? Down there? I'm much happier up here.'

Alice shot her brother a look and he reluctantly moved down to the business end. Alice told him to crouch down and hold the towel for her.

'Now, Kelly, don't push too hard,' Alice said, but Kelly had had enough and pushed with all her might.

'Jesus Christ!' Kevin roared, as the baby shot out and landed in his lap.

Alice smiled. 'It's a boy.' She clamped and cut the umbilical cord while Kevin stood in shock holding the baby until the little fellow peed on him.

'Argh, he's wet me,' Kevin said, and thrust him towards Alice.

Alice placed him on his mother's tummy.

'Did he come out of my stomach? Are you serious? Is this for real?' Kelly's eyes were wide with shock.

'Congratulations,' Alice said.

'That's the last time your mother's ever going to let you go out for sausages.' Kevin grinned, recovered from his initial shock.

As they all gazed at the baby, Kelly had another contraction and the placenta shot out, landing on Kevin's suede shoes.

'What the frigging hell is that?' Kevin screeched.

'Have I just had another baby?' Kelly roared. 'Twins? My mum's going to do her nut.'

'No, it's just the afterbirth,' Alice reassured them both.

'My shoes!' Kevin wailed. 'My five-hundred-quid Italian shoes.'

'Do you think I should call him José or Juan?' Kelly asked, staring at her unexpected baby in wonder.

The door burst open and two paramedics charged in. 'Bloody hell, it's like a crime scene in here. Well, Doc, you've been busy.'

They put Kelly and baby Juan/José on a stretcher and carried them out.

As they were leaving, Kevin called, 'Next time you go on holidays, keep your knees together.'

Alice looked at Kevin. He was covered with blood, as was she. 'I wasn't expecting that,' she said, and began to laugh.

'Bloody hell, I thought she had a stomach bug,' Kevin said, still gazing in dismay at his ruined shoes.

They were both laughing as the relief of everything ending well flooded over them.

'We'll have to call it a day. I can't really see patients in here today – they'll think I've murdered someone.'

'Good idea. I need a very long shower and some Xanax, followed by a stiff brandy,' Kevin said.

Alice looked at her watch. It was ten a.m. Adrenalin was coursing through her veins – she felt alive and alert. She knew what she wanted. She wanted to be with him. She wanted to run to him. She cleaned herself up, changed into a spare suit she kept at work, then texted him: *Where are you? Can I see you now?*

After a few minutes, her phone beeped. *I'm at the hotel. Can you come here?*

*Yes. On my way.*

*Use side entrance and ask receptionist for key to Suite 21 – it's empty. Will wait for you there. X*

Alice raced outside and hailed a taxi. Some part of her brain was telling her to stop, to think, but she was sick and tired of thinking. Her brain hurt from all the useless thinking and worrying and stressing. Right now, she wanted to let it go – and there was only one man she could do that with. Dan.

## Ben

Ben ordered a pint for David and a half for himself. He still had no capacity for alcohol. One glass of wine made him light-headed.

While he waited for his friend he pulled his purchases out of the bag. The leather-bound photo album was beautifully made. He had definitely chosen the right one. It was classy, like Alice. He had a couple of ideas for its use.

He checked the ingredients for breakfast. Yogurt, raspberries, blueberries and granola. Holly had told him that was Alice's favourite at the moment. He was going to get up early in the morning and make it for her. He wanted to surprise her with breakfast in bed. Holly had said she'd help.

Things were better with Holly. She was still a bit shy around him, but she was definitely warming up. Thank God for Jools, he thought. Since the day he'd come home she had been the same. She seemed to be the only one in the family who hadn't changed, although he did detect a watchfulness in her that hadn't been there before.

Everyone kept saying it was going to take time to settle back in but it was frustrating. Having lost two years of his life, he was eager to get on with things. He wanted to fix everything and push the past behind them.

In all the long, sleepless nights in Eritrea he'd never imagined that he'd feel like a stranger in his own home. He just kept thinking how wonderful it would be to be back.

Granted, he'd worried about Alice meeting someone else, but it hadn't happened. He didn't know if she'd had a fling or one-night stand – and he didn't want to. None of that mattered. What mattered was that no man had taken his place. What mattered was that Alice had been waiting for him. He had to focus on that. He had to remember that, even if she seemed distant and preoccupied, she hadn't moved on. She was still his wife, still his Alice, and even if it did take time, they'd make it work.

David waved from the door and bounded over. 'Hello, mate.' He threw his huge arms around Ben.

'Got you a pint.'

'Lovely.'

'Cheers,' Ben said, clinking his glass against David's.

David wiped some foam from his lip. 'So, how are things?'

'Good. I mean, I'm still adjusting, but I'm getting there.'

'Excellent. Well, don't put any pressure on yourself. I'm sure it'll take a bit of time to get back into real life.'

Ben nodded. 'Everyone keeps telling me to be patient, but it's frustrating. I've been waiting to come home for so long. I just want everything to be perfect. I want Alice and the girls to be happy and for us to be a proper family again.'

David coughed. 'Of course. I understand. I suppose, though, the two years you were gone will take a while to erase, as it were.'

'I don't think we'll ever erase them. The guilt of it is killing me.'

'Oh, mate, you didn't do anything wrong. You just had really, really bad luck.'

Ben rubbed his eyes with the heels of his hands. 'I should never have gone, David.'

David placed a hand on his shoulder. 'But you did and a terrible thing happened to you that was not of your doing.

Look, everyone's fine. You're back. You must stop blaming yourself, Ben, or it'll eat you up.'

Ben sighed. 'That's what my shrink says. I'm trying, but every time I jump when a door slams or I can't work something like the ridiculous new television, I see pity and fear in Alice's and the girls' eyes. It's as if they think I'm going to fall apart or have a breakdown. I want them to stop worrying. I want to look after them, not the other way around.'

David swirled his beer in the glass. 'They're just worried about you. It can't have been easy over there. They . . . Well, we all just want to help you ease back into life here. You've been through what I can only imagine as hell. We're just so happy to have you back home safely.'

Ben looked at his friend. 'Thanks. It wasn't hell. Don't get me wrong, it was mentally torturous but physically it wasn't. I just feel that when I get back to normal I'll be able to put it all behind me. I want to go back to work soon. I want to start earning money and looking after my family. Alice has had so much to deal with and I want to take that stress away from her.'

'She certainly did a good job of holding it all together. She was wonderful with the girls. But they were incredible too. They all supported each other.'

Ben chewed his lip. 'Alice is finding it difficult to let go.'

David's hand stopped in mid-air. 'What do you mean?'

'She's so used to doing everything that she finds it hard to let me take on some of the responsibilities. She tried to stop me putting the bins out the other night. I think she still sees me as weak and damaged.'

'Well, you're very thin, mate. We need to strengthen you up. Why don't you come to the gym with me? I can help you get those muscles back in shape.'

Ben smiled. 'I'd like that.'

They sipped their beer in companionable silence.

'I was worried she'd meet someone else,' Ben said.

'What?' David knocked his glass against the table as he put it down, spilling beer on his trousers.

Ben laughed. 'Sorry, I didn't mean to startle you. I'm just relieved that she wasn't with someone when I got back. It was my biggest fear. She's so lovely I was sure someone would snap her up.'

'Well . . . yes. She is . . . she . . .'

David's phone buzzed. It was Pippa. Ben thought he heard her say something about their son William and rugby, but David turned away and started talking very loudly. 'What? . . . Hospital called? Emergency? Right. I'm on the way.'

He turned to Ben. 'Sorry, mate, I have to cut this drink short. Problem with a patient.'

'Well, it was good to see you.'

'You too. Call me about the gym. Must dash.' David waved as he rushed out of the door.

*Alice*

Alice slipped through the hotel's side entrance, stopped for a moment to take a deep breath, then forced herself to walk slowly and calmly to the reception desk. Her adrenalin was still pumping from delivering the baby.

'Suite twenty-one, please,' she said.

The receptionist looked at her for a moment, then handed her the key. Alice took it and went to the lift. Her heart was beating like crazy as the lift rose to the fifth floor.

Although she had the key, she felt suddenly strange about walking straight in, so she knocked softly. Her shaking hands were trying to get the key into the slot when the door was flung open and there stood Dan. Her Dan. The smell of his aftershave, so familiar, was wonderful. He smiled at her, and Alice melted. She threw her arms around him and kissed him.

Dan pulled her in and slammed the door shut. They ripped each other's clothes off and were naked in seconds. Alice wrapped her legs around him and inhaled his scent. Dan . . . Oh, Dan. Her body tingled with desire. She didn't want to let go. She wanted Dan inside her, part of her, all over her. She relished feeling his weight on top of her. She was safe here – safe, secure and loved. They made love in a frenzy, then lay on the huge bed wrapped around each other.

'God, I've missed you.' Dan nuzzled her neck, then moved to get up.

'Don't.' Alice curled her body tightly around his. 'Stay with me. Please, Dan. Stay with me.'

Dan pushed her hair off her cheek. 'What's going on, Alice?'

Alice hid her face in his shoulder. 'I don't know. I'm completely lost.' She wanted to tell him that she loved him, that she wanted to move into his house and block out the world, to live with him in a bubble, no problems or heartache.

Dan had been her haven from the drudge and worry of day-to-day life. She knew it was wonderful that Ben was alive, but it was so hard. They were like strangers.

Alice looked into Dan's blue eyes. 'I don't know what's going on. Everything is a mess. I came here to give you back your ring and say goodbye.'

'Interesting way of going about it.' Dan smiled.

Alice blushed. 'I just . . . when I saw you . . . Sorry.'

'You don't have to apologize for greeting me with great sex.'

'No, I'm sorry about all of . . . well, everything that's happened.'

'There's nothing you could have done about it. I'm glad your husband's home and safe for the girls, but I'd be lying if I said I wasn't disappointed. It throws an almighty spanner in the works.'

Alice smiled. 'You can say that again.'

Dan moved to sit up against the pillows. He pulled Alice close to him. 'So, how do you feel about him?'

Alice was glad he couldn't see her face, which was buried in his chest. 'I honestly don't know. He's not the same man. He's changed. It's . . . Everything is different.'

'Do you love him?'

Alice winced, but she was determined to be as honest as she could. 'I love him as the father of my daughters. But I don't think I'm in love with him.'

'Is it terrible that I'm pleased about that?'

Alice didn't respond.

'I love you, Alice. I want you. I don't want to share you with anyone. I've been going crazy wondering if we were over.'

'I'm sorry. I just had to focus on him and the girls.'

'I understand. It hasn't been easy.' Dan paused. 'I have to ask, are you sleeping with him?'

Alice shook her head. She didn't want to admit to the terrible sex. It was too personal and it felt cruel to expose Ben like that. Here she was, lying again. Would she ever be able to tell the whole truth to anyone?

'Well, then, I think we should make up for lost time.' Dan wrapped his legs around her and Alice let herself go. She switched her mind off and used her body for release from the problems that threatened to crush her.

When Alice came out of the shower she found that Dan had ordered a snack.

She sat down and played with her food.

'Not hungry, darling? I'm ravenous after all that . . . physical exertion.' Dan put his arm around her. 'Now don't go feeling guilty. You did nothing wrong. You were a widow. We fell in love. There's no crime in that.'

'Then why do I feel so bad?'

'Because you're a good person who doesn't want to hurt anyone. But you have to tell him, Alice. You have to come clean.'

Alice played with the button on her jacket. 'I know, but I need more time. I need him to be stronger first.'

Dan put down his fork and sighed. 'Not seeing you is killing me, Alice. I want us to be together. I'm like a caged tiger, snapping at everyone. I'm driving Stella mad.'

'How is Stella?'

'Gutted. She loves your girls. She's worried she'll never see you all again.'

'She will. It's just . . . I need . . .'

'More time. Yes, I know.' Dan sounded fed up.

'I have to tell him when the time is right, but I'm terrified he'll hear it from someone else. Are you sure your friends won't say anything? If the newspapers get hold of this I'll die.'

Dan took her hand in his. 'Don't worry, Alice. I told you I spoke to everyone at the party in my house – no one will breathe a word. They understand the delicate nature of the situation.'

'Thanks.'

Alice glanced at the clock on the table. Damn, it was almost six. She stood up. 'I have to go,' she said.

'Not yet.' Dan stood up and pulled her to him.

'I have to,' she said.

'When will I see you again?'

'I don't know.'

'I need you, Alice.'

Alice pulled back. 'He needs me more, Dan. I have to stay with him for now.'

Dan's face darkened. 'I won't let you go.'

Alice gulped back tears and handed him the engagement ring.

He pushed her hand away. 'No.'

'I can't keep it.'

'Yes, you can. I'm not giving up on you. I want you to keep it. I love you and I'm not letting you go without a fight. I'll wait for you, Alice. I'll give you time, but I will not give up on us. No way.'

Alice nodded, unable to speak as tears streamed down her face. She grabbed her bag and rushed out of the room. She didn't want to give him up, but did she have a choice?

*Holly*

Mummy and Jools just had the worst fight ever. It was awful, really awful. It started because Jools found a text on Mummy's phone. We were all in the kitchen. Jools was on her iPad, and I was talking to Mummy about school. Daddy had gone to meet David for a drink.

Mummy's phone beeped. It was beside Jools. She looked at it, then snatched it up. 'It's from Dan. What the hell?' she shouted.

Mummy went red. She grabbed the phone from Jools.

'Oh, my God, Mum, you were with him today!' Jools screamed. *'Being with you today was amazing. To touch you again was mind-blowing. I love you. I'll wait for you,'* she read. 'How could you do this to Dad?'

I felt really sick.

Mummy snatched the phone out of Jools's hand. 'Stop it, Jools. That's private.'

'You said you were going to break up with Dan. But you're sneaking around meeting him and having sex! Why, Mum? Don't you get it? You're going to break Dad's heart.' Jools was shaking and she looked angrier than I'd ever seen her before in my life.

Mummy took a step back. 'Jools, what goes on between Dan and me and between your dad and me is private.'

'He's home. We've got our dad after two years of utter misery. He is back and he's so happy to be home and he loves us so much and now you're going to ruin it all because you're a selfish *bitch*.'

Mummy slapped Jools across the face. She looked really shocked – like she couldn't believe what she'd done. Jools stumbled backwards, holding her face.

'I'm sorry. God, I'm sorry. I didn't mean to do that,' Mummy gasped.

Jools glared at her. 'I hate you. How can you be so selfish? Dad needs us. You'll destroy him.'

Mummy wiped her eyes. 'I'm trying to break up with Dan, but it's not easy. I spent months and months picking up the pieces, minding you and Holly, worrying, working and heart-broken, and then I met someone, and he was kind and wonderful and I fell in love. I thought your dad was dead. I didn't do anything wrong, Jools. Ben was dead.'

'Yes, he was, but he's alive now,' Jools shouted. 'So when you run off and shag someone behind his back, that's *cheating*.'

Mummy's hand went up to her cheek and her eyes were really wide. She was white and her mouth opened but no words came out. Then she took a deep breath and said very quietly, 'I can't just turn my feelings on and off. I'm doing the best I can, Jools. I'm trying really hard, but it's not easy.'

'Yes, it is, Mum. Dump Dan and be with Dad.'

'It's not that simple.'

'She loves him, Jools. She can't help it.' I handed Mum a tissue. 'We all liked Dan and Stella. We can't just pretend they never existed.'

Jools turned her spiteful stare on me. 'Oh, typical you, Holly, always taking Mum's side. What's wrong with you both? Dad is back. He needs us.'

'I know that,' I shouted back. 'I know he wants everything to be the same as before, but it isn't, Jools. And Mummy isn't selfish. She did everything for us when Dad was gone. She was our person. She kept us together and did everything to make us happy again. She's been through hell, Jools.'

'So has Dad!' Jools snapped. 'So have I.'

'Girls, please don't fight. This situation is very complicated. I just need some time, Jools. I need to figure it all out in my head and I know your dad needs me. I'm here for him. I promise you that I'm doing my best, but I'm only human, so please don't shout at me and call me a selfish bitch.' Mummy wiped her tears with a tissue.

Jools sighed. 'I'm sorry. You're not selfish, but I'm scared. I'm scared Dad is going to find out that you were with Dan and that me and Holly were happy and that we liked Dan and that we were about to move into his house. I feel sick every time I think about it because I let Dad down. I moved on. While he was chained to a tree, I was in Dan's house planning which bedroom I'd sleep in and having a great time with Stella. Dad's my person. He's the one who gets me and I let him down. Don't you see? I let him down.' Jools bent over and sobbed as if her heart would break.

Mummy rushed over to her and threw her arms around her. 'Oh, Jools, no no no no. You didn't let anyone down. You've been so wonderful and brave and supportive. I'd never have got through this without you. I told Dad how fantastic you were and he's so proud and so grateful to you. You didn't let anyone down, ever.'

Jools's face was wet with tears. 'But I did, Mum, I did.'

I suddenly felt really angry. Angry with everything. Angry with the mess we were in, angry with life for giving us so much to deal with.

'No, you didn't, Jools,' I said crossly. 'You just chose to live your life and not be miserable all the time. We weren't wrong to move on, we *had* to. And . . . and . . .' I started to cry too

'. . . Daddy can't blame us for that and he wouldn't. He loves you, Jools, and he knows you love him. I liked Dan and Stella too, and I was glad Mummy met Dan. We thought Daddy was dead!' I said again, trying to get through to my sister. 'We thought he was gone for ever.'

'I just feel so guilty,' Jools said.

'You have nothing to feel guilty for.' Mummy hugged her again. 'You never stopped loving your dad.'

Jools sat down and put her head in her hands. 'I'm sorry for shouting at you, Mum, but you have to break up with Dan and give Dad a chance. Please don't hurt him. Please.'

Mummy looked utterly shattered.

I was going over to give her a hug when I saw him standing at the door. We all had our backs to him.

'David got called away, so I came home early,' Dad said.

## Alice

Christ! How much had he heard? Alice felt a pain shoot through her chest. She thought she was having a heart attack.

Jools and Holly froze. Ben stood in the doorway, not moving.

Alice knew she had to take control. 'Girls, why don't you go up to your rooms? It's getting late.'

Neither moved. Ben went towards Jools. 'Goodnight, darling.' He reached out to hug her. She fell into his arms.

'Goodnight, Dad.'

'Sleep well, Jools. I love you.'

'I love you too,' Jools said, her voice quivering.

Ben went over to give Holly a hug. 'Goodnight, Holly. I love you very much too.'

'Me too, Daddy, so much.' Holly followed her sister out of the room, but not before looking back at her mother. Her eyes were full of fear. Alice knew she had to make this better somehow.

She was shaken by what Jools had said. When she'd gone to meet Dan and they'd ended up in bed, it had never occurred to her that she was cheating: it was just being with Dan, like before. But Jools was right – before, she had been a widow, but now her husband was back and she *was* cheating. She had never been unfaithful to Ben in all the years of their marriage. Yet today she had been. Today she had gone behind her husband's back and slept with another man.

She was behaving as if she was still a widow, not married, but single. How could she have done such a thing and not even realized it? Alice took ragged deep breaths, trying to calm her heart rate and think straight.

When the girls left, there was silence. Alice stood still, afraid to move or speak. Ben closed the kitchen door softly and went to the fridge.

'I think I need a drink. Would you like some wine?' he asked.

Alice nodded. She watched as Ben poured two large glasses. She noticed that his hands were trembling. She sat down, afraid her legs would give way from under her.

Ben remained standing, leaning against the counter. 'So I gather there is someone else?'

Alice nodded.

Ben took a long sip of his wine. 'Do I know him?'

'No.'

'How long have you been together?'

'Six months.'

'Was it . . .' he stumbled over his words ' . . . Is it serious?'

Alice's mind was whirring. If he was asking if it was serious, he mustn't have heard Jools mention moving into Dan's house. 'It was getting there,' she said, treading softly.

'Who is he?'

'Dan Penfold. He's a businessman, he's . . . a . . .' Alice trailed off. Ben didn't need to hear how successful Dan was.

'Do the girls know him well?'

Alice swallowed. 'Not very . . . quite . . . They had got to know him better just recently.'

'I see.'

Alice cleared her throat. She had to make him understand that they didn't leave him behind: they were just trying to live life. 'The girls mourned for you so much, Ben. They were so sad, and so was I. We were shattered. Then I met Dan and he was nice to me and nice to the girls. Not in any way trying to be a father to them, just nice and kind. He has an older daughter they got on well with.'

'How did you meet him?'

Alice knew this was going to hurt, but she couldn't lie. 'A dinner party at David and Pippa's. He lives next door to them.'

Ben's whole face caved in. He looked as if he'd been punched.

'David set you up with him?' he gasped.

'It wasn't like that.' Alice was desperate to explain. 'David and Pippa invited me for dinner. They invited me out lots of times and most of the time I said no because I was too upset and low. They were just being kind, wanting to see if I was all right and trying to get me out of the house. They didn't know that anything would . . . well . . .'

'Happen,' Ben finished Alice's sentence.

Alice reached out to touch Ben's hand, but he pulled it back. 'Ben,' she said gently, 'I know this must seem awful, like a betrayal, but you have to remember, I believed you were dead.'

Ben looked up at her for the first time. 'I know you did. I know the girls did. I'm aware of that fact. I've thought about it every single day since I was captured. It torments me, it haunts me and it eats me up inside.'

Alice fought back tears. 'I'm sorry, I really am. It's just a mess, really. It's been such a shock for all of us.'

'Are you still seeing Dan?' Ben asked.

Alice paused. 'I've only seen him once since you came back.'

Ben took a long, deep drink, then asked, 'Do you love him?'

Alice covered her face with her hands. She didn't want

Ben to see her eyes. He had always been able to read them. He knew when she was lying.

'Jesus, Ben, I don't know. I mean, I just . . . I'm not sure about anything.'

'I see.'

Alice peeped through her fingers. Ben looked broken. 'Oh, Ben, I'm sorry. I never meant to hurt you. I'm so glad you're back. I'm so glad you're alive. The girls are so happy and it's wonderful. I'm still in shock, I think, and I need to get used to it all, and then . . . well . . . then . . . we'll see, I guess. I love you, Ben . . . I do. It's just different. Everything has changed . . . I think we both have to . . . I . . . we . . .' Alice didn't know how to finish the sentence because she didn't know how she felt or what was going to happen.

Her head ached and she felt sick with sorrow, guilt and loneliness. The strange thing was that, in the midst of everything going on, she felt incredibly lonely. She couldn't be with Dan and she was trying and failing to be with Ben. In the middle of all this drama, Alice was alone. No one could help her. It was something she was going to have to figure out by herself.

Ben moved towards the back door. 'I need a cigarette. This has been a lot to take in.'

Alice stood up and reached out a hand to him.

He ignored it. 'I'm not blaming you. I'm not angry. I knew it was a possibility. You're a beautiful woman – of course men would want to be with you. It's just a bit too real now.'

'Ben, I'm sorry . . . it's not . . .'

'It's okay. I just need to think.'

Alice watched as Ben walked slowly out to the garden bench and lit a cigarette. He stared at the sky as he exhaled long lines of smoke. Alice felt afraid. Very afraid. She knew she had hurt him and she hadn't meant to. She loved him: she just wasn't sure that she was still in love with him.

## Ben

Ben waited until they had all left the house for work and school, then sat down to Google Dan Penfold. He typed in the name and immediately hundreds of articles came up about him. Who the hell was this guy? Ben skimmed through Dan's Wikipedia page. Jesus Christ, he was a multi-millionaire property baron.

Ben zoomed in on a photo of him. He was older than Ben, but Ben could see that he was good-looking and his confidence jumped out of the photo.

Ben cursed. He hadn't imagined his rival would be so bloody successful. He felt his confidence sag. Before Eritrea he'd always been very sure of himself, proud of his achievements and full of self-belief. But those two years had knocked him. Now he saw how important it was that he regain his confidence if he was going to win Alice back.

Ben needed to talk to someone. He certainly wasn't going to call David. He knew it wasn't David's fault, but he couldn't help being annoyed that his best friend had introduced Alice to Dan. Besides, now he knew why David had run out of the pub when Ben had been spouting on about how great it was that Alice hadn't met anyone. He felt like a complete fool. He also felt incredibly alone. He badly needed to talk to the one person he could be totally honest with. He picked up his mobile and dialled.

'Morning, Benji,' Declan bellowed.

'You sound chipper.'

'I've been for a run and had breakfast already. I've decided to cut down on the boozing. Billy said it was making my nightmares worse and that I needed to calm down and start living a more normal life, as he so politely put it.'

'Good for Billy.'

'Ah, sure, he's a rock of sense. How are you? You sound down.'

Ben smiled. Declan knew him too well. 'I found out last night that Alice has been seeing someone else.'

'Shite.'

'Shite indeed.'

'Is it serious?'

'I don't know. I think it might be. Alice was cagey about how serious it is, which implies that it's serious.'

'Don't jump to conclusions. It might not be. It could well be a fling.'

'No, it's definitely more than that. It's been going on for about six months and the girls know him quite well. I think . . . I think Alice is in love with him.'

'Shite.'

'Yes.'

'How did she meet him?'

Ben winced. 'David introduced them. He's David's next-door neighbour.'

'Ouch.'

'Yes, that did hurt.'

'Mind you, if we're being fair, they did all think you were dead.'

Ben stirred sugar into his coffee. 'I know that. Rationally I know I have no right to be annoyed or upset, but I am. I want to punch someone – preferably this guy Dan. Alice said David was just being nice and trying to get her out of the house, but why the hell did he have to introduce her to an eligible single multi-millionaire?'

'Multi-millionaire?'

'He's absolutely loaded. Apparently he's worth over six hundred million.'

'Bollox.'

'My sentiments exactly.'

'Never mind, Benji. You're a tall, dark, handsome surgeon, who spent two years surviving in captivity only to escape like Indiana fecking Jones. Dan has nothing on you.'

Ben laughed. 'When you put it like that . . .'

'The only thing he has on you is six hundred million quid, but who cares about money? Alice married you because she loved you. You had a great life together. This guy probably swept her off her feet a bit – wining and dining and all that – but that's probably all it was, just a bit of spoiling and luxury. You've got years of history with Alice, don't forget that. This is just a flash in the pan.'

'Maybe.' Ben desperately wanted to think that was all it was, but deep down he knew it was more than that. He could read Alice like a book. She couldn't look at him last night when he'd asked her about Dan. He could see she was trying not to give too much away. She was definitely serious about him.

Ben rested his head against the cupboard. 'Why did it have to happen, Declan? Why did the bastards have to keep us there for so long? Everything is so messed up now.'

'We both know that looking back and asking why will drive us insane. Come on, Ben, you have to look forward. You can take this guy on. You just need to make Alice fall for you again. You need to remind her of who you are, how brilliant you are, how happy you two used to be and how happy you can be again. You can do it, Ben. Now, come on, fight for her. You're Indiana Jones, remember that.'

'Thanks, mate.'

'Anytime.'

'I wish you lived round the corner so we could go to the pub and drink pints and you could fix my life for me.'

'You're going to sort this out. You can do it. And remember, I'm only ever a phone call away. Seriously, Ben, if you ever need me, I'll be on a plane in a second.'

'Thanks, and likewise.'

Ben could hear Declan lighting a cigarette. 'My life is less complicated than yours. I'm a single man. But I know you'll work it out with Alice, I really believe it, but it's going to take time and effort.'

'I just feel so tired all the time, you know?'

'I do. It's not easy putting those two years behind us. Not easy at all.'

Ben said nothing. There was nothing to say. Eritrea would always be with them, but hopefully the effects would fade with time.

'I've decided to bring Billy and Sean to the welcome-home party in January.'

Ben groaned. He was dreading it. Theo Halston, the chief executive of the hospital, had insisted on throwing a party for the two men. Ben really didn't want a party. He'd kept putting it off until Halston had finally pinned him down to a date. Ben felt that a party was ridiculous and embarrassing. He just wanted to be with his family and get back to work, instead of repeating his story over and over again to people he barely knew.

'It's a bloody pain in the arse, but let's just have a few drinks and try to get through it. I presume you're bringing Alice?'

'Definitely.'

'It'll do her good to see you back in your old workplace with the nurses falling all over you. A bit of jealousy is no harm. Right, I'd better go, I've got an appointment with my shrink. She says I'm "doing very well considering". Considering I was chained to you for two years, it's a fecking miracle I'm normal at all.'

They both laughed. It felt good to laugh.

'Good luck with the shrink and thanks again.'

'Anytime, mate.'


Ben woke up drenched in sweat, his heart racing. He slipped out of bed and went down to the kitchen. He pulled on his coat and shoes, went out to the garden and sat on the bench. He glared at the tree, whose bare branches shimmered in the moonlight. He lit a cigarette and shivered in the cold. His head ached from the nightmare he'd just had. It was the same dream every time: they were escaping and suddenly, out of nowhere, Eyob appeared. He held up his rifle, aimed it at Ben's face and pulled the trigger.

Ben wondered if he'd ever sleep properly again. Alice had offered him sleeping pills, but he didn't want to take them. He was afraid of becoming muddled and groggy. He needed to be clear-headed to figure out how to fit back into his old life and win his wife's affection.

It was hard trying to find his place again. Everyone had moved on. Alice was so independent now: she never asked his advice or looked for him to pay a bill or help around the house. He felt useless. He longed to go back to work.

Jools had a tutor to help her with her schoolwork. Ben had offered to fill in, but Alice said things were going well with the tutor and she didn't want to 'rock the boat'. She told him to relax and put his feet up, but that was the last thing he wanted. He was lost with nothing to do. When he'd offered to cook dinner last week, he'd had a panic attack in the middle of doing it, and by the time it had passed, the chicken was burnt. They'd all eaten it and pretended it was nice, but that was almost worse. He wanted them to treat him like they did in the old days. He wanted them to make gagging noises and say it was 'disgusting'. But they were still being kind and gentle with him and it was beginning to drive him crazy.

The back door opened. Ben turned around to see Jools coming out to him. He was relieved. Jools was the only one who treated him the same way. She was pulling her coat on over her pyjamas.

'Can I have one?' She pointed to the cigarettes.

'Certainly not. They're bad for you.'

'Come on, Dad, I smoke too, you know.'

'Since when?'

'Since you died.' Jools smirked.

'Sorry about that.'

'Dad!' Jools cried. 'Stop bloody apologizing. It wasn't your fault you got kidnapped.'

'It was my decision to go, though, and your mum did ask me not to.'

Jools pulled a cigarette out of the packet and lit it. 'Yes, but Mum never wanted you to go anywhere. She wanted all of us at home, safe. I know it's because her parents died, but she was a pain about it.'

Ben shook his head. 'She was right, Jools. I shouldn't have gone to Eritrea, it was selfish. I went because I wanted adventure. I was restless and only thinking about myself.'

'So what? Everyone's selfish in their own way. You mustn't feel bad, Dad – it's stopping you being happy. It's over now. We've got you back and that's all that matters.'

'I'm so glad to be home. I used to lie awake at night in that

355

tent and worry about you so much. I knew you'd think I'd been killed and I hated you not having a dad.'

Jools blew out a line of smoke. 'It was shit. We were all devastated. Mum was so sad all the time, but she was amazing too. She was so good to me and Holly. In a weird way, the whole thing made me and Mum closer. But in the beginning Mum was like a zombie. Kevin moving in really kept us all going. He was brilliant.'

'How did you and Holly cope with it all?'

Jools looked away. 'Holly read zillions of books and followed Mum around like a lost puppy.'

Ben closed his eyes. He felt sick. 'And you, Jools?'

'I just kind of got on with it. It's a bit of a blur.'

Ben knew his daughter too well. 'Jools, come on, tell me the truth. I can take it. It's me, Dad, you can talk to me.'

'I was okay, honestly,' Jools said, as tears fell down her cheeks.

'Jools.' Ben mopped them with the back of his hand. 'There were times when I thought I'd never see you again that I wanted to die. I know it was awful for you. Be honest with me.'

'Well, I did some silly things, but that's all over now.'

'Like what?'

'Nothing, stupid stuff.'

'Jools?'

Jools stubbed out her cigarette with her slipper and slowly pulled up the sleeve of her coat.

'Oh, Jesus.' Ben felt sick as he looked at the zigzag of scars on his daughter's arm. He had caused this. He forced himself to remain calm. He wanted Jools to talk to him. But all he really wanted to do was pull her to him, hold her and never let her go.

'I needed to feel pain. The cutting helped me release the pain inside. Does that make sense?'

'Yes, but it's only ever temporary. Have you stopped? Please tell me you've stopped.'

'Yes.'

'God, Jools, I'm sor—'

'STOP!' Jools put up her hands.' Don't say it. It's over, Dad. We need to look to the future now. I want us to be happy again.'

'So do I. But, Jools, do you promise never to cut yourself again?'

'Yes. I want to wear short sleeves. I spent the whole summer roasting in long ones. Besides, the reason I cut was because I thought you were dead, but you're not. I'm happy now, Dad. But you don't seem happy. What's wrong?'

Ben lit another cigarette. 'I am happy, darling. I'm back with you, which is all I dreamt of. I'm just adjusting to it, as are you and Holly and Mum. It's a bit of a shock for you all, having me walk back into your lives. It'll take a little time to adjust and get back to normal.'

'How are you and Mum getting on? Really?' Jools asked.

Ben shuffled about. He didn't want to talk to his daughter about his problems with her mother. 'Fine.'

'Dad, I'm eighteen. I can vote, join the army, drink, buy a house, get married and get a tattoo. You don't have to protect me.'

Ben smiled. 'Please don't get a tattoo.'

'I will if you don't talk to me. I'll get a huge one that says "My dad came back from the dead". So, how are you and Mum?'

Ben put his hands into his coat pockets for warmth. 'She's changed. So have I, but I can't seem to get close to her.

She's always so busy. We haven't had a proper chance to reconnect.'

'So, go away for a holiday. I can keep an eye on Holly.'

'I suggested that, but she said she was up to her eyes with work and looking after you two, and lots of other excuses. I don't think she wants to be on her own with me, to be honest.' Ben turned to Jools. 'She told me the whole story about Dan.'

Jools took a long drag of her cigarette. 'Mum didn't even want to go to that dinner party, but Holly and I made her. She needed to start living again. She'd been so sad, Dad. She was so heartbroken. We wanted her to be happy. Anyway, that's where she met Dan. He was nice to her and they got on well.'

'Was it very serious?'

Ben watched as Jools paused, searching for the right words. 'Quite . . . not really . . . kind of.'

'Is he a nice person? Alice said he is.'

Jools nodded. 'Sorry,' she whispered.

'For what?'

'For liking someone else. I never loved him or anything, but I feel bad that I even liked him.'

Ben hugged her. 'Jools, I'm genuinely glad that someone was nice to you and Mum and Holly. I'm glad you had a nice time after all that grief. You have nothing to be sorry for.'

'I love you, Dad.' Jools clung to him.

'Oh, Jools, I love you too. And I'm not angry with anyone about Dan. It's only to be expected. Your mum thought I was dead. She's a beautiful woman. I knew she would have met someone.'

Jools put her hand on his arm. 'She loves you, Dad. You should have seen how upset she was when she thought you were dead. She was absolutely devastated. Dan was just someone who came along and was nice to her. You need to make Mum fancy you again. Do nice things for her and . . . I don't know . . . tell her she's fabulous and buy her presents and stuff. It works for me.'

Ben kissed his daughter's forehead. 'Thanks, Jools. Very good advice. Now, I don't want you to worry about anything. Everything is going to be fine. And you're right, we all need to look to the future and leave the past behind.'

Ben walked Jools back to her bedroom, then went downstairs, made himself a cup of coffee and took out the old photo albums. It was when he was looking for a pen in Alice's bag that he found it. He felt a hard square box and pulled it out. What the hell?

He stared at the Cartier box. Christ, it looked like Alice and Dan were more serious than she was admitting. With a sinking heart, Ben flipped open the box and stared at the enormous diamond sparkling in the moonlight. He shook his head, and then a slow smile spread across his face.

He put the box carefully back into the bag, found a pen and sat down. Ben pulled out the photos he needed, making notes for each one. He knew what he had to do.

*Holly*

Daddy decided to cook Christmas dinner. He said he wanted to give Mummy a break. Jools and I helped him. It was fun. We all went shopping together and bought everything we needed.

We spent ages chopping and preparing everything. Daddy seemed happier, less quiet. He was more fun too. It was just in little things, like he did silly dances with us in the kitchen. Before, he'd always worked up until Christmas Eve and Mummy had always decorated the house and cooked the turkey and everything.

It was so nice to see Daddy messing about and laughing. Mummy was usually the one who made a big fuss about Christmas, but this year she was so busy with work she wasn't home much, so Daddy did it all. He came home with big bags full of new decorations and we hung them everywhere.

Daddy asked me to help him make a trifle – it's Mummy's favourite dessert. We did it together and it was nice, just him and me making something for Mummy. It felt less awkward when we were doing something than just sitting around trying to make conversation. I felt more relaxed with Daddy like that. The first trifle was a disaster but Daddy just laughed and threw it into the bin and we started again. But it was a real laugh, not a forced fake one, like he's been doing since he came home.

Kevin called in on Christmas morning with presents.

When he saw all the decorations he said it was like 'Santa's grotto'. He asked where Mummy was and Daddy said she was upstairs having a shower.

Jools asked Kevin what Axel had given him for Christmas and Kevin said 'a pain in my arse'. Daddy said he was dying to meet Axel, that we'd told him all about him. Kevin said, 'I wouldn't hold your breath. His other "gift" to me was chlamydia. I think our relationship is about to end.'

I didn't know what chlamydia was, but Daddy had that face where he looks shocked but wants to laugh too.

'What's chlamydia?' Jools asked.

'It's an STD,' Kevin said.

'Oh!' Jools was shocked. 'Gross.'

I didn't know what STD was either. I decided to ask. Daddy coughed, and Kevin said, 'It's what you get when your boyfriend has been with other guys.'

'Can girls get it too?' I was worried Mummy might have got one from Dan.

'Yes,' Kevin said.

'Does it hurt?'

'Yes.'

'Are you going to break up with Axel?'

'Probably.'

Oh, my God, what if Mummy gives Daddy chlamydia and they break up?

Daddy said he thought that was enough about STDs and asked Kevin to taste the trifle as it was his favourite dessert too. Kevin said it was nice but needed way more sherry, so I poured in a few more drops, but Kevin tipped my elbow and lots went in. It looked a bit soggy, but he said it tasted perfect and that the whole point of trifle was to drown the sponge in booze.

Daddy poured Kevin a glass of wine and made a toast. He

said that he wanted to thank Kevin for being so brilliant with us and that he was 'for ever indebted to him'.

Kevin blushed and said it had been a pleasure. It was nice to see Daddy and Kevin getting on so well. Daddy used to be a bit impatient with him but now they're like real friends.

Kevin asked Daddy what he'd got Mummy for Christmas and Daddy said that he'd bought her a diamond ring and that he was working on another present, but it wouldn't be ready for a while.

Daddy showed us the ring. Jools looked at me and I looked at the floor. Kevin took a gulp of wine.

'You see, there are three diamonds – the bigger one is Alice and the two smaller ones on either side are you girls.'

We told him it was beautiful and he seemed pleased.

'I know it's not an enormous diamond, but even if I had six hundred million quid, this is the ring I'd buy Alice.' Daddy winked.

It's such a relief that Daddy knows about Dan and that he didn't go crazy about it. Well, he knows almost everything. Jools told me that Mummy didn't tell Daddy about the engagement but that he knows she and Dan were in a serious relationship and he's not cross with us but he is determined to win Mummy back.

'This ring is perfect, Dad,' Jools said.

'Mummy will love it,' I agreed.

'You've got great taste,' Kevin said, holding the box up so that the ring caught the light. 'It's the perfect ring for Alice.'

Daddy took it back, put it into his trouser pocket and smiled at us.

He gave Mummy the ring before dinner. She gasped.

'Isn't it stunning?' Jools said. 'Isn't it the most beautiful ring you've ever seen?'

'It's . . . it's lovely. Wow, Ben, I really didn't expect you to buy me something so big. I feel bad now – I just got you clothes and some books.' Mummy was flustered.

'It's about new beginnings,' Daddy said, watching her closely. 'You're the larger diamond in the middle and the girls are the two smaller ones. It represents my family. I thought it was very you. Not flashy or ostentatious, just elegant. It goes well with your wedding ring. I got it in the same jeweller's. You remember the eccentric guy in Hatton Court who kept telling us about his gout?'

Mummy smiled at the memory. 'Yes, of course I do. When he found out we were medics, he took off his shoe and sock to show us his foot, then gave us a discount on the ring because you were so nice to him.' She kissed Daddy's cheek and then put the ring on. It looked lovely on her hand.

'It's gorgeous,' Jools said.

'It really suits you,' I added.

'It really is you,' Kevin agreed.

Mummy looked at it and nodded. 'It's exactly what I would have chosen myself. Thank you, Ben.'

Mummy tried to help with dinner but Daddy told her she wasn't allowed to move from her chair for the whole day. 'I want you to relax. You've always done Christmas dinner. It's time I did one.'

He had tried really hard so we all ate everything even though it wasn't very nice.

'Gosh, the sprouts are rock hard,' Daddy said.

'They're just a bit crunchy.' Kevin tried to chew one.

'Very crunchy.' Jools giggled.

'Exceedingly crunchy.' I snorted and we all laughed.

'I reckon you could play ping-pong with them,' Kevin said.

'And the turkey's bone dry.' Daddy looked at the shrivelled meat.

'It just needs a lot of gravy,' Jools said.

363

'God, I forgot all about the gravy. Sorry, everyone.' Dad looked sheepish.

'It's fine. I like my turkey cremated,' Kevin said.

'I love the way it sticks to the top of my mouth,' Jools cackled.

Daddy was laughing so hard, he had to hold his stomach.

'Don't mind them, Ben. It's lovely. The first time is always tricky,' Mummy said, laughing too.

'It was a heroic effort but I'm recommending that you stick to surgery and leave the cooking to Alice,' Kevin suggested.

'Can we please move on to dessert now?' Jools asked.

'Good idea.' Daddy got up and went into the kitchen.

When Daddy came back in with the trifle, Mummy clapped. 'My favourite!'

'And the good news is that I've tasted it and it's edible,' Kevin said.

'You've gone to so much trouble, it's . . . I'm . . . Thank you, Ben.' Mummy got up and hugged Daddy. He held her and kissed her hair. I felt all warm inside. Jools nudged my foot under the table and grinned.

## *Alice*

A ring! She couldn't believe it. She put it on. It was beautiful. Smaller than Dan's but much more her, if she was honest. It was exactly the kind of ring Alice would have chosen for herself. But it felt as if it was burning her finger. She felt like a fraud. The guilt of not having broken up with Dan yet was eating her up.

She would tell herself, 'I'll do it', but once she rang or texted him, she lost her conviction and wanted him all over again. That day when she had met him in the hotel had been so wonderful. She'd felt her problems melting away as she lay in his arms. She just wanted to be with him, blocking out all of her worries. He felt like an addiction. He was her safe place, her haven from the madness around her. And it didn't help that Dan knew that. Each time they talked, he managed to talk over and around her reasons for giving him back the ring, telling her not to draw a line under it yet. Not yet. He painted pictures that swirled around her head like confetti – images of a perfect life with him, of travel, beautiful houses, comfort and great sex. It was a seduction, a temptation, and she seemed powerless against it.

Alice was trying very hard to block Dan out and stay in the present. Ben had gone to so much trouble. She could see how hard he was trying and she was grateful, very grateful, but it didn't change the way she felt about him. She just didn't feel the same any more. She loved him, really loved him, but the spark was gone. He was like a really good friend she adored, but the physical side was dead.

Maybe if she gave up Dan she could try to get it back, but she dreaded sex with Ben. It was so intimate that all their problems seemed to be heightened when they were alone and naked together. She felt completely exposed. It was as if someone was screaming, 'You two don't work any more.'

But she had promised herself and the girls that she would try harder. She had to: she owed it to them. Seeing Jools so angry the other day had been a real eye-opener. This whole situation could devastate the people she loved most, maybe even split them apart. There was no way she could let that happen.

Alice went over and hugged Ben. 'Thank you for making this Christmas so special. It's wonderful to have you home.'

Alice saw Jools and Holly beaming, and her heart sank. Much as she wanted her marriage to work, she wasn't sure she could stay with Ben in the long term, and her daughters' hearts would be broken again.

Alice pushed down the fears and forced herself to stay in the present. One day at a time, she told herself.

They were playing a lively game of charades – Kevin, Holly and Alice against Ben and Jools – when there was a knock on the door. Ben went to open it and walked back into the lounge with Harold and Helen. They had brought wine and flowers for Alice and Ben, selection boxes for the girls.

'We thought we'd pop in with some gifts.' Harold was full of fake bonhomie.

'I'm not eight,' Jools muttered, when she saw the selection box.

Alice gave her a warning look. She wanted to tell Harold where to shove his presents, but it was Christmas, he was

Ben's father and she didn't want to upset anyone. She stood up, shook her father-in-law's hand and was air-kissed by Helen.

Harold barely acknowledged Kevin, which infuriated Alice. 'Will you have a drink?' she asked, planning to do some deep breathing exercises in the kitchen to keep her temper in hand.

'A cup of tea would be lovely, thank you, dear,' Helen said.

'Yes, tea,' Harold agreed.

'I'll make it.' Holly got up and went into the kitchen before Alice could say anything. She sat down again and prepared to be civil. She could hear her mother's voice in her head saying, 'Bite your tongue, Alice', which made her smile.

'So how are you, Dad?' Ben asked.

'Fine. I must say, this is a very happy Christmas with you home safely. The last two were a bit on the grim side.'

'They certainly were,' Alice agreed.

'I imagine it wasn't much fun in Eritrea either.' Kevin tried to make a joke.

'No, Santa Claus couldn't find us.' Ben smiled.

'Yes, well, you're here now and all is well.' Harold's tone was firm.

'I don't even remember the first Christmas. It's a complete blur,' Jools said.

'You were still in shock, poor things,' Kevin said.

'Thank God for Kevin or we wouldn't have had anything to eat. You bought everything and cooked for us that year. You were great,' Alice said.

'David and Pippa were really nice too. Remember, Mum? They came round with loads of presents and food to put in the freezer so we wouldn't have to cook for the whole Christmas holidays,' Jools said.

Alice smiled. 'Yes, they did. They were so thoughtful.'

'Where were you, Dad?' Ben asked.

Alice looked at her husband. His jaw was set. Uh-oh.

Harold coughed. 'I wasn't feeling well. We just went to Helen's daughter nearby for a bite to eat and straight home.'

'Yes, he had a bad cold and we didn't think it was wise to pass it on to the children.' Helen backed up her husband.

'So you didn't call in to see my wife and children on Christmas Day when they were alone and broken-hearted.'

'I phoned, of course, but I felt it was wiser to stay away. Alice was very emotional and I thought it best to leave her alone.'

Ben walked over to his father. 'So you thought it was a good idea to leave my widowed wife and two young daughters alone on Christmas Day and not even call in to check up on them?'

Alice was cheering inside, Go, Ben!

Harold stood up. 'I don't like your tone. I came the following Christmas and ended up being asked to leave.'

'That's because you were mean to Mummy.' No one had seen Holly coming into the room carrying a tray of cups and saucers and the teapot.

'Now, Holly, that's not true.' Harold was angry now.

'Yes, it is,' Jools said quietly.

'I merely pointed out that Alice should have discouraged you from going to Eritrea.'

The muscle on the side of Ben's cheek was throbbing. Alice only ever saw that when Ben was incredibly angry.

'Alice did discourage me. In fact, she begged me not to go. She pleaded with me, but I didn't listen because I'm pig-headed, like you, Dad. I went because I wanted to have an adventure. Well, I certainly got one, didn't I? So do not blame my wife for any of this. It was entirely my fault.'

'Men who are content at home don't go looking for adventure,' Harold snapped.

Alice watched as Ben's fury rose to the surface and exploded out of his mouth. 'How dare you say that? My wife is wonderful and I was very happy at home. But I'm greedy, I wanted more. I wanted the perfect home *and* adventure. I didn't think about Alice and the girls, I only thought of myself when I agreed to go to Eritrea. And those two years in captivity were my punishment for being such a selfish git. And never in my wildest dreams would I have thought that you could let me down and not look after your own daughter-in-law and grandchildren. You let me down badly and I'm not sure I'll ever forgive you.'

Alice was in shock – she didn't know whether to step in and stop Ben, or jump up and down and cheer. It was amazing to hear Ben defending her, making it clear to Harold that it was all his own idea to go away.

Harold's face was puce. 'How dare you? I have always supported you. I worked long and hard to send you to the best schools. I've been there every step of the way. I knew that Alice and the girls weren't alone – *he* was here. He moved in the minute you were gone.' Harold pointed at Kevin.

Ben moved over to where Kevin was standing. Putting his arm around his brother-in-law, he said, 'I know Kevin was here and I will always be grateful to him for looking after my family while I was gone. Kevin kept them going. Kevin helped them get back on their feet. I will spend the rest of my life trying to pay him back for all he did. I'm so disappointed in you, Dad. I expected more of you.'

Alice was thrilled to see Ben stick up for Kevin and for really understanding how much Kevin had done.

Harold grabbed his coat and gloves. 'I did not come here to be insulted. They weren't the only ones who were suffering. I believed my only child was dead. There is no worse agony to befall a man.' Harold's eyes were wet, and although Alice really didn't like him, she felt sorry for him. He adored Ben and to have Ben berate him must really hurt.

Alice tried to stop him leaving. 'Don't go, Harold. Sit down and have a cup of tea. Don't leave angry.'

Harold moved away from her towards the door. 'Helen, we're leaving.'

Ben stepped forward. 'Don't go, Dad. I apologize for shouting. It's Christmas, come on, sit down.'

'I will not stay a minute longer in this house. I'll talk to you when you find your manners and your respect.'

With that, Harold stormed out of the house, Helen following in his wake.

'Way to go, Dad!' Jools high-fived Ben. 'It was about time you told Granddad the truth. He's always so rude to Mum. And Kevin.'

Ben grinned. 'That was what you call pent-up anger coming out.'

'You were on fire.' Alice smiled warmly at him.

'Anger is always better out than in,' Kevin said. 'I thought it was very chivalrous of you to defend your wife. Well done, and thank you for what you said about me.' Kevin raised his glass in a toast.

'I felt a bit sorry for Granddad,' Holly said. 'He's just a person who doesn't know how to deal with feelings. He looked really upset.'

Ben put his arm around her. 'Don't worry, I'll let him cool down and I'll let myself cool down, and then I'll call him and apologize again for shouting, but not for what I said.'

'I'm glad you're not cold like Granddad,' Holly said, hugging Ben. 'Mummy always said you got your mother's genes, which is lucky for us.'

370

'I doubt you'd be here if Dad was like Harold.' Alice laughed. 'Cold and aloof is definitely not my type. Thankfully, your dad is nothing like that. In fact, he's the opposite, lovely and warm and kind.'

Ben grinned as Alice leant in and kissed him on the lips.

## *Ben*

Declan put another pint in front of Ben. 'Get that down your neck.'

Ben was feeling a bit light-headed already. 'Steady on, I'll be on the floor soon. I don't want to arrive drunk at our welcome-home party.'

'Relax. You're supposed to get drunk at welcome-home parties. You need to relax and have some fun, Benji. Come on, cheers. Here's to 2015 being a year when we don't get kidnapped and chained to each other.'

'Hear, hear.'

They clinked glasses and Ben took a sip of his beer. It felt good to be sitting in a pub with Declan, catching up face to face.

'So, how have the first few weeks back at work been?' Declan asked.

Ben put his glass down. 'I have to say, it's really good. I was starting to go crazy sitting around the house. I need to work – I missed it. I'm rusty, though. I've got two years of catching up to do. But the buzz of operating is still very much there.'

'You must be a legend at the hospital after Eritrea. I'd say they're all over you.'

Ben smiled. 'Not quite, but I am getting a fair bit of attention, particularly from the female staff.'

'Any hot ones?'

'Lots, but I'm not tempted.'

'You're not normal, Benji,' Declan said, shaking his head.

Ben grinned. 'Maybe not, but I have one focus, and that's getting Alice to fall in love with me again.'

'How are things going?'

Ben ran his hands through his hair. 'Things are better, but she's still distant. It's an uphill battle, but one I'm determined to win.'

'Any sign of your man Dan?'

'No, but it's not over. Every now and then she gets a call or a text and she leaves the room. It's not often, but it's still happening.'

'How's sex?'

Ben shifted on his stool.

'Come on, it's me. Talk to me.'

'We haven't had any in a few weeks. I'm leaving her alone for the moment. She needs space and I'm giving it to her.'

'Don't give her too much – she might disappear into it.'

'On the positive side,' Ben said, anxious to change the subject, 'I'm getting on really well with the girls. We're spending lots of time together. I took them camping last weekend, and although Jools protested at first, we had fun. I wanted to spend time with them away from phones and tablets and TVs.'

'Did Alice go?'

'Yes. She spent the first day reading her book, but the second day she came for a hike with us and we had a nice time. It was old-fashioned fun, toasting marshmallows by the fire, telling stories and laughing.'

'Reminding her how nice it is to be a family again.' Declan patted Ben on the back. 'Good man, you're playing it well. You might consider mentioning one or two of the women throwing themselves at you, though. A bit of jealousy works wonders.'

Ben smiled. 'Maybe I will. Anyway, how are you?'

'Never better. I've decided what I'm going to do with my life. I'm telling Theo tonight at the party that I'm not coming back here. I'm staying in Dublin and I'm going to specialize in paediatrics. I can't leave my da again. Dublin is where I belong.'

'I'm happy for you, mate. You'll be fantastic.'

'It feels right, and if there's one thing I learnt from being stuck in that hole it's that life is short and you have to live it the way you want to and follow your heart.'

'Speaking of hearts, any romance?'

'I've stopped shagging every girl that looks sideways at me and I'm looking around for someone special now. Although tonight is kind of a mini-holiday, so I might have some fun.'

'You'll meet someone special. Even though you're half crazy, you're a decent catch.'

Declan grinned, then looked up and waved. Ben felt a hand on his shoulder.

'There he is, the main man. Howzit going, Ben?' Billy enveloped Ben in a bear-hug.

'Good, thanks, Billy. How are you?'

'Feckin' brilliant. Great to be in London.'

Ben was distracted by the large lump of hair sitting on Billy's formerly bald head.

'I see you're checking out my new roof.' Billy pointed to his head.

Ben was speechless. It looked very odd.

'Thanks for rushing off and leaving me to pay the taxi, Da,' Sean said, coming in behind his father. He greeted Ben: 'Good to see you, man.'

'Ben's just noticed Da's thatch.' Declan grinned. 'He's still not been able to muster up any words to describe it.'

374

'I preferred him bald,' Sean said.

'Well, I prefer me not bald. Can you believe it, Ben, they took the bit of hair I had at the back of my head and put it on the top? I feel like George Clooney.'

'George Clooney's granddad.' Sean snorted.

'You look smashing, Billy,' Ben said kindly.

'The women will be lining up,' Billy said.

'Yeah, to borrow it.' Sean laughed as Billy smacked him on the back of the head.

'I hope your children have more respect for you,' Billy said to Ben. 'How are they?'

'Really good, thanks. Jools is in her final year, which is hard to believe, and Holly is as sweet as ever.'

'And Alice?' Billy asked, lowering his voice as Declan and Sean argued about football beside them.

'Things are better, but it's very slow, to be honest.'

Billy squeezed his arm. 'You hang in there, son. That woman loves you. She's had a tough few years and she got distracted, but she loves you. Keep trying, she's a good one.'

'Thanks, Billy, I will.'

'Romance her, Ben. Bring her back to the beginning and remind her of how things were and how you used to be.'

Ben smiled. 'That's exactly what I'm going to do, Billy. I'm working on it.'

'Good lad. How do you think Declan's doing?'

'He seems good. A lot calmer, less manic,' Ben said.

'He is, thank God. I let him go mad for a while, but then I took him aside and had a chat with him. He was drinking too much and his nightmares were getting worse with the alcohol. I was worried about him. He was very low some days. But he's steadier now. He's focused on his work and he's back running and eating well and not shagging a different young one every night.'

'Are you talking about me?' Declan asked.

'He's just saying he's glad the revolving door of women has stopped.' Ben smiled at his friend.

'Poor Da – he didn't know who was going to be at the table for breakfast,' Sean said.

'Don't mind him, he loved it,' Declan said. 'He used to charm them all, cooking them bacon and eggs.'

'You need to get your own apartment,' Sean said.

Declan shook his head. 'No, I like living with Da. I'm not moving out until I find my Alice.'

How ironic, Ben thought. I need to find my Alice, too.

When they arrived at the party venue, a cheer went up and everyone rushed over to them to shake their hands and welcome them. Although a lot of the staff had met up with Ben over the last few weeks, some hadn't, and none had seen Declan. He was soon surrounded by colleagues and duly regaled them with stories about Eritrea.

Ben saw Alice in the corner, talking to Theo Halston. As he was making his way over to save her from one of Theo's inevitably long and boring stories, he bumped into Sarah Langton, the new American anaesthetist he'd worked with earlier that week.

'Hey there, are you enjoying your party?' she asked, flashing her perfect teeth at him.

'It feels a bit odd, actually, because I've been back working for a few weeks. I think it's more for Declan, really.'

'Were you guys buddies before you went to Eritrea?' Sarah asked.

'Not at all. In fact, I'd only met him once, briefly. But we certainly got to know each other very well in Eritrea.'

'How well?' She raised an eyebrow in a flirty way.

Ben laughed. 'Not that kind of well.'

She winked at him. 'You know, everyone just thinks you guys are awesome. The way you survived and escaped. It's like a movie script.'

Ben leant towards her. 'It wasn't like a movie at all. We just about made it through in one piece.'

Sarah put her hand on his arm and spoke into his ear. He could smell her perfume and felt her cheek next to his. 'Here's the thing, Ben. You're a handsome, successful surgeon who survived captivity. You're a hero to everyone, so just go with it. You should be milking it. Have you seen the way the women look at you? They drool when you walk by.'

Ben laughed. 'I doubt it.'

'Honey, open your big brown eyes a little wider.'

Alice came over to them. 'You're late,' she said. 'I've been stuck with Theo for twenty minutes.'

'Sorry, got a bit side-tracked catching up with Declan.' Ben introduced the two women. 'Alice, this is Sarah Langton, the new anaesthetist I'm working with.'

'Nice to meet you, Sarah.' Alice shook her hand. Ben watched as Alice took in Sarah, from head to toe. The classic women's once-over. What was it Declan had said – 'A bit of jealousy does no harm'?

'Great to meet you too.' Sarah flashed her pearly-whites at Alice. 'You do realize you're the envy of every woman here? Ben is like a total god in the hospital. Yesterday I heard two nurses talking about him and one said, "I find it so hard to concentrate when he looks at me with those eyes."'

Ben laughed. The drinks he had had with Declan had loosened him up. He wasn't embarrassed, he felt flattered.

Alice smiled tightly. Sarah moved on, but before Alice could say anything, Ben was immediately surrounded by Declan and three nurses asking him if it was true that he had fought a wolf with his bare hands to save Declan's life.

Ben laughed. 'Declan's winding you up.'

'But it's incredible that you survived. You really are heroes,' a pretty dark-haired nurse said, batting her eyelids at him.

Alice nudged in beside Ben. 'I'm Alice, Ben's wife,' she said pointedly.

Declan winked at Ben.

The nurses barely gave Alice the time of day as they continued to focus on Ben, Declan and their exploits.

After about ten minutes, Alice tapped Ben on the arm. 'I think I might go. Everyone here just wants to talk to you and Declan. They're behaving as if you're rock stars or something. It's all a bit mad.'

Normally Ben would have asked her to stay or gone home with her, but he was having fun and enjoying spending time with Declan. He felt really good for the first time in ages, relaxed and happy. 'Okay, darling.'

Alice seemed a bit taken aback. She'd clearly been waiting for Ben to ask her to stay. 'Right, well, I'll be off then.' She pulled on her coat.

'Are you leaving, Alice?' Declan asked.

'I'm just cramping Ben's style tonight.'

Ben pretended to talk to the nurses, but he was listening to Alice and Declan.

'Ah, don't mind the nurses, they can't help themselves. They're all in love with Ben,' Declan said.

Alice frowned. 'Well, maybe they need to be reminded that he's married.'

'Maybe you need to be reminded of that too,' Declan said evenly.

Alice's eyes widened. 'I do . . . I am . . .'

'He could have any woman here, but he wants you. Remember, Alice, no man is perfect. No man is immune to attention.'

'I know . . . I can see . . . I'm not stupid . . . but . . . Well, some of the women just seem a bit over the top.'

'Do they? Ben survived two years in Hell. He's a hero. It's an intoxicating combination.'

Ben felt it was time to step in. He appreciated what Declan was doing, but he was worried he'd go too far.

He turned to face them. 'I'll walk you to the car,' he said to Alice.

'I forgot that part – he's a gentleman too.' Declan glared at her.

'I know that.' Alice glared back.

'I'll be back in ten minutes,' Ben said.

'Bye, Alice.' Declan waved at her.

She walked away, frowning.

## Holly

Stella sent us a text asking us to meet her. She said she had something she wanted to give us. Jools didn't want to go. She pretended she didn't want to see Stella, but I knew she did. Jools adores her and I knew she missed her but felt disloyal to Daddy if she had any contact with her.

Eventually I persuaded her to meet Stella just this one time and say goodbye to her properly. She deserved that. She had been so nice to us. Jools was really grumpy about it, but I could tell it was because she was nervous about seeing Stella again and getting upset.

Stella suggested that we meet in this cool café that was near her gallery. When we arrived, she was sitting at a corner table and waved to us.

We walked over slowly. Stella stood up and hugged Jools. 'I'm so glad to see you. I've missed you.'

I saw Jools's eyes well with tears. She hugged Stella back. She was too upset to speak.

Then Stella kissed me and I thought I might cry too. 'I'm so glad you came,' she said. 'I've been dying to see you.'

Jools looked embarrassed. 'I wanted to call you loads of times, but I felt weird about it all after Dad came back. It felt disloyal. I'm sorry.'

Stella squeezed her hand. 'Don't worry, I completely understand. Your whole world was turned upside-down. It's been a shock for everyone. How are you guys getting on?'

Jools rolled a sugar cube between her fingers. 'Good, great. He's our dad and we thought he was dead and he's not and it's . . . Well . . . It's a miracle.'

Stella smiled at me. 'How are you, Holly?'

'Fine, thanks,' I said, feeling like I wanted to cry. It was really sad, sitting there with Stella without Mum and Dan. We'd had some really nice times together. I'd blocked them out but now that she was in front of me, all the lovely memories came back. 'It's a bit strange too, though, especially for Mum.'

Stella looked down at her coffee. 'My dad's very cut up. He thought he'd met "the one" and then, just when everything was perfect, your dad came back. I mean, I'm really happy for you,' she added quickly, 'but naturally I feel really sorry for my dad. He loves Alice and you guys too.'

Jools was close to proper tears now. 'I know, but Ben's our dad and he's Mum's husband so she has to choose him. It's not fair to Dad if Mum stays with Dan, and I know it's not fair to Dan either but . . . what can we do? He's our dad.' Jools began to cry.

Stella gave her a hug. 'Of course you have to be with your dad. It's just really difficult. I hate seeing my dad so unhappy and I loved having "sisters".'

That was the comment that got me. I started crying too. People began to look at our table.

'God, what a mess,' Stella said, handing us napkins. 'What a complete bloody mess. Here, I wanted to give you this.' Stella handed us a framed photo. It was the selfie we took on the night we went to the Chiltern Firehouse. We were all smiling and looking so happy.

'I wish things were different,' I said.

'What? That Dad wasn't alive?' Jools snapped.

'No, of course not. But that no one had to get hurt.'

'Me too,' Stella said. 'It's not easy for anyone. I just wish that things hadn't got so serious between Dad and Alice. It makes it harder for him to accept that he might lose her.'

'He has to let go, Stella. He has to stop texting and calling her.' Jools wiped her eyes. 'Dad has suffered enough.'

I stayed quiet. There was nothing else to say.

'Hello there.' We turned to see Dan standing behind us. I almost had a heart attack. Jools's mouth hung open.

'Hi, Dad! Why don't you join us?' Stella said.

It was obvious they'd planned it. I felt very uncomfortable.

Jools found her voice. 'This is not cool. I'm sorry, Dan, but we can't see you. Come on, Holly.' She stood up to go, pulling me by the arm, but I was frozen to the spot.

Dan looked upset. 'Jools, come on, it's me, Dan.'

Jools shook her head. 'It's not right. Talking to you is like cheating on Dad.'

'Please, girls, I've missed you. I just wanted to see you and say hello. Please, just five minutes?'

Jools looked at me and I nodded. She sat down again.

'How are you?' Dan asked.

'Fine,' Jools said.

'We miss you all, don't we, Stella?'

Jools gritted her teeth. 'Look, I know it's hard for you and Stella but you have to leave us alone. We have to concentrate on Dad now. I know you love Mum but you have to let her go, Dan. She needs to be with Dad.'

Dan spread his hands wide on the table. 'It's not that easy. I love your mum. We were about to get married and spend the rest of our lives together, remember?'

'Of course we do,' Jools said. 'But that's in the past now.'

'You don't just fall out of love, Jools. I want to give you all a great life. I know your dad is back, and I'm so happy for you girls. I'm not trying to interfere in your relationship with him.'

'But you are,' I said quietly. 'By calling Mummy and texting her.'

'Your mum texts and calls back too,' Stella said. 'It's not just Dad.'

Jools froze. I put my hand on her leg under the table to calm her down.

'I love her, Holly, and I think she still loves me too. Look, all I want is for Alice to be happy,' Dan said.

'She loves Dad. She wants to be with him,' Jools said, but she didn't sound convinced.

'I'm not trying to upset you, but the bottom line here is that I want to spend the rest of my life with Alice and I'm not giving up on her. I think we can find a way where we'll all be happy. I'm not trying to take your dad's place. I just want to be with the woman I love.'

I could feel my hands shaking. I felt so mixed up inside, but I was angry too. 'But you are taking his place. You're taking up his place in her heart. You're not giving her a chance to be with Daddy. You're always in the background, calling and texting. If you really loved her, you'd give her space and let her make her own mind up. That's true love.' I couldn't believe I'd said so much.

Jools squeezed my hand under the table. 'We have to go,' she said.

Stella and Dan stood up. 'Can I please have a hug?' Dan asked, and he just looked so sad.

We hugged them both quickly, and as we turned to leave, Dan said, 'Just remember, if she does decide to be with me, I'll look after all of you, just like I promised.'

Jools hustled me out of the door and when we got outside she turned to me, smiling. 'You were amazing in there. I was so proud of you.'

I was literally dumbfounded. Jools had actually given me a compliment.

## Alice

Alice stared at the two rings, sitting side by side in their boxes on the bedside table. They represented two very different men and two very different sides of her life. She knew what she had to do. She knew she had to do the right thing. Her head told her to focus on Ben and her family . . . but every time she thought of Dan, her heart skipped a beat.

Things with Ben were improving. He was making a huge effort and she could see that the girls were more comfortable with him now. Jools acted as if he'd never been away and Holly was finally relaxed in his company. Alice could see how hard Ben had worked to make that happen and he was really trying with her too, but she couldn't let go. When they had sex, she missed Dan. When Ben kissed her or touched her, she felt awkward and tense.

It would destroy a part of her, but she was clear that there was only one solution: remove Dan from her life. She felt she could do it this time. They were meeting tonight, to talk, and she had insisted they were in a public place, so she couldn't give in to her physical desire for him, like last time. She had to stay in control. It was impossible to keep living this double life. She knew she had to make a choice and live with it. What she was doing now was hurtful and wrong. It couldn't continue.

Ben came into the bedroom as she was dressing. 'You look nice.'

'Oh, thanks.'

'Where are you off to?'

Alice avoided eye contact. 'I just need to pop out for an hour.'

Ben froze. 'Pop out where?'

Alice didn't want to get into an argument before she met Dan. She was upset enough as it was. 'Just out.'

'Are you meeting Dan?'

Alice pulled up the zip of her boot. 'Yes.'

'I see.' Ben's jaw set.

'I'm going to meet him to break up with him for good. Okay? Happy now? I'm giving him up for you.'

Ben looked into her eyes. 'I don't want you to stay with me out of a sense of pity or duty.'

Alice looked away. 'It's not that, it's . . . We're a family and I have to focus on that.'

'We're not a family if one of us wishes they were somewhere else all the time.'

'I don't.'

'You check your phone a hundred times a day, you switch off during most of our conversations and you're constantly distracted.'

Alice felt anger bubbling up inside her. 'Jesus, Ben, I'm doing my best. It's not easy when your dead husband walks through the door. I'm trying to adjust. Give me a break here.'

'You're not the only one it's difficult for, Alice. We're all adjusting.'

'Well, maybe I'm going to take longer than you. Maybe I changed more than you did. Maybe I had to change to get through the mess you left behind.'

Ben closed his eyes. 'You have to let it go, Alice. We can never put this behind us if you don't let go. I'm sorry. I hate myself for what I did, but I can't change it. All I can do is try to make it up to you, but I can't do that if you won't let me. I know I was selfish. Jesus Christ, I've apologized a million times to you and the girls. I know I was an idiot. I've regretted it every day since the day I walked out of here and got on that plane. I've tortured myself about it, but I can't undo it. I don't know many ways to say I'm sorry. The girls have forgiven me. Why can't you?'

Alice yanked on her other boot and stood up, shaking with anger. 'Maybe it's because I sat here and watched their hearts breaking. I spent two years holding them up, supporting them and trying to fix their heartbreak. I had to make sure they didn't spiral into depression or go off the rails. They were so shattered and so fragile emotionally, I was terrified for them. I did everything I could to keep them safe and secure, and I think I did a bloody good job. They're really well adjusted despite all of the turmoil.'

Ben paused. 'Did you know Jools was self-harming?'

Alice stood still. 'What?'

'She's been cutting herself.'

What the hell was he talking about? Jools didn't cut herself. 'Bullshit.'

'When was the last time you saw her arms?'

Alice thought about it. She had noticed that Jools always wore long sleeves but she'd put it down to a teenage fashion thing. She'd never suspected anything. Had she really missed it? Self-harm? Oh, Jesus.

'Her arms are always covered because they're marked with scars.'

'How do you know?'

'She told me.'

Alice's legs began to shake. She sat on the bed. How had she missed it? How could she not have known that Jools was hurting herself? She'd thought she'd been on top of things. She'd thought she knew everything. She'd thought she'd protected them and given them all the emotional support they needed.

'How long has it been going on?'

'She said she did it on and off for about a year. She stopped a few months ago.'

'Poor Jools.' Alice began to cry.

Ben came over and tried to put his arm around her but she moved away. She didn't want him near her. She was furious that he had dumped this on her, right now, and clearly thought she was at fault.

'I suppose you think I did a bad job, missing the fact that my daughter was slicing her arms open?'

'No, I don't. I just want you to stop blaming me. We can't move forward if you don't forgive me, Alice. I'm not perfect, but neither are you.'

Alice narrowed her eyes. 'Are you seriously going to try to turn this on me? Are you trying to say I messed up?'

'No!' Ben stood up and went to light a cigarette.

'Don't you dare light that thing. I'm sick of the house stinking of cigarettes. You know I hate the smell. I put up with it at first, but you have to go outside if you want to smoke. It makes me feel nauseous. And, by the way, I know Jools smokes. I didn't miss everything. I'm not a bad mother.'

Ben put the cigarette down. 'I never said you were. I just want you to stop being angry. You're so tense all the time that I can't talk to you. I want to get close to you again, Alice. Stop pushing me away.'

'I'm not.' Alice was defensive. 'I'm just trying to deal with everything that's going on and make sure the girls are okay and earn money and look after everyone.'

Ben placed his hand on her arm. 'You don't have to do

everything on your own. I'm here. I can help. I'm back now. You don't need anyone else. Let Dan go.'

Alice felt herself beginning to panic. She was having trouble breathing. It was all too much. She had to get out of there. She picked up her coat. 'I have to go.'

Ben put out his hand to stop her, but she brushed past him. 'I love you, Alice. I love you more than any other man possibly could.'

Alice was crying as she ran down the stairs.

Dan was sitting in the window of the café, typing into his BlackBerry. As she approached, Alice paused to observe him. He was so confident and strong and sexy. It was going to be so difficult to let him go. Why was life so cruel? What had she done to deserve so much upheaval and pain?

As if sensing he was being watched, Dan looked up and saw her. A slow smile spread across his face and Alice felt her stomach plummet. It was going to be so hard to give him up. He represented ease and no worries, like a slice of perfection she could shelter in whenever things got rough. Life with him would be uncomplicated, she was sure of that. He was so attentive, so in love with her, it would all be so easy. And that ease was incredibly tempting, to fall into it, let herself go and give herself up to it. She felt her resolve crumbling, her mind starting to wonder if there was an alternative . . . An image of Jools popped into her head. How could she have been so caught up in her romance that she had missed her daughter's self-harming? The guilt of that burnt in her chest. She dug deep within herself to find courage, then put her shoulders back and walked to Dan's table.

When she reached him, he stood up and pulled her into his arms. She rested her face in his neck.

'Oh dear, this is going to hurt, isn't it?' he whispered.

'Yes,' she said, trying not to cry.

They sat down opposite each other and held hands. They stared into each other's eyes, not speaking.

'Thank you.' Alice broke the silence.

'You don't have to thank me.'

'Yes, I do. You were so wonderful to me. I was so happy with you. You are such a good man.'

'Oh, God, those past tenses are killing me.'

'I have to . . . I have to . . .' Tears spilt down Alice's cheeks. 'I don't want to, I really don't, but I have to . . .'

'I know.' Dan wiped away her tears with his hand. 'I know, darling.'

'I wish it was different. I'm so confused and angry and tired. I hate this. I hate letting you go. I'm so sorry, Dan.'

'Hey, you're an incredible woman. I'm very glad you came into my life. We had a great time. But you have to give your marriage a go, I get it. He's a lucky man.'

'I don't even know if it's going to work. I don't know if I love him enough. I don't know anything any more. I feel as if I've been robbed of happiness again.'

'I know that feeling.' Dan smiled sadly.

'Oh, Dan, this is so unfair to you. I'm so sorry.'

'Stop apologizing. It's not your fault. None of us could have foreseen what happened. Just one of those things, as my own father would have said.'

Alice reached into her pocket, took out the Cartier box and placed it on the table in front of him.

'I bought that for you. It's yours.'

'I can't keep it.'

'You can, Alice. I'm saying you can. It was intended as a lifelong gift and that's just what I want it to be.'

Alice gulped back tears. 'No, Dan, I really can't. I know you want me to, but as long as I have it in my possession, in my house, it says that my heart is split in two, and I can't live like that. I have to choose one life and live it. It's wrong to keep it, disrespectful to you and to Ben.'

'But you can't erase me out of your life. We happened, Alice. We were real. I love you, and I want you to keep a symbol of all that. Don't discard it. You may eventually change your mind.'

She could see that he was getting angry. Why shouldn't he be angry? she thought. He's become the fall guy in a situation not of his making and that he can't control, which he must hate. His insistence was probably a desire to exert some control over things, but that was a luxury she just couldn't give him. 'Please don't be angry, Dan,' she said. 'I don't want to leave here with bad feeling between us. But I need you to understand that I have to give you up, which means I have to give up this gift. It's important that I do that.'

Dan sighed impatiently. 'All right, Alice. I don't really understand, but if it's important to you, I'll go along with it.' He looked at her sadly. 'Alice, is this what you really want, in your heart of hearts?'

She couldn't meet his eyes. The burning sensation in her chest was back and it was taking all her strength to hold herself together. Into her hands she whispered, 'No.'

Dan reached across the table and grabbed her hands, kissing them, holding on to her. 'Then, please, choose us. I know it won't be easy, but you just say one word to me right now, Alice, just say yes, and I promise you, this time next year all the hard bit will be long over and you'll be wondering why you even considered going back to him. You'll be happy, Alice. I'll work so hard to make sure the girls are happy, too, give them whatever they want. Stella is one hundred per cent behind us. We can be happy – you just have to say the word. That's all. I know I'm the man for you, Alice. I know I can make you happier than he can. Stop fighting it and just accept that it's the truth, even if you feel bad for admitting it. Put this ring back on your finger and don't even go back there. Come home with me now. We'll sort it out.'

He was staring at her, willing her to give the 'right' answer, willing her to choose him.

'Dan, if Ben hadn't come back, I would have married you and lived out my life with you. But he did come back. I can't change that, and nor can you. And I made a promise to him on our wedding day that we would do this for better or worse. This is the worst worse we've gone through, but I have to try to see it through. I owe it to my family.' She drew his hands towards her and kissed them. 'I have to let you go, Dan. I'm so sorry.'

Dan pulled his hands away and sat back in his seat. He looked weary and angry – a man who had given it his all, only to be rejected. 'Okay. There's nothing more I can say or do. You've made your decision. Go home and give it your best shot. If for some reason it doesn't work out, which I don't think it will, call me.'

Alice nodded, unable to speak now as the tears ran down her cheeks. They stood up, embraced, and Alice gave Dan a final kiss. Then she walked out of the restaurant and away from the life she wanted to live.

# *Holly*

Mummy knocked on my bedroom door and asked if she could speak to me. I was lying on my bed, reading. She had her serious face on and I was terrified she was going to tell me she was leaving Daddy for Dan. I felt sick and panicky. I sat up, gripping my duvet because I was so scared of what she was going to say.

'Holly, I need to ask you if there was anything I missed while Daddy was away.'

'What do you mean?' I was puzzled by the question.

'I mean, did you have any problems I missed, like issues in school or with friends or with grief in general?'

'No, Mummy, nothing I didn't tell you about. I did have to have the calculator near me all the time, but now that Daddy's back I don't need it. Why are you asking?'

Mummy was twisting her hands together and I could see she was trying not to cry. 'I may have missed something with Jools. I feel terrible about it and I want to make sure there's nothing I failed to notice with you. Did you ever feel so sad that you couldn't cope and wanted to . . . well . . .'

It suddenly hit me: she knew about Jools cutting herself.

'How did you find out about Jools?'

'My God, you knew?' Mummy was crushed. 'How did I not see it? You were just a little girl and you knew.' She looked so shocked. 'Christ, how bad a mother have I been?'

'You're a brilliant mother,' I said. 'Jools was very secretive and I only knew about it because I walked in on her one time. That's all.'

She took a deep breath and sat down on my bed beside me.

'How did you find out?' I asked.

'Dad told me. But why didn't you say anything at the time, Holly? You should have told me, pet. It's dangerous, she –'

'Don't blame Holly.'

Jools was standing behind us in the doorway.

'I made her swear not to tell you. I never wanted you to know. You had enough to deal with and I knew you'd freak out.'

Mummy stood up and went over to Jools. 'Of course I'd freak out. Jesus, Jools, you could have killed yourself.'

Jools rolled her eyes. 'I was careful.'

'I'm so sorry I missed it. I should have noticed. I should have protected you.'

'Oh, God, don't get all emotional, it's fine. It's over. Dad shouldn't have told you.'

'Have you really stopped?' Mummy asked.

'Shortly after you met Dan. I don't know why, everything seemed to settle down and the house was calmer and less sad and . . . I just didn't need it any more.'

Mummy bit her lip. 'I wanted to tell you both that I've ended it with Dan. I met him and gave back the ring and told him it was really over.'

Jools was smiling. I was glad but I felt sorry for Dan. He must have been so upset.

Mummy was staring at Jools. 'I can't bear to think of you in so much pain that you cut yourself. I wish you'd told me – I could have helped. I'm your mother – it's my job to notice – and I'm a bloody *doctor*. How did I miss it? I'm so sorry.'

Jools shook her shoulder. 'Stop it. Stop blaming yourself.

394

I was an idiot. Now I'm fine and it's over. You were brilliant when Dad wasn't here. You did everything for us, Mum. You were the best mother in the world. You have nothing to be sorry for.'

That set Mummy off because Jools never says nice things to her. Mummy sobbed and sobbed.

Jools put her arm around her and leant her head against Mummy's. She looked like she was the mother comforting the child.

'It's okay, it's okay now, it's okay, Mum,' Jools said over and over. 'You're fine, I'm fine, Holly's fine, Dad's fine. It's all okay. We'll be okay.'

Mummy nodded, but she kept crying. She cried like her world was ending.

## Ben

Kevin sat opposite Ben in the coffee shop, read through the list and circled one name. He handed the piece of paper back to Ben.

'Why not Venice?' Ben asked.

'She went there with Dan.'

'Oh.'

'It should be Paris. She loves Paris and it's where you got engaged. That's the place.'

'I promised to take Alice to Paris as soon as I got back from Eritrea. I was worried going there now might remind her of that promise. But you're right. It's full of good memories. It's a place where we were very much in love.' Ben fidgeted with his pen. 'How do you think she is now?'

Kevin paused. 'When they first broke up she was upset, but in the last two weeks she's been calmer. She's less distracted and more present. I think she's slowly coming back to herself.'

Ben looked at his brother-in-law. 'Is she coming back to me?'

Kevin put his hands up. 'I can't answer that because I honestly don't know. She doesn't talk about it. But she seems lighter and less weighed down. I think the guilt was eating her up. Alice is not the cheating kind, as you well know. I think she was overdosing on Irish Catholic levels of guilt.'

'I'm sorry to ask you this, but I have to know. Is it really over?'

Kevin nodded. 'To the best of my knowledge, yes.'

'Well, that's something,' he said.

'She's trying, Ben. She really is.'

'I know, but she still feels far away. She's still distant and not really with me.'

'She's had a lot of stuff to deal with. I mean, I can't even imagine how hard it is to have grieved the death of someone only for them to turn up again. You knew she was alive, but she never for one moment thought you had survived. The report from the Foreign and Commonwealth Office was very clear that you and Declan were dead. Harold organized that awful memorial service with the empty coffin, then Alice had the ceremony for you in the garden. They were tough times. While Alice was trying to deal with your death, she went very close to the edge, Ben. She had to put your memories away to survive.'

'And I had to cling to our memories to survive.'

Kevin looked at his watch. 'I have to go, sorry. We've ten more patients to see. But we've covered everything, haven't we? And it's a really good idea. I'm rooting for you.'

'Thanks, Kevin, for everything.'

Kevin squeezed Ben's shoulder and disappeared out of the door.

Jools padded outside in her slippers and coat and sat beside Ben on the garden bench.

'Another nightmare?' she asked.

'Yes.'

'Will they ever stop?' she asked.

'The psychiatrist thinks so. They're fewer and less frequent already, so it's going in the right direction.'

They smoked in companionable silence.

'I hate that tree,' Jools said.

Ben was surprised. 'I thought you liked it.'

'It's just a constant reminder that you used to be dead and of sad times.'

Ben stubbed out his cigarette. 'I hate that bloody tree, too. Sometimes I feel I can't see the future for the tree. We need to leave the past behind and focus on moving on.'

'I agree.'

Ben jumped up. 'Let's cut the bugger down.'

'Seriously?'

'Yes. Do you think Mum will be cross?'

Jools thought for a moment. 'No. It's a sad tree. It's a tree that reminds us all of death.'

Ben smiled. 'Let's get the saw from the shed.'

Thankfully, the tree wasn't very big. It still took them an hour and a lot of puffing and panting to trim the bigger branches, then chop through the trunk.

As the tree fell sideways, they clapped.

'Goodbye and good riddance,' Ben said.

It felt good to cut the tree down. Ben was taking back control of his life and eliminating the negative reminders of what had happened. It was cathartic to feel that he was cutting the past out of his life.

He went over to deal with the roots and saw something shining in the moonlight. He bent down and pushed back the mud. It was a little metal box.

'What is it, Dad?' Jools peered over his shoulder.

Ben showed her the box.

'Gosh, I'd forgotten all about that. Mum buried it with the tree when we planted it. I think there was a letter inside.'

Ben tried to open the catch, but it was stuck. He went into the kitchen, Jools following.

Ben got a knife out of the kitchen drawer and prised open the box. Inside was an envelope. It said *Ben* in Alice's big loopy writing.

'I'm tired after all that. I'm going to bed. I'll leave you to read it in peace. Night, Dad.' Jools kissed him and went upstairs.

Ben sat down. He opened the letter, unfolded it and began to read.

*My darling Ben,*

*How I wish my last words to you weren't angry ones. How I wish I could go back in time and tell you that I love you before you walk out the door and out of our lives.*

*I'm sorry I was angry with you. I know you were just looking for adventure. I understand that you felt restless. I was just so scared of losing you and now I have.*

*How am I going to live without you? You're my best friend, my rock, my everything. Who am I going to talk to, confide in, ask for advice from, laugh with, love?*

*I always looked around at other couples and felt smug. None of them had what we had. None of them were as close as we were. None of them loved each other like we did.*

*God, Ben, I love you so much. I wish I'd told you that more often. I wish I'd told you every day. You were the best thing to ever happen to me. We were so happy, Ben. Do you remember our wedding day? We were so in love.*

*And then the girls! Our two little miracles. Jools looking so like you and Holly like me, both of them a mixture of our personalities. You were such a great dad. I'm so angry that the girls won't get to have you in their lives as they grow up. You always knew what to say to Jools and how to handle her when she was being difficult. She worshipped you. Her heart is so broken, it's painful to look at her.*

*And Holly, she's like a lost kitten. She loved you so much. You were her hero. Oh, God, Ben, what am I going to do without you?*

*You were my hero, too. I was so proud of you. So proud to be your wife. So proud that you chose me. I should have told you that.*

*There are so many things I regret. So many things I want to tell you. I'm so lonely, Ben, I think my heart is actually broken. I can't do this without you. I need you. I'm lost, Ben. I miss you so much. I love you, I love you, I love you.*

*Alice*

## Holly

Mummy and Daddy had a big fight about the cherry tree. Mummy was really cross when she saw that Daddy had chopped it down. But Daddy said he was back now and he didn't want a constant reminder of the bad days. Mummy said it wasn't his decision to make and he should have asked her first.

Daddy said he had made an executive decision. He was glad it was gone and Jools had hated it too. Mummy asked me what I thought and I said that I kind of agreed that, now Daddy was back, we didn't need it.

Mummy's mouth went all tight. She said it was amazing that Daddy had 'waltzed back in' and started changing things without even asking her opinion.

Daddy said he was sorry if she was upset, but he'd found a very special letter buried underneath. Mummy stopped talking then. Daddy said the letter was the most beautiful thing he'd ever read. Mummy looked a bit sad. Daddy said he would cherish it always. Mummy said nothing. Daddy said he hoped that some day she'd feel the same way again but Mummy pretended to look for something in the fridge.

Jools and I looked at each other. Neither of us had seen what Mummy put in the box. It was private. I wonder what the letter said.

*

Daddy took us to the ballet for Mummy's birthday. Daddy used to hate the ballet and never wanted to go. Mummy loves it and thinks it's 'magical'. Daddy used to say it was silly men 'jumping about in tights with their balls hanging out'.

But this year he brought us all to the Royal Opera – including Kevin – to see the Bolshoi Ballet perform *Swan Lake*.

Mummy was really surprised but happy. She said it was very thoughtful and she'd always wanted to see the Bolshoi. Daddy said he remembered her saying that years ago and that was why he'd booked the tickets. I could see Mummy was touched. I was so happy with Daddy for doing something so nice. He's trying so hard to be the best husband and he's doing a really good job.

Me, Mummy and Kevin thought it was amazing. Kevin kept looking into his opera glasses to get a closer look at the dancers. He spent the whole time staring at the lead male dancer and sighing.

Mummy hugged Kevin and told him that his prince would come. She said he deserved to be with someone amazing and that she was delighted Axel was out of his life because he wasn't nearly good enough for him.

Jools spent most of the time texting her new boyfriend, Rupert, and Daddy pretended he was enjoying it until the third act when he fell asleep. I saw Mummy turn to say something to him. When she saw he was asleep she smiled and took the programme from his hand.

Rupert came over last night to meet everyone. Even Nora stayed late to meet him. She stood at the front door with her coat on, looked him up and down, and muttered, 'All brawn and no brain.'

Mummy shushed her but Kevin laughed and said, 'Give me brawn over brain any day.'

Rupert smiled blankly. Thankfully, he didn't understand. We knew what Nora meant because she says the same thing whenever she sees a really good-looking man or woman. I think Nora is secretly jealous of all very good-looking people.

Jools gave Nora a dirty look. 'Weren't you on your way home, Nora?' she said.

Nora started to take off her coat. 'I think I'll stay for a bit. I'd like to get to know Rupert better. I've a few questions for him.'

Jools looked panicked. 'What?'

Nora patted her cheek. 'Don't worry, I'm only messing with you. But I will say this.' Nora turned her razor-sharp eyes on Rupert. 'This girl means the world to me. If you mess about or do anything to upset her, you'll have me to answer to.'

Rupert's eyes widened. 'Well, I . . . of course I wouldn't dream of . . .'

Mummy took charge. 'Thanks, Nora. We'll see you in a couple of days. Bye for now.'

Jools pretended to be annoyed but I saw her winking at Nora as she left.

Kevin thought Rupert looked like Brad Pitt and acted all funny around him. Jools said Kevin was embarrassing. Kevin kept offering Rupert cups of coffee and asking him questions about his fitness regime and if he had any brothers. Rupert is very good-looking but he's not very bright. Mummy was talking about a young Down's syndrome patient she had seen, and Rupert said, 'You have to be careful, Mrs Gregory, people might think you're racist. You can't say brown syndrome, it's African American.'

Daddy choked on his coffee and started laughing, which set Mummy off too. They couldn't stop. It was nice to see them laughing together.

Jools stormed off in a huff, Rupert following behind, asking, 'What did I say that was so funny?'

When they'd left the room, Daddy wiped his eyes and said, 'Where did she find him?'

'He joined the school this year,' I told him.

'Where was he before that?' Daddy asked.

'Having a lobotomy,' Mummy said, and they were laughing again.

I thought it was a bit mean to say that, but Mummy and Daddy thought it was hilarious.

Mummy seems happier now. She's not working as much and she's not all tense around Daddy. Daddy's the one working hard. He's back full-time at the hospital, but he always takes weekends off and won't go in unless it's an emergency.

I've only heard him having a nightmare once in the last two weeks, which is great. He looks better too: he's not skinny any more and his eyes are smiley, not sad. He laughs a lot and is less serious than he used to be. He spends more time with us than he did before too. It's so wonderful to have him back. I just wish Mummy would love him the way she used to. Then everything would be perfect.

## Alice

Ben leant down and kissed Alice. 'See you later, darling. I'm meeting David in the gym after rounds but I'll be home for dinner.'

'How's the gym going?'

'Can't you tell?' Ben flexed a muscle.

Alice smiled. 'Sorry. Of course I can see the results.'

Ben squeezed his still slender arms. 'It's only been three weeks but it's definitely helping me regain strength, and it's fun being with David.'

Alice was glad Ben was in touch with David again. She knew he'd frozen him out when he'd discovered that David had introduced her to Dan. Pippa had called and said how upset David was. But Alice felt she couldn't interfere because it was about Dan.

So Pippa had suggested they all 'bump into' each other over brunch. It had worked out really well, and although Ben had been a little cool at first, he had soon mellowed. He had been touched by how much the girls loved Pippa and David, and how close they had become.

By the end of the brunch David had asked Ben if he wanted to take him up on his offer to go to the gym together, and Ben had said yes. Pippa had squeezed Alice's hand under the table. Their plan had worked!

'Do you have a busy day, darling?' Ben asked.

Alice nodded. 'Full schedule. But I'm hoping to be back by seven.'

'Would you like me to cook tonight?' Ben asked.

Alice smiled.

'What?' Ben asked.

'You never used to ask me about work and you never used to offer to cook.'

Ben laughed. 'Every cloud has a silver lining.' Then, turning serious, he added, 'I promised myself that if I got out of there alive, I was going to be a better husband and father.'

Alice did up her watch strap. 'You weren't so bad before, you know.'

'There was room for improvement.'

'There is room for improvement in all of us.'

'Not in you,' Ben said.

Alice frowned. 'Don't do that, Ben.'

'What?'

'Put me on a pedestal. I'll only disappoint you.'

Ben picked up his wallet. 'No, you won't. After all these years, I know all of your flaws and I'd still choose you every time.'

Alice blushed. Ben went downstairs to have breakfast while she finished getting dressed.


Kevin and Alice sat in her surgery sipping coffee before the day began.

'Dan sent me a text yesterday,' Alice said.

'What?' Kevin stared at her.

'He asked how I was doing.'

'Did you reply?'

'Yes.'

'What did you say?'

'That I was okay.'

'Are you?'

Alice looked at her brother. 'Yes.'

'Do you miss him?'

'Yes. But not in the awful, pain-in-my-chest way that I used to. It's more of a dull background ache.'

'You seem to be getting on better with Ben,' Kevin said, without looking at her.

'I am. It's still hard, but I feel that we're making progress.'

'He's making a huge effort, Alice.'

'I know, and I really appreciate it. I'm trying, too.'

'But you're not there yet?'

'No.' Alice sighed. She wondered if she'd ever get there. Things had improved a lot – she felt more comfortable around Ben and he was being really lovely to her – but she was holding back. She didn't know why but she just couldn't let go. They hadn't had sex in ages and she was stressed about it but just couldn't go through with it. It was as if, since breaking up with Dan, she was blocked.

She missed Dan more than she cared to admit. She hadn't told Kevin the part where Dan texted: *I'm moving to New York. I need a change.* She had replied: *God, this is hard.* He sent back: *Yes, that's why I'm moving continents.*

She had wanted to call him, to talk to him, but she hadn't. She knew it wasn't fair. What was there to say anyway? 'Goodbye . . . good luck . . . I miss you . . . I wish . . .'

It hurt like hell to know he was leaving. Alice had needed to be alone after the texts. She had locked herself into the bathroom, drawn a bath and cried into it.

Kevin put his hand on her arm. 'I really believe you made the right decision, Alice.'

'I know.' Alice knew she had had to choose her family,

especially when it had made the girls so happy. But her own feelings were separate from that, and they weren't so straightforward.

'Will we run through the day?' Kevin asked.

'Yes.' Alice welcomed the distraction of work. 'Actually, hang on, how was your date?'

'It was pretty fantastic, actually.'

'Oh, good! Was he nice?'

'Very, very hot.'

'Kevin, forget hot, was he a nice person?' Alice asked.

'Oh, don't get all big-sister on me. He had the body of Adonis and he was nice too.'

'What does he do?'

'Now I feel like I'm talking to Mum!'

'Seriously, does he have a proper job?'

'Yes, actually, he does. He's a stripper.'

'What?'

'Ha! Gotcha. He's a sports teacher.'

'You mean he has a real job?'

'Yes, and his own apartment.'

'Wow! That's great.'

'I know.'

Alice beamed at him. 'I'm really glad for you.'

Kevin raised his hands. 'Hold on – it's been one date, we're not getting married!'

Alice laughed. 'I'm just glad you had fun. You deserve lots of it after having to listen to me moaning and crying for the past two and a half years.'

'Yes, I do, and I plan to make up for lost time.' He winked. 'Now, let's get back to the patient list.'

After a long day of dealing with patients, Alice was getting ready to go home when Kevin popped his head round the door. 'Lilly's here. Will you see her? She says she has bad stomach pains.'

Although Alice was tired, she was very fond of Lilly. 'Sure, send her in.'

'I think her dementia is worse and she's as deaf as a post. Norman's with her but sure he's so old he can barely stand up straight. I'll bring them in now and call you in fifteen minutes with some "emergency". Otherwise you'll be here all night. Poor Lilly doesn't know what day it is. She keeps asking me if I saw the royal wedding and didn't Diana look stunning.' Kevin rolled his eyes and disappeared to call Lilly in.

Norman held Lilly's arm as they shuffled into the consulting room. Alice welcomed them and asked them to sit down.

'How can I help?'

'Lilly has pains in her stomach and she's bleeding from . . . well . . .' Norman coughed '. . . from her . . . from her posterior.'

'I see. Let's pop you up here, Lilly, so I can examine you.' Alice raised her voice so Lilly could hear. She led her to the examination table and helped her to lie down.

Alice felt Lilly's stomach, then explained that she had to do a rectal examination to make sure there was no blockage.

'WHAT?' Lilly shouted.

'I need to examine your rectum,' Alice said.

'I can't hear you. Speak up.'

Alice raised her voice. 'I'm going to have to put my finger into your bottom to check for blockages.'

'What's she saying about my bottom, Norman?' Lilly asked.

'She needs to examine you, darling,' Norman bellowed,

looking increasingly uncomfortable as he shuffled about at the far side of the room.

Alice helped Lilly to roll over and tried to position her as best she could. She put on some gloves and then gently placed her finger in Lilly's rectum.

'NORMAN!' Lilly roared. 'Stop that immediately. Get it out of there. You know I don't like it when you stick it up there. If you insist on having sex, please put it in the front door, not the back.'

Alice avoided Norman's eye and bit the inside of her cheek to stop herself laughing.

'Norman, I've told you before, if you want to stick it up there, go and find a lady of the night to do it with. Front door only!' Lilly shouted.

Alice pretended to sneeze as laughter escaped.

When Alice and Kevin got home, they were still laughing about it. Ben was reading some medical reports in the kitchen. Alice filled him in on the story.

Ben threw his head back and laughed. 'That is a classic.'

Alice giggled as she poured them all wine. 'I felt sorrier for Norman, to be honest. He was mortified.'

Jools came in. 'What are you all laughing about?'

'It's just a story about one of my patients,' Alice said, hoping Jools wouldn't demand to hear it.

Thankfully, Ben's phone rang, distracting them. Alice could hear a woman's voice at the other end. Ben chatted to her for a while, laughing a lot.

'Yes, it was tense . . . You were fantastic, though, very cool under pressure . . . Well, thank you, what a nice compliment . . . Of course I'll be there . . . Yes, I promise to wear the surgical hat you gave me . . . ha-ha . . . No, I like it, it was very thoughtful . . . ha-ha, yes . . . It should be an interesting day.

I'm looking forward to it too . . . I'll bring the coffees . . . No, I insist, it's my turn, you're far too generous . . . A latte, right? . . . You don't need low-fat milk . . . You are not! You're almost too thin if you ask me . . . All right, I promise . . . Great, see you then . . . I will . . . Bye.'

Kevin looked at Alice and raised an eyebrow.

'Who was that?' Alice asked.

Ben put his phone down. 'Sarah Langton, the new anaesthetist.'

'The one I met at the party?'

'Yes.'

'Oh.' Stupid cow. How dare she call and give Ben compliments – and why the hell was Ben being so flirty?

'Did she buy you a surgical hat?' Jools asked.

'Yes, it's a bit of fun. It says "Survivor" on it.' Ben took a sip of wine.

'It sounds ridiculous,' Alice snapped.

'I think it sounds cool,' Jools said, looking up from her Facebook page.

'When did Sarah start at the hospital?' Kevin asked.

Ben rubbed his chin. 'About ten weeks ago. She makes a nice change from William Gilbert. He was a terrible bore. Sarah's quite the opposite, full of fun. She's also extremely good at her job, the best I've worked with.'

'What age is she?' Kevin asked.

'That's the amazing part. She's only thirty-seven and she's at the top of her game.' Ben sounded impressed.

Alice slammed the fridge door. She hated Sarah now – good-looking, thin, smart, successful and a practised flirt by the sound of it. Alice wanted to go to the hospital now and shove the stupid surgical hat into Sarah's big mouth.

'I bet she looks younger than her age – Americans always do. They take way better care of themselves than English people,' Jools said. 'They're also really into Botox. The Kardashians get it. Do you think Sarah's had any work done?'

'I don't think so. She looks very natural,' Ben said. 'She's very fit and healthy.'

Alice felt rage flooding her body. She wanted to shout at Jools to stop being ridiculous and to tell Ben to stop wearing a stupid hat that said 'Survivor' on it and, most of all, to tell Kevin to stop smirking across the table at her. She didn't care about some stupid Barbie from California with her low-fat lattes.

She started banging pots and pans loudly as she made a start on dinner. She'd sign up for those Pilates classes tomorrow. She'd been planning to do it for months. It was about time too. All these months of feeding Ben to make him put on weight had meant she'd put on weight, too.

Stupid bloody American gym bunny with her tiny waist and perfect teeth and tan. Alice glared at Ben, who was laughing at something Jools had said. His smile lit up his face. Now that he had put back some weight and the haunted look was gone from his eyes, he was handsome again. A little more lined than before, greyer around the temples, but very attractive. The handsome hero.

Alice hadn't really looked at Ben properly since he'd been home. She had avoided it. She hadn't stared at him and examined his face and really seen him. But now she did, and what she saw was a good-looking, kind and brilliant man. No wonder American Barbie and all the nurses were flirting with him. Well, they could just back off. Ben was her husband. He belonged to her.

Alice looked down at her stomach. She slammed down a pot. 'I'm going for a run,' she announced.

'It's lashing rain,' Kevin pointed out.

'Sounds like a plan to me,' Sarah said, smiling at him.

They ordered another round, then another and another. Ben felt fantastic. The drinks were giving him a nice buzz.

Sarah was good company – smart, funny, charming, flirty. He liked her. He liked her a lot.

She leant forward and laid her hand on Ben's thigh. 'I think I'm a little drunk.' She giggled.

Ben smiled through his happy alcohol haze. 'Me too.'

'We deserved a drink, though. That was one hell of an operation. You rocked it, Ben. You were on fire today. Awesome job.' Sarah raised her glass to clink with his.

They both drank deeply and then Sarah put her hand higher up on Ben's thigh. It felt good, too good. Ben knew he had to move. He stood up and said he was going to pop out for a cigarette.

Sarah followed him. It was dark and they were tucked away behind some beer kegs. Ben lit his cigarette and Sarah reached in to have a puff.

As she handed the cigarette back to him, she looked into Ben's eyes, then slowly moved towards him and kissed him. Ben didn't resist. He closed his eyes and kissed her back. Softly at first, then more passionately. Sarah's hand reached inside his trousers. God, it felt so good.

She leant her body against his, turning him on.

Alice, thought Ben, through his foggy haze. Alice.

'I want you,' Sarah whispered.

Ben groaned, and then, using every ounce of willpower in his body, he pulled away. 'Sarah, I'm sorry.'

'Oh, come on, don't stop now. I'm horny as hell.' She kissed his neck.

'I can't . . . I'm –'

'Married. Yeah, I know. But I won't tell anyone.'

Ben pushed her back. 'It's very, very tempting, but I can't.'

Sarah put her hands on her hips and stared at him. 'Are you kidding me? I need a cold shower now! Your wife's a lucky woman. I hope she appreciates what she has.'

Ben smiled. 'I'm the lucky one.'

'Oh, please, don't tell me how great she is. I'll barf.'

Ben laughed.

Sarah ran a hand across his chest. 'You're missing out, Ben. I'm sensational in bed.'

Ben exhaled deeply. 'I have no doubt you are. So I'm going to use every single scrap of resolve that I have to force myself to leave.'

'I'm going to stay here and get drunker,' Sarah said, as she walked back inside. 'I'm sure someone else will find me irresistible.'

'Every man in there.'

'Except you,' she said, shaking her head as she pulled the door open.

On the way home, Ben rang Declan. He needed to talk to him, to hear his voice.

'You sound a bit pissed, Benji.'

'I am.'

'Great! You need to loosen up and have some fun. Good night?'

'Yes, but I got into a bit of a situation with Sarah.'

'The American anaesthetist?'

'The very one.'

Declan whistled. 'Kudos, mate, she is one hot bird.'

'I know.'

'So what was the situation?'

'Bit of kissing and groping outside the pub.'

'No way. Did you shag her?'

'No. I managed to stop it going too far.'

'Jesus, Ben, maybe you should have just shagged her. No one would have known.'

'I'd know.'

'You'd get over it.'

'I love Alice.'

'We're not talking about love, we're talking about sex, and you're not getting any at home. We men have our needs.'

'Christ, it was bloody hard to walk away. But it was the right thing to do.'

'She really is hot.'

'She certainly is!' Ben said, remembering her body pressed against his.

'Jesus, I'm horny just thinking about her. Alice is a lucky woman. You're a better man than me.'

Ben laughed. 'Things are better with Alice. We're making progress, getting closer. I don't want to mess it up.'

'But you're not getting any action, are you?'

'No.'

'You know what? Maybe you need to stop waiting for it to happen and just go for it,' Declan suggested. 'Birds like it when men take control.'

Ben took out his front-door key and leant against the porch. 'You might be right.'

'Is everything set up for Paris?' Declan asked.

'Yes. The girls have been wonderful. They've helped me plan it all. Kevin's been great too.'

'Good luck, mate. I'll be thinking of you.'

'Thanks. Better go. I'm outside the door now.'

'Get in there and screw your wife's brains out.'

Ben laughed and hung up. The house was quiet. It was late and the girls were in bed. He went to the bedroom. Alice wasn't there, but he heard music from the bathroom.

Ben walked in. Alice was lying in the bath. It was dark except for the flickering light of a candle. She was leaning back, listening to music. She opened her eyes. They stared at each other, saying nothing.

Ben didn't hesitate. He kicked off his shoes and climbed into the bath fully clothed.

'Oh, my God, what are you doing?' Alice gasped.

Ben pulled her to him. 'Making love to my wife.'

They lay on the bathroom floor, side by side, their chests rising and falling with their breathing as it slowed. The tiles were wet. Ben's soaking clothes were strewn around them.

'Wow,' Alice said. 'That was –'

'Amazing,' Ben finished, with a grin.

'I was going to say unexpected.' She smiled. 'But, yes, it was pretty amazing too.'

'Maybe we should hang out in the bathroom more often.' Ben kissed her shoulder.

Alice didn't pull away. She seemed at ease for the first time. Ben wanted to punch the air. The sex had been good, really good. He hadn't been gentle or hesitant or apologetic, he had taken complete control and Alice had responded to him as she used to, with passion. Their bodies had moved in rhythm, like the old days. It had been fantastic.

Alice sat up and reached for her robe. 'I fancy a drink and a cigarette after that.'

'You don't smoke.'

'I know, but I feel like sharing one with you tonight.'

'Sounds good.'

'Come on, then.'

Ben lay where he was. 'I'll follow you down.'

'Okay. I'll get the wine.'

As he watched his wife pad barefoot out of the bathroom, Ben smiled and whispered, 'Yes!' Declan had been right: what he'd needed to do was take control. Bring on Paris.

# Holly

Jools and Rupert are doing a science project together. Nora said it's a bit like the blind leading the blind – not in front of Jools obviously. Nora would never hurt Jools's feelings. Even though she tells her off sometimes, she adores her.

When Daddy was away, Nora was constantly saying how great we were, but now that he's home she's gone back to grumbling at us, a bit more like the old days.

She said she doesn't need to compliment us now because Daddy does it every second of every day. It's true: he tells us how amazing we are all the time. He's always saying how he feels so lucky to have such fantastic daughters. It's really nice. It makes me feel brilliant inside and I know Jools loves it too, although she told him he's not allowed to cuddle her in front of her friends because it's just 'not cool' and she's an adult now and he needs to respect that.

Jools and Rupert's project is on 'How to Make the World Safer'. When Daddy asked them what they were going to do, Rupert looked all pleased with himself.

'We're testing the safety of scrum caps.'

'What?' Daddy looked as surprised as I felt.

'It was Rupert's idea and it's totally genius,' Jools gushed.

'Thanks, babe.'

'Do you mean the scrum caps you wear when you play rugby?' Mummy asked.

'Totally,' Rupert said.

'How exactly are you going to test them?' Daddy asked. I saw him winking at Mummy, who tried to keep a straight face.

'Well, at first Rupert wanted to put on the different caps and run into a wall, but I thought it could be dangerous. I mean, if one of the caps wasn't good quality, he could get concussed or brain-damaged,' Jools said.

'Would this be something you've tried before?' Daddy asked, hiding his smile behind his coffee cup. Mummy snorted into her laptop, then pretended to cough.

'No,' Rupert said. 'But I realized Jools was right and it could be dangerous. I could, like, fry my brain doing it. So we've decided to put watermelons into the four different types of scrum cap and drop them from Jools's bedroom window and see which gets more smashed up.'

'I was wondering what all the watermelons were for,' Nora said, pointing to the four big fruits sitting on the kitchen counter. 'I thought you were on some new mad diet.'

'Well, it's certainly an original concept, but I'm not sure how scientific it will be,' Daddy said.

Jools tapped her sparkly nails on the kitchen table. 'It's fine, Dad. We don't need to spend a month becoming expert scientists, staring at stuff through microscopes in pee-wee dishes. It's just a boring project and we've got our idea and we're doing it. Don't start being all Mr Surgeon and suggesting hard things to do. Science is your thing, not ours.'

Daddy laughed. 'I won't interfere.'

Jools stood up. 'Come on, Rupert, let's go. I'll throw them out of the window and you stand below and take videos and photos.'

'Cool.'

'Hold it right there, missy.' Nora blocked their exit. 'Who exactly is going to clean up the smashed watermelons?'

Jools and Rupert looked at each other.

'You hadn't thought about that, had you? Well, it's a good thing I have a brush, a pan and mop here for you. Now, off you go.'

They left carrying watermelons and scrum caps.

'Make sure you stand back, Rupert,' Daddy called after them. 'You don't want a flying watermelon landing on your head.'

Mummy started to laugh. Daddy, Nora and I joined in. It was kind of funny. Jools is bonkers.

Daddy has been planning a big surprise for Mummy for ages. He asked Kevin, me and Jools to help. He wants it to be perfect. He's taking her to Paris, where they went when he proposed to her. I think it's really romantic, but I'm worried. We were all talking about it together when Mummy was out running one night, and Kevin said, 'I've been thinking about it and maybe you should wait a bit and ease Alice into it.'

Daddy did not agree. 'No, Kevin. I realize now that I've been too passive. I've spent six months tiptoeing around. It's time for action. I need to remind her of what was and what can be. She's in a kind of life-limbo. I want to push her out of it and back into the real world.'

'I understand, but she might need more time, Ben. It's been a very difficult few years for her.'

'It hasn't been easy for Daddy either.' Jools sounded cross.

I didn't say anything. My stomach hurt. I was really worried that Paris might not go well and Daddy would be so disappointed.

'I know,' Kevin said. 'Ben, you've been brilliant since you got back. I can see how hard you're trying to make things perfect for everyone, but Alice has had so much shock and pain to deal with, I just think it's going to take her longer to get back to normal.'

'But that's just it. I don't want her to get back to normal. I want her to see that we have a new life, a different life – possibly a better one. I know this guy Dan was a multi-millionaire and he spoilt her and treated her like a princess, but I'm going to look after her now. I want her to see that I'm back, I'm here and I'm going to take care of things.'

'She's just scared. It's hard for her to let go. She's been looking after everything on her own,' I said. I wanted Daddy not to rush things. He needed to give Mummy time.

'I understand, sweetie.' Daddy reached out and held my hand. 'But she needs to let go if we're to have any chance of moving forward. I love her. I love my family. I want us to be together for life. I want to be a better husband, father and friend. I know what I want to do.'

'I admire you for it,' Kevin said. 'To be honest, I prefer you now. Maybe Eritrea wasn't such a bad thing after all.'

'Kevin!' Jools shouted. I gasped.

Daddy threw back his head and laughed. 'Only you would say that, Kevin. I wouldn't go quite that far but I'll take the compliment.'

'I'm serious. You're like a nicer version of yourself. I really want things to work out for you. I'm on your side, Ben. I'm rooting for you.'

'I should think so!' Jools said.

Daddy looked a bit emotional then. 'Thanks, Kevin, that means a lot to me.'

Kevin took a sip of his coffee. 'Right. Change the subject before I get all gay and weepy and you stop liking me again.' He asked Jools about Rupert and she talked a lot about how great he is.

The conversation about Mummy made me worry. What if

Kevin's right? What if Daddy is pushing Mummy too soon? What if she doesn't like the trip? What if she wishes it was Dan taking her to Paris on a private jet and staying in the most expensive hotels and all that? What if it all goes wrong?

I'm scared that if it doesn't go well, Daddy will be heart-broken. He's put so much work and thought into it. I'm praying every night that Mummy sees . . . that she gets how much Daddy loves her and how much he wants her back.

## Alice

Ben was being secretive and Alice was worrying. He kept going out to make phone calls and snapping his laptop shut when she came into the room. He had a glint in his eye and seemed particularly happy and upbeat.

Since the night they'd had sex in the bath, Alice had seen Ben in a different light. She'd stopped looking at him as a man who had lived through two years of trauma and needed to be nursed back to health and started seeing him as a strong, capable man. The man he used to be.

The sex had been good, really good. He had caught her completely by surprise and taken control. She'd felt dominated, but in a very sexy way. She hadn't had time to think or tense up or worry about not enjoying it or comparing Ben to Dan. It was fun and hot and she'd felt their bodies come together like they used to. It had been familiar and different. Ben's body was more like the old Ben's too. He was less thin and fragile. He was stronger and sturdier. She wasn't afraid he'd break. It had reminded her of old times.

But since that night Ben had pulled back. He'd seemed preoccupied all the time and hadn't tried to have sex with her again. She was worried that he was becoming distant and uninterested in her. Now that Ben wasn't trying to have sex with her, she wanted him more.

\*

When she arrived at the surgery on Friday morning, Kevin was waiting for her at the door. He handed her a coffee.

'Thanks. So what does today look like?' Alice asked.

Kevin didn't answer.

'Kevin?'

'What?' He jumped. 'What is it?'

'I just asked about the patients we have today.'

'Oh, uhm . . . well . . .'

'What's going on with everyone today?' Alice asked. 'The girls were all jittery this morning, too.'

'Okay, sit down, Alice.'

'Oh, Jesus, is it bad news?'

'What? No!' Kevin smiled. 'It's good news. You have no patients today. You are booked in for a hair appointment at nine thirty. Then we are going home to pack. You will be picked up at eleven thirty and taken to St Pancras, where you will get the Eurostar to Paris.'

Alice was totally confused. What was he talking about?

'Ben's taking you to Paris, on a little trip down Memory Lane.'

'I don't understand. Why didn't he just tell me?'

'He wanted it to be a surprise and he wants you to have time on the train, alone, to read this.' Kevin held up a beautifully wrapped package.

'I hate surprises.'

'I know you do, but, Alice,' Kevin put his hands on her shoulders and looked into her eyes, 'for once in your life, go with it. Stop thinking and just feel. Trust your heart.'

Kevin put the package back into his bag and led Alice out of the surgery to the salon.

As the car drew up outside the house, Alice picked up her suitcase, then put it down again. Turning to her brother she said, 'Thanks for absolutely everything. You are the best brother a girl could wish for.'

'Stop, you'll make me cry and I am not going on a date with puffy eyes.'

'It seems to be going well with this guy.'

Kevin shrugged. 'So far, so good. Now go to Paris and enjoy yourself.'

'I'm scared,' Alice said.

'I know. Ben's an amazing man and you're an incredible woman. You've both been to Hell and back, but you made it. Whatever happens, you'll both be okay. Ben's a survivor and so are you. Just do what feels right for you. Stop overthinking everything. Go with your gut and trust your heart.'

'I love you.'

'Ditto. Now get your arse into that car.'

Alice sat back in the first-class train compartment and pulled out the package. She was afraid. She put it down on the table and studied it. She sipped her champagne and tried to calm her nerves. 'Trust your heart,' Kevin had said – what was expected of her from all this?

With shaking hands she carefully undid the wrapping. Inside was a book. On the front was a photo of Alice on her wedding day, laughing into the camera. Her eyes shone with pure joy. The title of the book, in thick silver lettering, was *THE WAY WE WERE*.

Alice opened the cover and was transported back to her first date with Ben. David had taken a grainy photo of them kissing in the corner at a party and there it was, reminding her of that very first kiss. The pages took her through their courtship, graduations, wedding, honeymoon, pregnancy, the birth of Jools and Holly, moving into the old house, then the new house, photos of their parents, their friends, their workplace, their parties, their birthdays, Christmases, Hallowe'ens, holidays ... The memories jumped off the pages. They showed her a life full of happiness, joy and love.

In every photo Alice was smiling, laughing or looking adoringly at her husband or her children.

The final two pages of the book were two letters on opposite sides, facing each other. Alice gasped. One was the letter she had written to Ben and buried under the tree. She knew Ben had retrieved it, but she had never wanted to see it again. Now she read it and remembered, feeling once again the pain and heartbreak that she had poured out onto the page.

On the other page was a letter dated 'Christmas 2013 – 14 months in captivity'. It was a letter Ben had written to her in Eritrea.

*My darling Alice,*

*I'm writing this letter while chained to a tree. The idea of spending a second Christmas here without you and the girls is excruciating. I want you to know that I'm sorry. I'm sorry for not listening to you. I'm sorry for putting myself in a dangerous position that has now caused so much pain. I'm sorry for being a selfish git and thinking I needed more adventure in life. I'm sorry for not realizing that I had it all. I had everything a man could possibly want – a beautiful wife I adore, two wonderful daughters, a happy home. I'm sorry for not telling you how much I love you every day. I'm sorry for not appreciating you more. I'm sorry for not telling you how proud I am of you and what a wonderful mother, wife and doctor you are. I'm sorry for being dismissive of Kevin, who is so important to you and the only family you have left. I can see now how much you need him and what an important person he is in your life, how kind and generous he is to you and the girls. I'm sorry for not helping you more. I'm sorry for not being the husband you deserve.*

*I swear to you that if I get out of this hell-hole, I will be a better man. I'll treasure you and I will never leave your side. I promise I will be a better father, more involved, more affectionate, more present. I will love you the way you deserve to be loved – completely, unconditionally and passionately.*

*If for some reason I don't make it, Declan has promised to deliver this letter to you. I want you to know this – meeting you was the best thing that ever happened to me. I loved you from that very first date, when you made fun of my floppy hair. I love your smile, your sense of fun, your sense of humour. I love the way you never take yourself seriously. I love the way you throw your head back when you're laughing and that you laugh loud and free. I love the way you cry unashamedly at films. I love the way you chew your lip when you're concentrating. I love the way you feel passionately about so many things – even The X Factor!*

*Thank you, Alice. Thank you for coming into my life. Thank you for being my rock when my mother died. Thank you for giving me our two magnificent daughters. Thank you for putting up with my difficult father. Thank you for being the best person in the world to go through life with. Thank you for being my best friend, my lover, my cheerleader and my wife. I am so proud to be your husband. Thank you for saying yes when I asked you to marry me. I love you, Alice, with all my heart. I love you in this life and I will love you in the next.*

*Ben*

Alice sobbed loudly into the little cocktail napkin that had come with her champagne. People were staring at her, but she couldn't stop the tears. Eventually an older lady sitting across the aisle came over to her.

'Madame, are you all right? Can I 'elp you?'

Alice wiped her nose. 'I'm fine, thank you. I'd just

forgotten. I'd forgotten all of it. I blocked it out so I could survive and move on. But now . . . well . . . now I remember and it's just really . . . really . . . sad . . .' Alice collapsed in tears as the woman patted her gently on the back.

The car drew up in front of the Hôtel Petit Maurice on rue du Bac in St Germain. The driver came around to her door and opened it. ''Ere we are, Madame.'

Alice climbed out and stood in front of the hotel. In the many years since she'd been there, it hadn't changed. It was the same quaint, charming, slightly rundown place they'd stayed in to celebrate their engagement.

The receptionist rushed out to greet her and made a great fuss of taking her bags upstairs.

'Is my husband here?' Alice asked.

'Yes, but 'e 'ad to go out to arrange some things.'

Alice looked around the room for signs of Ben. There were none. This was a separate room. What was going on?

'Monsieur Gregory ask me to give this to you.' The receptionist handed her an envelope.

Alice sat down on the bed and opened it. Inside was a map of Paris with three destinations, marked 1, 2 and 3.

There was a note attached: 'Go to number 1 at 6 p.m.'

Alice had a shower and applied concealer to her puffy eyes and make-up to her red face. She got dressed in the outfit Kevin had chosen for her – a cream dress with a navy waistband and a navy cardigan to wear over it. Kevin said it was fresh, pretty but sexy, too, because of the side slit.

Alice nervously put on a third layer of lipstick and looked at her watch. Time to go. She got into a taxi and pulled up close to the square du Vert-Galant. It was when she saw the weeping willows that she remembered. Ben had brought her there on a picnic all those years ago.

She'd been to Paris before with her parents. She'd even been to Île de la Cité, but she'd never visited this park. Ben had read about it being romantic and he'd suggested they go there. They'd sat under the weeping willows by the Seine and marvelled at the stunning view. You could see the Louvre and the Pont des Arts. Alice looked down at her instructions. It told her to look for the pink-and-white checked rug. She saw it to the left. In the middle of the rug there was a mini bottle of champagne and a glass with an envelope attached: *Drink this and watch the river.*

Alice sat down on the rug in the warm spring sun and poured herself a glass of champagne. She felt nervous, excited and afraid. She tried to do what Kevin had said, switch off her mind and just enjoy the moment. As she sipped her drink, she remembered lying there with Ben. They had lain on the grass all afternoon, talking and planning their future. So carefree, so full of hope and aspirations, so clueless about what life was really going to be like.

Alice leant back on her elbows and watched the boats sailing down the Seine. They had been so naïve, young and happy. That's what she remembered most – happiness. It was before her parents had died, before children had come along and mortgages, bills, responsibilities, mid-life crisis and Eritrea.

Something caught Alice's eye. It was a boat with a huge sign: *Two Can Play That Game, Alice!* The boat was playing the Bobby Brown song as it passed by.

Alice sat bolt upright as it all came rushing back. It was the first song she and Ben had danced to. She could picture Ben now, dancing around the tiny apartment, all arms and legs, bumping into the other guests and knocking over their drinks. She had loved how Ben danced – as if no one was watching, completely uninhibited, which seemed at odds with his stiff English upbringing and made it even more charming.

Alice got up and ran down to the water's edge. People around tut-tutted about the loud pop song, but Alice sang along.

The boat was soon out of sight and Alice suddenly felt very alone. She was on the sidelines, looking on. It was how things had been lately, she thought. She'd become more of an observer and less of a participant.

Alice walked slowly back to the rug and glanced down at her instructions. It was time to move on to the second place. She strolled back through the park and got another taxi, which brought her to the place Saint-Germain-des-Prés, to Les Deux Magots, as instructed. As she approached the café, the manager came over to her and led her to a table at the side of the terrace. There, waiting for her, was a glass of chilled Sancerre and a large chocolate éclair.

There was a note under her plate: *Last time, we shared one. You deserve a whole one. Bon appétit!*

Alice dug her fork into the éclair and savoured the chocolate mousse filling. It was delicious. She remembered arguing with Ben over the last piece and how he had pretended to eat it, only to pop it into her mouth at the last moment.

Alice hadn't eaten an éclair in years, possibly decades. It tasted so good. She could feel the alcohol and the chocolate relaxing her. She sat back and watched the people at the other tables – couples kissing, couples arguing, groups of friends talking animatedly about something, tourists bent over maps, children eating ice-creams . . . and she, Alice, a woman sitting alone, trying to figure out what the future held.

As she sat contemplating, a violinist came and stood

beside her. She thought she recognized the music, but she couldn't place it. What was that song?

'Oh, my God, Brad, that guy's playing Madonna's "Get Into The Groove"!' an American woman at the table behind her said.

Alice looked up, and the violinist winked at her. It was her favourite song. She began to laugh. How had Ben done this? It was incredible. Alice forgot her inhibitions and sang along. When the musician finished, he kissed her hand. '*Bonne chance*, Madame. Your 'usband is a very romantic man. But hees choice in music is terrible.'

Alice grinned and waved him goodbye. She asked for the bill, but instead she received another note: *Be at the Pont des Arts at 7.55 p.m. sharp.*

Alice got out of the taxi and walked up to the bridge. It was where Ben had proposed to her. She hadn't hesitated, just thrown her arms around him and said yes. She'd known he was 'the one'. She had been so sure, so positive. Not even a second of doubt had crossed her mind. Oh, to be that girl again. Alice hadn't been sure of anything in a long time.

In the middle of the bridge, dressed in a tuxedo, stood Ben. Alice stopped and looked at him. He smiled at her. He looked so handsome. She didn't see his grey hair or the lines under his eyes, she saw the young Ben, the man she'd fallen in love with.

Ben held out his hand and Alice moved towards him, slowly at first but then faster. He silently pulled her close.

'I was worried you wouldn't turn up. I think I was more nervous now than the day I proposed.'

'How could I not turn up? This day was just . . . perfect.'

'Did you like the book?'

433

'I loved it. I hadn't thought about those things in years. When I thought you were dead, I tried to block it all out because it hurt so much to remember. But now . . . now it's wonderful to be reminded of all those happy times.'

'I've missed you, Alice.'

'I've missed you too.' She said it, and she meant it. In that moment, she knew just how much she meant it. She had been trying to replace what she missed most, which was Ben. So simple, and yet it had taken her so long to figure it out.

'I know things are different,' Ben said, kissing her forehead. 'We've changed – we're older and wiser and bruised and battered from the last two years, but I love you more than ever. Our past is our past, and now I want to build a future with you and the girls. A new beginning. Will you come with me?'

*Will you marry me?* In her head, Alice could hear Ben's proposal, a lifetime ago. But there was still a lifetime to go, and she had to decide how she wanted to live it. Dan had offered her a shimmering mirage of perfection, but what would it have been like, really? She would have had to tuck herself into his life, which was so busy and scheduled and demanding. And no life carries on worry-free. That's not possible. Alice could read the last two years now with a clarity that had escaped her for so long: she had fallen in love with a man, yes, but perhaps more so with what he represented, the idea of freedom and ease and letting go of all of her responsibilities for a change.

But was that really Alice? Was that who she was and how she wanted to live her life? Looking into her husband's eyes, she knew now that the answer was no. It wasn't her. She was a woman who liked to work hard, challenge herself and share the ups and downs of her life. That was what she'd had with Ben. They had been through so much but she knew now that

434

they could weather any storm if they stayed together. They were a team, a unit, a couple. Ben couldn't offer her the gilded life that Dan could, but he could offer her a real life, based on love and the solid foundation of their amazing history.

Alice nodded. 'Yes, Ben. Absolutely yes.'

Behind them a busker sang Jacques Brel's 'Ne Me Quitte Pas' – Ben's final surprise. They swayed to the song, lost in each other, kissing and laughing.

As the Eiffel Tower light display lit up the Paris sky, Alice danced with the man she loved.

# Acknowledgements

This book was one I had wanted to write for a long time, but I was nervous about the Eritrean scenes and the surgeries. Some very brave and fascinating people helped me with my research into Eritrea. They have asked not to be named.

A big thank-you goes to:

James Murphy, for his invaluable expertise and insight into the world of surgery. Any and all mistakes are entirely my own.

Paul Carson, for his help in researching the life of a GP – the patient stories in the book are *all* completely fictional.

Rachel Pierce, a truly wonderful editor who makes every book better.

Patricia Deevy, for her ideas, input and cheerleading.

Michael McLoughlin, Cliona Lewis, Patricia McVeigh, Brian Walker and all the team at Penguin Ireland for their continued support and help. To all in the Penguin UK office, especially Tom Weldon, Joanna Prior and the fantastic sales, marketing and creative teams. To Julia Murday and Celeste Ward-Best for their hard work on the publicity.

To my agent, Marianne Gunn O'Connor, for always knowing the right thing to say.

To Hazel Orme, for her wonderful copy-editing and for being such a positive force.

To my friends, for always being there.

To Mum, Dad, Sue, Mike and my extended family for their constant support and encouragement.

To Hugo, Geordy and Amy, by far my greatest creations. (Special thanks to Hugo for the idea for Jools and Rupert's science project!)

And, as always, the biggest thank-you to Troy.